VANQUISHED
HOPE TARR

"A touching story of salvation and renewal in authentically
depicted Victorian London."
— *Best-selling author, Madeline Hunter*

Jewel Imprint: Sapphire
Medallion Press, Inc.
Printed in USA

DEDICATION:

To my mom, Nancy Louise Tarr, for her steadfast support
and unconditional mother's love, with heartfelt appreciation.

Published 2006 by Medallion Press, Inc.

The MEDALLION PRESS LOGO
is a registered tradmark of Medallion Press, Inc.

Copyright © 2006 by Hope Tarr
Cover Model: Anna Ward
Cover Illustration by Adam Mock

Printed in the United States of America

10 9 8 7 6 5 4 3 2 1
First Edition

ACKNOWLEDGEMENTS:

Vanquished is my first sale after a three-year hiatus from the romance-publishing industry, and as such represents a renaissance of sorts, both professionally and personally. Like most rebirths, writing the book brought its share of Dark Nights of the Soul and painful, uncertain times. I would be remiss indeed if I failed to thank the following loved ones and colleagues for their gifts of love, support, and encouragement.

Foremost, I would like to express my heartfelt appreciation to Earl Pence. Seventeen years of steadfast, loving partnership is no trifling gift, and the resulting wonderful memories are more than ample to fill any writer's treasure chest to brimming.

Love and thanks to my mother, Nancy Louise Tarr, for giving me safe haven, encouragement, and a mother's unconditional love, all when I needed them most.

To Marvin and Clara Pence, my second family, I miss you more than any words can express.

Warm thanks go out to my best friend, Lisa Davila for making me laugh and letting me cry at turns, and to Susan Shaver and Nancy Greer for being two of the best gal pals on the planet.

I also would like to thank Terri Wright (writing as T.A. Ridgell), Lori Pepio, Pamela Moniz, Paul Lewis, Karen Derrico, Carole Bellacera, and Christopher Whitcomb for understanding as only other writers can.

Many thanks to Kathy Liu, a romance reader living across "The Pond," for her help in sleuthing answers to my questions on the British suffrage movement from London-based collections. That said, any errors in the book are entirely my own.

Lastly, I would like to thank Helen Rosburg, Leslie and Wendy Burbank, and the wonderful staff at Medallion Press for their vision in giving a publishing home to Hadrian and Callie's rather unique love story.

PROLOGUE

"I may first of all broadly state the somewhat self-evident proposition that prostitution exists, and flourishes, because there is a demand for the article supplied by its agency."

—WILLIAM ACTON, *Prostitution, Considered in its Moral, Social, and Sanitary Aspects*, Second Edition, 1870

Covent Garden, London
Winter 1875

Another sharp gust of wind knifed its way through the boy's thin woolen jacket and trousers, drawing a shiver that ran from the top of his hatless head to the tips of his thinly shod feet. The snow beating down on his cold-chapped skin didn't help matters, either. The great fat flakes might look soft as feathers, but they felt more like

1

stinging nettles. Before the night was over, he'd be soaked through—assuming he didn't freeze to death first.

It wasn't yet seven o'clock, but for Harry Stone the misery of it all made it seem at least midnight. Taking shelter on the columned portico of Saint Paul's, he surveyed the scene through eyes watery from the cold. The square that had been bustling a few hours before was rapidly approaching deserted, the flickering gaslights casting their oily glow on the handful of porters carting away crates of left over fruits and vegetables. As soon as the last of them was on his way, Harry would steal inside the darkened market and scavenge the stalls for what leavings he might make a meal of. But that would not be for a while yet.

He slipped a cold-numbed hand inside his coat, feeling for his gin flask. His stiff fingers worked the stopper free, and he brought the bottle to his lips, draining it in one long, sweet swallow. Propping a shoulder against the column, he savored the spirit warming his insides even as he practiced his failsafe antidote to misery of any kind—taking photographic pictures in his mind. *Snowy Night in the Square of Venus* he would call it, this photograph he could have captured had his camera survived its angry clash with plaster and wood. With its lodging houses and Turkish baths, playhouses and gaming dens, Covent Garden was said to boast the most whores of any quarter of the city. Being the son of one of them, Harry well believed it.

Not that he meant to walk the streets begging for long . . . or at least not forever. Someday somehow he meant to save up enough to buy a camera, a proper one this time, and set up as a real photographer. Like his idol Roger Fenton, whose documentary images of the Crimean War were known the world over, he would take big pictures, important pictures, pictures that made you feel and see things as you hadn't felt or seen them before.

But more than any static scene, it was the people he ached to capture with a camera's unerring eye. *Ode to the Shadow People*, he thought to call it, this series of photographs he couldn't seem to stop firing off in his mind. By now Harry knew them all, had heard or could piece together their stories. The tall blonde known as Poxy Polly, so named because of the sore at the side of her mouth that never seemed to heal. The pretty little Italian Maria who, with the help of a vinegar-soaked sponge, managed to grow a new maidenhead every night. Then there was Randy Roger, just a handful of years older than Harry but looking more forty than twenty on account of the opium he couldn't seem to smoke enough of. Like it or not, Harry was one of them now, one of the shadows.

Self-portrait of a boy leaning against a column. Head bowed, shoulders folded inward, hands shoved into pockets the subject's stance . . . everything about him said he'd rather be anywhere but there. Only it wasn't a portrait, not a real one, as you couldn't see the face beyond a forehead covered with shaggy blond hair, a suggestion of finely molded nose, the tip of a squared-off chin—features recollected from a memory that seemed to grow more blurred with each passing day.

Harry hadn't looked into a mirror in more than a year.

Before glancing at his reflection hadn't been so much a daily ritual as an unavoidable occurrence. Growing up in Madame Dottie's Palace of Pleasure, mirrors had been in abundant supply unlike the sherry and champagne and fancy foods that were brought out only on special occasions or when an important client called. Great gilt-edged pier glasses covered nearly every wall; more mirrors hung from the ceilings of the bedrooms where women like his mum had entertained their "guests." And then there were the special mirrors his friend, Sally, had pointed out to him. On the outside they looked to be made of regular reflecting glass only the backs were really windows that let the people in the next room see inside. When he'd asked why anyone would want to be looking in, or have someone looking in on them, Sally had laughed and explained that people basically fell into one of three groups: performers; peepers; and those who fancied a go at both from time to time. At the time, Harry hadn't understood what she'd meant.

He did now.

A torque of his belly pulled him back into the present. The last of the produce wagons was just pulling off. It cleared the thoroughfare, and Harry spotted a tall man in a top hat and greatcoat cutting through the empty square.

Heart thrumming, he shoved away from the column and hurried down the slick steps to the street. Putting himself dead center of the man's path, he looked up into the blunt-featured face and forced his cold-stiffened lips into a smile. "Spare a coin so a poor lad can sup tonight?"

The man didn't smile back, only glared at him from beneath bushy eyebrows, the jutting forehead drawn into an unmistakable frown. With his fierce eyes and stone-carved features, he reminded Harry of one of those Methodist do-gooders, the sort who preached against the evils of drink on East End street corners and spooned up thin soup at the Christian Mission on Whitechapel Road. But beneath all that piety, Harry sensed an edgy hunger not unlike that he'd seen in the faces of some of his mum's best customers Heaven and hell, saints and sinners—only the finest of lines separated the two.

He glanced at the substantial-looking cane the man wielded, at the large hand wrapped about its knob, and backed away. "Sorry, guv, my mistake. I'll just be on my way then." He turned to run, thinking to lose himself in the labyrinth of castoff crates and rubbish bins.

"Hold. Hold, I say!" From behind, a gloved hand took firm grip of his shoulder.

Equal parts terrified and furious, Harry wheeled about. "Hey leave off, I said I was sorry."

The staying hand fell away. "You mistake me, young man. I mean you no harm. I only want a word with you." The hooded eyes regarding Harry were shrewd but not unkind.

Harry ran a practiced eye over the man's broad-shouldered if slightly stooped frame. His coat and hat were both finely made, and the knob of his walking stick looked suspiciously like gold.

"All right then," he finally said, "but it'll cost you."

The weathered face fell at that, whether weighted by pity or disgust Harry couldn't quite say. With a sigh, the man reached inside his coat's breast pocket. "I presume this will suffice?"

He pulled a five-pound note from his money clip and held it out. *A fiver!* Harry felt his mouth drop open. Closing it, he answered with a mumbled "right-o" and pocketed the bill before anyone watching them might see.

"What is your name, young man?"

Harry hesitated. Giving up your name was a tricky affair, especially when your business with the asker wasn't yet clear. "Depends on who wants to know."

"Mine is William."

Harry wavered a moment more. "The name's Harry."

That he didn't offer up his mother's surname of "Stone" was a matter of both principle and practicality. William, if indeed that was his real name, hadn't given up his. If things got dicey, he might take it into his head to snaffle the old gent's purse and make a dash for it, in which case volunteering his surname would be pretty bleeding stupid.

Solemn eyes settled on Harry's face. "How old are you, Master Harry?"

Old enough was Harry's standard reply, but something in William's manner prompted him to give a more sober answer. "Fourteen, I think, maybe fifteen." Dragging the toe of his boot through the snow, he found himself admitting, "I'm . . . I'm not exactly sure."

Voice gentle, William asked, "Have you any parents, any

relative who might give you succor?"

Harry couldn't say what "succor" was, but he felt his eyes watering in a way that had nothing to do with the cold. "Only me mum, and she's dead." He looked sharply away, ashamed by the cracking of his voice. "Of the typhus," he added because at least typhus was a respectable ailment unlike the pox, which peppered you with putrid red legions and drove you mad as a March hare. Of course, considering what his mum had been, she might have had the pox, too. But no, Sally had assured him it was typhus that had carried her away, and Sally was the one person in the world he trusted not to lie.

You had to trust someone.

"I see," William said. Making himself meet that kind, knowing gaze, Harry could almost believe he did. "What if I were to tell you that, if you come with me now, I will help you secure employment in the country where you will receive wholesome food, clean clothing, and a warm bed?"

"Workhouse, you mean." Harry spat on the snow-covered cobbles to wash the detested word from his mouth. Everyone knew workhouses were terrible places where children were made to work all day and pray all night—and beaten soundly if they failed to do either in sufficient quantity.

A pained look crossed William's weathered face. "Roxbury House is not a workhouse, far from it. It is an orphanage established and operated by the Society of Friends—the Quakers. Commensurate with its mission of placing orphaned boys and girls in Christian homes is reaching out to those who have fallen into sin and preparing them to embark on productive, God-fearing lives."

Harry shrugged though inside his heart was drubbing his chest like a mallet. "What's that to do with me?"

"As it happens, the orphanage finds itself in need of an able young man to serve as assistant to the groundskeeper. The position would entail plenty of fresh air and exercise while working in the gardens and about the property."

The only air Harry had ever breathed was London air, heavy with coal dust and ripe with rubbish. As for gardening, he doubted he'd know a radish from a leek. Yet when he closed his eyes at night, the vision he summoned to send him to sleep was one of rolling green fields and cobalt-blue skies; of milk thick and creamy and still warm from the cow; of groves of apple trees where a boy might make a feast of fruit plucked straight from the branches.

William bent to him, his gaze boring into Harry's. "Might you be that able young man?"

The snow was falling faster now, feathering William's shoulders with silver, the silver of . . . angels' wings? Harry held his breath without knowing why.

Might you be that able young man?

Might he? Harry reached inside himself, searching his bruised soul. A chance for a new life, a chance for something clean and good—could such a chance truly be within his grasp?

Almost afraid to believe, he found his voice and mumbled, "As able as the next, I expect."

Seemingly satisfied, William nodded. "For tonight you

will come back with me to my house, where my dear wife will see to your supper. Tomorrow we shall set your feet on the path to a new start in life."

Without another word, he turned and set off in the direction of James Street, the tip of his cane leaving chink marks in the mounting snow. The scene reminded Harry of a story he'd once been told about a little boy and girl, lost in the wicked forest, who'd scattered a trail of breadcrumbs behind them so that they might be found.

I want to be found.

Heart pounding, Harry ran after him, thin soles skidding on the sticking snow. "Hold. *Hold!*"

Gulping down great mouthfuls of icy air, he raced on, ignoring the fiddle music, raucous laughter, and occasional shriek pouring out of the doorways of the gin palaces and brothels he streaked past. He caught up with William at Long Acre as he was climbing inside his carriage, an impressive black-lacquered conveyance, not unlike the ones Harry saw depositing well-heeled theatergoers at the entrance of Drury Lane.

He launched himself at the open door before the caped driver might close it in his face. Breathless, he fell back against the tufted leather seat across from William.

The older man regarded him with sober, searching eyes. "Well then, young Harry, am I right in thinking you are prepared to put your wicked ways behind you?"

Before he might answer, the carriage door slammed closed. He felt the small vibration, the finality of it, in every cell of his quivering body.

But when William reached out to him, it was only to hand him a carriage blanket and to point out the two flannel-wrapped bricks set on the floor beneath his seat. Enfolded in the warm wool, feet propped atop the heated bricks, Harry let his head drop back against the leather squab. Inhaling the comforting scents of fine leather, cigars, and bay rum, he felt his eyes drifting shut. When he opened them again, the carriage was at a standstill and a hand, firm but gentle, was shaking him to wakefulness.

He shook it off and scrambled upright, horrified he'd let himself fall asleep in the presence of a stranger. "Where . . . where are we?"

If William was offended, he gave no sign of it. Sitting back against the seat, he folded his gloved hands over the knob of his walking stick. "My house on Downing Street. Number ten, to be precise."

Ten Downing Street; why that direction should strike Harry as familiar he couldn't say, for lifting the leather window shade and peering out onto the quiet, elegant street, he could be certain he'd never been there before in his life. A plain-faced woman of middle years threw open the black-lacquered front door for them before the lion's-head knocker need be raised. When she whisked away William's wet coat and hat and then shooed him off to the library fire with dire predictions about the effect of the damp on his ague, Harry knew she must be William's "dear wife." As for Harry, he soon found himself wrapped in a homey quilt and bade to sit on a bench before the kitchen fire, a bowl of savory stew and wedge of crusty bread pressed into his hands. Afterward he was placed in the care of a plump, pleasant-faced maid who ushered him up the grand staircase to his room, which smelled so wonderfully clean that for a moment he just stood breathing in the freshly laundered scent. Though he'd expected to lie awake brooding on the queer turn his life had taken, he fell into exhausted slumber the moment his head hit the goose-feather pillow.

The next morning, bathed, fed to bursting, and wearing scrupulously clean if ill-fitting clothes, he stood on the train platform at Victoria Station, a coach-class ticket to Kent clenched in his fist for fear he might otherwise lose it.

"The Almighty loves the sinner as well as the saint," William told him just before he boarded. "Be a good lad, work hard, love the Lord and you will surely prosper."

In later years when Harry would recall his first and only meeting with William Ewart Gladstone, then Britain's prime minister, it would be with a mixture of amusement and awe. For it was in that unlikely encounter on a bitter winter night with the man known as the People's William that Harry Stone had begun to die . . . so that Hadrian St. Claire could be born.

CHAPTER ONE

"Your denial of my citizen's right to vote, is the denial of my right of consent as one of the governed, the denial of my right of representation as one of the taxed, the denial of my right to a trial by a jury of my peers as an offender against the law; therefore the denial of my sacred right to life, liberty, property . . ."

—SUSAN B. ANTHONY, *United States of America v. Susan B. Anthony*, 1873

Westminster, London
February 1890

Votes for women now. Votes for women NOW!"

The protestors' voices pitched higher still, *shriller* still, or so it seemed to Hadrian as he hurried across Westminster Bridge, the wind tearing at his greatcoat and scarf and threatening to rip the bowler from his head. Stepping out onto the crowded street, he tightened his grip on his camera, a German-made Anschütz with a shutter mechanism capable of arresting motion to one-thousandth of a second. He'd put the equipment to good test that afternoon at St. Thomas Hospital photographing a newly discovered medical anomaly. The poor bastard had been born with an enormous scrotum, tumor-mottled skin, and a chronic palsy that would have rendered traditional photographs little better than a blur. Even so, using his talent to turn a fellow human being into little better than a circus freak hadn't sat well with Hadrian, and the subject's sad-eyed patience in holding any number of humiliating poses had made him feel like the lowest of beasts. Now frozen, footsore, and famished, he couldn't reach his studio soon enough.

But to do so he first had to run the gauntlet of suffragists who'd overtaken Parliament Square. They'd camped out for coming on two days now, creating a bloody nuisance for pedestrians and conveyances alike. Dressed in somber grays and serious blacks, the fifty-odd females picketing beneath the gray wash of winter sky might just as easily pass for a funeral procession as a political rally were it not for the placards the women held aloft and the noise they emitted—especially the noise.

"Miss Caledonia Rivers to speak on the subject of female emancipation . . . Caxton Hall in Westminster . . . tomorrow evening . . . seven o'clock sharp."

Dodging traffic to cross to the sidewalk, Hadrian could

only shake his head. That any woman fortunate enough to possess a roof and four walls would march about in the bitter air struck him as a sort of perverse self-indulgence, a foolishness on par with going slumming in the stews or touring prison yards to observe the convicts picking oakum. He had no patience for it, none at all and when one bug-eyed female had the audacity to try and stuff a pamphlet in his already full hands, he swallowed an oath worthy of his Covent Garden days and darted inside the square's gated entrance.

He realized his mistake at once. Apparently not content with clogging the sidewalks, the damnable females had made camp within the park proper. A platform had been erected in the center of the green and several more dark-clad women busied themselves lighting the torches set about its perimeter. Giving them broad berth, he kept his head down and his sights trained on the opposite end of the wrought-iron gate.

The blare of a bobby's whistle from outside the park walls instinctively sent him swinging around—and barreling into a female's soft body. "Oof!"

Hadrian stared down in horror. The woman he'd knocked off her feet now sprawled at his, feathered hat askew and skirts bunched. On the frost-parched grass beside her, a leather briefcase crammed with papers stretched wide open.

He went down on his knees beside her. "Madam, are you all right?" Unleashing his grip on the camera, he slid an arm beneath her shoulders.

She jerked at his touch. Obscured by a netted hat veil and framed by wire-rimmed spectacles, her green eyes flashed fire. "It's 'miss,' actually." She elbowed her way upright and yanked down her skirts—but not before Hadrian caught sight of a pair of appealingly trim ankles. "And I would be in fine fettle, indeed, had you seen fit to mind where you were going." Broken ostrich feather dangling, she got to her knees and began collecting her papers.

Courtesy toward women was deeply ingrained, one of the few values Hadrian possessed, and the only claim he could make to being a gentleman by deed if not by birth. And so, rather than point out that she had bumped into him as well, he held out his hand to help her to her feet. "Allow me."

Beneath the weight of that atrocious hat, her head snapped up. "I believe I have had quite enough of your *help* for one day."

She'd barely got the declaration out when the demon wind kicked up, scattering vellum sheets to the four winds.

She leapt to her feet. "My papers!" Hiking up her skirts, she gave chase across the park. Over her shoulder, she shouted, "Well, don't just stand there. *Do* something!"

With a muttered prayer that his camera would still be there on his return, Hadrian abandoned it to run after her. Hell-bent on cheating the wrangling wind, he plucked one sheet from its skewer of wrought-iron fencepost and another from the foot of the statue of the late Benjamin Disraeli. At the lady's insistence, he retrieved two more from the upper branches of one very tall, very scratchy oak tree. Breathless, bruised, and sporting a tear in his coat, he shoved the last of the papers in his pocket and climbed down. Dropping to the hard-packed ground, he scanned the square for signs of his erstwhile victim, but she appeared to have vanished.

He was on the verge of giving up and going on his way when he spotted her, down on all fours and buried shoulder-deep in the boxwood hedge. Coming up behind her, he tapped her smartly on the back. "What the devil do you think you're about?"

From beneath the branches, her muffled voice answered, "Collecting my papers naturally." She crawled out, feathers hanging at half-mast and a clutch of vellum in one grubby glove.

This time she accepted his hand up without argument. Standing face to face, he saw she was tall, though no match for his six-foot-four frame. The novelty of looking a woman more or less in the eye had him peering beyond the blur of veil for a closer study. No great beauty, he decided, nor was she any green girl. If he had to make a stab at guessing, he'd peg her at thirty-odd, perhaps a year or two older than himself, and a spinster judging by the "miss" as well as the dreary clothing. And yet the sage-colored eyes beneath the slash of dark brows were both expressive and arresting, and the full mouth and softly squared jaw completed a pleasing enough picture.

Caught up, it took her discreet cough to remind him of the papers bulging from his pocket. Handing them over, he said, "I think this is the lot."

"Thank you." She took them from him, her gloved fingertips brushing his, and improbably he felt the warm tingle of her touch shoot straight to his groin. Stuffing the papers inside her case, she spotted the mud and dried leaves festooning the front of her coat. "Oh dear, I'm a mess" she said, swiping at the muck with her soiled glove. "I never can seem to manage the trick of remembering a handkerchief."

He fumbled in his pocket. "Here, have mine." He pressed the square into her palm, again experiencing that peculiar surge of heat.

She accepted with a grateful smile and bent to brush away the dirt. "Thank you—again." Straightening to her full, glorious height, she handed back his handkerchief.

Feeling in better spirits, he shook his head. "Keep it. Really, it's the least I can do after mowing you down like so much lawn grass."

She laughed then, a soft airy tinkling that made him think of the wind chimes his landlady insisted on hanging by his backdoor. "All right then . . . if you're sure." She stuffed the wadded ball of linen into her coat pocket and turned to go. Stopping in her tracks, she looked back. "Mind you don't lose *your* papers."

"My papers? Oh . . . quite."

Good God, he'd left his best camera out in the open and, worse yet, had been on the verge of forgetting it entirely. What the devil was the matter with him? Jogging over to retrieve it, he thought of his flat, empty save for his cat, and realized he was no longer so very eager to reach it—at least not alone.

"I'm not always such an oaf, you know," he called back, wracking his brain for something clever to say, some pretense to hold her.

From a few feet away, she cupped a hand to her ear. "Sorry?"

"I said I'm not always such an *oaf.*"

"Oh." She paused in mid-step, appearing to consider that. "Well, I'm not usually such a harridan, either, except when I'm nervous—or in this case, late."

"I don't think you're a harridan." Camera in hand, he closed the space separating them in three ridiculously long strides. "It's these protestors, taking up the whole bloody square as if they own every brick and statue, spewing their rubbish at all hours that have everyone on edge. I only cut through the park to avoid them."

Mouth lifting into a pretty smile of full pink lips and straight white teeth, she nodded to the park beyond them. "It would seem you've rather failed in that regard."

"Yes, I suppose I have." Looking back over his shoulder, he saw they were the object of a good many whispers and gawking stares. Their mad dash must have made an amusing spectacle indeed. Ordinarily that realization would have set him fuming but rather than care, he found himself saying, "There's a tea shop just around the corner. Allow me to make amends by buying you a cup?"

She shook her head, looking adorably shy and far younger than she had at first when she'd still been tight-lipped and cross. "That isn't necessary. And I've an . . . engagement to keep."

Ah yes, presumably the engagement for which he had made her late already. A decent fellow would accept defeat and send her on her way. Yet the mental image of how splendid she would look freed from all those ghastly clothes and wearing only his bedsheet prompted him to press, "As you're late already, why not postpone it altogether, at least until you've thawed?"

She shook her head, causing the broken hat feathers to careen like a torn sail. "I can't. I really must be going." The firming of her mouth told him he'd been too forward, that this time she really did mean to go.

"Ah well, perhaps we'll *bump* into one another again sometime." He fished inside his coat pocket for one of his business cards as a pretense to asking her name.

"Yes, perhaps we shall," she allowed but there was no hope of it in her eyes. She turned to go and Hadrian knew there would be no more keeping her, that this really was goodbye.

Before she could take a step, a squat woman with salt-and-pepper hair and a man's plaid muffler wrapped about her short neck rushed up to intercept her. "Good Lord, Callie, are you all right? I was outside the gate and only just heard what happened."

Beneath her veil, the woman—Callie—flushed bright crimson. "Calm yourself, Harriet. I am perfectly fine. I took a bit of a tumble, and my briefcase spilled." Her shy-eyed gaze shifted to Hadrian. "This gentleman was kind enough to help me."

From behind horn-rimmed spectacles, Harriet's beady eyes dropped to the camera case in Hadrian's hand. "I don't know what rag of a newspaper you're with, sir, but if your scheme is to scare up scandal and rubbish by waylaying Miss Rivers and photographing her in disarray, then you'd best think again."

Taken off-guard, Hadrian demurred when from the vicinity of the stage someone with a bullhorn belted out, "Miss Caledonia Rivers to make her address. Five minutes, ladies. Five minutes . . ."

Callie Rivers. Caledonia Rivers. It was then that the fog inside Hadrian's head lifted. His mystery woman was one of them, a suffragette! And not just any suffragette, but their leader! Seeing her through new eyes, he took in the spinsterish coat, the awful hat, and the leather case containing the oh-so-important papers, and asked himself how a piquant smile and a pair of pretty ankles had turned him into such an absolute idiot.

He stared at her, feeling like a Biblical figure from whose eyes the scales had just fallen. "Your pressing engagement, I take it?"

She answered with a brusque nod, at once prim and proper and utterly businesslike. "Quite."

Now that his initial shock was fading, he could at least appreciate the irony of the situation. The first woman to pique his interest in years was the celebrated champion of a cause he'd come to loathe.

"Lest we part as strangers, my name is St. Claire. Hadrian St. Claire." By this time, he had the sought-after business card in hand and his shock firmly in check. Handing her the card, he said, "I'm not a reporter. I'm a photographer. I have a studio not far from here on Great George. Portraiture is my specialty."

She tucked his card into her pocket with nary a glance. "I'm afraid I'm not terribly fond of having my photograph taken."

"Pity. You'd make for a most intriguing subject." And because he had absolutely nothing to lose—now that he knew who and what she was, what possible interest in her could he have—he looked directly into Caledonia Rivers's beautiful, mortified eyes and added, "I should have recognized you from the newspaper etchings, but they hardly did you justice. You're far prettier, and far younger, than I would have supposed."

Beneath the veil, the stain on her cheeks darkened from pale pink to dusky rose but, to her credit, she didn't look away. "I think you mock me, sir."

"On the contrary, miss, if either of us is the subject of mockery, I rather think it is me." He nodded toward a clutch of young women watching them and giggling behind their gloves.

Harriet skewered him with a sharp look before giving him her back. "Callie, we really must be on our way." She hooked her plump arm through her friend's and began leading her away.

"Ladies." He tipped his bowler to them both, but it was Caledonia Rivers whom he followed with his eyes as she hurried toward the platform, creased and muddied skirts trailing the pavement, broken hat feathers caught up in the fingers of the wind.

So that was Caledonia Rivers, the celebrated suffragette spokeswoman making headlines in all the newspapers. What was it the press was calling her these days? Ah yes, The Maid of Mayfair. Unlike so many of her suffragette sisters whose reputations skirted the fringe of respectability, Caledonia Rivers was said to be so very good and virtuous—and yet not too good or too virtuous to indulge in a bit of a flirt in a public park, the little hypocrite.

He'd only paid her the compliment to torture her, and yet in his roundabout way he'd spoken nothing but the truth. The flesh-and-blood woman with whom he'd passed the last delightful few minutes scarcely resembled the stern-faced amazon the newspapers made her out to be.

As for the "maid" part, he was deucedly sorry he wouldn't have the opportunity to test that out for himself.

❦

"Harriet, you've missed your calling entirely. Why, you should have been a detective," Callie teased after they'd mounted the platform, her crumpled speech clutched in one hand. "I just supposed that case of his held business papers."

Harriet shrugged. "I know a thing or two about cameras is all, but if I'd been thinking straight, I would have known that fancy German model would be beyond the touch of the Fleet Street boys."

By now Callie was well acquainted with most of the press photographers by face if not by name. She was quite confident she'd never seen Mr. St. Claire before today. No, him she would have remembered most particularly.

"I still don't trust him," Harriet went on, face screwed into a frown. "He had lecherous eyes."

Remembering how that blue-eyed gaze had seemed to peel away her layers of clothing to expose the curves she took such pains to harness and hide, Callie dropped her eyes to the papers she was supposed to be collating. "Really, and I thought him a rather pleasant young man."

Pleasant although admittedly forward and possessed of enough wicked charm for ten men but then with those striking looks, he was likely accustomed to getting what he wanted from women. But looks and charm aside, she'd had no business dallying with him—and in plain view in the midst of the rally, no less. Such behavior, although entirely innocent on her part, was dangerous indeed, fodder for the scandal sheets, and the surest way to set tongues to wagging within the Movement as well. With the new Parliamentary suffrage bill slated to come before the Commons by the month's end, now was the very worst of times for her to take foolish risks. Ever since the press had branded her with that absurd sobriquet, Maid of Mayfair, her enemies in the Conservative opposition had kept even closer watch than before, determined to catch her up in some scandal or embarrassment. Certainly they'd all come too far, fought too hard, to have some selfish slip-up on her part bring their collective hopes and dreams crashing down like the proverbial house of cards. Her mentor, Mrs. Fawcett, the members of the London Society for Women's

Suffrage of which Fawcett was president, the women braving the cold within the park's ironwork gates—everyone was counting on her to see them through to victory.

She would not, must not, let them down.

Yet it had been a long time since someone, a man, had told her she was pretty.

Humming a dance hall tune beneath his breath, Hadrian walked westward to where Bridge Street became Great George. Preoccupied with mentally fleshing out the details of Caledonia Rivers's veil-blurred visage, he took his customary shortcut through the alley behind his studio. By the time the sound of two sets of heavy footfalls reached his ears, it was too late. He looked back over his shoulder to the pair of familiar hulking figures closing in and felt his mouth go dry. Sam Sykes and his fellow debt collector, Jimmie Deans. *Damn!*

Trapped, the best he could do was plant his camera behind the nearest rubbish bin and turn about to face them while hoping his legendary luck would hold. "Don't tell me you lads have come to have photographic portraits made?" He forced a smile even as he wondered how many teeth they intended on leaving him.

Thumbs in their pockets, Sykes and Deans drew up before him. "Best wipe that shite grin from your face, St. Claire before I'm minded to wipe it off for you," Sykes warned. "Your account is three months past due, and Bull wants his four hundred pounds, or else." Expression dour, he shook his shaved head. "You know Bull's terms as well as I do."

Bull was Bull Boyle, former pugilist and now proprietor of the Mad Hare Gaming Emporium in Bow, an establishment Hadrian heartily wished he'd never stepped inside. As for his "terms," the basic code was a pound of flesh for every hundred pounds past due. A code which, in retrospect, Hadrian really ought to have considered more carefully before playing not one or two, not three, but four hands of baccarat against the house at one hundred pounds per match—on credit. Only there'd been fresh dry plates and a new tripod to purchase and the rent on his studio to pay, not to mention his friend, Sally's orphans relying on him to carry them through to the spring.

Stalling, Hadrian said, "Tell Bull I need more time, another two weeks, and then I'll pay him what I owe him at double his rate."

Sykes spat onto the cobbles at Hadrian's feet. "Talk, St. Claire. It's always talk with you. I'd just as soon cut out that clever tongue of yours as waste me time hearing any more of your lies." He reached inside his open coat and drew a carving knife from his belt. "Jimmie, time to get to work."

Deans stepped forward and with impressive swiftness for one so bulky, seized Hadrian, pinning him against the stone wall. "Should we start with his ears or his nose?" He shoved his bulldog face up to Hadrian's, so close that Hadrian could count the black hairs sprouting from each nostril and all but taste the leeks on his breath.

Holding the knife so that the metal caught the glimmer

of waning light, Sykes considered the question. "Oh, I dunno mate, you decide."

Good God but they meant to carve him up like a Christmas goose. Sweat trickling down his back, Hadrian said, "I can get the blunt, but I need more time." Inspiration struck and he added, "I've a big commission about to come in."

Sykes cocked a bushy brow and jabbed the point of the blade into Hadrian's Adam's apple. "How big?"

Hadrian sucked in his breath as sticky warmth trickled down his collar. "What would you say if I told you I was to photograph the Prince of Wales?" As lies went this one was a corker and yet he was counting on Sykes and Deans to be too ignorant to know that the London firm of John Mayall held exclusive rights to photographing members of the royal family.

"I'd say you were a bloody liar, that's what."

"Suit yourself, but I can't very well take the photograph if I'm in hospital, now can I? Who knows but Bertie might be minded to ask why I've had to beg off, and in my delirium I might accidentally whisper a name or two in the royal ear, if you take my meaning."

Deans, the slower-witted of the two, looked to Sykes for reassurance. "He's bluffing, ain't he Sam? He don't really know the Prince of Wales . . . do he?"

Hadrian shrugged, the movement possible now that Sykes had withdrawn the knife. "Who's to say that I don't? Either way, it's your call, mates. Of course if I do, I doubt Bull will thank you for being the ones responsible for having the police pay him a little impromptu call. Why, there's no telling what the bobbies might find if they turn over the place, now, is there? And Bull, well, I wouldn't be surprised if he took it in his head to collect his own pound of flesh—or two." He punctuated the latter statement by dividing a knowing look between the henchmen.

Sykes spat again and then wiped his mouth on his sleeve, considering. "All right, St. Claire. You win—for now. You can have your two weeks but after that . . ." He sliced a finger across his throat in the age-old gesture.

Expression grim, Deans fingered the scar slashing his stubbled jaw. "Bull ain't going to like it."

An eye on Hadrian, Sykes shrugged. "Two more weeks and then it'll be five hundred pounds he owes, not four. In the meantime, we'll let him keep his eyes and ears. Bull has plenty o' trophies in the pickle jar as it is." He poked a thick stump of forefinger in the vicinity of Hadrian's face. "But mark me, St. Claire, we'll be back to collect and, fancy friends or no, you'll pay up or we'll finish you."

Hadrian watched them back out of the alley. Once they'd disappeared into the encroaching twilight, he took off his hat and swiped a gloved hand across his sweating brow. In the distance, he could make out bits and pieces of a speech in progress.

"Distinguished colleagues . . . guests, sisters . . . brothers."

Despite the tunnel-like echo of the bullhorn, the female voice rang out full and rich, confident and strong. A feminine voice—yet the voice of a natural leader.

Caledonia Rivers's voice. Who could have guessed that

bumping into the suffragette would prove to be the nicest part of his day?

It was coming on twilight when Callie stepped up to the makeshift podium amidst the flash fire of press-photographers' cameras. As always when she was about to speak, her stomach fluttered and skipped as though an entire brigade of butterflies had taken residence within. Inside her fur-lined leather gloves, her palms were damp with perspiration.

Yet she also knew that as soon as she began, any nervousness would melt away as her gaze and heart connected with the collective of the crowd. In this case it wasn't much of a turnout as rallies went, just about fifty-odd, and most of them recognizable as LWSS members and representatives from the other member organizations comprising Millicent Fawcett's newly formed National Union of Women's Suffrage Societies. But then again, after standing about in plummeting temperatures and rain-soaked fog for two days now, perhaps the already converted were more in need of inspiration than anyone.

Before beginning, she took a moment to push her borrowed spectacles higher on the bridge of her nose. The eyewear was an accessory, a crutch of sorts, the corrective glass replaced with clear. It was foolish, she knew, but for whatever reason looking out at the world from behind the barricade of spectacles bolstered her self-confidence.

"Distinguished colleagues, guests, sisters. And brothers," she added, nodding toward her friend, Theodore—Teddy—Cavendish, who smiled and saluted her from the back of the crowd.

Looking out onto the green, she took note of the running noses and cold-pinched faces and decided on the spot to cut her speech by half. The bullhorn proved to be more encumbrance than boon. Halfway through, she handed it to Harriet and made do with her own raised voice.

Afterward, she spent a good quarter of an hour shaking hands with women who came up to meet her, society ladies and tradesmen's wives, women of independent means and women who hadn't a penny apart from what their husbands gave them in allowance. Women who had never known a day of toil in the whole of their lives and others who had known little but. By the end of it, her fingers felt so numb she could barely feel the eager hands pumping hers and she was keenly aware that her nose had begun to run. Without thinking, she reached into her coat pocket for her handkerchief, but the rumpled linen square she retrieved wasn't hers. Seeing the "H.S." embroidered on an upper corner, she stuffed it back into her pocket unused, a flush working its way across her wind-chapped face.

Her vice president, Lydia Witherspoon, was the first to greet her when she stepped down. "Well done as always, Callie. But are you quite sure you're well? You look a bit feverish."

"Do I? It must be the effects of the wind, not to mention the coffee Harriet has plied me with for fear I'd fall asleep mid-sentence." Eager to change the subject, she turned to her secretary, already busy gathering up their things. As soon as Lydia had moved on, she leaned in to Harriet and confided, "I'm afraid I may have no voice left for tomorrow night."

Harriet paused from her packing. Looking up, she grinned broadly. "I hope you find it because we're expecting two hundred or more."

Two hundred or more. Callie suppressed a sigh. Now that her address was concluded, she felt a profound weariness tugging at her, an exhaustion that went beyond mere physical fatigue. How lovely it would be to go home and curl up beneath the covers with a cup of tea and a book, perhaps one of those sweetly foolish penny dreadfuls she hadn't picked up since her schoolgirl years, when she'd still believed in fictions like *True Love* and *Happily Ever After*. But these days leisure was beyond her reach, a self-indulgence for which she simply hadn't the time. She had any number of tasks to attend to before she could seek out her bed, and neither novel reading nor daydreaming about handsome young photographers could be counted among them.

Yet when Harriet groaned and announced, "Oh no, here he comes," Callie's heart leapt into her throat. Hadrian St. Claire, he'd come back! She turned about eagerly. But instead of the handsome photographer, it was Teddy walking briskly toward them, his bottle green coat and plaid trousers making him easy to track in the twilight.

Swallowing her disappointment, Callie fixed on a smile. "Teddy, I spotted you earlier. How good of you to come."

"I wouldn't have missed it for the riches of the world." All smiles, he reached for her hands, planting a kiss atop each in turn. "By Jove, that bit about 'uniting to break the yoke of patriarchal serfdom' really had them going."

From the corner of her eye, Callie caught Harriet rolling her eyes. "If you'll excuse me, those placards won't jump back into the boxes by themselves."

As soon as Harriet was out of earshot, Teddy said, "She's warming to me, I can tell."

Callie couldn't help but smile. "I shouldn't hold my breath if I were you."

"Why not, what the deuce's wrong with me?"

Callie allowed herself a brief disloyal glance at his mustache, the tips waxed so that they stood out like handlebars. Every time she'd tried imagining kissing the small pink mouth beneath, she found she simply couldn't. Kissing Hadrian St. Claire, however, required no imagination at all. Thinking of what the press of those firm lips upon hers might feel like, she felt a wave of warmth roll through her in spite of the sharp air.

Thoroughly ashamed, she reached up to check that her veil was still in place. "Not a thing. It's only that our Harriet is a very serious sort and prefers those about her to behave in kind."

"Be serious, so that's the way to win over the old harridan. But what I'd much rather hear is the way to win *you* over. I don't suppose you've any hints in that department, hmm?"

"Oh, Teddy, you have won me—as a *friend*," Callie said,

not bothering to keep the exasperation from her voice for as many times as he'd asked her to be his wife, she still wished she might give him a different answer.

In spite of his garish clothes and effete ways, Teddy was in so many ways the perfect companion, steady and uncomplicated and, she suspected, easily as lonely as she was. Most importantly, he didn't have a cruel bone in his body. And though she suspected what he liked most about involvement in the suffragist cause was that his participation in it irked his straight-laced father to no end, his support of her was as ungrudging as it was unconditional.

As always, he took her refusal with good grace. "Then as a *friend*, I trust you'll allow me to see you home before you catch your death." Turning serious, he added, "Really old girl, you look fit to drop, and Harriet can manage without our help, mine especially."

Relieved to have the awkward moment past, she allowed herself to be persuaded. "In that case, yes."

She hooked her arm through his and together they walked out to the street corner where in short time Teddy hailed a hansom. Leaning back against the cracked leather seat, Callie let her eyes drift closed, vaguely aware of him giving the driver her directions and settling a carriage blanket across her lap.

"You're so good to me, Teddy," she said, yawning into her glove, even as the part of her that could never quite settle down to contentment demanded that surely there must be more to life than that.

Unbidden, an image of warm blue eyes pushed to the forefront of her thoughts, joined in short order by a fine strong nose, molded jaw glistening with a hint of golden stubble, and a firm, masculine mouth.

Oh, Callie. Always wanting more, hasn't that ever been your fatal failing?

She forced her attention back to Teddy, settled into the seat across from her. Gazing into his dear, plain face, she chided herself for acting the part of a perfect idiot.

Steady, uncomplicated, and kind—what more could there possibly be?

CHAPTER TWO

"A *free* man is a noble being; a *free* woman is a contemptible being. Freedom for a man is emancipation from degrading conditions which prevent the expansion of his soul into godlike grandeur and nobility, which it is assumed is his natural tendency in freedom. Freedom for a woman is, on the contrary, escape from those necessary restraining conditions which prevent the sinking of her soul into degradation and vice, which it is all unconsciously assumed is her natural tendency."

—Victoria Woodhull and Tennessee Claflin, *Woodhull & Claflin's Weekly*, 1871

Later that evening Hadrian stood at his washstand, scouring the silver nitrate solution from his hands. Drying in his studio's dark room were the photographs of the medical anomaly. Looking past the misshapen features to the man's eyes, Hadrian had felt an eerie kinship. Reflected in their dark depths was the very same expression he'd seen when he'd peered into his shaving mirror to bathe the dried blood from his throat.

Hunted, didn't he know just how that felt?

While he'd processed the pictures, he'd reviewed his options for raising the five hundred pounds needed to settle his debt with Boyle. Short of robbing a bank, the only possibility he could come up with was to ask his barrister friend, Gavin Carmichael for another loan. When he'd shown up on Gavin's doorstep a year ago, Gavin had greeted him like a long-lost brother rather than an old orphanage chum he hadn't seen in fifteen years. It was Gavin who'd helped him settle on his new name, Hadrian after the great Roman emperor who'd started out life as an orphan, and St. Claire because they'd both agreed it had a certain cachet—a solid, old-money ring certain to put people with real money at their ease. He'd ferried Hadrian around to soirees and theater receptions, to rich old biddy's "at-homes" and to his gentlemen's club, putting him in the path of every well-heeled friend and acquaintance he could come up with. While Gavin made do with letting a shabby suite of rooms at the Inns of Court, he'd fronted Hadrian the money to set up in Parliament Square. How then could he ask such a friend for five hundred pounds more, a sum that as a junior barrister Gavin likely didn't have anyway, to bail him out of a situation brought on by nothing more than his own recklessness? No, he'd let Sykes and Deans flay him alive before he'd stoop so low as to take advantage of his friend any further.

Brave sentiment that and yet the clang of the shop bell below gave him such a start that he very nearly knocked the washbasin from its stand. *Get hold of yourself, man. When Boyle and company come for you, it won't be through the front door.*

But it was late, past six o'clock, and with the exception of the Parliament, which would reconvene at nine for the evening session, the government offices and area shops would be dark by now as his too should be if only he'd remembered to turn his sign over to CLOSED. Heart drumming, he stripped off his apron and hurried down the stairs. Seeing neither Boyle nor his henchmen but a well-dressed man of late middle age pacing his shop floor, he let his lungs expand with relief. "May I help you, sir?" he asked, stepping forward.

"That depends." The gentleman turned about and Hadrian saw that this was no apple-cheeked shopkeeper or government clerk but a senior statesman or government official of rank, the very sort of well-heeled client he'd set up shop hoping to attract.

"Are you St. Claire?" he asked, gaze flickering over Hadrian in such a way that he was reminded he hadn't taken time to roll down his shirtsleeves or put back on his tie.

"I am."

Like a phrenologist feeling the bumps on a skull to infer mental faculties and character, Hadrian examined the gaunt, weathered face for the clues housed within flesh and bone. A high forehead etched with deep lines almost always meant the subject was a worrier. The long, thin nose and flared nostrils bespoke of arrogance, an absolute belief in his superiority to others. The down-turned mouth betrayed bitterness—life might owe him everything, but so far the rewards received had been less than satisfactory. But as always it was the eyes more so than any other feature that gave away the subject and meeting those icy gray orbs, so pale they appeared opaque, Hadrian read—merciless.

"Josiah Dandridge, MP for Horsham." The introduction was not accompanied by the customary extension of hand.

Glancing down, Hadrian saw that the attaché case Dandridge carried was covered in Moroccan leather and embossed with the Parliamentary seal. "And how may I assist you, Mr. Dandridge?"

"How, indeed?" Dandridge strolled over to the display case where Hadrian set out samples of his most popular item, the pocket-sized portrait photographs known as *cartes de visites*. Tapping on the glass, he asked, "This portrait is the same displayed in your shop window, is it not?"

Coming up beside him, Hadrian glanced down at the portrait card of Lady Katherine Lindsey and nodded. "Lady Katherine is my bestselling 'PB' at the moment."

The PBs, or Professional Beauties, were society ladies who consented to have their portraits displayed for sale in shop windows all over London. Only in Lady Katherine's case, in return for Hadrian's turning over to her half of the money from every copy sold, she'd agreed to sit for him exclusively. What she did with her share he'd never asked, although she would hardly be the first highborn woman to have secret money troubles.

"You show a remarkable talent for bringing out your subject's underlying vulnerability."

Hadrian looked away from Lady Katherine's striking visage, the dark intelligent eyes openly defiant and subtly sad, and thought, *you, sir, could be a very dangerous man.* "I doubt the lady in question would take kindly to hearing herself described as vulnerable. Lady Katherine is one of the most independent-minded women I've ever known."

Beneath the overhang of salt-and-pepper brows, Dandridge's wintry eyes hardened to chips of ice. "You speak of female independence as though it is some sort of virtue. Pray do not tell me you are one of those dewy-eyed idealists who would see the vote handed over to a pack of hysterical, ranting women?"

So Hadrian wasn't the only one set on edge by the suffragist protest in the square. Hoping to steer their interchange toward a possible commission, he shrugged and said, "Politics have never interested me."

"Yet you must have some convictions, some principles you wish to see advanced?"

Why a man such as Dandridge should care about the state of his conscience was a mystery to Hadrian but regardless he answered honestly, "I leave principles and convictions to men with the money and time to pursue them. For those of us who must work for a living, the only interest we can afford to serve is our own."

The lined face relaxed measurably. "So, St. Claire, you

are a pragmatist at heart. How refreshing."

The MP resumed walking about the room, pausing to examine the framed photographs lining the studio walls. Tempted as Hadrian was to inform the arrogant bastard he was closed for the night, he strained for patience. He needed money, he needed it desperately, and if a potential patron with influence and tin-lined pockets had a mind to keep him standing about after hours, there was nothing to be done but bite back his ire, smooth the scowl from his face, and await his pleasure like the lackey he'd sworn never again to be.

Dandridge stopped before an eight-by-seven-inch platinum print of a female nude lying supine atop a bed of fringed pillows and Oriental carpeting, a cone of chiaroscuro light playing with the shadows framing the curve of one alabaster breast.

"Very fine," he said at length, his back to Hadrian. "The clarity of the foreground is impressive and the setting shows a far greater attention to detail than one normally sees."

At least there was no faulting the fellow's taste. The classically inspired scene had been a true labor of love, the fruit of a fortnight of experimenting with various props and lighting effects and poses until he finally hit upon the composition that matched the mental picture he'd been carrying about in his mind. At one time he'd thought to enter it in the Photographic Society's annual exhibition, but now it occurred to him that the picture might be put to a more practical purpose.

Biting back his pride, he ventured, "If you'd care to

purchase it . . ."

With a shake of his head, Dandridge dispelled any hope of that. Turning to Hadrian, he remarked, "I can't help but notice that your subjects are all females."

Hadrian shrugged but inside he was wary. "I like working with women for many reasons, not the least of which is that they are generally better disciplined about keeping still."

"I see. And do they, in turn, like *working* with you?" When Hadrian didn't immediately answer, Dandridge turned back to the nude, his gloved finger stabbing the spot where her drape dipped to reveal that perfect breast. "That woman must have liked you very much indeed to allow you to photograph her in such a . . . vulnerable state."

"Justine is a professional model and accustomed to posing for painters."

"Yet I wonder, has any portraitist before managed to elicit from her such a sweetly dreamy countenance, such unaffected sensuality?"

Hadrian folded his arms across his chest. "I wouldn't know." He had, in fact, taken the girl to bed on any number of occasions, but he'd be damned before he'd expose his private life to satisfy a stranger's prurient curiosity. At the end of his patience, he added, "It's late, Mr. Dandridge. Perhaps you should tell me how I can be of service."

"Very well, then. What I have in mind is for you to make me a photograph such as this only I've a very particular model in mind."

So finally they were to get to the bottom of all this

hemming and hawing. The old goat must have a mistress set up somewhere and wanted a nude portrait of her. Feeling on firmer footing, Hadrian walked over to his pine worktable. "If you'd care to take a seat, we can discuss the specifics of—"

"I want the most damning photograph you can possibly make. Beyond that I shall leave the details in your capable hands."

Hadrian halted from pulling out a chair. "If this is meant to be some sort of joke . . ."

"It's no joke, of that you may rest assured. I want the subject stripped bare, St. Claire. I want her utterly denuded and humiliated, exposed to the world for the filthy slut I know her to be."

Hadrian shook his head and turned away. "If it's a private detective you want to spy on your mistress, I have a barrister friend who can recommend you to one of the better firms."

"Damn it, man, I don't want some snitch's blurred snapshot. I want a portrait, a portrait such as only someone with your expertise can make, and I am prepared to pay handsomely for it."

Desperation warring with decency, Hadrian turned back. "How handsomely?"

Dandridge's smile would have befitted Lucifer himself. "What say you to five thousand pounds?"

Five thousand pounds! Hadrian's mouth went dry. To someone such as him, it was nothing short of a fortune. For a handful of seconds, he allowed himself to imagine Sykes's and Deans's crestfallen faces when they learned he'd cleared his debt with Boyle, that they wouldn't have the pleasure of carving him up after all. He glanced down at his hands, still stained with the silver nitrate solution that never seemed to come entirely off, and considered all he might accomplish if he could afford an assistant to help with developing the exposures and maintaining the apparatuses and generally keeping the shop in good order. Who knew, but perhaps down the road he'd even bring on another photographer to handle the commissions too small or too mundane to interest him.

Finding his voice, he said, "That is a very large sum, Mr. Dandridge. Even if I agreed, what makes you think the lady in question will consent to sit for me at all, let alone disrobe to do so?"

Dandridge raked his gaze over Hadrian as though he were assessing goods at Fleet Market. "Don't be overmodest, St. Claire. You're devilishly handsome, and you have a certain rough charm that is not without appeal. I'd wager you can be persuasive indeed when it serves you. If even half of the rumors circulating about you are true, you'll have the slut spreading her legs for both you and your camera within a fortnight. Unless, of course, she fancies girls—some of them do, you know."

Hadrian tried to ignore the ice water trickling its way through his veins. "Them?"

"Suffragists." Dandridge spat out the word. "They are like a plague of locusts descended on the nation, a cancer that spreads with the growth of a single cell. And like a cancer, our only hope for a cure is to root them out, starting with their leaders."

Half-hoping Dandridge would withdraw his offer, he pressed, "And you think to accomplish so much with a single photograph?"

"Not just any photograph, St. Claire, but *the* photograph, the one that will take down Caledonia Rivers once and for all."

Caledonia Rivers! Like exposures brought out in the development process, the impressions took ghostly shape before Hadrian's mind's eye: a tall statuesque form swathed in an old-fashioned coat, a proud head hidden beneath a monstrous hat, the sweet curve of a strong but utterly feminine jaw blurred by a black web of veil. Best of all had been those magical few moments before he'd known who and what she was when ignorance truly had been bliss, and he'd stared at her like a child on the lookout for a falling star, wishing with all his might for the wind to lift up that veil and reveal the woman beneath.

But if he accepted Dandridge's bargain, he would be exposing far more than the lady's face. "Why must it be her?" he asked, the words sticking in his throat.

"Caledonia Rivers is young, she is well-born, and unlike her suffragist *sisters*, she possesses a reputation that is presently above reproach. As president of the London Society for Women's Suffrage, she is one of three suffragist leaders to meet privately with the prime minister before their infernal bill is brought back before the Commons at month's end." Dandridge paused to take out his handkerchief and mop the

43.

sweat from his brow. "Bring her down and you bring the whole bloody Movement down with her. Reveal her for the foul slut she is and any self-respecting Member who otherwise might have been persuaded to cast his vote for extending the franchise will withdraw his support. The bill will die in the House without ever making it to a final reading. But mind you there must be no ambiguity, no uncertainty at all. The photograph must be damning, indisputably so. I mean to see Caledonia Rivers not only ruined but vanquished. Vanquished, St. Claire, I'll settle for no less."

Callie's aunt-by-marriage, Charlotte—Lottie—greeted her inside the entrance of her townhouse on Half Moon Street. In a single glance, she took in her niece's ruined hat and rumpled, mud-stained clothes, and gave a rueful shake of her elaborately coiffed silver curls. "Good heavens, Callie, you look as though you've been run over by a coach and four."

Callie looked up from working cold-stiffened fingers out of her gloves. "Now don't fuss, Auntie."

"But I'm concerned about you, my dear. You work too hard by half. It wouldn't hurt you to take some time for yourself, get out a bit. The new Gilbert & Sullivan operetta is playing at the Strand and the *on dit* is that it's positively delicious."

"Honestly, you're as bad as Teddy." Callie reached up to unpin her hat. Glad to be rid of the beastly thing—what had she been thinking to let the milliner talk her into such a monstrosity—she handed it to their maid, Jenny, along with her gloves.

All brisk efficiency, Jenny set the articles on the hall table and moved to help Callie with her coat. Frowning at the stains, she tossed the coat over her arm. "I'll take this upstairs and give it a good brushing." As she started toward the stairs, a treacherous scrap of white fell from the coat onto the parquet tiled floor.

Face afire, Callie dove for the handkerchief but Lottie, spry for her age, reached it first. "Oh my, what is this?" Straightening on creaking knees, Lottie looked from the crumpled linen to her niece, her lovely, lined face an open question. "Whoever is H.S.?"

Feeling like she'd been caught with her hand in the honey pot, Callie found herself babbling, "No one . . . a man . . . I met in the square. Not met really. Bumped into, I suppose you could say." She glanced at Jenny, eyes bright as buttons. "Admittedly I'm selfish as winter is long, but what I'd like most now is to pour a nice cup of scalding tea directly down my throat." Hoping the maid would take the hint, she put an arm about her aunt's slender shoulders and steered her toward the parlor.

But Lottie was not about to let her off that easily. The older woman had scarcely settled herself on the silk-covered settee before insisting, "Do tell me more about this H.S. How were you introduced? What sort of profession does he practice? Is he in sympathy with the Cause?"

With a sigh, Callie sank into the overstuffed wingchair

by the fire, her habitual spot. "Truly there's nothing to tell. His name is Hadrian St. Claire. He's a photographer of some sort. Apparently he has a studio not far from Parliament Square. We literally ran into one another in the park."

"Well, don't leave me hanging on tenterhooks, dearest. Do go on."

Feeling the beginning of a headache building at the backs of her eyes, Callie took off the spectacles, which had belonged to her uncle, Lottie's late husband, and kneaded the bridge of her nose.

"There is absolutely nothing more to tell. He was kind enough to give me his handkerchief and help me collect my speech and then he was on his way." In the interest of sanity, hers, she saw no earthly reason to mention the very improper invitation to tea which, she assured herself, she never would have accepted.

Lottie busied herself with plucking nonexistent pieces of lint from her skirts, but Callie could see the wheels of her aunt's mind working fast and furious. "It's only good manners that you return his handkerchief to him. After it's been laundered and pressed, of course."

"There is no need. He told me to keep it." Recalling the way his tweed overcoat had fitted to his broad shoulders as only fine tailoring could, Callie added, "I'm quite sure he must have a drawer full at home."

"Even so, I don't suppose there are all that many photographic shops in Parliament Square. I'm sure we could find his without great difficulty."

Callie thought of his card, presumably still tucked safely out of sight in her coat's other pocket, and sank deeper into the comforting cushions. Out of the corner of her eye, she spotted Jenny at the door. Grateful for the reprieve, she beckoned the maid to enter.

The girl approached with the tea tray and handed Callie one of two rose-patterned cups and saucers. "I went ahead and fixed it with plenty of cream and three lumps, just the way you like it, miss."

"Lovely." Callie wrapped her cold hands about the warm porcelain and sniffed the steam with genuine appreciation. Darjeeling, her very favorite. "Jenny, has anyone told you you're a pearl beyond price?"

Crossing the room, Jenny let out a laugh. "Can't say as they have, miss, leastways not lately."

Lottie accepted her cup. Sipping her tea, she waited until the girl had gone before asking, "By the by, how did your speech come off?"

Only too glad to steer the conversation toward a neutral topic, Callie propped her feet on the needlepoint footstool. "Well enough, I suppose, running noses and racking coughs aside."

"Theodore was there to hear you, I've no doubt."

Callie nodded. "Beyond the few press photographers who'd no choice but to show, Teddy was our sole representative of British manhood, I'm afraid"

"He is undeniably devoted to you, Callie."

Callie sighed into her teacup. "You know I adore Teddy,

truly I do, but I simply don't have those sorts of feelings for him. For all his protestations of undying devotion, every time I've turned him down, I've got the impression he is nearly as relieved as I am."

To her surprise, Lottie didn't disagree. "Theodore is a dear boy but yes, I expect the two of you would never suit. I can't quite put my finger on it, but there is something . . . oh, no matter." Lottie regarded her niece with serious eyes. "But as that handkerchief you're guarding so closely attests, Theodore is hardly the only unattached young man in London."

Callie stiffened. "And by eligible you mean marriageable, of course."

Lottie rolled her eyes. "Shackles of matrimony, instrument of women's oppression, legalized prostitution—is that all or have I left off one?"

Callie smiled in spite of herself. "Perhaps, but I believe you've touched on the basic tenets."

Lottie set her cup and saucer on the marble-topped lamp table. "I know you find this difficult to fathom, but marriage to the right person can be a very satisfying experience. My dear Edward, God rest his soul, was a most agreeable companion—and lover."

"Aunt Lottie!" Callie very nearly spilled tea onto her lap, for despite more than a decade of such frank woman-to-woman talks initiated by her thoroughly modern aunt, she'd yet to feel comfortable discussing such an intimate topic.

"Well, he was." Lottie settled back against the cushions, dreamlike expression making her look younger than her sixty-odd years. "Sexual congress with someone we care for deeply is one of the highest expressions of our humanity, a precious opportunity to connect with the divine while we're still firmly rooted on this earth."

Carried back to her own narrow escape from the parson's trap, Callie tightened her grip on her cup's porcelain handle. "Then perhaps you'd explain why it is the sex act brings out the beast in such a great many men."

The look her aunt cast her conveyed both sadness and pity. "Lovemaking can and should be pleasurable for both man and woman. When passion is tempered with caring and patience, the result can be highly satisfying for both partners."

Partners, once Callie had thought that was what she and Gerald would be after they'd wed. Not master and slave, conqueror and conquered but soul mates walking side by side on the journey of life. But those fairytale illusions had been torn away with brutal force, so that now the mere thought of placing herself in such a vulnerable—helpless—position ever again was enough to send a bolt of panic shooting straight through her. Yet there'd been a handful of moments, a blink of time, really, when she'd stared into a stranger's irreverent blue eyes and felt herself carried away from all that.

"I expect I shall have to accept your word." Knowing it was fruitless to argue the point, Callie pushed aside the stool and rose. "You won't mind if I go upstairs? My speech for tomorrow night's assembly could do with a bit of polishing."

"Of course not, dear." She had one foot over the threshold when Lottie called her back. "Callie."

Callie slowly turned about. "Yes, Aunt."

"You can't hide out behind those spectacles forever, you know. You're going to have to talk about it one of these days."

"Perhaps . . ." The concern she saw in her aunt's softly lined face almost undid her. Almost, but not quite. "Only not tonight."

Not tonight—and if Callie had her way, not ever.

Seated at Hadrian's table, Dandridge unlocked his attaché case and removed a string-tied bundle. Sliding it across to Hadrian, he explained, "Press coverage and publications of the Rivers woman from the past year. Familiarize yourself with them."

Hadrian glanced down at pamphlet topping the stack. *Musings from the Mouths of Slaves: A Treatise on the Subjugation of Women.* Penned by redoubtable Miss Rivers herself, I see."

Dandridge snorted. "Miserable radical rot, but you'll have to stomach it if you're to carry out your assignment."

His *assignment*. In light of it, Hadrian thought back to the impromptu meeting in Parliament Square, marveling at the difference a few hours could make. Then Caledonia Rivers had been a pretty face to which he'd yet to attach a name, an attractive stranger he'd asked to tea with a mind to taking her to bed. When he'd handed back her papers, she'd smiled at him as though he were a knight in shining armor rather than a scapegrace photographer who'd only reclaimed a few wrinkled sheets from the wind.

But staring across the table into the MP's hardened eyes, the happenstance encounter seemed sinisterly providential, as if the Powers That Be had conspired to deliver the lady into his devil's hands. But first he had to find a way to infiltrate the fortress of what he suspected was a regimented and rather complicated life.

"Exactly how do you propose I approach her? Were I to proposition her outright, I'd put her onto me for certain."

"That's been taken care of." The MP slipped a hand inside his coat's breast pocket and pulled out a sealed letter. "Consider this your entrée into Miss Rivers's inner circle."

"Unless you want me to break the seal, you'll have to do better than that."

"Millicent Fawcett is president of the National Union of Women's Suffrage Societies, as well as Caledonia Rivers's mentor. The Fawcett woman recently embarked on a month-long lecture tour of the United States, which is all to the good, ours at any rate. This letter informs her protégée that she is to submit to you taking a series of photographic portraits for display as part of the planned march on Parliament. The march will coincide with the third and final reading of the suffrage bill."

"So the letter is a forgery?" It was more statement than question.

"Of course. Does that shock you?"

Hadrian thought back to his bygone days of purse snitching and sundry forms of petty theft, and shook his head. Tossing the letter aside, he eyed the open case. "I assume a forged letter and reading material isn't all you've brought?"

"Quite." Dandridge withdrew a wad of fifty-pound notes from the lambskin lining and handed the money over to Hadrian. "Half now, and half on delivery of the photograph."

Hadrian hesitated. *Blood money*, he thought, and stretched out a stained hand to take it. Heart pounding, he flipped through the stack before tucking it inside his vest. "This is a great deal of tin, Dandridge. What makes you so certain I won't take it and disappear?"

"Greed, for one. If twenty-five hundred pounds can improve your life, only think what transformation five thousand can bring about." Dandridge snapped the case closed and rose. "Of course there is the instinct to preserve life, in this case your own." He looked down at Hadrian, gaunt face granite hard. "Play me false, St. Claire, and yours will be but one more body that turns up in the Thames."

His second death threat in as many hours—what the devil had he come to? Watching Dandridge cross to the door, it occurred to him that even Harry Stone, miserable little bugger that he'd been, hadn't been someone men had wanted to kill.

"Wait." Hadrian shot up from the table.

Dandridge turned around and for a handful of seconds Hadrian considered returning the money and calling the whole bloody business off. But it was too late for that.

Whether or not he kept the money, he knew too much to be let off the snare.

"Once I have the photograph, how shall I contact you?"

Dandridge opened the door and cold air rushed the room, chilling the perspiration dampening Hadrian's brow. "When you have it, I'll know. And I'll be in touch."

The shop bell knelled, signaling the MP's departure—and the sealing of their devil's bargain. Hadrian sank back into his seat. Staring out the frosted glass of his shop's window, he traced the bump on his left palm where years before a sliver of camera lens had embedded. He'd had to crawl on his hands and knees at the time. The scar served as a reminder of how far he'd risen in life—and how far he still might fall.

Yet his agreement with Dandridge involved a great deal more than bedding a woman and taking risqué photographs of her. He had just signed on to ruin her life. Despite his past as a whore's son, a beggar and a pickpocket, he'd never felt so low as when he'd felt the weight of Dandridge's money in his hand.

The best he could hope for was that Caledonia Rivers wouldn't be someone he'd have to work too hard at hating. To harden himself, he mentally cataloged her more obvious faults. Foremost, she was a suffragist and not just any suffragist but one of their leaders. And then there was her privileged status. Dandridge had said she was "well-born," which, in a word, meant *rich*. Hadrian recalled the bored society females who'd set foot inside his studio since he'd opened. With the exception of Lady Katherine, they'd been uniformly pampered and petty, oblivious to the plight of those whose duty it was to serve up their suppers and tend to their toilette and sweat out their lifeblood in their husbands' factories so that madam might have a smart, new carriage—and a brace of virile young footmen to go with it.

Feeling marginally better, he glanced down to the pamphlet topping the pile. The title alone went a long way in helping to flush out his image of Caledonia Rivers as a sanctimonious do-gooder, a toffee-nosed snob so far removed from the common man's plight that she wouldn't recognize real life if it bit her on her bustled ass.

Speaking of her ass . . . what *would* she look like out of her clothes? *Full-figured*, he thought, recalling the split-second feel of her breasts crushed against his chest, and though he usually fancied a lither form, he had an inkling the extra flesh suited her. As for her face, from what he'd seen of it she'd looked to be passably pretty, dark-haired judging from the brows arching above those rather magnificent eyes and fair-skinned as any English rose could hope to be.

Not that her appearance mattered, not in any meaningful way. Be she pug-faced and plain or a classically featured stunner, Caledonia Rivers was a means to an end, his ticket out of hell, and his last hope for salvaging the future he'd worked so hard to create.

Caledonia Rivers was just another commission to him—and it was time to get to work.

CHAPTER THREE

"This morning I had a deputation from the Working Men's Association . . . I dare say when it has to be done I can do it, and it is no use asking for women to be taken into public work and yet to wish them to avoid publicity. Still I am very sorry it is necessary, especially as I can't think of anything to say for four speeches. The first of these trials is to be next week. It is a tough and toilsome business."

—Elizabeth Garrett, first female candidate for the Marylebone School Board, 1870

Built to serve as the City Hall for Westminster, Caxton Hall set on the north side of Caxton Street, its proximity to Parliament making it a popular rallying point for political gatherings, including the suffrage cause. Accordingly, the Great Room was filled to overflowing by the time Hadrian forded his way inside, the several-hundred-odd attendees, mostly women, packed like kippers pressed into a tin. Standing at the back of the room, he shifted from foot to foot, the camera strap digging into his shoulder. Although he'd brought along the apparatus mainly for show, he found himself wishing he'd fought for a spot in the press box upfront. Wedged between a broad beast of a woman wearing whore's red and a dowager who smelled of talcum powder and sour apples, he would have sold his soul for a spot of fresh air—if he hadn't sold it to Dandridge already.

Dandridge. Shoving away from the wall, Hadrian swept a searching gaze about the room, half-expecting to glimpse the MP darting out from behind one of the potted palms or peaking out from one of the tiered boxes—a foolish and rather paranoid fancy. Men like Dandridge didn't soil their hands with their own dirty work, let alone expend their time and self-importance lurking about the enemy camp.

The sudden buzz of several hundred female voices had him returning his gaze to the stage in time to see the marigold velvet curtain draw back. Amidst a firestorm of clapping and the smoky flash and pop of press cameras, Caledonia Rivers stepped out onstage accompanied by a small birdlike woman of middling years. The latter led the way to the lectern, note card in hand. "My dear friends, colleagues, and sisters, it is my pleasure and privilege to introduce her among us who has distinguished herself as the oracle for delivering our message to the masses . . ."

Hadrian scarcely registered the rest of the stilted introduction, his attention riveted on the oracle's quite pretty face. Unlike most of the women in attendance, Caledonia Rivers was bare headed, her dark hair swept back from her temples and pinned into a knot at the nape of her elegant neck. Freed from the heavy outerwear of the previous day, she appeared both slender and statuesque, a splendid amazon approaching the podium, speech in hand.

"Good evening, ladies and gentlemen. I stand before you tonight not to make pretty speeches but to address the fundamental question of why we are here. Because we want the vote, you might well answer. Indeed, we are here because we seek universal suffrage, the inalienable right of every member of a free and self-governing society to have a say, a *voice*, in that governance."

She paused to cast her spectacled eyes out onto the assembly, and Hadrian was hit by the unnerving notion she was looking directly at him. Meeting the head-on heat of her gaze, he felt his heartbeat quicken even as he told himself he was being absurd. He stood at the very back of the room out of range of the domed electrical chandelier anchored overhead. Surely she couldn't see him. Yet he couldn't shake the feeling that the raw silk of her voice was directed solely at him.

"Yet how often I am asked by men and some women, too, why it is that we suffragists insist on making all this fuss and bother about national reform when, for the most part, our individual lives are led in our home parishes and boroughs, the circumstances of which have far greater bearing on our immediate health and happiness than those matters concerning Britain and her policies at home and abroad. To those of you who may harbor such doubt, whether openly or in secret, I answer you this: the sole pathway to civil rights, higher education, and equal status for women rests with the parliamentary franchise."

A groundswell of applause and shouts of "here, here" had Hadrian looking about the room, which seemed to be vibrating like the current housed in an electrical pole. Be they young or old, beautiful or plain, rich or poor, the women's faces were uniformly animated, eyes glowing like beacons as they stared raptly ahead. He swung his gaze back to the lone figure standing at the podium. Despite her height and regal bearing, Caledonia Rivers struck him as very small, very young, and very feminine to stand at the eye of such a storm.

A skilled speaker, she waited for the din to die down before continuing, "This is not, ladies and gentleman, a unique or sudden revelation. It was in 1867 that the Honorable John Stuart Mill, Member for Westminster, presented to parliament the first petition to grant universal suffrage to women householders. That petition, which bore no less than fifteen hundred signatures from women throughout Britain, was defeated in the Commons by 196 votes to 73."

Predictably a chorus of boos and hisses greeted that pronouncement.

Caledonia Rivers lifted an ungloved hand, motioning for silence, and Hadrian found himself wondering how that white palm and tapered fingers might feel against his flesh. "I grant you that in proportion to the millions of Englishwomen who reside in this country or its possessions, fifteen hundred signatures may not seem a very great number. However, when we reflect on how few women are encouraged, dare I say *allowed*, to express political opinions independent of their husbands, fathers, brothers, and in some instances adult sons, it becomes evident that every woman who succeeds in doing so should be regarded as the representative of a considerable body of opinion . . ."

Hadrian thought her latter point rested on rather shaky ground. If women as a sex were too simpleminded to form their own opinions, let alone to put forth those opinions without wavering, then why the devil should the government give them the vote? But, he reminded himself, it wasn't what he thought that counted, but rather what Caledonia Rivers thought—of him. He composed his features into a mask of mild interest and listened on.

"That we acknowledge a woman as our sovereign gives the lie to the conventional wisdom that would disqualify women for government. Where female sex is no obstacle to the higher privileges of political life, it cannot be to the lower, including the vote."

She paused to sip from a glass of water, her tongue sliding over her full bottom lip, and Hadrian felt a warm, answering ache in the vicinity of his groin. "Yet throughout the seventies we have seen almost annual parliamentary debates concerning the issue of female suffrage, with at least three of the private bills put forth by our good friends such as Lord Brassey going to a second reading. Each time we have petitioned and each time we have waited, waited with patience and in good faith, only to have our hopes dashed by that vocal minority who would continue to oppress us." Her voice was pitching incrementally higher, a sign she must be approaching the finale. "Ladies and gentlemen, I stand before you today to say that I, for one, am done with patience, done with waiting. I stand before you and beseech you to join your voices with mine in demanding of our distinguished representatives: 'Votes for women—*now*'!"

A heartbeat later "Votes for women NOW" roared throughout the assembly, and Hadrian felt the collective thunder, the *thrill* of it, resonating inside his very chest. It was as if a fever, a contagion, swept the room. The benches, the chairs, the other makeshift seats—all were deserted. To a person, the crowd surged to its feet, ignited by the words, the *power*, of one woman. Even women whom he felt certain would under other circumstances be the very pictures of propriety stamped and clapped, hooted and hallooed like fishwives at Billingsgate Market. One reed-thin matron dressed in the mauve of half-morning punched her gloved fist into the sky and let out a piercing wolf whistle worthy of a pugilist proclaiming victory in the ring.

He swung his gaze back to the platform. Behind the lectern, Caledonia Rivers stood very quiet and very still. Staring out onto the churning crowd, occasionally acknowledging a familiar face with a small nod or wave, she'd set her mouth into a tight smile that never wavered. The smile didn't reach her eyes, which looked uncertain, he thought, and perhaps just a little afraid.

She knows all this fuss and bother is a necessary evil of winning, but she doesn't fancy it, not a jot, he thought to himself, and the vulnerability he saw in her wary gaze gave him heart that his own victory might be won as well. Caledonia Rivers might be an orator on par with any statesman he'd ever heard. He didn't for a moment doubt she was genuinely, passionately committed to her cause. Clearly she was highly intelligent and highly educated. In all likelihood, she spoke several languages and spoke them fluently. All in all, she exuded the sort of social polish one didn't acquire but rather was born to—along with the silver spoon stuck straight up her ass.

But though Caledonia Rivers might be as cultured as a prize pearl, beneath her armoring of tightly coiffed hair, high-buttoned shirtwaist, and the voluminous umbrella of those very stiff, very starched skirts, she was still a woman with a woman's weaknesses and desires. It was the woman within, and not the leader without, to whom he would appeal, woo, and ultimately win over.

So when the crowd finally began to thin, roughly half heading for the exit doors and the other half queuing up stage-side for the chance to shake the hand of their heroine, Hadrian didn't hesitate. Gaze trained on the pooled electric light hitting like a halo atop his quarry's dark head, he pushed a path toward the stage.

Callie looked up from the genteel older lady on whose program she'd just scribbled her autograph and felt her heart stumble over itself. Striding toward her, looking coolly confident and yes, just a trifle amused, was *him*, the blue-eyed Adonis from the park. Hadrian St. Claire. The photographer she'd thought never to see again, whose handkerchief and business card, even now, lay at the bottom of her dresser drawer. The drawer which, she would dissolve with shame if ever forced to admit, housed her small collection of most cherished mementos.

She sucked in her breath and tried to focus on what the woman before her was saying. Something to do with an invitation to address her ladies' association in Hampshire but beyond that she couldn't be sure. Nonetheless, she made it a point to smile and nod, fobbing off making any immediate commitment by directing her to Harriet, waiting in the wings with appointment book at the ready.

The woman moved on only to have several more file through along with a reporter from the *Times* seeking a quote. By the time she broke away to look about again, the room had cleared considerably. Hadrian St. Claire appeared to have left as well. The depth of disappointment that observation stirred set off a bevy of warning bells. Really, why should she care in the slightest one way or another? The man was nothing to her, a virtual stranger. Yet she did care, she cared a lot or easily too much judging from the hollow feeling overtaking her despite that she stood amidst a room chockfull of supporters. Dear Lord, she must be lonely and desperate indeed to latch onto a stranger and make him the answer to filling the empty place inside her. *Pathetic, Callie, well and truly pathetic.*

A hand settling on the blade of her shoulder sent her spinning about, and she found herself face to face with Hadrian St. Claire. The speech papers slipped through her fingers, which suddenly felt as nerveless as her knees.

"Oh dear, I seem to be making a habit of this." She dropped to the stage floor.

Grinning, he followed her down so that they were both squatting, heads bowed and knees brushing. "Yes, we must make a pact to stop meeting this way."

Between them, they managed to gather the papers and after some awkward shuffling, she had them back in hand, a messy stack. He offered her a hand up and personal touch that it was, she felt the heat of him flare up through her fingertips. "How did you get here?"

Stepping back, he cast a sheepish glance back to the set of side stairs leading up to the stage, gold-tipped lashes grazing the high planes of his cheeks. "I've never been terribly good about waiting in queue. Dash it, I've never been any good about waiting at all. Are you put out with me?"

He looked at her then, another of those melting, too-long looks that set her to wondering if he might just have the capacity to see through her clothes, some sort of special radiographic power endemic to photographers, this one at least. Her hands, which had remained steady throughout her speech, were at once trembling and chill. And low in her belly, the shameful liquid warmth she had fought against pulsed and pooled.

She drew a steadying breath and reminded herself that giving way to madness such as this exacted a heavy, heavy toll. The last time she'd given her passions rein to rule, she'd come bloody close to ruining her life. At times such as this, though, with a handsome-as-sin stranger staring at her as though he must know what she looked like beneath her shift, it was all too easy to forget. Easy to forget it was the mind, the *intellect* that must rule the heart and body, not the other way around. Easy to forget that never again must a man, any man, be trusted.

Reaching for the shield of her reserve, she cleared her throat. "On the contrary, I am only surprised to see you here at all. From your remarks the other day, I would not have thought you a proponent of our cause."

"My remarks?" Hadrian felt the heat rising between them, too, although any reciprocity of feeling had no place in his plans. Immersed, he stared at her while he scoured his sex-soaked brain for some recollection of what he might have said to warrant such a starchy response. A great deal had happened in the past twenty-four hours, none of it good, and while he carried with him a clear mental picture of every detail of her from wind-kissed cheeks to broken hat feather, he couldn't recall a single word he'd said.

"I believe it was something to do with spewing rubbish and rot?" She arched one dark half-moon brow, waiting.

Damn but if his mouth hadn't gotten the better of him

yet again. When the devil would he learn? "In that case, I hope you'll accept my most sincere apology. It's only that suffrage for females is a new notion for me, I freely admit it." He paused before adding with a slow smile, "And well, if you'll pardon my saying so, you don't fit my mental picture of what a suffragist should look like."

She bristled at that remark just as she'd known she would. "Just what do you imagine a suffragist should look like?"

He glanced toward her secretary, the one with the mannish manner and hawkish gaze, standing at the opposite end of the stage. "Rather I imagine what a suffragist is not. You're altogether too young and too pretty to be spending your evenings in stuffy lecture halls."

"My age and looks are of no consequence." But the blush limning those lovely high cheekbones told him the compliment struck home.

"In point, Miss Rivers, your image is the very thing that brings me here tonight." Feeling the urgency of dwindling time—he caught someone, the secretary, no doubt—hinting they would shortly be locking the doors—he said, "Is there somewhere we can speak in private?"

Nibbling her bottom lip, she hesitated. "Very well, there is a greenroom backstage."

She turned and started off toward the partitioned curtain, leaving him to follow. Backstage, she opened the door to what served as a waiting room for visiting speakers and entertainers, a tray of tea biscuits and a pitcher of water set out on the marble-topped sideboard.

Leaving the door ajar—did she really imagine he meant to pounce upon her—she asked, "What is it you would say to me?"

Amused at her skittishness, he said, "As I may have mentioned the other day, a great deal of my work is portraiture." He reached inside his jacket pocket for the forged letter Dandridge had supplied. "As it happens, my most recent commission is to photograph you."

Her eyes widened, and she gave a fierce shake of her head, the motion knocking the spectacles halfway down her nose. Pushing them back, she said, "That cannot be."

Rather than argue, he handed her the counterfeit letter of introduction, hoping the forger had possessed an able hand. She broke the seal, unfolded the paper, and began to read, spectacles slipping down her nose once more only this time she didn't seem to notice. Even with head bowed, the shock coursing through her was a palpable thing. He could read it on her face, feel it in the sudden stiffening of her stance.

She refolded the letter, very slowly, very carefully, and looked up. A less confident man would have taken her stricken look as a grave injury to his pride. "I cannot credit it," she said at length, looking so forlorn that suddenly, inexplicably, he wanted to reach out and hold her. "She said nothing of this before she left, not a word. This . . . command comes as so contrary to her character, I cannot fathom it."

Thinking quickly, Hadrian said, "If a series of photographs is what is needed to tip the scales of public opinion in your favor, then surely sitting for me is not so great a sacrifice given all the many sacrifices you must have made up until now?" The gentleness in his voice caught him by surprise. What the devil did he care for her so-called sacrifices?

"This letter is dated more than a week ago and yet you made no mention of it the other day when we met." Her keen-eyed gaze settled on his and though he'd been over warm all evening, Hadrian was only now conscious of the sweat soaking his collar.

"Yes, well, if you will recall, there was the small matter of the elements to deal with, in our case the wind, and errant papers to collect. By the time I knew who you were, that dragon of an assistant was ferrying you away as though fearful I meant to debauch you in the public park." He smiled at her then, the same reassuring smile he used to comfort crying children and other portrait subjects edgy at having their picture made.

She smiled back though it occurred to him that her eyes looked wistful, even a trifle sad. "Harriet is my secretary and as dedicated to our Cause as any of us. If she seems a bit protective at times it is only because the press has not always been kind."

Were we in different circumstances, I would be kind to you, Caledonia. Kind indeed. Startled, he realized he'd let his mind wander. What was she saying now?

"What I don't understand is why she would select you. Given your remarks the other day, you hardly seem a supporter."

Hadrian hesitated. He needed a hook and he needed it

badly. The hall tonight, though packed, had shown a striking absence of men. Beyond the handful of photographers, representatives of that less-than-kind press, he'd looked to be the only male in attendance.

"What would you say to our striking a small bargain?"

Behind the glasses, her eyes narrowed. "What sort of bargain?"

"We will divide our session between your sitting for me—your sacrifice, if you will—and my submitting to your instruction on the finer shades of female equality? Should you succeed in winning me to your point, I will not hesitate to spread the word to other males who might be persuaded as well, including a barrister friend of mine who has the ear of those influential in the Fleet Street set." When she didn't answer, he cocked his head to one side, trying to read the thoughts behind those clear, soulful eyes. "You are very quiet suddenly, Miss Rivers, and looking at me rather strangely, I think. Come now, do we have a bargain or do we not?"

She hesitated, biting at her bottom lip in a way that had him hardening. "Yes, Mr. Rivers, I believe we do. I will call on you at your shop at noon tomorrow, if that is acceptable to you."

So she'd kept his card after all. Hadrian hid his smile. The woman had played into his hands entirely. More time in her company meant that much more time to carry out his plan, and if the prelude to seduction meant putting up with her prosing on about her blasted cause, then so be it.

Vanquishing her, it might prove easier than he'd first

thought. "I shall spend what remains of this evening counting the hours."

She held out her hand. Amused she meant to seal their agreement with a handshake as a man would, he reached out to take it. Encouraged to find it cold and faintly shaking, he carried their clasped hands to his mouth, brushing a quick kiss atop her smooth white one.

She jerked away as though he'd burned her. "Don't count, Mr. St. Claire, but rather *read*. Barbara Leigh Smith's *A Brief Summary, in Plain Language, of the Most Important Laws Concerning Women* is an excellent starting point as it is both comprehensive and concise. You will derive far greater benefit from reflecting on Mrs. Smith's wise words than conjuring elaborate flatteries. You may see my secretary on your way out, and she will furnish you with a copy." She cast a meaningful glance toward the side door.

So he was being dismissed. What cheek! Suppressing a groan, he reminded himself that his goal was to win her trust. "You do yourself a disservice, miss, if you believe my remark was anything but completely candid." With that, he started for the door.

Her voice called him back. "On the contrary, Mr. Rivers, it is you who do me the disservice."

That set him off his guard. He felt his smile slip and with it his some of his self-assurance. Turning about, he said, "Sorry?"

"You must think me a perfect simpleton indeed if you expect me to credit such rubbish, charmingly put though it may be."

Hadrian relaxed, feeling once more on firmer footing. The estimable Miss Rivers was flirting with him whether she recognized it or not. "Quite the contrary, miss, I am coming to understand that there is nothing of the simple about you."

Simpleton, I must be an utter simpleton.

Thrashing about her bed later that night, Callie allowed she had acted the perfect idiot. Only an idiot would agree not merely to sit for Hadrian St. Claire like some bloody trained monkey, but also to be cajoled into acting as his tutor. As if she gave a fig for what he thought, the thick-skulled man. *Rot and rubbish indeed!*

As for the letter of introduction, whatever could Millicent have meant by directing her to fritter away precious hours posing for a portrait when there was so much of critical importance to accomplish in over the next few weeks? Were her mentor still in England, Callie wouldn't hesitate to plead her case. As it was, the breadth of a great wide ocean stood between them. She briefly considered telegraphing a message but the lecture tour of the United States was a hectic affair involving a great deal of travel by train—did she really want to trouble Millicent with a matter that was, well, trifling?

And it *was* trifling, or at least should have been. Photographs, people sat for them all the time nowadays. Why, you could scarcely walk into a public park on a Sunday and not encounter at least one photographer, passersby patiently queuing up for shilling photographs of their babies, wives, and sweethearts. Yet the thought of having her imperfect image captured by a camera's unforgiving lens dredged up all the old insecurities.

God, would it never be over? She closed her eyes and rubbed a hand over her throbbing forehead. Ten years, and yet at times such as this, when it was night and she was alone, it might have been just the other day, the memory lodged in her consciousness like a deep-seated splinter.

It was springtime in the countryside, a lovely twilight evening. Lilac and early roses scented the air; the breeze was a silken caress against her face and bare shoulders, welcome balm after the stifling confines of the ballroom. She was nineteen and about to be married to Gerald, one of the season's most sought-after bachelors. Even her parents were thrilled—this once she'd managed to please them. Yet something was wrong, or at least not quite as it should be, she could *feel* it. On pretense of her dance slippers pinching, she'd sought solace in the garden. Being careful of her gown, a pale pink affair with far too many ruffles and bows for someone her size, she perched on the edge of the stone bench and slipped off her shoes. Above her, the balcony doors opened. Cigar smoke drifted downward, choking out the scent of roses.

"So, old sod, how does it feel to be about to be leg-shackled to last season's leavings?" It was Gerald's best friend, Larry, his speech a telltale slur.

Cheeks flaming, she slunk back into the shadows and

waited for Gerald to defend her.

Instead, he answered, "Oh, she's a milcher, to be sure, but with a splendid set of tits and a dowry beyond generous, I can bear marriage to a beast." He paused to take a puff. "The old gaffer must be desperate to be rid of her."

Chuckling, they stubbed out their smokes and went inside. Numb, she'd sat on the bench for what had seemed like hours. Eventually she got up, walked back in, and carried on with the evening as though nothing were amiss. It wasn't until the following morning that she called her parents aside and told them the engagement was off. When they declined to agree, she packed her bags and boarded the next train leaving for London and her Aunt Charlotte. She'd lived with Lottie ever since.

Every morning for the past ten years now, she'd scraped her thick waist-length black-brown hair into a tight bun, tucked her offending bosom into high-necked shirtwaists, and hid her curvy hips beneath layers of petticoats and skirts. She'd embraced spinsterhood and then the suffragist cause with the same enthusiasm, the same passion that other women applied to the roles of wife and mother. Instead of home and hearth, she'd chosen to fight as a soldier would fight, for a just and noble cause. Progress, albeit incremental, was being made. In a fortnight there would be the closed-door meeting with the prime minister, Lord Salisbury, who already had expressed some sympathy with their cause. Success was in sight, she could *feel* it. And if she hadn't found happiness exactly, at least she could claim contentment.

Or so she'd thought.

But at times such as tonight when all her restless energy spiraled toward a decidedly physical sort of pinnacle, content was the very last thing she felt. In the lonely stillness, she registered the rhythmic ticking of the bedside clock, which suddenly struck her as loud to the point of earsplitting. She thought about turning up the bedside lamp and reading for a while, or perhaps jotting a note or two in her journal but couldn't summon the self-discipline.

No, there was only one remedy, as shameful as it was inevitable. Closing her eyes, she slipped a hand beneath the covers and focused on conjuring "him," her fantasy lover. Though admittedly make-pretend and sketchy on details, he was real to her all the same. When she put her mind to it, she could all but feel the weight of him in the bed beside her, the warmth of his breath striking the side of her throat, the soft press of his lips as he trailed heated kisses over her body, a body which he miraculously found to be perfect in every way.

No matter how hard she'd set her mind to it, though, she could never fathom his face. The one time she'd tried to force it, the blankness assumed Gerald's features as she'd last seen him, bleary-eyed and sneering, which of course ruined everything.

The only part of him she'd ever been able to see clearly was his hands. Strong hands. Warm hands. Knowing hands, the palms broad but not too broad, the fingers long and sensitive, beautifully shaped. Even the fingertips had been meticulously attended to; the nails were clipped short, dustings of golden hair on the backs. And his knuckles, or rather the image of them stroking her cheek, her throat, the curve of her breast, was all it took to bring the throbbing between her thighs building to crescendo.

Only when she could bear it no longer, when the restless, budding ache was simply too urgent to ignore, did she give in and find herself with her fingers. But tonight was different, tonight was a first, for it wasn't her own too soft palm kneading her mons or her own too slender digits slipping inside her swollen to bursting sex, but the hands of a flesh-and-blood man.

Hadrian St. Claire's hands.

Stifling a cry, Callie fell back against the mattress and came.

"Hold on, Mum. I'm coming."

Head pounding from where he'd hit the wall, Harry crawled toward his mother, folded into the dusty corner like a schoolboy's broken paper missile. The floor between them was aglitter with glass, the only remains of his camera's shattered lens. Powdering the planks like new-fallen snow, it looked crystalline. Pure.

"Don't cry anymore, Mum. I'm here."

Reaching her, he stuck out a bleeding hand to comfort her, but she shoved him away, the angry red mark on her cheek matching the flash of her eyes. "Wicked ungrateful boy, only look what a muck you've made of things. Couldn't leave well enough alone, could you? Had to stick that bleedin' contraption of yours where it didn't belong."

"But Mum, he hurt you, he—"

"No buts." Dropping her voice to a whisper, she said, "One word from him, and I'll lose my place, and then we'll both be out on the streets." She slid her gaze toward the man standing in shadow, watching them from the far side of the room. Watching, always watching.

"You should mind your mother, boy." Footfalls came toward them, the shiny black shoes stopping within inches of Harry's bleeding fingers. "Get up." Before Harry could move, the man reached down and grabbed him by the back of his collar, jerking him to his feet.

"Please sir, no. Take me. I'll do anything you fancy. Anything." Mum stumbled to her feet, tugging on the man's coat sleeve.

Hard fingers bit into the back of Harry's neck. "But I don't fancy you, you slattern. It's him I want."

Like a scruffed kitten, Harry found himself dragged across the room to the bed, the big brass four-poster where his mum entertained her clients.

He tried digging in his heels but it was no use. Tossed atop the mattress, he twisted to look back at his mother. "Mum . . . Mummy . . . please."

She turned her battered face up to the man. "You won't hurt him bad, will you?"

Hurt him bad, hurt him bad, hurt him bad . . .

It was then that the last of the fight left him. Harry squeezed *his eyes closed and waited.*

Hadrian awoke amidst sweat-drenched sheets. Shaking, he reached for the gin bottle by his bed, pulled out the cork, and knocked back a healthy swallow. It was the dream again, the one that had haunted him for years only not for some time. Indeed, he'd been halfway to believing it was a thing of the past, a milestone he'd finally moved beyond. As always, it came as a rapid-fire flash of images with feelings attached like strings to balloons. No, not balloons—too benign an image, that. More like a black fog of terror and shame, a demon perched silently on his shoulder, awaiting the opportunity to strike.

The earlier encounter with Caledonia Rivers must have rattled him more than he'd cared to admit. Raking a hand through his damp hair, he tried telling himself that however good and noble she might be, he owed her nothing. Regrettable as is was that he must ruin her, *vanquish* her to placate Dandridge and save himself, that's how it went in a dog-eat-dog world. He couldn't afford to let guilt make him soft, not now when he had everything to lose and so very much to gain.

Forgive me, Caledonia. Nothing personal, but I can't go back. I won't go back.

No going back.

CHAPTER FOUR

"O do not praise my beauty more,
In such world-wide degree,
And say I am one all eyes adore;
For these things harass me!"
—THOMAS HARDY, *The Beauty*

"Do try to relax, Miss Rivers. You're looking stiff as a board."

Head buried beneath the light-blocking cloth cover, Hadrian studied his "subject" through the camera's viewing portal. Owing to the high caliber of his apparatus, he rarely required posing devices such as a headrest or clamp. Had Caledonia Rivers managed to stay reasonably motionless, they should have managed quite nicely. In the course of the past two hours, however, he'd shot easily a half-dozen photographs, each one worse than its predecessor. Already the close atmosphere in his studio's staging area was choked with the acrid odor of magnesium powder—which hardly set the scene for seduction.

Seated in his posing chair against a backdrop of painted-canvas woodland, she lifted her chin in an age-old gesture of defiance. "I am doing my best to cooperate, sir. You did caution me to hold still just as I cautioned you that I am not accustomed to sitting idle."

At wit's end, he threw back the cover and straightened. Really, she could be the most infuriating of women. "You're not sitting, idle or otherwise. You're *posing*. Think of it as a task, your job, if that helps you."

"I beg your pardon." She lifted her eyes to his face despite his express instruction to settle on a spot just beyond him and not look away.

Shoving hands in his pockets—what better way to stave off the temptation of shaking her—he came around to the front of the camera. "I only mean that you don't strike me as a woman who relaxes much. What with the whole great world in want of saving, and you alone responsible for its salvation, there mustn't be a great deal of time for leisure, let alone amusement."

"Right is not done by shirking one's duty, Mr. St. Claire." All at once, the stiff-lipped look she'd worn since her arrival slipped. "Oh, blast. I have shown myself to be a dreadful subject, I know. I have tried your patience sorely."

Oh, she had tried his patience, all right, only not in the way she thought. From the past hours spent in her prickly presence, it was abundantly clear that seducing Caledonia

Rivers, the so-called Maid of Mayfair, was not going to be a matter of a few hours or even a day.

"It is only that I have never so much as had my portrait painted let alone sat for something as . . . unforgiving as a photograph." She looked down, pretending sudden interest in the long-fingered hands laced in her lap. Sitting there so hesitant and unsure, she seemed more girl than woman, so much so that Hadrian hadn't the heart to point out that she'd moved—again.

Stepping over the striking cord, he closed the small gap between them. "You should make it a point to smile more, Miss Rivers." Reaching her, he lifted her chin on the edge of his hand, pleased when she didn't shy away. "You're quite lovely when you smile. Ah, now she blushes. Tell me, don't you think of yourself as pretty?" Resisting the urge to touch his thumb to that enticing cleft, he dropped his hand. "You are, you know, despite the pains you take to hide that fact."

Her high forehead folded into a frown. "I am hiding nothing."

"Nothing? Tell me, if I may be so bold to ask, who dresses you?" He let his gaze slip over her seated form from primly coiffed head to sensibly half-boot-shod feet.

She looked at him as though he'd sprouted a third eye. "I dress myself. Why do you ask?"

"That frock you're wearing is positively funerary."

Her half-moon brows arched. "And just what is the matter with my gown?"

"Rather you might ask what is right with it in which case

I would reply in all honestly—nothing." He softened the statement with a smile.

She answered with a huff. "A woman is more than an ornament to grace the arm of a man, sir."

"You'll never grace the arm of anyone if you persist in dressing like a drab."

She shot up from her chair. Tall though she was, he topped her by several inches, which for whatever reason pleased him enormously. "You are honest to the point of pain, sir, as well as abominably rude."

Inexplicably invigorated, he answered, "In that case, I'll not hesitate to point out that the way you wear your hair, scraped into that tight little knot at the back of your head, brings to mind a maiden aunt."

"I have a maiden aunt, and I'll have you know she is quite the fashion plate."

"Then you would do well to emulate her. As for those spectacles, are they strictly necessary?"

She hesitated, biting at her lip, confirming what he'd suspected—the eyewear was a bit of stagecraft, a screen for her to hide behind. "Only if I wish to see."

"You look like a woman who sees far too much already. Take them off, won't you."

She made no move to do so, but then he was coming to understand that obedience was nowhere in her nature. He admired her for that. Under other circumstances, he might even consider her a kindred spirit.

But of course he had a job to do.

Conscious of her gaze on his face, he reached out and gently lifted the wire frames from her face. He folded the glasses and handed them back, making sure their fingertips brushed. "Ah yes, better now. You have lovely eyes, beautifully shaped. My only regret is the impossibility of recapturing their color with pigments and paints. Such a vivid green, especially now that I've made you angry."

Cheeks limned in rose, she shook her head. "I am not angry. Anger would be pointless, a waste of my energy."

He started to postulate another use for all that famous energy of hers, but stopped himself in time. What the deuce had taken hold of him? All she need do was storm from his studio, and the game would be up before it had even begun. Could it be that part of him, some small core of decency buried deep within the rotten apple he'd become, was goading her in the hope she would do just that? Was it possible he might be trying to save Caledonia Rivers from . . . himself?

Whatever his motive might be, it required all of his reserve not to reach out and touch that blush-tinted cheek. "I beg to differ. You are angry and rightly so. I am once again too frank. I have offended you. In future, I will endeavor to curb my tongue if not bite it outright."

All this talk of tongues had her flushing rosier still, suggesting her thoughts were not quite as proper, as *pure*, as she would have him believe. "No, no don't alter anything on my account. I shouldn't wish for you to behave other than comes naturally to you." The telling blush deepened, and her gaze dropped to study the space between their feet. "What

I mean to say is that more and more of late I find myself surrounded by persons who tell me what they suppose I would wish to hear. That becomes . . . tedious." She raised shy eyes to his face, and he felt something inside his chest gave way. "Your plain speaking took me aback at first, I admit, but I am finding it refreshing, a welcome change. I would be pleased if we could continue on as we are, with our discourse modeled on complete honesty."

Complete honesty. Some emotion, guilt, perhaps, took a chokehold about Hadrian's throat. "In that case, allow me to repeat that I find you attractive, quite attractive indeed, and hang your high-minded ideals, I'll make no apology for it. But then again I'm a man, Miss Rivers, and thus a slave to my baser instincts, my bestial nature. I cannot help myself or so those infernal tracts of yours would have us all believe."

Eyes glowing like embers, she regarded him. "Infernal tracts, indeed. I wonder, sir, if you are as open to instruction as you would have me believe."

He took another step back. "There is only one way to find out. As they say, Miss Rivers, fire away."

She slipped back into her seat. "Very well, then. I thought we would employ the Socratic Method with you, as the student, posing questions based upon what you have read."

Clever girl, he thought, to turn their first session into a quiz in order to discern whether or not he'd done his homework. Fortunately he had. He thought back to the pamphlet she'd pressed on him the night before. What a dreary affair that had been, a great deal of sanctimonious drivel though he'd hunkered down and plodded through it anyway. True, it wasn't very long but it was *dense*, a comprehensive listing of all the British laws pertaining to the social, political, and economic status of females. Sprinkled throughout were testimonials from various women—some provided their true names but most improvised aliases such as "Mary B" or the ubiquitous "Mrs. Smith." Some of the information was new to Hadrian—was it really the case that a husband held the legal right to imprison his wife in pursuit of his conjugal rights? For the most part, though, the contents confirmed that which he'd known before but, until now, hadn't given a great deal of thought. Yes, he'd realized that when a woman married everything she owned, inherited, or earned became the sole property of her husband. But as most of the women he'd known as Harry Stone owned, inherited, and earned nothing or the nearest thing to it, the law had never caused them any great concern. As for the women who came to his studio to have their portraits made, dressed to the nines and with servants in tow, they didn't appear to suffer overmuch— except perhaps from boredom.

"I do wonder, given womankind's softer, more sentimental nature and innate aversion to warring, might extending the vote to females not place the empire at grave risk? Given the less demanding education of girls, was it an unwarranted fear that some female voters—barring present company, of course— might lack sufficient intellect to fully grasp the issues?"

Eyes very green, very angry, and very much focused on his face, she answered, "If women as a sex are averse to war, perhaps that is a good thing. Men, as history bears out, seem to have entirely too great a fondness for it. As to the supposed intellectual inferiority of women, why not throw open the doors of the presently all-male public schools and universities to girls and young women and let their academic record as a sex set the issue to rest once and for all? Instead, men—barring present company, of course—contrive to keep women ignorant and oppressed."

Hadrian backed up to the camera. Positioning the lens, he leaned in to frame his shot. "Better . . . much better. Now, mind you hold that position. Quite as still as you can manage." He took the striking cord in hand and pulled. The flash flared, illuminating Caledonia Rivers in a burst of actinic radiance. "Ah, better now. You should allow yourself the luxury of temper more often, Miss Rivers."

She stared at him aghast. "You're taking my picture . . . *now?*"

He slipped out from the cover long enough to smile at her. "No better time than the present. Do you know your eyes turn from sage to dark green when you're in a passion?" Passion. He'd chosen the word deliberately and the blush climbing from her throat to her cheeks told him he'd found his mark. Enjoying himself immensely, he added, "Why, they are glittering like emeralds."

"I am not in a passion, as you say."

Ducking back beneath the sheet, he called out, "Suit yourself, Miss Rivers. You were saying?"

"Er . . . ah yes. And once a woman is wed, her very body

belongs to her husband. Should she be moved to deny him, he has the right—the *legal* right, Mr. St. Claire—to hold her captive until she surrenders as well as the right to force her. Legalized rape, if you will, how as a civilized man can you countenance that?"

"So you are an advocate of Free Love, then?"

Looking adorably flustered, she hesitated before answering, "If a woman must marry, then she should be able to follow her own inclinations and sensibilities in selecting a mate. As it stands now, far too many gently born women are as good as sold to the highest bidder, trading their liberty for a title and a name. Should she leave her husband and seek a divorce, she forfeits any right not only to her property but to see her children, if that is the husband's wish."

"If she left them in the first place then perhaps she doesn't deserve to."

The scorching look she leveled him might have melted his camera's lens. "And what of all the men who leave their wives and families or, barring that, keep mistresses?

"I'm the very last person to claim that the world is fair, Miss Rivers. On the other hand, I expect you'd be rather shocked at the number of married women who manage to navigate a way around the rules." He thought of the wayward matrons he'd helped in that regard and was glad for the cover that hid his smile.

She rose from her chair. "I think you are deliberately goading me."

Uncovering himself and straightening, he made no move

to deny it. "And what of you, Miss Rivers, what do you advocate when it comes to managing intimate relations between the sexes?"

She flushed that delectable shade of pale pink that had him thinking of summertime peaches but to her credit, she didn't look away. "It is my personal belief that . . . sexual congress should be reserved as an expression of the deepest regard and esteem, that it should only take place between two persons whose minds and souls are prepared to meet on the highest of planes."

Sexual congress . . . ah, they were getting somewhere at last. "And must those two people be married before their souls meet on this highest plane, do you think?"

"Preferably."

"Preferably, but not always?" He took a step toward her.

"On occasion there are special circumstances that keep one soul apart from its mate."

"And yet you also countenance divorce?"

"If you mean an easement of the current divorce laws to afford fair and equitable access, then yes, I do."

"So then you as good as admit that a woman who marries for love may be mistaken in her inclinations?"

A cloud crossed her face. "When a man is courting a woman, there is much about his nature he may choose to conceal."

He studied her for a moment before asking, "May not the same be said of the woman?"

"A gently bred young woman is reared to please in all

things, to be docile and quiet in company. If she presents herself as other than her true self, it is not artifice or wiles that lead her to do so but a simple ignorance of who her true self is."

"I cannot help but observe that your theories all speak to high-born women. What of women in the merchant class or even the so-called lower orders? Those women who are not *gently bred* as you say, do your high-minded theories apply to them as well?"

She shrugged, which did interesting things to the high slopes of her breasts beneath the shirtwaist. "I suppose so but—"

"You suppose?"

Her hesitation helped to peg her as exactly what he'd been hoping for, a toffee-nosed society bitch who considered the so-called "lower orders" to be almost a separate species. Ruining her—he just might enjoy it after all.

"For a woman who is otherwise so firm in her convictions, you demonstrate a delightful ambiguity when it comes to relations between the sexes. On one hand, you say women should choose for themselves who and how they shall love and yet when that freedom leads them astray, you assume they must have been seduced against their wills."

Her eyes glittered, her cheeks flushed. She was looking very angry now and, it occurred to him, very beautiful. "I made no such claim. You are twisting my words."

"On the contrary, I am but mirroring them much as a photograph depicts only that which the camera lens sees."

"I believe our session is at an end. I really must be on my way." She looked past him to the shop door as if willing it to open.

He backed up. "I have enjoyed our conversation, Miss Rivers. I have enjoyed it immensely. If nothing else, our discourse has served to show just how far off the mark my thinking still is. You have quite a challenge ahead of you; I trust you see that now. I confess I cannot wait for our next session."

"Another session!" She paused in collecting her things to stare at him, mouth falling open. "But surely two hours suffices to make a single portrait?"

He shook his head. "Photography is not merely a medium for artistic expression and documentary, Miss Rivers. It is a process for uncovering truth. To do so, we mustn't exhaust ourselves—or in any way attempt to hurry that process along. I will spend this evening developing the images we've taken thus far, but I have the innate sense that today was but the beginning of our journey. We shall require several more sessions at least before I arrive at a composition that will do you justice."

"Several more!"

He nodded. "Indeed. Still, I suspect you are not comfortable here, not yet, at any rate. And I rather fancy capturing you as I first saw you, brisk and busy in Parliament Square, not posing amidst a contrivance of painted scenery and props. Fortunately, I can set up out-of-doors easily enough."

"But it is winter."

"As it was the other day, when you and your suffragette sisters held your frosty vigil. Unless, of course, you are worried to be seen in public with me. I wouldn't want to sully that sterling reputation of yours, after all."

She lifted her chin, a habit of hers; or so he was coming to see. "What nonsense . . . though I can't come tomorrow as I've meetings all day."

"The day after, then?"

She hesitated, and then nodded. "Very well, then. I believe I am free on Wednesday after ten o'clock? Will that do?"

Feeling much like a cat with a very delectable canary in its sights, Hadrian could barely conceal his satisfied smile. "Excellent. As it is winter, midmorning is when the light is at its best."

The London Women's Suffrage Society had its headquarters at Langham Place. Accustomed as Callie was to coming in to the clicking of typewriter keys and the ringing of the telephone, she walked in to find the office quiet as a tomb.

Sober-faced, Harriet descended on her before she had the chance to get her coat off. "Callie, there you are. I was on the verge of sending someone out to search for you."

Callie glanced over her shoulder to the women volunteers, usually so brisk and busy, sitting silent and sullen at the conference table. Heart sinking, she turned back to Harriet. "Something's gone terribly wrong, hasn't it?"

"I'm afraid so." The secretary nodded to the folded newspapers stacked on Callie's desk. "You'd best read for yourself."

Callie drifted over to her desk where she spent the next few minutes perusing the articles recounting the recent rally and her last night's speech. Reading on, she felt her face flushing, not with embarrassment this time but anger. They'd been skewered by the *London Times*, the *Globe*, and the *St. James's Gazette*, but as they were staunchly Conservative publications, she'd half-expected that. It was the lukewarm coverage in the Liberal *Westminster Gazette* that really set her blood to boiling. A pity Hadrian St. Claire wasn't about now. Were he inclined to embroil them in one of the sparring matches he seemed to thrive on, she would have been more than ready to take him on.

Slapping her gloves down on the desk's scarred surface, she let out an unladylike oath. "Bloody, bloody, *bloody* hell!"

Coming up beside her, Harriet waited for the storm to settle before reaching out to take her coat. "How did it go with the photographer chap this morning?"

Callie hesitated. Her session *à deux* with Hadrian St. Claire had been the most stimulating few hours she'd spent in a long while, but she could hardly say so. "It seems I'm not a terribly good portraiture subject, otherwise we might have finished today."

Harriet turned to hang her coat on the rack by the door. "I still think you should have taken someone along with you."

In no mood to be criticized, Callie reached up to unpin

her hat. "I fail to see what taking two people away from our work would have accomplished when there's so very much of it to be done. At any rate, I'm too old to require a chaperone. I've been on the shelf for years." Glancing back at the conference table where the women had resumed working, she dropped her voice to a low whisper and added, "Mr. St. Claire is a professional. He photographs any number of respectable ladies, and I can't think he ravishes them all."

True enough and yet his slightest touch while posing her had rendered a rush of sexual heat so hot, so scalding, she'd walked back to the office rather than taking a hansom, glad of the bracing winter air.

Harriet turned back to her, looking less than convinced. "I only hope that is so. With a man like that, one never knows."

Declining to press what precisely Harriet meant by "a man like that," Callie said, "Have no worries, I can more than manage Hadrian St. Claire."

What she didn't say, indeed would have dissolved with shame to admit, was that the person most in need of managing was herself.

CHAPTER FIVE

"Whether we consider that women ought to be especially devoted to what is beautiful or to what is good, there is much work in the interests of either to be done in politics; and if the ladies were only to take schools, workhouses, public buildings, parks, gardens, and picture galleries under their special protection, and try to send to Parliament a few members who would work efficiently at such subjects, the rest of the community would have cause to be glad of their help . . ."

—HELEN TAYLOR, *The Claim of Englishwomen to the Suffrage Constitutionally Considered*, 1867

Setting up in Parliament Square, Hadrian congratulated himself that moving his second session with Caledonia out into the open was nothing short of brilliant. The air was cold, more brisk rather than bitter; the sunshine, though tepid, sufficed to keep the damp at bay. And of course the square was but a short stroll from his studio, a critical consideration given that seduction was his game. The spoiler was that he must use passion as a weapon to destroy, to *vanquish* as Dandridge put it. Were it not for that, he couldn't have rushed Caledonia Rivers back to his rented rooms quickly enough.

"Mr. St. Claire, hullo there."

He finished unfolding the legs of his tripod and looked up to find his quarry hailing him from the other side of the park. Watching her approach, he found himself admiring the manner in which she carried herself. Shoulders back, spine straight, steps neither mincing nor hurried but well, purposive. How she would move once he got her out of those oh so cumbersome clothes and into his bed was a delicious discovery waiting to be made. The prospect alone set his groin to aching.

"Good day." Reaching him, she extended her gloved hand as a man might, an idiosyncrasy he was coming to view with a certain degree of fondness.

"It is, isn't it?" He enfolded her slender hand in his, holding on a second or two longer than was strictly necessary.

She had on another of her hideous hats, but of course he'd known she would. A few wisps of hair had escaped and standing in full-on sunshine as she was, he saw that what had looked to be near black indoors was shaded with strands of rich mahogany. Even the woman's damnable hair color was complex, confounding, and not exactly as it appeared at first glance.

93

Remembering himself, he pointed to the statue of the great American president and emancipator, Abraham Lincoln; along with being situated in a fortuitous spot of sunlight, the obvious parallel appealed to him. "I thought we might begin by standing you over there."

"Right, then." She walked over to the bronze and turned about, arms held out at her sides as if to embrace the day in all its glory. "Like this?"

"Let's have a look, shall we?" He slipped beneath the camera cloth and brought the aperture of the lens to focus on her head and shoulders.

Hers wasn't, strictly speaking, a beautiful face, at least not in a classical sense of strict symmetry and form, but there was beauty in it, a subtlety, a nuance, a *passion* that spoke to his artist's soul. He especially fancied her chin, rather too square for fashion but softened by that slight and rather beguiling cleft. The other day in his studio when she'd lifted it to dress him down, he'd imagined putting his thumb there, just *there*, and gently drawing her face upward so their mouths might meet.

"I don't suppose I could persuade you to part with the hat?" he called out though it was a foolish question. He well knew what her answer would be.

She responded with the anticipated shake of her head. "It *is* winter, Mr. St. Claire."

Ah, well, it was worth a try. At least she'd left off the spectacles. That was something, he supposed. "In that case, do pull back the veil . . . yes, that's the way, only a bit more like . . ."

He ducked out from behind the camera and came toward her. Reaching out, he smoothed down the one side of the netting that had lifted with the wind and caught a whiff of some delectable scent, rosewater and cinnamon, or so he thought. Just a light touch, he fancied, and likely dabbed behind the shell of that delectable ear. It took only a handful of seconds for him to pin the veil back in place and yet standing close to her as he was, it was all the time needed to make him hard.

He stepped back, grateful for the concealing folds of his overcoat. "There, much better now. You've beautiful eyes as I've said before. It's a pity to hide them."

She arched a brow. "You're a master of flattery, are you not?"

Annoyed, he turned and walked back over to his camera. Never in his life had he met a woman so averse to compliments. Over his shoulder, he tossed off, "The customary response to a compliment is thank you. You might try it sometime."

She opened her mouth to reply when children's laughter had her turning away toward a trio of small boys kicking about a rugby ball. Hadrian had noticed them earlier when he'd arrived to set up but other than the proximity of their play and its potential for disruption he hadn't given them much thought. But now he looked back at Caledonia. Judging from her rapt expression and soft smile, she must genuinely like children—yet another paradox since it seemed she'd chosen not to have any of her own.

The ball bounding between them caught the leg of the

tripod, catching him off-guard and nearly knocking the camera to the ground. For a split second, the sight and sound of a shattering camera lens ripped through his memory, resurrecting a sharp, primitive pain.

One of the boys rushed up to Caledonia, damp blond hair sticking to his flushed cherub's cheeks. "Crikey, miss, I'm that sorry. We didn't mean it. We was only playing."

Hadrian whirled to confront the pintsized offender. "Mind what you're about, you little bugger," he shouted, rather louder than he ought, although already the anger was ebbing, leaving in its wake the familiar soul-sinking emptiness.

The boy stopped in his tracks. Bottom lip trembling, he backed up to Caledonia just as his two mates approached. The other two boys took one look at Hadrian and halted.

Over the top of the child's towhead, Caledonia sent Hadrian a scorching look. "Really, Mr. St. Claire, it was an accident. They were only having a bit of fun, weren't you lads?"

The trio nodded in unison. A tall, lanky boy in a stocking cap and corded trousers patched at the knees chanced a step forward to scoop up the ball. Adam's apple bobbing, he swallowed and said, "We didn't mean no 'arm, sir, honest we didn't." He nodded to the blond-haired boy, the smallest of the lot, on whose thin shoulder Caledonia's gloved hand now rested. "Ned 'ere isn't a very good kicker is all."

"Oliver Tuttle, you take that back or else." Fear apparently forgotten in the need to uphold masculine pride, the boy, Ned, deserted his protector's side and took a step forward, hands fisted.

"Or else what?" Oliver, a good head taller, approached until the pair was all but butting heads.

The corners of Caledonia's mouth curled upward, the sight of which stalled the sharp reply Hadrian had been about to make. "I'm a crack punter or at least I used to be. Maybe I could give you lads some pointers?" Her warm-eyed gaze encompassed the group.

Ned's eyes widened to saucers. "But . . . you're a girl."

Oliver elbowed him in the ribs. "She's a lady, idiot."

Her smile broadened to a full-on grin that revealed the pretty dimple Hadrian had so far seen only once before, on their very first meeting. "I may be a girl but it so happens I grew up playing a great many rough and tumble games girls are not always encouraged to play." She reached out for the ball, and Oliver reluctantly surrendered it.

Aware that he'd become an onlooker to the scene, Hadrian backed up to his camera. Slipping beneath the cover, he leaned in to frame his shot.

Blissfully oblivious to his scrutiny, Caledonia raised the ball high above her head, and then dropped it. Catching it neatly atop her right foot, she kicked upward. The ball shot skyward, a perfect punt, its release coinciding with a sharp blast of wind. Like a stiff breeze to a ship's sail, the bluster caught beneath her skirts, showing a goodly portion of stocking-clad leg from trim ankle to shapely knee.

Peering through his camera's viewer, Hadrian froze. All he need do was flex one finger and he would have, if not the damning photograph Dandridge demanded, a very promising start toward it. And yet he kept his hands still, letting the moment pass.

She tugged down her skirt just as little Ned, hand tented above his eyes, stared across the square to where the ball landed on the ground, a tiny dot. Swinging back around to Callie he exclaimed, "Gorm, you're . . . good."

Caledonia laughed. "I shall take that as a compliment. I used to be a fair hand at cricket, too, though I'm a better batter than sprinter—having to run in skirts puts girls at a decided disadvantage," she added with a wink.

The two older boys trotted off to retrieve their ball, but Ned hung back. "Girl or not, you can play on my team anytime," he lisped, lifting worshipful eyes to Caledonia's face. He shuffled away and then stopped, turned about, and launched himself at her skirts, arms outstretched in a bear hug.

"Thank you, sweeting. That is by far the nicest thing anyone has said to me in quite sometime."

Blinking back tears, she ruffled his hair and bid him go and join his friends. With a final squeeze, the child sped off. She watched after him for a long moment, her wistful expression pulling at Hadrian's heart, the sadness in her profile a palpable thing, something he felt echoed in the aching emptiness of his own heart.

"You like children, don't you?" It wasn't really a question so much as something to say, a reason to breach the silence.

As if suddenly remembering him, she turned back. "Yes. Does that surprise you?"

"A little," he admitted, leaning forward to focus the lens

on her eyes.

Wasn't it the American philosopher, Mr. Thoreau, who'd said the eyes are the window to the soul? If that were even half the truth, Caledonia Rivers must have a beautiful soul indeed. A less cautious man might find himself falling headfirst into those smoky green pools, so earnest and so sad.

"Because motherhood is womankind's sacred calling, no doubt?" The edge to her tone told him that he'd struck a nerve, that on some level she was hurting.

He thought of his mother, who'd spent half her time drunk on gin and the other half spreading her legs for any man with the requisite quid to spend. If motherhood had been her calling, sacred or otherwise, she'd hid it well.

Slipping out from under the cover, he shook his head. "Watching you with that lot, I couldn't help thinking what a wonderful mother you'd make."

She dropped her gaze to the frozen ground. "I rather think it's a bit late for a family. I'm coming on thirty." She gave up her age as one might reveal a dirty secret or at least something of which to be more than a little ashamed.

"That's not so very old."

Looking off into the distance, she shook her head. "A family would be a distraction if not an outright obstacle to continuing my work. It wouldn't be fair to anyone, the children especially."

The cold-blooded practicality of her response grated on him, perhaps because his own mother had made him feel nothing but a nuisance. "Ah, the noble cause for which no sacrifice is too great."

He'd anticipated another of her sharp-tongued retorts but instead she regarded him for a long, quiet moment before asking, "What of you, Mr. St. Claire? There must be something you care about, something for which you'd sacrifice almost anything?"

Her assumption that he harbored some innate nobility was so far off the mark he was moved to laugh. Surely those canny eyes of hers could see through him to who and what he really was?

He made a point of taking out his handkerchief and using it to dust his camera's lens. "Sorry to disappoint but I'm afraid my own survival consumes my every selfish waking moment."

"There must be something or someone you care for?"

Her steady-on gaze had him scouring his brain. Gavin and Rourke were more blood brothers than friends; certainly the closest he had to family. He cared for Sally, too, though the boyhood ardor he'd felt for her long ago had faded to friendship. Beyond that . . .

"There was a time when I fancied myself a future Roger Fenton, but that was a long time ago." Catching her questioning look, he added, "Fenton was the photographer who documented the Crimean War; but my idea was to make a photographic record of the poverty in England, London particularly."

He didn't miss how her eyes lit up. God, those eyes, they had a way of catching at the light, at a man's heart, at *his* heart, as no others ever had. "You still could, couldn't you?"

He shrugged and tucked the handkerchief back in his pocket. "Commissioned work pays, charity doesn't. At any rate, the world has martyrs aplenty. We self-interested sorts exist to keep things in balance."

She shook her head, looking not so much angry as disappointed, as though he were a hopeless case indeed. "Why is it I suspect you are baiting me?"

He grinned. "Why, Miss Rivers—or Caledonia, if I may be so bold—I'm sure I cannot say."

"If you must call me by my given name, call me Callie. The only time I am called Caledonia is when I've got myself into mischief of some sort."

She smiled then, a soft, easy smile that had him going undercover again, not because capturing the image would bring him any closer to bedding her but because for whatever reason he wanted to hold this moment for all time.

"Very well, then, Callie it is. Should you mean to go on plumbing the depths of my black-hearted soul, best call me Hadrian."

He pulled the striking cord. A muffled pop confirmed that her image, that *smile*, was embedded on the proving plate, part of history's record, theirs at least.

Straightening, he looked over the top of the camera and asked, "So tell me, *Callie*, what think your parents of your determination to remain husbandless and childless? Or do you have siblings sufficient to keep the family nurseries stocked?"

It was as if a veil had fallen over her face. Looking not so much at him as through him, she answered, "I have an older brother I haven't seen in years. He and his wife have twins, both boys, a fact that pleases my parents enormously—carrying on the family name and all that."

"What are your parents like?"

She paused a moment before answering. "Staid, conventional. Father is the penultimate *pater familia*. Mother runs the household with an iron fist, yet wouldn't dream of picking up a newspaper and forming an opinion of her own. Aside from the occasional holiday, our contact is limited to correspondence, sketchy at best. I suppose it's fair to say my family doesn't approve of me." She kept her tone matter-of-fact, and yet he sensed the state of affairs caused her some degree of pain.

"It's their loss, I'm sure," he said not because he was working to woo her but because, quite simply, he felt it must be true.

"What of you? Do you have family here in London?"

He shook his head, marveling at how neatly she'd managed to turn the tables on him yet again. Sticking to the story he and Gavin had come up with when he'd resurfaced in London the year before, he said, "I'm an only child."

True enough, at least so far as he knew, though as a boy, he'd dreamt of having a brother just as he'd dreamt of living in the country. It wasn't until he'd left London and his past behind and made a fresh start at Roxbury House that he'd come close to realizing either dream.

"An only child and a boy at that, you must have found yourself fawned over by a great number of aunts and uncles and grandparents."

The happy family portrait she was painting was such a stark and cruel contrast to the circumstances of his actual upbringing that he felt the old buried bitterness rising up. "Hardly. My mother was a . . . widow actually." He thought of the other women who'd worked in Madame Dottie's, Sally especially, and for whatever reason was moved to embellish, "I had a number of aunts who spoiled me after a fashion. After Mum—Mother—died, I lived in an orphanage for a while."

"I'm sorry. I didn't mean to pry." Her eyes were sad—sad for him.

He shrugged to indicate it wasn't important, and yet for whatever reason, being the object of her pity hurt him, rather profoundly. "It wasn't a bad place. Quite the contrary, in fact. It was in the country, and in time I made three friends there, one of whom lives in London now."

"And the other two?"

"There's a big, braw Scot, Patrick, though we called him Rourke after his surname. The last I heard, he was somewhere in northern Scotland working on the railways. The little girl, Daisy, was adopted by a husband/wife acting team and whisked off to parts unknown."

"So you were left all alone?"

The way she said it brought back how very much it had hurt to find himself abandoned yet again. "For the most part, yes." He punctuated the admission with a shrug and then busied himself with changing out the exposed plates for blank ones. Aware of her watching him, he looked up and asked, "What are you thinking now?" not because he was playing her but because for whatever reason he genuinely wanted to know.

She turned to face him, a smile on her lips—lips he suddenly wanted to kiss rather badly. "That it is growing markedly colder not to mention coming on time you fulfilled your end of our bargain."

He'd wager the whole of his twenty-five hundred pounds that wasn't what she'd been thinking at all but rather than press, he said, "Time to pack up and pay the piper, is it?" Straightening, he stepped away from the camera. "Ah well, it is cold, I'll grant you that. The lens of my camera is starting to fog. What say you to that cup of tea I promised the other day—Callie?"

When he'd invited her back to his flat for tea, he hadn't really expected her to agree. As a rule, well-bred women such as Caledonia Rivers simply did not consent to go to a man's lodgings, even if those lodgings did set above a shop. In point, he'd prepared himself for, if not a battle precisely, mulish, unequivocal refusal. Instead she'd sent him a worried look, a longer than usual pause, but in the end, she'd nodded that brisk nod of hers and answered "very well then."

But then beneath those high-necked shirtwaists and stiff, starched skirts, Caledonia was a woman after all.

As he was a man.

They walked back in silence, a state that seemed to suit them both. Once indoors, Hadrian kept his shop's sign on CLOSED and twisted the key in the lock. He turned about to find Callie roaming his studio, making a show of perusing his framed works even though she'd surely seen them when she'd sat for him before.

As if sensing his eyes on her, she moved away from the wall to face him, and he felt something inside him give way as though he was about to steal something he'd no right to so much as touch. "These are very fine. I meant to say so the other day. I am no expert in the photographic arts, but you are very talented."

He regarded her, arms crossed. "There are those who say that photography is no art but craft at best."

She smiled at him, that small Mona Lisa smile of hers that did funny things to his insides. "If you'll pardon my saying so, you don't strike me as a man who cares overmuch for what others say."

"True enough, and yet I think I might care a great deal what you say, what you think." The moment the sentiment escaped, he would have given the world to reclaim it although, oddly enough, he'd meant it—every word.

She surprised him by asking, "Precisely how does it function?"

"Sorry?"

She crossed the room toward him. "The mechanics of the thing, it boggles my mind how something viewed through the lens of your camera can be transformed into a

105

physical representation I can hold in my hand, perceive with my own eye?"

Ridiculously pleased she should care, he beckoned her to over to the camera he'd just set down on the worktable. Pointing to the pertinent parts, he explained, "The process requires the alignment of three components: light; a closed chamber with an opening through which light can pass; and a light-sensitive medium—in this particular case, a glass plate coated with a gelatin emulsion containing light-sensitive salts."

She nodded. "But how do you get the image to fix?"

A canny question, that. How to keep the image from fading away was the very conundrum that had bedeviled early pioneers such as Sir Humphrey Davy and Thomas Wedgwood as far back as 1802. "After exposure, I use a chemical agent to fix the image, and then the plate is left to dry."

Her brow furrowed. "It sounds a rather lengthy process."

He shrugged. "Minutes give or take."

She shook her head, face quietly lovely in the midday light, eyes reflecting an almost childlike wonder. "To think that in mere minutes you can make something that will last forever, perhaps change the world forever."

"Changing the world, that's your mission, not mine." And yet there'd been a time not so very long ago when he'd thought to employ his photographic skills to do just that. "At any rate, nothing really lasts forever, does it?"

Idealist that she was, she took issue with that as he'd known she would. "What of the Parthenon, the Tower of

Pisa, the . . . ?"

He tamped down the urge to seal that lovely open mouth of hers with his own. "As I haven't seen any of those places with my own eye, I'll have to take your word for it. Though I've seen a photograph of the tower at Pisa—wasn't it leaning, and quite precariously, in fact?"

She laughed then, releasing that lovely wind chime sound he hadn't heard since their first haphazard meeting. "Well, then, several hundred years or more . . . give or take." Shrugging, he said, "My work will end up in the rubbish heap long before then."

"Why do you say that?" She cocked her head and regarded him.

"It's the shadow side of human nature, I suppose, to value only what has cost us dearly. Much of my portraiture work involves tintypes, and they carry little artistic weight, I'm afraid. Galleries snub them and many of the more established photographers refuse to make them altogether on the grounds that something so easy to produce and therefore accessible to the so-called masses couldn't possibly be high art."

"That seems foolish."

"Ah well, perhaps and perhaps not."

He doubted the likes of Fenton had ever to worry over where to find the funds for the coming month's rent. Certainly he'd never had to sell his soul to a devil like Dandridge. And it wasn't just his soul Hadrian had bartered but Callie's, too. The latter made him truly sad.

Before melancholy might soften him, he seized on the

opportunity to say, "But really the only way to understand the process is to undertake it oneself. Perhaps you'd care to try your hand at picture making?"

His motive in issuing the invitation was twofold. On the one hand, he was genuinely eager to share his life's passion with a bright and willing pupil; on the other, the large closet that served as his darkroom was upstairs—as good an excuse as any to lure her into his private rooms.

She hesitated. "You should know I've never been terribly . . . artistic."

"You'll be taking a picture. No watercolors or sketchpads, I promise. Ten minutes, surely you can spare that much for science?"

He was openly teasing her but rather than take offense, she smiled. "All right, then, if you're sure you won't mind my bumbling about."

"Bumble away, Miss Rivers, but first let me see about that tea I promised."

CHAPTER SIX

"The history of mankind is a history of repeated
injuries and usurpations on the part of man toward
woman, having in direct object the establishment of
an absolute tyranny over her."
—Seneca Falls Declaration, 1848

It was cold in his upstairs flat, or at least chilly.
Hadrian closed the door behind them and turned
about, making an effort to see his surroundings as
Caledonia Rivers was seeing them, the furnishings sparse
and uniformly secondhand—a rope bed tucked behind a
teakwood screen, the table where he took his meals, a divan
covered in moth-eaten velvet that served as a staging area for
his more intimate boudoir portraits.

Seeing her rubbing her hands together, he moved to make
good on his promise of tea. He had a small gas cook stove, a
gift from Gavin he'd felt almost embarrassed to accept but in

the end had, mostly to forestall a fight. Thankful for it now, he lit the paraffin burner, filled the kettle from the tap and set the water to boil, and then measured out what he hoped was the right amount of tea leaves for a proper pot.

She drifted over to his table and bent to inhale the fragrance from the centerpiece of roses, which he'd got from the local flower seller at an extravagant price. Later, if the afternoon followed according to plan, he would be dragging one of those blood red blooms across her very white, very bare skin.

But first there was the pretense of tea to be got through. Accordingly, he poured the boiling water into the china teapot he'd begged from his landlady along with the dainty teacups and saucers she'd sworn to break his arm over if he so much as chipped. Tossing the oven mitt aside, he called out, "You'll have to tell me how you take your tea."

"With cream if you have it and sugar, lots."

He didn't have cream, only milk. Hoping it hadn't spoiled, he opened the door to the icebox and gave the pitcher a sniff. Satisfied, he poured a small measure into both cups, dropped in several lumps of sugar, and then carried them out to the living area.

He found Callie seated on the divan and petting Dinah, who'd seen fit to hop up on her lap. Charmed at the sight, he handed her a cup. "So it's not only children you're fond of. Apparently small, furry animals find favor with you as well?"

She accepted her tea with a nod of thanks, sniffing the steam before venturing a small sip. Putting down the cup, she said, "I'm very fond of animals of all sizes, horses especially though I haven't ridden in some time."

He thought of the horses stabled at Roxbury House, most of them too old or infirm to be ridden. Like lost children, the orphanage had provided them safe haven. Helping the groom who tended them had been one of his chief pleasures.

Slipping onto the cushion next to her, he took a sip of his tea and teased, "Shall I photograph you on horseback next? Rather like a general commanding her troops."

He felt her tense; whether from his flippant remark or his nearness or both, he couldn't say. She gave a quick glance to the watch pinned to her shirtwaist. "My lesson, I almost forgot."

"An eager pupil, the very best kind." He set his tea on the table next to hers and got up, gesturing for her to join him at the camera he kept stationary on its stand.

Lifting the camera cloth, he motioned for her to slip beneath. She hesitated and then ducked under.

Arranging the cloth to cover her head and shoulders, he couldn't get beyond the lovely floral fragrance of her hair. "Looking through that small screen shows you what the camera lens sees. That is how you frame your shot."

A few seconds passed and then her muffled voice called out, "Ah, I see now. But it's so very small."

He smiled at that. "Beyond that, the direction of the main light is the most important factor in establishing the overall look of the picture. The stop otherwise known as the aperture of the lens is responsible for controlling how much light is let in. Too little light, and the picture will be shadowed; too much and you risk blighting your image with flares—light that appears as streaks or stars." To demonstrate, he reached around to the camera front, fiddling with the focus.

Caught up in the lesson, she couldn't know how her amazing bottom tilted upward, a bare inch from pressing against his groin. Leaning in, she shifted position, and her hip brushed his thigh. He felt his mouth go dry with anticipation, with want. *Bad show, Hadrian.* In this cat-and-mouse game he was supposed to be the predator, the one on the hunt. He wasn't supposed to feel things in response—that was most definitely not allowed.

Clearing his throat, he continued, "The very first thing to be done after checking your equipment is to position your subject—in this case, me."

Slipping out from beneath the cover, she straightened and turned to look at him. "You are my subject?"

Thinking how delightful she looked with her hair mussed, he nodded. "Unless you fancy photographing inanimate objects such as that now empty divan, I suggest you place me in any position you will. I promise I'll not move so much as a muscle. Unlike some persons, *I* can hold still."

"Is that so? We shall see about that, shan't we?" The sudden smile breaking over her face, delightfully devilish, had him grinning in return, temporarily forgetting that this wasn't sport but a game he must, at all costs, win.

He walked over to the divan, swung back toward her, and stretched his arms out at his sides much as she had done earlier in the park. Only they weren't out-of-doors in the public eye any longer, but rather tucked inside this very small, very private space. "Do with me as you will."

She hesitated and then crossed toward him. Only Hadrian didn't move, only stood there staring her straight in the eye, for getting her to touch him *was* the object of the game, after all.

"Very well, sit."

He shook his head, refusing to budge.

Exasperated, she pressed a light hand against his chest, pushing against him. He pretended to sprawl back against the seat, which had her shaking her head and laughing with delight.

Enjoying himself, he said, "But the photographer is not only a scientist. He or *she*," he added purposefully "must also view the scene with the eyes of an artist, taking into account any number of small details that contribute to the overall composition of the piece."

"What sort of details?"

"Subject contrast, for one. By way of example, setting my white shirt against a white backdrop would yield very poor contrast whereas setting it against a black backdrop would result in a contrast that was maximal but perhaps overly stark. By way of striking a happy medium, taking up one of those blooms from that vase on the table might make for just the proper point of interest."

Taking the hint, she glanced back to the table. Going over to it, she plucked one of the roses from the chipped earthenware vase. She returned, snapped off a portion of the thorny stem, and handed it to him. "This would look smashing tucked into your lapel, don't you think?"

She really was beginning to catch on. "I can't see myself as you can, so I think you'd best do this for me," he said both because it was true and because coaxing her into touching him was the aim of the exercise.

She fixed it in his buttonhole and then stood back to study him. "I think I'd like your arm draped along the sofa back."

"Like this?" He kept his arm deliberately stiff, creating an awkward if not unnatural angle.

"No, not quite, more like . . ."

A hand on his wrist, she bent over him, her full mouth pursed in concentration, peppermint-spiced breath fanning his face, her amazing bosom rising and falling beneath the starched shirtwaist. Hadrian sobered, suddenly realizing how very much he wanted to lean up and kiss her. Not because kissing her, seducing her, was his job, but because under other circumstances, honest circumstances, it would be his very great pleasure.

And because he wasn't a good person at all, because he was a very bad fellow indeed, when she turned to adjust the bud in his lapel, he contrived to brush her breast.

She jerked back her hand as though she meant to slap him. Bracing himself for the blow, he caught sight of the pinpoint of crimson on her index finger and realized she'd pricked herself.

He hadn't counted on that any more than he'd counted on his reaction. Though he hadn't even touched her skin to skin, already his cock had begun to thicken and thrum. The flash of awareness in her eyes told him she'd felt it, too, that the possibilities of that brief contact weren't lost on her, either setting his fevered mind to wonder what diorama of pictures she might be playing out inside her own mind.

Looking up into her furious face, Hadrian said, "No need to break the crockery over my head. It was an accident, I assure you."

"Accident or not, a gentleman would beg my pardon." Taking in that dark-eyed gaze and moist, trembling mouth, it wasn't anger Hadrian read so much as naked yearning, unadulterated desire.

"But then again I'm no gentleman, am I, Callie? And I never beg." He reached for her hand and took her bleeding finger inside his mouth.

"I think your cat may be jealous of me." Lying atop Hadrian on the divan, her chin resting lightly on his chest, Callie glanced above them to where the black-and-white cat perched on the sofa back. Tail flicking and ears pinned, the feline looked poised to pounce.

Hadrian followed her upward gaze. "No one fancies being usurped, and Dinah's got spoiled from being on the receiving end of my undivided attention."

Pushing up on one elbow, Callie smiled down at him, feeling deliciously wanton and wholly alive for the first time in . . . well, *forever*. Abed or the nearest thing to it with a man who was not nor would ever be her husband was the very last place she should be, and yet she couldn't find it in herself to regret it for so much as a moment. "I can't say as I blame her."

He slid his hand to her nape, pulling her back down to him and capturing her mouth in another of those long, languorous kisses that set her pulse pounding, her *sex* pounding, so that she wanted to rip off every stitch of his clothes if only she dared. Pulling back, he said, "In the event you've failed to notice, my attention, like my eyes and lips and hands, has been occupied solely with you for the past hour or so."

Despite his declaration that he was no gentleman, once he'd brought her down atop him, Hadrian had acted nothing but, not pressing her for more than she was willing to give nor undoing so much as a single button of hers.

"An hour is it? I suppose I never did get 'round to taking your picture."

Grinning, he reached up and stroked the side of her face. "You can take my picture or indeed anything else of mine whenever you wish, though it would be a shame to bury all this beauty beneath a cameraman's cloth. You belong in front of the lens, not behind it."

She slid kneading fingers into his hair. "Now you really are laying it on with a trowel."

"You don't believe me?"

She settled her head on his shoulder, such a lovely feeling, that. "Simply say I think you're rather guilty of gilding the lily. Only in my case, the lily is more in the way of being a rather stout weed."

"Oh, Callie, what am I to do with you?" He turned his head, pressing a kiss to the top of her head. "You're a very sensual woman whether you care to admit it or not. You also happen to be lovely to look at, to touch." He slid his hand down her spine to the swell of her bottom beneath the padding of her wrinkled skirts. "A great many men would pay dearly for the privilege of taking you to bed."

Stunned, Callie felt heat rushing her cheeks. She wasn't sure at which she was more appalled, Hadrian's scandalous statement or the traitorous thrill that shot through her at the thought that a man, this man, might covet her that much.

Instead of rising up in indignation as well she ought, she turned her face up and asked, "Would . . . would you pay for me?"

Looking down into her eyes, he didn't hesitate. "Yes, I would. In fact, I believe I'm paying even now."

"How so?" She licked dry lips, very much aware of the slow, sweet ache drumming the moist space between her thighs. A single word from her and Hadrian would move to release that ache and bring her satisfaction that until now had existed only in her dreams, and yet she held back.

"There are all sorts of ways of paying one's dues, Callie," he said, somber gaze steady on her face. "Those who can afford to do so pay with pounds sterling. And those of us who cannot, we pay with our flesh. But then I think you already know that. After all, that is why you came back here with me, isn't it?"

Rather than answer that, she rose up over him, touching her lips to brow, his eyelids, the sensitive spot where the pulse struck the side of his throat. Even with clothing separating them, the sensation of touching a flesh-and-blood man after a decade of self-denial and empty fantasies was nothing short of exquisite. Eyes on his face, she said, "I love touching you. Do you mind it terribly?"

"Touch me anywhere you like. Anywhere but my heart," he added on a whisper and let his head drop back against the cushion.

Hadrian was buttoning on a fresh shirt when the shop bell sounded from below. Callie, back so soon? He'd seen her to the door mere minutes before. Had she left something behind? Better still, perhaps she'd decided she wanted more from him than kisses?

Anticipation thrumming through him, he called out, "I'm upstairs, love," trusting his voice to carry through the half-open door.

Footfalls, rather heavier and slower than he remembered hers being, announced her presence on the stair landing. Without turning around, he said, "Decided to come back for another photography lesson after all?" He whirled about, welcoming smile withering when he saw who it was darkening his door.

Cane in hand, Josiah Dandridge stepped across the threshold. "I believe I shall leave any photographing to you, St. Claire."

Despite the cheerful fire he'd got going earlier for Callie's sake, Hadrian felt as though the temperature in the room had dropped a good ten degrees. Without preamble, he asked, "Why are you here?"

Leaning on his cane, Dandridge paused in plucking off his leather gloves to survey the two teacups set on the table, their contents barely touched. "A picture of the Rivers woman frolicking in the park like an inmate escaped from Bedlam with her skirts blown beyond her knees may not be the piece de resistance I am paying you to produce, but it constitutes a promising beginning to building the case against her. I want it."

So his initial instincts about being followed hadn't been pure paranoia after all. "You've set someone to watch me."

The older man dismissed the question with a flick of his hand, the thin fingers gnarled like the trunk of a knotted oak, the top liberally dusted with dark hair yet to turn full gray. Hadrian stared at the appendage for a long moment, disgust and something more—anxiety—taking root in the pit of his stomach. It was only a hand, after all, and an old man's hand at that. Why it should bother him he couldn't say but there was no dismissing that it did.

I'm overwrought. I haven't been sleeping. Yes, that must be it . . .

"How long will it take you to develop it?"

Hadrian hesitated, weighing the merits of claiming the image had been destroyed in the proving process. But no, a green-behind-the-ears assistant could be expected to make such a mistake but not an experienced photographer.

"I'm afraid that's impossible. No such image exists."

That got the MP's attention. "The devil you say."

Hadrian crossed his arms. "Had I attempted to make such a photograph, Miss Rivers would have been on to me in an instant. She is no fool, after all."

Indeed, Callie was no fool. Nor was she the ruthless, cold-hearted bitch he once might have made her out to be. Instead he'd found her warm and loving, gracious and kind. True, she was passionate about her beliefs, opinionated to the point of obstinacy even, but those were small sins compared to what Dandridge had in store for her. What she could have done to warrant the MP's very personal hatred Hadrian couldn't begin to imagine. Surely pushing a suffrage bill through Parliament wasn't the whole of it.

Another mystery yet to be answered was why the devil he'd let her off so easily that afternoon. Lying pliant in his arms, it would have been easy enough to strip off those confining clothes of hers and seduce her—and in full view of the camera he'd set up, no less. With one pull of the striking chord, his debt to Dandridge would have been paid in full. And yet, as in the park, he'd prevaricated only . . . why?

Dandridge assessed him through narrowed eyes. "She is a handsome woman, is she not?"

Careful to keep his expression blank, Hadrian answered, "Some might find her so."

"It is not the opinion of 'some' that interests me. How do *you* find her?"

Meeting Dandridge's gaze, he chose his words with care. "She is passably attractive, though the clothes she chooses to wear cannot be said to flatter."

Without warning, Dandridge brought the tip of his cane down hard onto the floor, sending Dinah scurrying. "Then get her out of them, by God!"

Hadrian held his ground. "It's as yet early days. We've had but two sittings so far. Had I proposed she strip off so much as a glove, she would have fled out that door never to return, let alone promise to return again tomorrow."

Dandridge aimed a knotty index finger at Hadrian. "I may not comprehend the menial mechanics of a camera but I am something of an expert in human nature, St. Claire, and I detect a wavering in your resolve."

Despite the battering of his heart, Hadrian managed a shrug. "You must be imaging things. Beyond the blunt her photograph will fetch, Caledonia Rivers means nothing to me."

His words had the desired effect. Dandridge backed down. "Mind you keep it that way." Cane in hand, the MP made to leave. Halfway out the door, he turned back. "The suffrage bill comes before the Commons for a final read in precisely thirteen days. I must have the evidence in hand well before that."

"As you shall."

"I hope so, St. Claire. For your own sake, see you do not fail me."

Carriage skirting the Victoria Embankment, Dandridge pushed aside the window curtain and peered out. Sighting the shadowy yet unmistakable form stamping his feet at the base of the riverside road, he touched the tip of his cane to the carriage ceiling, signaling his driver to pull over. A moment later, the door opened. The conveyance dipped as a hatchet-faced hulk in a worn tweed coat and shapeless hat climbed inside.

Sam Sykes pulled the door closed and settled into his seat, setting springs creaking. "Good day, guv."

"You took long enough." Dandridge turned to his newest retainer and felt his nostrils twitch in recoil. *Leeks*, he rather thought, *or was it garlic?* Whichever, it was flavored with the unmistakable pungency of unwashed flesh. He'd always been fastidious, a failing of his, he supposed. Yet he'd never understood why being born in the gutter apparently compelled one to carry the stench of the stews about wherever they went.

And yet persons such as Sykes had their uses.

Dandridge waited until the carriage continued onward before asking, "What do you have for me?"

Settling back against the leather squab, Sykes blew on

cold-chapped hands the size of small hams. "She spent close on to two hours in there alone with him."

"You're quite sure?"

"Oh, aye, I stood watch from across the street, though it were cold enough to freeze the balls off a brass monkey. Saw 'em go in together and then him leave the shop sign turned to closed. A couple minutes later a light came on in the upstairs window, but the shop below stayed dark. She didn't come out 'til nigh on three o'clock."

Dandridge paused to stare out to the elaborate ironwork standards ranged along the riverside, their fierce-looking dolphins coiled about the bases, before asking, "Alone?"

Sykes shrugged. "Well, not alone exactly. He was standing just inside the door."

"How did you find them?"

"Sorry?"

Teeth gritted, he prompted, "Was she flushed? In a state of dishabille—undress?"

"Oh, she were buttoned-up proper, with one of them big fancy hats on and a boxy coat that went clear past her ankles. He was in his shirtsleeves, but he had on his breeches and they was buttoned, too—I looked."

Putting aside his disappointment, Dandridge picked up the string-wrapped bundle on the seat beside him and handed it across to Sykes, careful not to let his gloved fingers come into contact with any part of the henchman. "I see. Keep a watch on them until you receive further instruction."

Sykes's thick lips stretched into a gap-toothed grin. He

stuffed the money inside his coat. "Oh, aye, I will. In fact, you might say as it'll be my pleasure."

"Well, well, this is an unexpected pleasure. I've never known you to sneak off shopping on a weekday before."

Callie started. She looked up from the display of gentlemen's business cases she'd been perusing to find Teddy standing beside her. Blast, but she'd as good as forgotten he clerked at Harrods.

Finding her smile, she said, "Yes, well, I need to purchase an attaché case."

Ever since leaving Hadrian's studio hours earlier, she'd been obsessed with the notion of giving him something, a memento, by which to remember her. An attaché case seemed to strike a reasonable middle ground between the practical and the personal; personal, to be sure, but not embarrassingly so. Earlier she'd noticed that the leather case he carried along with his camera was worn to the point of shabbiness. Likely he'd been so buried beneath commissions he hadn't given a thought to replacing it.

Teddy frowned, twisting one end of his waxed mustache as he was wont to do when puzzled. "But didn't Lottie just give you a crack case for your last birthday? If it's worn, we'll make good on it, you've only to bring it in."

Callie cleared her throat. Dear Lord, was it ever her lot in life to be caught out over even the smallest deception?

Choosing her words with care, she said, "It's not for me. It's a gift . . . for a . . . colleague."

"I see." The wounded look he sent her made her think he did see the situation in all its sordid truth.

Fighting back a blush, she pointed at random to the display shelf and said, "That black one is awfully smart."

"You have excellent taste." All at once the dutiful clerk, he walked over and popped open the case. "The lining is lambskin, not the green baize of the less dear models. Not that there's anything wrong with baize—"

"I'll take it," she interrupted, desperate to break away if only to be alone with her thoughts and the truly momentous, disastrous, and altogether wonderful course her life had careened toward since earlier that afternoon. "How soon might I have it engraved?"

"The gent responsible for our leatherwork has a few items in queue before yours, but I'm not without influence." He snapped a suspender and added, "I can put in a word on your behalf—important friend waiting and all that. It should be ready by tomorrow, late morning. Will that do?"

"Oh Teddy, that would be so good of you. You're quite certain you don't mind?"

"Quite." He clicked together the heels of his polished shoes. Looking down, he said, "I lay off work in a few minutes. Any chance of you joining me in the tearoom upstairs?"

"I wish that I could but I haven't time." What with the hours she'd already spent with Hadrian, she'd need every remaining minute of the evening to catch up.

"Don't give it another thought, old girl. It's only that . . . well, dash it, I miss you, Callie. I miss you dreadfully. We scarcely see each other these days."

She waved a hand, hoping to appear matter-of-fact rather than what she was—a guilty person, a loose woman, a liar on the verge of being caught out. "With the suffrage bill set to be reintroduced, I've been so busy lobbying potential backers I haven't had a moment to myself. But in a fortnight and a day, this business will be resolved one way or the other, at least until next session, and then we'll have a nice long catch-up, I promise." She summoned what she hoped passed for an easy smile, even as she felt her heart sinking like millstone tossed into a stream.

A fortnight and a day. What she didn't say, couldn't bear to think on was that her photographic portrait soon would be finished as well. That meant she would have run out of reasons for seeing Hadrian St. Claire.

CHAPTER SEVEN

"The suffrage is the right of all women, just as it is the right of all men, and although the immediate need may not be felt by the happy and the prosperous—by the women with kind husbands and comfortable homes—we insist on it on behalf of the solitary, the hard pressed, and the wronged; we insist on liberty so that all may share the blessings of liberty."

—MARY LEE, *South Australia Register*, 1890

The encounter with Dandridge had shaken Hadrian mightily. He was still in a filthy mood the next afternoon when Callie breezed inside his flat, brown-paper-wrapped parcel tucked beneath one arm. She stopped in her tracks when she saw him seated at the window, cat in his lap. "Hadrian, are you quite all right?"

Unshaven and unwashed, he knew he likely looked like

hell, perhaps stank even worse and yet he couldn't resist. "Why do you ask?"

"Because you seem, well . . . not quite yourself."

He had a mind to point out that she didn't really know him, at least not outside of bed, but of course he couldn't say such a thing, not at this stage at any rate. Setting Dinah down, he rose stiffly as an old man might. "We had an appointment. Do you imagine yours to be the only time of value?"

What remained of her smile faded to bewilderment. "Of course not. She glanced back to the door. "I can come back another time if you'd rather. If the light isn't good or . . ."

Ordinarily a ten minute or so infraction wouldn't have fazed him in the least, but since Dandridge had admitted to having him watched, he felt vulnerable in ways he could scarcely own. Mired in such a state, it was easy enough to convince himself that the MP and Callie were cut from the same cloth. Political persuasions aside, they were all too willing to rampage over others to achieve their precious ends. No sacrifice was too great so long as it was made by somebody else, somebody beneath them.

"The light is fine. Sit down." Without waiting for her to answer, he pulled out a chair. "Now tell me about this meeting of yours, the one that was so important you must be late."

She set her package on the table and slipped into the proffered seat. "It was a lecture on the plight of East End women and girls given by Mrs. Catherine Booth who with her husband founded the Salvation Army. Owing in no small part to Mrs. Booth's guiding hand, the Salvation Army gives women equal responsibility for preaching and welfare work."

"How . . . inspirational." Voice dripping with sarcasm, he scraped out a second chair and took his seat.

She hesitated. "Indeed, it was. In fact, Mrs. Booth recounted a case just last week of a young woman, a girl really, who came to the shelter seeking refuge from her father who meant to sell her to a house of prostitution to make ends meet."

Hadrian thought of his childhood friend, Sally, now the madam of the house where he'd grown up. It had been a hard life but at least they'd never starved. Not until he'd left to strike out on his own had he known real hunger. The memory of that gnawing belly ache would stay with him for the rest of his life. Sometimes in his dreams he felt it still.

In his dreams.

He rolled his shoulders. Taut as they were, they barely moved. "Brothel, workhouse, everyone's version of hell-on-earth takes its own shape. Better that than she should starve and her family along with her."

She paused in pulling off her gloves to stare at him. "Hadrian, you can't be serious."

"Indeed, I am wholly so."

She dismissed his comment with the flick of her hand, not unlike Dandridge had done the day before—more fuel to the fire. "Better she should be given refuge and trained for some gainful employment, some useful occupation that provides a true service to society."

For whatever reason, the way she said *society* set his teeth on edge. "There are those who would say that prostitution provides a necessary service, a safety valve if you will."

He was being unpleasant, deliberately so, risking his mission and his very life into the bargain. But the old recklessness was coursing through him potent as any drug and for the life of him he couldn't bring himself to care. In truth, he hoped she would take it into her head to simply get up and walk out. Better yet, run while she still had the chance.

Run Callie, run.

Slapping her gloves atop the table, she shot back, "Easy for you to say so, a man." Man, she all but spat out the word. "Did you know that, in England alone, as many as forty-odd percent of unmarried women live in dire poverty, a condition that makes them vulnerable to succumbing to prostitution and sundry other degradations."

Good, he'd got to her at last, that was his aim after all. "What would someone like you know of whoring?" That he didn't say prostitution but rather the coarser term was a measure of just how far beyond control he was. It should have been a warning sign but for the moment he was past caring. As it was, he was a heartbeat away from shouting at her: *If you want to know about whoring, ask someone who knows. Ask me.*

She flushed but to her credit held his gaze. "I have read accounts of women who must walk the streets to feed themselves."

"Accounts, is it? Tell me, Caledonia, have you ever condescended to speak to such a woman? Face to face, that is?"

"No, not exactly."

"Not exactly?" Fingering the glass fragment buried in his palm, he made no attempt to strain the sarcasm from his tone. "Tell me, what manner of recompense are such women paid to give their testimonials? Five shillings? As much as ten? More perhaps but then such titillating gossip would be worth a great deal, wouldn't it, for spinsters too gutless to allow a man near enough to touch them, really touch them."

Cheeks dyed a wind-chapped red, Callie pushed back from the table, and rose. "For whatever reason, you seem determined we should be at odds. You are in a foul humor, and I've no mind to be made the butt of it so much as a moment more." She snatched up her parcel in shaking hands and turned to go, leaving her gloves lie.

Like a drunk who'd just come to, he took a stumbling step toward her. "Caledonia. Callie." He reached out to touch her but something in her ramrod straight stance called him to take his hand back.

Bottom lip trembling, she shook her head. "Mind you don't say a word more, not a single flipping word. Hang your bloody photographs and . . . *hang* you."

With that, she turned her back on him and stalked off. He steeled himself for the requisite slamming of the door but when she only drew it quietly closed, he knew in his heart she meant never to come back, that this was farewell, not merely goodbye. The very worst part was that he couldn't fault her for it. Not a jot. If he had so much as a drop of decency left, he would let her go, let her save herself, and accept whatever consequences came his way.

Yet somehow, he couldn't resign himself to bidding her farewell. Not just yet. Not like this.

"Callie, hold." He vaulted out into the hallway. Catching her on the stair landing, he took firm hold of her shoulders.

Whirling about, she struggled to shake him off, the parcel falling to the floor. "Take your bloody hands off me."

He held firm, absorbing her hurt, her anger, the heat of her all but searing his palms. "Callie, please. Don't go. Not like this."

"If I do leave now, whose fault is it? First you insult me. No, worse yet, you skewer my intelligence and challenge my commitment, and impugn my honor by suggesting that I or my associates would bribe, actually *bribe*, other women to lie to advance our political ends. You poke fun at my . . . inexperience and in the next breath you manhandle me as you might some sort of . . . street woman. Just who the bloody hell do you think you are?"

Who indeed? Harry Stone? Hadrian St. Claire? Somehow the two had gotten all mixed up in his head. "I think I'm the man, the *lout*, who owes you his most humble and heartfelt apology. I should never have spoken to you as I did." He let his hands fall away though even bristling with anger she felt so good, so right, in his arms.

"Why did you?" She held herself stiff and apart from him but at least she wasn't fleeing.

Choosing his words with care, he answered, "I had a visit the other day from a . . . patron, a very influential patron, displeased with my services. I've let it rattle me rather more than I should."

Her expression softened. "I gather he is a very important client? Or perhaps I should say 'she'?" Beneath the brim of her hat, one dark brow edged upward, a frame for the unspoken question in her eyes.

"No, it was—is—a man." Did he imagine it, or was that relief flickering across her face? "As for his importance, I venture to say he considers himself of great consequence indeed."

God, but the melting expression in those big soulful eyes of hers very nearly wrecked him. "Hadrian, tell me true, have you been neglecting your other commissions to work on my portrait? If so, I shall telegraph Mrs. Fawcett directly and ask her to engage another photographer. I'm sure she'll—"

"No, no need to do that." Heart racing, he took a moment to gather himself before continuing in a calmer voice, "Really, I've managed everything. The gentleman left with my complete assurance that the photograph I deliver shall be more than worth the wait."

The tenseness about her mouth eased into that tentative half-smile he found so utterly disarming. "It will be all right then, won't it?"

Oh God, as if anything would ever be all right again? "Yes, well, we shall have to wait and see." Desperate for distraction, he looked down to the fallen package at their feet. He bent to pick it up. "What is this?"

She hesitated, gnawing at her bottom lip. "It's a gift . . . for you," she added, rather unnecessarily, though her discomfiture was endearing all the same.

"I can't say as I've done anything to merit presents, unless it's a lump of coal, but shall we go open it?"

They walked back inside, his hand resting lightly on the small of her back, his palm fitting the curve of her as though it belonged there.

He set the parcel down atop the table and reached for the scissors to cut the cord. "It's been a very long time since someone's given me a present."

Arms folded across her breasts, she said, "I hope you don't think me forward. It's only that after the other day, well, I wanted to give you something, too."

He paused in ripping away the brown paper to look up at her. "Callie, what we shared together, that was hardly charity on my part." Rather than risk embarrassing her further, he turned his attention to stripping away the remainder of brown paper. He lifted out the contents, a proper businessman's case every bit as handsome as the one he'd seen Dandridge carry. His gaze shot to hers. "Oh, Callie, you shouldn't have."

"I know it's not the sort of gift a woman normally gives to a man she's only just met but I thought . . . rather, I saw that yours was . . . is rather well-used, and I thought . . . it was a whim, silly of me, really, but I thought you might like to have it."

Touched, he traced the tooled leather with a single finger.

"You've had it engraved with my initials."

She nodded. "The gentleman in the men's shop at Harrods was kind enough to take care of that for me. Unfortunately he couldn't get to it until today."

So that was it, her real reason for arriving late. She'd stopped to pick up his present, the present he so ill deserved. *Oh, Callie, forgive me.*

Mired in his misery, he was vaguely aware of her rambling on, "I didn't know if you had a middle name, so I settled on H.S. If it's not right, or if you prefer your old one, you needn't use it. I shan't be offended, truly. I just wanted . . . I just wanted to give you something."

H.S.—be it Harry Stone or Hadrian St. Claire, either way it served. He dragged his gaze up to her face. Feeling as though his blackguard heart might cave at any moment, somehow he found his voice. "It's splendid." *You're splendid.* "It was . . . very good of you to think of me." Christ but how stiff he sounded, how formal, rather like the hoity-toity set he spent so much of his time aping but whose manners he could never quite carry off. "I shall be proud to carry it. Thank you."

"I'm glad you like it." Looking anything but pleased, she glanced down at the watch pinned neatly to her bodice. Like the spectacles she'd recently left off wearing, he suspected the timepiece was mostly for show. "I should be going." She turned away.

"Callie . . . wait up, will you . . . please."

She turned slowly toward him. "Yes, Hadrian?"

He hesitated, wondering what the devil he might say to her to ease the hurt, to make it all right between them again, at least as all right as things could be under such circumstances. "There's something, a place, I want to show you. Think of it as my gift to you, if you will." At her perplexed look, he elaborated, "A lecture, no matter how well intentioned, is no substitute for the genuine article."

"Hadrian, what are you proposing?"

"Before you take this cause of yours any farther, why not venture out and meet some of these so-called East Enders for yourself?"

The hired hansom took them as far as Covent Garden Market. Hadrian paid the fare and directed the driver to let them out at the Russell Street entrance. Stepping inside the enclosed market, Callie saw that the aisles were largely deserted, the vendors' goods picked over from that morning. Hadrian explained that while some costers were packing up for the day, others would remain until dark to draw what custom they might from the early-evening theatergoers.

Hadrian had a camera slung over his shoulder but so far he'd yet to remove it from its case. Wondering why he'd brought her if not to take pictures, Callie strolled down the line of food stalls, the displayed delicacies ranging from pineapple, lemon, and other imported fruits to hot cross buns and jellied eel. She was debating whether or not to purchase a paper cone of roasted chestnuts when a woman's high-pitched voice drew her attention to the other side of the room.

Standing before a seller of hot pies, the tall blonde shrilled, "For the love of God, Tim Brody, 'ave a heart. Girl's gotta eat, don't she?"

From behind the stall, the apron-clad merchant shouted back, "You're no girl, Pol, and 'aven't been for years. Now take your poxy hide out o' me sight before you chase away any more customers." Reaching over, he dealt the blonde a hard shove.

Watching in horror, Callie caught at Hadrian's coat sleeve.

The woman righted herself, stepping back to straighten her worn velvet bonnet with great dignity. "I'm going, aren't I, but mark me, ye'll pay for that if not in Heaven then in 'ell."

Clutching a thin, fringed shawl about bony shoulders, she turned and staggered across the aisle, nearly careening into Callie and Hadrian. Looking up, her scowl lifted into a crooked smile. "'arry Stone, why bless me soul. Where've you been keeping yourself, love? I 'aven't set eyes on you in ages."

Hadrian froze. Recovering, he tapped the side of his nose and said, "I'm afraid you've got the wrong fellow, but here's something for your trouble." He dug into his pocket and pulled out several one-pound notes.

Eyes darting from right to left, Polly snatched the money and stuffed it down the front of her gown. Fingering the crusted sore at the side of her mouth, she shifted her gaze to Callie, looking her up and down. "Ah, so that's the way 'o it, now." She threw back her head and laughed as though someone had said something funny indeed. "Oh, nay trouble at all. My mistake, guv." She winked and continued on her way, but not before Callie caught the backward glance she sent them.

As soon as she was out of earshot, Callie leaned in to Hadrian and whispered, "Was that woman a—"

"Streetwalker," he finished for her.

"I thought as much. Poor thing, she looked so fragile and thin and unwell."

Jaw set, he nodded though she couldn't miss how he avoided looking her in the eye. "Poverty, disease, and childbirth are of greater menace to the typical London prostitute than the Ripper ever was—or the lack of voting rights, for that matter."

Ah, so now they'd got to the crux of why he'd brought her. Whatever had she been thinking to presume to be his teacher when it was clear, and painfully so, how very much she had to learn. "If your aim was to show me what a spoiled, unfeeling wretch I am, then point taken."

She'd expected him to crow like a rooster but instead he turned and looked at her for a long, thoughtful moment before saying, "I don't think you're spoiled or unfeeling. If anything, you're one of the kindest, most feeling women I've ever had the privilege of knowing."

Stunned as much by the warmth in his eyes as by the unexpected compliment, Callie was at a loss for words. "Thank you," she finally said, and without thinking took hold of his arm.

They left the main market building for the outside, Hadrian occasionally pointing out some structure of note—an orphanage for Jewish children, a soup kitchen, a gin palace that fronted for a thieves' academy. Hand resting in the crook of Hadrian's arm, it never occurred to her to feel frightened. So absorbed was she in all she saw, including the newly revealed depth to the man walking beside her, she came close to stepping on the wraithlike form sprawled on the sidewalk at her feet.

"Spare a coin, lovey?"

Startled, Callie looked down. Slumped against one of two pilasters announcing the gated entrance to an imposing brick building of several stories, the woman was of indeterminate age, the lower-left portion of her face wrapped up in a scarf and pitifully sagged, putting Callie in mind of a balloon with half the air let out. At her side were a moth-eaten tabby cat and several boxes of matches. Callie didn't know what to make of her. The match sellers she'd seen were girls, not adult women, and certainly not wizened creatures such as this poor soul.

She was about to reach into her reticule when she spotted the empty flask in the woman's hand. She snapped the bag shut. "I will not finance your addiction, madam, but if you wish, I will gladly hire a hansom to convey you to the Salvation Army shelter. There you will find a hot meal and refuge." And medical attention, she almost added, but thought better of it.

The woman coughed and spat a wad of yellow sputum

on the pavement near Callie's foot. "Ha! Bloody Methodist do-gooders, I'll rot in 'ell before I let 'em get their filthy mitts on me."

Wordlessly Hadrian reached into his pocket and took out his money clip. The woman's hazed eyes brightened when he handed her a bill.

She snatched it up as though afraid he meant to take it back. Looking down at the money in her hand, she blinked, and then stared up at Hadrian, cracked lips breaking into a broad grin. "A fiver! Oh thank ye, sir. Warms the cockles of me heart, it does, to know there's still such a thing as a true gentleman—and true Christian charity."

Shocked to her core, Callie would have repeated her offer of transportation and safe haven only Hadrian cut her off. "Leave her be," he said, tone sheathed in steel, and taking firm hold of her arm he steered them away.

It wasn't until they crossed to the other side of the street that Callie had the presence of mind to break free. Indignant, she choked out, "What could you be thinking to give that woman money when you know she will only use it to buy more of the very spirit that enslaves her?"

He turned on her then, hard fingers biting into her arm. "What if she does, poor devil? If a flask of Mother Geneva can carry her away from her pain for a few hours, then I for one look upon it as money well spent."

Stunned to be the one under attack when she was so obviously in the right, Callie shot back, "In case you've failed to notice, it is winter. If she should fall asleep in this weather with gin thinning her blood, she may well freeze to death."

He responded with one of his infuriating shrugs. "Who are we to say that might not be a blessing?"

Could he really be that callused to the loss of a human life? "A blessing! Dear Lord, have you no human feeling at all?"

His mouth dipped downward; his eyes were as bleak as the soot-stained sky above. "Have a look about you, Callie. Can you not see where it is we are?"

Without waiting for her answer, he took hold of her shoulders, turning her so that she was facing across the street to where a clutch of women clustered about a rubbish bin. Hands outstretched, they took turns catching the warmth from the feeble flames coming up from the grate.

"That large and undeniably handsome brick building across from us is the Bryant & May Match Factory. Those women standing outside the entrance all work there as once did that poor devil we just passed."

She angled her head to look back at him. "What of it?"

"Have you never heard of a condition known as phossy jaw?"

As much as it irked her to admit ignorance, she admitted, "No, I haven't."

Sliding his hands from her shoulders, he blew out a breath. It hovered between them for a handful of seconds like pixie dust, a small cloud of crystallized air. "The yellow phosphorous in which the match-heads are dipped is highly toxic," he explained, sounding much as he had when he'd first taken her through the mechanics of photography. "Prolonged contact causes all manner of maladies—burns to the skin, shortness of breath, jaundice. And, in advanced cases such as that woman's, it eats away at bone until teeth and sometimes even pieces of jaw can be pulled out."

"Dear Lord." Callie fought nausea as the few bites of breakfast toast she'd had threatened to come up. She searched Hadrian's face, studying the resolute set of his own lovely squared jaw, before asking, "Is there no cure?"

He shook his head, confirming what she'd already suspected. "Phossy-jaw is fatal, I'm afraid, a cancer of the bone, so no, she is beyond help except for what numbing comfort there's to be found in a bottle. As for the others . . ." He shrugged again, but the intensity of his gaze holding hers told her he was far from past caring. "The company could substitute red phosphorous instead, which is essentially harmless."

"Allow me to guess—yellow phosphorous comes less dear?"

His expression lightened although she had the disconcerting suspicion that inwardly he was laughing at her. "Ah, Callie, you begin to catch on. Beyond that, improving working conditions would go a long way in minimizing the problem if not eliminating it altogether. Better ventilation to increase the flow of fresh air, a separate room where the workers might take their meals rather than eating at their benches, shorter shifts. But then implementing such measures would gnaw away at the owner's profits as surely as yellow phosphorous gnaws away at bone." He jerked his head toward the afflicted woman slumped against the wall. "And God knows we can't have that."

She was coming to see that he cared a great deal more

than he let on. "Perhaps at first but surely healthier, happier workers would be more productive in the long term?"

"True, but then, that is at the very heart of the problem. Most people cannot see beyond the here and now. It takes a true visionary to look beyond present circumstances to the future. It takes someone like you."

Had he just paid her yet another compliment? Callie stared at him, trying to decide. Pulling her gaze away, she said, "Excuse me," and started back across the cobbled street.

From behind her, he asked, "Where the devil do you think you're going?"

Not stopping, she called back over her shoulder, "Why, to talk with those women, of course. I'd like to hear firsthand what their conditions are and, more to the point, for what improvements they're striking. Perhaps I can be of some help to them."

He caught up beside her, made as if to grab hold of her elbow again but this time she moved away before he could. "Leave it alone, Callie."

"Rubbish. I'll just dash over and chat for a few minutes and then we'll be on our way."

"Not on your own, you won't."

She whirled about, blocking him with a hand against his chest. "We are women. We settle things not by brawling, but by talking. It is men who use their fists to force their way whereas women employ reason to appeal to one another's sensibilities."

He looked down at her hand, the palm flattened against his

sternum. Even though they wore winter coats and gloves, the intimacy of the gesture, and the perfect ease with which she'd touched him, caught her off-guard. She took her hand away.

"You are standing in the middle of Bow, Callie, not some Mayfair drawing room. I've known women who thought nothing of hammering away at one another like prize pugilists. Survival of the fittest is the only rule that applies here, or do you dismiss *Origin of the Species* outright simply because Darwin was a man?"

"We shall see." Leaving him standing on the sidewalk, she turned and walked toward the factory's smoke-charred façade.

Reaching it, she ran a practiced eye over the group congregated about the dustbin. It didn't take her more than a moment to pick out the leader, a rail-thin woman who stood slightly apart from the clutch of shivering bodies. Despite the blustery day, she wore a decades-old bonnet and only a thin calico shawl over her dress, but her air of authority was unmistakable.

Callie cleared her throat, though the women's stiffened stances and wary expressions told her they were well aware of her approach. "Hullo there. May I inquire as to which one of you is acting in the capacity of leader?"

Predictably, the woman with the calico shawl turned to face her. She might have been twenty-five or forty-five, it was impossible to tell. Lines bracketed the corners of her hard eyes and tightly drawn mouth, and the skin stretched over her sharp-boned face was the color of parchment.

"That would be me." The woman planted a knobby fist on either hip and ran her gaze over Callie with a slow thoroughness calculated to intimidate. "Who is it that wants to know?"

Callie stood her ground, the women in the circle stabbing her with hard, appraising stares that ran the gamut from envious to openly hostile. Plain and simple though her clothes might be, in this company they stood out as costly to the point of decadence. Then there was the matter of her name. While the Movement included women of all classes, there were still those working women who viewed the fight for suffrage as the pursuit of the privileged. If any of these women were of such a mind, then owning up to being Caledonia Rivers might well prove more liability than boon.

"For now, perhaps you might think of me as an interested bystander."

The woman scowled. "Then you'd best stand somewhere else. It's serious business we're about, and we've no time for curiosity seekers—or mealy-mouthed do-gooders, either . . ."

The rest of whatever she'd meant to say erupted into a hacking cough. In the throes of it, she pulled a handkerchief from her skirt pocket and, without apology, spat into the worn folds. She stuffed it back inside her pocket but not before Callie glimpsed the bright bloom of blood.

Lifting her gaze to the woman's worn face, she said in her most matter-of-fact tone, "Fair enough. If I say that I am sympathetic to your plight and that I have some experience in organizing protests, would you speak to me then?"

"She don't look like a strikebreaker, Mum."

Callie looked down to the small girl tugging at her skirt.

Wide, intelligent eyes peered up at her from a thin, white face.

Addressing herself to the child, she answered, "That's because I'm not. I'm what people call a reformer—a person who works to try and make things better." Ignoring the snickers behind her, she squatted down until she was eye-level with the child. "And may I ask your name?"

"I'm June Brown. And she's me mum." She pointed to the leader.

Glancing back over her shoulder, Callie saw the mother's gaze soften as it rested on her child. *She's the joy of her life*, Callie thought and beyond all reason she felt a pang of envy.

She turned back to the little girl. "I'm pleased to meet you, June Brown. I'm Caledonia. Caledonia Rivers."

Sudden silence surrounded her, making it obvious they knew exactly who and what she was. Beneath her breath, one woman hissed, "Bloody suffragist," but Callie ignored her and held out her hand to the child.

June laid her tiny hand trustingly inside, and Callie felt her heart squeeze in on itself. She could well understand why Mrs. Brown would resign herself to slaving in the living hell of the match factory to keep this precious being fed and clothed.

"I'd be pleased if you'd call me Callie."

Brown eyes solemn, June nodded. "All right then. I like Callie better anyway."

"So do I." Smiling, Callie straightened and turned to face the women who'd moved in to form a circle about her. For a handful of seconds Hadrian's warning flashed through her mind, then she dismissed it. To a woman, the strikers were too tired, too dispirited, and, she suspected, too weak with hunger and despair to raise a hand in violence—particularly to someone who, though an outsider, was willing to help.

The leader stepped toward Callie and extended her hand. "I'm Iris. Iris Brown."

"Mrs. Brown, my pleasure." Callie grasped the roughened hand firmly in hers.

Iris Brown looked down at their clasped hands for a long moment before letting go. Apparently coming to a decision, she turned to indicate the others. "This lot is Doris, Jenny, Annie, Martha, and Old Emma."

"Ladies." Callie acknowledged each woman in turn, expensive kid leather joining hands with moth-eaten wool and bare, chapped skin. Breaking away from the last of the women, Callie asked, "May I ask then what terms you are proposing in order to resume work?"

Iris produced a folded paper from beneath her shawl and passed it to Callie. "I suppose it wouldn't hurt for you to have a look. We've nothing to hide."

"Thank you." Callie unfolded the limp paper and read through the list of demands, a half-dozen or so items scratched out in block letters and with the poor spelling and grammar characteristic of young children. Even so, the women were clear about what changes they wanted implemented. Elimination of the current system of fines—three pence to one shilling for talking, dropping matches, or going to the loo without the permission of the shift manager; a half-day's pay in punishment for lateness. Although the "offenses" were so minor as to be absurd, the fines didn't seem to Callie to be overly harsh . . . until someone explained that a week's wage was only five shillings.

Five shillings! From the little she'd read of sweatshop labor, she'd understood that working conditions in the factories were substandard at best, abysmal at worst. Even so, she hadn't realized the situation was this bad.

She skimmed the rest of the demands—a separate room in which to take meals so that the women wouldn't have to eat at their workbenches, an increase in pay to six shillings a week, and a half-day off every other Saturday so that they could spend more time at home with their families.

Handing back the paper, she said, "These all seem quite reasonable. What did the factory owner say when you met with him to present your grievances?"

Iris snorted. "I don't know as I'd call it a meeting exactly. Said he runs a business, not an almshouse, and that anyone who don't care for the way things are is free to go elsewhere. Then he fined me a week's wages for having the cheek to show my face at his office door. It meant June going without milk for a full week. Toward week's end, I had to keep her home from school; she hadn't the strength to walk."

This time Callie couldn't hold back. "But that's . . . that's outrageous."

Old Emma spoke up, "Hardcastle ain't exactly known for 'is Christian feeling, miss."

"Mr. Hardcastle is the proprietor, I take it?"

The women nodded in unison.

Old Emma turned her head and spat into the gutter.

"Aye, and a miserable unfeeling wretch he is, as was his father before him."

The young woman introduced as Doris confided, "We call him Mr. Hard-Arse behind his back." She grinned broadly, revealing a patchwork of missing and brown teeth, a smile sadly out of step with her smooth, youthful face. "Why, when he caught Peg Yardley saying so, he docked her a full day's wages. Peg, God love her, said it was worth it to see the bugger's face go afire."

Tepid laughter made the rounds, but there was no real mirth in the women's faces, only misery.

A broad hand settled on her shoulder. "There are some things on which you can't put a price."

Callie whipped about to find Hadrian standing behind her, so close that were she to back up a step, she would find herself pressed against him. That thought alone sent a little shock of electricity shooting down her spine, making her shiver in a way that had nothing to do with the cold.

Doris shook her head, liberal patches of pink scalp showing through her thin brown hair, yet another effect of the phosphorous poisoning or poor nutrition or perhaps both, Callie suspected. "If we strike and fail, this time it's sure to be the sack for all of us." She brightened. "Then again, as they say, 'naught ventured, naught gained'."

Nothing ventured, nothing gained. Callie looked down at little June, who was stroking the top of Callie's kid leather glove with the reverence usually reserved for small, furry animals, and prayed the adage would hold true.

CHAPTER EIGHT

"Wherever a noble deed is done, 'tis the pulse
of a hero's heart is stirred. Wherever the right hath
triumph won, there are the heroes' voices heard."
—MARY LEE, *South Australia Register*, 1890

air wages for women, now. Fair wages for women
NOW!"

Carrying makeshift placards, the women marched
up and down the factory walk, their carrying voices beginning to attract the attention of passersby.

From inside the gated entrance, the proprietor, Mr.
Hardcastle shouted out, "Shove off or I'll call the bobbies on
you bloody bitches, and don't think I won't."

Balanced atop the vegetable crate that served as a
makeshift speaker's platform, Callie called back, "We are on
the public street, sir, and well within our rights. If anyone is

disturbing the peace, it is you."

"Is that so?" He elbowed the barrel-chested foreman next to him.

With a grin, the foreman shoved away from the wall and sauntered though the open gate to the protestors. He stopped before Iris Brown and, reaching across, wrenched the sign out of her grasp. "Take this, bitch." He hefted the placard high and brought the end of the wooden handle down atop Iris's head.

"Mum!" Screaming, June rushed over to her mother, who'd folded to her knees, blood spilling onto the cobbles.

Mayhem broke out with more men pouring out from the factory doors, converging on the women with fists and clubs.

Caught up in the chaos, Callie didn't see the shop foreman coming toward her until hard hands encircled her waist, pulling her off the crate and flush against his thighs. "What's a tasty bit o' crumpet like yourself about making mischief 'ere?" His thick-lipped mouth covered hers in a foul-breathed kiss.

"No!" Callie drove her knee upward, catching her assaulter in the groin. With a howl, he dropped back to clutch himself.

Looking beyond him, she searched the sea of flailing bodies for Hadrian, but he was nowhere to be found. She started forward but a dark shape blocked her way.

The foreman hefted a heavy hand. "Bloody bitch, you'll get your comeuppance, I'll see to that." The backhanded blow caught her squarely across her cheek. She staggered, the gate at her back breaking her fall.

"Bastard!"

The fist whizzing past caused Callie to duck only this time the blow wasn't meant for her but for her attacker. Bare knuckles connected with the man's bulbous nose in a cartilage-crushing crunch that dropped him to his knees.

Sidestepping the fallen man, Hadrian rushed to her side. "Come, we've got to get you out of here." Throwing an arm about her shoulders, he steered her away from the scene.

Digging in her heels, she said, "But I can't just leave them. I—"

Somewhere in the near distance a police siren blared. Hadrian tightened his hold. "Callie, for bloody once do as I say. Take hold of me and run. Run, Callie, run!"

Hadrian led them through a maze of winding streets, concealed courtyards, and rubbish-strewn alleyways, navigating like a seasoned ship's captain charting his course around a storm. Later Callie would marvel at how he seemed to know without stopping to think just which way to turn—but for the moment all she could manage was to fill her lungs with great gulps of icy air and run for dear life.

They ducked into a gin shop alley just as a police wagon sped by. Breathing hard, Hadrian leaned back against the crumbling stone wall. "I think we managed to give them the slip. We'll rest here . . . for . . . a moment."

Callie fell back next to him, one hand pressed to the invisible knife stabbing at her side. "What . . . what just happened?"

He turned to look at her. Like her, he'd lost his hat. Sweat streamed the side of his face, darkening the golden hair at his temples. "It seems Hardcastle made good on his threat and sent someone to call out the bobbies after all."

"But that's outrageous. It was he who ordered those men to come after us. Oh, Hadrian, he must have planned it all along." And she, Callie, had stepped right into his trap, leading the other women to follow. She shoved away from the wall. "I have to go back and explain."

He grabbed her arm, pulling her back. "Don't be a fool or a martyr either. You can't very well help if you're jailed alongside them, now can you? Tomorrow you can post bail, give a statement if you like. For now, leave it."

Leave it. How many times in the span of the past few hours had he told her to do just that and how many times had she brushed aside his objection, assuming she knew what was best. Now instead of being at their liberty, Iris Brown and the others were beaten and on their way to incarceration.

Thinking of June Brown cradling her mother's bleeding head in her small lap, she felt perilously close to crying. "I was only trying to help them and, dear Lord, look what I've done. Thanks to me, they're worse off than they ever were."

"Hey, you." He wrapped an arm about her, his body an anchor of comfort against a world gone suddenly to sea. "It's not all bad."

Fighting tears, she shook her head. "Isn't it?"

Eyes fixed on her face, he said, "You gave those women hope, a sense of purpose. Because of you, they were able to stand tall and proud, perhaps for the first time in their lives. They may not have prevailed today but because of you they may do so tomorrow or the next. At least now they'll have the tools, the resolve, to try again."

She fitted a hand to her forehead, damp with perspiration despite the raw air. "I doubt that will afford anyone much comfort tonight as they're lying on a hard jail floor with throbbing heads and empty stomachs."

He looked at her with the same mixture of tenderness and weary resignation she might have shown little June. "Sometimes it's the beauty of the struggle that makes an action worthwhile. I should think a warrior princess such as you would own the truth in that."

"I don't feel much like a warrior, even less a princess."

He laid his hand along her cheek. Now that they'd stopped running, the place where she'd been hit had begun to throb. Tracing the bruise that was surely taking shape by now, he looked into her eyes and said, "My brave, beautiful Caledonia, whatever can I do to make you see the wonderful truth of who you are?"

Callie didn't think first, only acted, a condition that was becoming more and more frequent since Hadrian had come into her life. "You could kiss me."

"Could I now?" He smiled but his eyes boring into hers were disconcertingly sober.

"Yes." Lifting her face to his, she felt something cold and wet strike the tip of her nose.

Hadrian must have felt it too. He pulled away to look up. She followed his gaze to the sliver of white sky visible through the arc of sagging rooftops. Blast, but it was snowing.

Unwinding his woolen scarf, he wrapped it about her neck. "We'd best save that kiss for later. For now, I have to get you inside somewhere safe and dry until this business blows over. Fortunately I know just the place."

It was coming on twilight when they reached Hadrian's friend, Sally's house. The streets in this part of the city were not only narrow and winding but poorly lit. The new electrical lights had yet to make it this far eastward, and from what Callie could see maintenance of the old gas fixtures was spotty at best. That left large patches of darkness relieved only by the odd lit window or doorway. In contrast, the gabled house Hadrian led her up to was glowing like a Christmas tree, Chinese lanterns festooning the gated entrance and the three tiers of windows, splashing their gaily colorful iridescence onto the bricked courtyard and cobbled street.

Sally Potts was a prostitute, Callie could see that straightaway. Unlike the ragged, careworn creature she'd encountered in the market, the woman who answered Hadrian's knock, or rather three sharp raps, was plump and handsome, her low-cut taffeta gown suited for evening though it was barely four o'clock.

They stepped inside the entrance hall, the walls decked with flocked paper and pier glasses, the etched glass sconces fired with electric, not gas. Closing the door behind him, Hadrian said, "Callie, this is an old friend of mine, Sally Potts. Sally, I'd like to introduce Miss Caledonia Rivers."

Callie stared, she couldn't help it. Face paint, lots of it. A prodigious quantity of powdered bosom protruding from a square-cut bodice. Red hair, obviously dyed, elaborately curled and piled high with combs. Likely the woman was at best a few years Callie's senior, and yet the elaborate artifice made her seem at least a decade older.

"Never say old, not in my line of work." Jabbing Hadrian in the side, Sally tossed back her head and let out a loud laugh.

"Mrs. Potts, a pleasure." Extending her hand, Callie bestowed the title as a courtesy though she heartily doubted the woman had ever been married.

Sally turned curious eyes on Callie, making Callie aware of just what a mess she must look, hatless and with her unpinned hair falling wild about her shoulders. Despite Sally's frank appraisal, though, she appeared neither unfriendly nor unkind. "Any chum of Harry's is welcome here."

"Harry?" Was it Callie's imagination, or did Hadrian stiffen beside her?

"Oh, did I say 'Harry'? Bless me, I meant to say Hadrian. Lud, I'd forget me own name some days if there weren't friends to remind me of it." Again that thunderbolt of laughter, this time rather studied, or so Callie thought.

Hadrian cleared his throat. "We're in a spot of trouble, Sal. Oh, nothing too serious, mind, a bit of bad business over at the match factory. Might we stay here until the heat dies down? Just an hour or so, and then we'll be on our way."

Sally shrugged, the motion causing her breasts to slip even farther out the top of her low-cut gown. "Stay as long as you like. Business always drops off the beginning of the week. It's not like I can't spare the room."

Hadrian glanced toward the scarlet-carpeted stairway. "Something with a window facing out onto the alley would be just the thing. Just in case."

"No problem; I have a solution."

Hadrian and the woman exchanged knowing looks, and Callie felt her heart lodge in her throat. *They're lovers*, she thought, and even as she told herself she shouldn't care, that what she'd had with him so far had only been a silly kiss and a bit of a fumble, after all, the stab of anguish she felt was a very real thing, a warning that history was about to repeat itself if she wasn't careful.

Sally led them upstairs, taffeta skirts swishing. At the top, she turned down a long, sconce-lit hallway. Following closely behind, Callie heard the sound of a slap, and then a woman's giggle, coming from behind one of several closed doors. Face heating, she ventured a look over her shoulder at Hadrian, but he didn't meet her eyes.

Sally stopped at the closed door at the very end of the corridor. Opening it, she stood back and announced, "Here we are, loves, my very favorite room in the house." She shot

Hadrian a wink. "As you can see, the window faces out to the alley. Not the best of views, mind, but practical at times and not so high you can't climb out if the need arises. In the meantime, I'll send up some refreshments and a beefsteak for the lady's eye."

"Thanks, Sal. You're the best," Hadrian said, and Callie didn't miss the easing of his taut features. For the first time it occurred to her she hadn't been the only one in danger of being carted off to jail.

Sally tossed back her head, painted lips parting into a smile of tobacco-stained teeth. "Oh aye, that's what they tell me." Catching Callie's eye, she sobered and said, "I'll send one of the lads off to check out the situation and then knock on your door to give the all clear. Three sharp raps."

She pulled the door closed behind her, leaving Callie and Hadrian alone once more. Callie hazarded a glance about. The still air was scented with perfume and sex; the carpet a plush cloud beneath her feet. A big four-poster bed dominated the room's center. The counterpane was done up in crimson velvet that matched the window curtains and bed canopy. A large mirror hung over the gilded dresser.

Now that the aftershock of fear was draining from her blood, she felt the chill of cold, hard reality setting in. She, Caledonia Rivers, was hiding out in the bedroom of a working brothel, a tart's boudoir. Even her questions over Hadrian's obvious friendship with the madam faded to the edges of her mind as she struggled to absorb this incredulous fact.

I don't care. I shan't allow myself to care.

She turned to find Hadrian standing beside her. He'd set the camera down and was stripping off his gloves, the right one split at the stitching. Grimacing, he pulled it off.

She saw the torn flesh of his knuckles and felt her heart turn over. "You're hurt."

He tossed the gloves aside with a shrug. "I've been hurt a great deal worse than this. Growing up as I did produced an elephant's thick hide."

"In the orphanage, you mean? Fighting with the other boys?"

He shook his head. "On the streets such as the ones we walked today. I lived on my own for almost a year. After that, the orphanage seemed a rather tame place."

"You were put out on your own after your mother died?" She looked up at him, her heart aching for the lonely, lost boy he once must have been and the secretive man standing before her whom, she suspected, wasn't entirely sure how to either trust or love.

He hesitated, and then shook his head. "I was a runaway. I heard about her death months afterward from . . . from a mutual friend. By then, it was too late to mourn her, at least properly."

Callie thought of her own parents, whom she hadn't seen in more than a year. Though they'd never been a close family, still she didn't care to think of the day when they would pass from her life altogether. To lose one's parent when still a child would be devastating indeed. "Oh, Hadrian, I am so sorry."

"I'm sorry, too—sorry I haven't done a better job of

taking care of you today."

Reaching out, he touched her face with gentle fingers, probing the bruise blooming on her cheekbone just below her eye. Callie shivered, not because the spot throbbed (although it did) — but because being touched in this way, by this man, made her feel small and feminine, cared for and cherished. For the first time in a very long time, someone, a man, was taking care of her and though the circumstances were considerably less than ideal, it still felt so very right, so immeasurably . . . *good.*

And yet the part of her that insisted she could manage perfectly well on her own prompted her to say, "Taking care of me isn't your job. I don't need a keeper."

He dropped his hand and stepped back to look at her, no doubt put off by her strident tone. "What do you need, then?"

It was a leading question designed to discomfit, and yet for a moment she paused to consider. What did she need? The answer, crystal clear, came to her as though someone, unseen, were whispering in her ear.

I need a lover. I need you to be my lover.

The bruise beneath her eye wasn't the only part of her that throbbed and ached and while a raw beefsteak or a cool cloth might answer to that, the only cure for that other, deeper ache was this man.

For the first time in perhaps in her entire adult life, she walled off her mind with its niggling self-doubts and persistent insecurities, and allowed herself the freedom to feel. Instead of moving away, she lifted her face to his, offering him her mouth for the second time that day. "I need you to kiss me, Hadrian. On the lips as a lover would. As you did the other day."

"Callie," he said, his voice a raw whisper. He caught her by the shoulders, holding her fast. Lips, butterfly light, landed on her eyelids, her cheeks, the pulse point at the side of her throat. "Callie." He moved to her mouth, kissing bottom and top lip in turn, running his tongue along the seam, teasing them apart. "I'm wrong for you, Callie, so bloody wrong and yet this feels so—"

"Right, I know. I know, I feel it, too." Eyes open, she reached up and laid a hand on either side of his neck, the muscles going taut beneath her fingertips. "Right or wrong, I don't care anymore. I want you. I just want you."

She opened her mouth for him. Later she might look back and rue her foolish, wanton ways but for the present she didn't care to think, only feel. Hadrian St. Claire was kissing her, kissing her as no man had kissed her ever before, and when she felt his tongue slide inside her mouth to twine with hers, the sweet joy of it, the soul-deep sensation of feeling well and truly alive, eclipsed everything else.

He found her breast with his hand, torn knuckles brushing the sensitive tip. Even through her layers of clothing, she felt herself harden, felt the sweet ache of it all the way down to the throbbing core of her sex.

"Please." She shivered and arched against him, wanting more, wanting all of him.

He wrapped an arm about her waist and deepened the kiss, tongue stroking hers, teeth gently nipping at her bottom lip even as his clever fingers found the fastenings fronting her coat.

"Callie." Breathing hard, he unfastened the few buttons it took for him to fit a hand inside, and then found the smaller buttons of her shirtwaist and unfastened them too. He covered a palm over one camisole-covered breast. "So beautiful," he whispered and set his thumb to circling her nipple, calculated torture.

Without breaking contact, they backed across the room. Callie bumped up against something, and realized it must be the mattress against the back of her thighs. A whore's bed and yet she couldn't wait to crawl between those sex-scented sheets and make love with Hadrian as until now she'd only made love in dreams.

Outside their door, three sharp raps sounded. Sally's high whisper announced, "Coast is clear. Shall I still send up that beefsteak?"

Like guilty children, they broke apart. Hadrian glanced to Callie. She shook her head and a moment later he called back, "I think we're set, Sal, but thanks just the same."

Looking back to Callie, he shook his head. In a whisper meant for her ears alone, he said, "It's just as well. I told you before I'm all wrong for you. I'm the very last man you should let near you. I ruin everything I touch."

"I don't believe that."

He rested his head against her forehead, breathing hard. "You should. In fact, you should consider it fair warning."

"Maybe I don't care for being warned. I'm a grown

woman. I know what I'm about."

"Do you?" Hadrian pulled away. Walking over to the window he pulled back the velvet drapes and looked out. "It's almost dark. The streetlamps are just coming on." He dropped the curtain and turned to her. "In this world where night is day, Sally's patrons will begin arriving before much longer. We should go now before someone sees you."

Oh God, he was turning her away. The bitter disappointment of it came out in a brittle laugh. "It's rather late to worry for my reputation, wouldn't you say, though I seriously doubt I run the risk of encountering anyone I know in this place."

"You think not?" He turned back inside. "Don't be a fool. Sally's clients ran the gamut from prosperous tradesmen to London's upper crust, including several Members of Parliament and a cousin to the Lord Mayor of London. There's no telling who you might encounter if we stay."

He crossed the room toward her. Laying a hand atop either of her shoulders, he turned her toward the room's sole mirror, which hung in plain view of the bed. "That mirror may look ordinary enough but the glass it holds is two-way. Even now, someone could be in the next room watching us." Sliding an arm about her waist, he pulled her to him, her back fitting against his chest. Reaching around them, he cupped her breasts. "Watching me do this and . . . this." He flicked his thumbs over her nipples, once, twice . . .

Callie moaned and leaned back against him, the now familiar hardness pressing against her buttocks.

"Perhaps listening to the soft sounds you make when I touch you there and . . . there." He slid one hand down from breast to belly, settling the heat of his palm between her thighs.

Crushing his hand to her, Callie stared into the mirror, to the flush-faced, disheveled woman who was her and yet very much a stranger, and asked, "And if I said I didn't care?"

"You may not care at this moment, but I think you'd care very much tomorrow and the next day and all the days after." He pressed a kiss to the side of her neck and let her go.

The sudden absence of those arms holding her must be among the loneliest feelings in the world. To go ten years without being touched was to know want of the silent, suffering sort, but to have known a man's touch, Hadrian's touch, and then have it suddenly withdrawn was nothing short of torture. Even if he was acting for her good, his withdrawal released all the old insecurities. What would a man like Hadrian St. Claire possibly want with her? She was past her prime, on the shelf, a dried-up spinster. The kissing, the fondling he'd done out of pity and, she suspected, convenience—whatever animal instinct the confrontation on the street had aroused in him had demanded satisfaction, and she'd happened to be the only willing female at hand.

She turned away from the mirror, fumbling with her buttons. "You're quite right." She struggled to push the words past the knot of hurt blocking the back of her throat. "You'd best take me away from here. Take me home now."

Home. Sitting in the worn wing chair in his flat later that night nursing swollen knuckles and a glass of gin, Hadrian asked himself how what had started out as a bad day could have ended so very much worse. The answer was to be found in his poor judgment but then that was hardly new. Hauling Callie off to Bow had set the wheels of disaster in motion. What business was it of his whether or not she understood how the proverbial "other half" lived? Yet if he were going to be honest with himself, his motive in taking her there had been more than didactic. Short of confessing his true name and past, it had been his way of doing just that. When Polly had called out his true name in the market, a part of him had felt almost, well, relieved.

As it was, the day's events had worked out in his favor, or at least they could have had he pressed his advantage. He'd had a camera with him, after all. Though only a portable, he could have used it to capture any number of damning images including the piece de resistance, a photograph of Callie being hauled off to jail. Instead he hadn't taken so much as a single shot, whisking her away from harm instead.

Afterward, when they'd paused in the alley to catch their breath, taking her in his arms to comfort her had seemed the most natural thing in the world. Like breathing, he hadn't given it so much as a second's thought. All he could seem to do was to fall into the welcoming sweetness that was Callie.

Again at Sally's, he'd let yet another golden opportunity

slip away. Given the seediness of the setting, even a grainy photograph of Callie in partial disarray would have sufficed to satisfy Dandridge, ending the game in Hadrian's favor then and there. But when he'd reached for her with a mind to tumbling her back on the bed, he hadn't been playing the game, not in earnest. He hadn't been playing at all.

He glanced over to the table where the case she'd given him earlier set untouched and knocked back the rest of his gin. Ordinarily self-examination was something he avoided like the proverbial plague but now he was aware of a deeply profound discontent, a roiling restlessness. Whoever Hadrian St. Claire was, he didn't much like him. He didn't like him at all.

And owing to his behavior, in all probability Callie no longer liked him, either. On the carriage ride to her aunt's house in Half Moon Street, she'd kept her gaze trained on the tightly folded hands in her lap or the dark streets visible though the hansom window—anywhere but on him. He'd hurt her feelings and he felt horrible about it and yet wasn't hurting her, *vanquishing* her, precisely what he'd set out to do?

There was no getting around it—the woman was working her way under his skin. Like the sliver of lens glass lodged in his palm, the only remedy was excision. He would cut Callie out of his heart. It was the only way, the only chance, for either of them.

CHAPTER NINE

"We do not remember days; we remember moments."

—Anonymous

Harry lay on his stomach, breeches yanked down to his ankles and head twisted at an odd angle. The counterpane smelled musty; it was made of some sort of shiny, satiny stuff patterned with clusters of roses and a trelliswork of ivy. He traced the raised needlework with one finger, connecting the leaves and branches with the odd stain, making a game of it in his mind.

Out of the corner of his eye, he saw his mother standing by the scarred nightstand, tears tracking her cheeks. "Here, this'll make it go easier." She handed a cobalt-colored glass jar to the man and turned to go.

Eyes squeezed closed, Harry listened to her retreating

footfalls. The bedroom door closed softly, but he felt the vibration of it, the finality, all the way inside his chest.

The bed dipped, and a hard knee shoved between his legs. He tried to rear up but he was pinned, as helpless as a wild animal caught in a hunter's snare. Burying his face in the pillow, he gritted his teeth. "You can't make me like it."

Ugly laughter greeted that statement, and then the cold, wet smear of grease slathered fingers between his buttocks. "My dear boy, I don't give a tinker's damn if you like it or not. But if you fight me, it'll go hard with you and that slut of a mother of yours. Now be a good lad, and it'll be over soon enough."

Be a good lad, a good lad, a good lad . . .

Blunt pressure and then a sudden knife-sharp pain seared through him, threatening to rent him in two. He squeezed his hands into fists until the nails drew fresh blood from his palms, bit down on his bottom lip until he tasted the metal of blood there too. Anything, anything, to keep from crying out.

A big hairy hand reached around the front of him, fondling his balls. As if it had a mind of its own, his cock stiffened. In his ear, hot breath hissed, "You said I couldn't make you like it only I think you do like it, my little whore."

My little whore, whore, whore . . .

Another few blunt, burning thrusts, a hoarse shout of triumph and release, and then it was over. The mattress dipped then steadied as the man climbed off him. Harry curled onto his side, cool air brushing his backside. Hot cheek pressed to the pillow, he listened to the sounds of clothing being adjusted, a satisfied grunt, and then footfalls heading back to the bed. He tensed, waiting. Please, God, no more.

Paper, a five-pound note, floated down to the vacant patch of pillow by his head. "Next time show a bit more enthusiasm, and I'll make it ten."

Next time, next time, next time . . .

He waited until the door closed, then stuffed the money beneath the pillow and rolled onto his back. Beyond that, he couldn't muster the energy to move. How long he lay staring up at the ceiling he couldn't have said. It might have just as easily been hours as minutes, but at some point a soft knock sounded outside the door.

"Mum?" He pushed himself up on his elbows.

"No, it's me. Can I come in?" The whispered voice coming from the hallway belonged to his friend, Sally, one of the new girls and three years his senior.

Sally, how could he face her now or ever again? He flopped back down on his back without answering, hoping she would give up and go away. No such luck. The door opened partway, and she slipped inside. "You all right, Harry?"

He found solace in sarcasm. "Bloody grand. The best day of my life, don't you know it?" He fixed his gaze on the ceiling but not before he noticed her face was free of paint, which could only mean she wasn't seeing any "gentlemen callers" today.

She sat down on the bed beside him. "He hurt you, didn't he, the lousy bugger?" Her tone was a soothing balm of outrage and loyalty.

He dropped his gaze from the cracked plasterwork and turned on his side to look at her, hot tears of shame rolling down his cheeks. *"Oh Christ, Sal, Jesus Bloody Christ."* Digging the heels of his hands into his eyes, he willed the back flash of images to stop.

"First time's always the hardest." She reached down to pat his shoulder, the bodice of her castoff gown dipping open. Through the waterfall of tears, he caught an eyeful. Breasts, big as melons and tipped with nipples the soft pink he'd seen in a rainbow just the week before.

He shook his head. *"There isn't going to be a next time. I like girls. I like you, Sal."* All at once, the tears stopped and against all odds he found his smile.

He reached up and slipped a hand inside her gown. Soft and supple as he imagined a cloud might feel.

"I like you, too, Harry, but you know we can't. House rules and all." Despite her protest, he noticed she didn't pull back.

"No pay, no lay," he repeated, heartily sick of Madam Dottie and her rules.

Sally nodded, solemn as if they sat in a church pew instead of half-naked on a whore's bed while he played with her breast, the nipple hardening beneath his thumb.

But not as hard as Harry's cock, miraculously come to life and standing out straight as a pikestaff.

"Oh, what the 'ell." She lifted his shirt, looking at him long and hard before taking him in her hand. *"My, you're a big lad,"* she said, licking her lips in a way that had him shivering.

He dropped his hand. *"Is it . . . all right, then?"*

She giggled. *"Better than all right, I'd say, so long as you know how to use it."* Her hand began moving up and down him, *smooth, sure strokes that had him pulsing against her palm.*

She lifted her skirts and moved to straddle him. Other than her stockings and garters, she wasn't wearing undergarments. He stared at the triangle of dark hair between her full thighs, at the dark core of pink inner lips, and felt his mouth go dry.

Arching his hips, he poked around her thighs, sweat breaking out on his forehead when he didn't immediately hit home. "Easy, ducks, it's not a race." She reached down between them and guided him to her.

"Will it hurt you?" he asked, going still, reminded of his own stinging bum. Sally might be a girl, but she was his friend, too. He didn't ever want to make her cry.

"No, silly, I'll like it." She came down on him hard, taking him full inside her, or at least he thought so—he still hadn't chalked up the courage to look down.

Lying still, he closed his eyes and let her ride him, thinking nothing in his life had ever felt this nice, this good. Then she did something with her hips and pleasure so stark it bordered on pain bolted through him. He came, losing himself inside her.

Afterward they lay facing each other atop the sheets. Hands pillowed beneath her tousled auburn curls, Sally was the first to speak. "He'll be back for more, you know he will."

"I won't be here when he does." Reaching beneath the pillow, he pulled out the money he'd stowed there. "Come away with me, Sal. I'll take care of you."

She shook her head. "My place's here, at least for the time and sure there's worse places I could end up. Only promise me that someday when you're a fine gentleman, a photo . . ."

"A photographer," he said to save her from stumbling over the word.

She smiled, but her eyes were sad. "Yes, that. Promise me you'll visit me sometimes, will you? And you can take my picture again, if you like."

"I swear I will."

The first lights of dawn streaked the coal-fogged sky when, belongings tossed into an empty pillowcase and the five-pound note folded into his pocket, he climbed out the bedroom window under Sally's watchful eye. He waited for her to give the all clear, three sharp raps on the window pane, before skirting the ledge of gabled roof. Reaching his chosen spot, he dropped down into the alley.

Straightening, he turned to look up at the window but the room had gone dark. "I won't forget you, Sal, I swear I won't. Someday I'll be back, you'll see." He turned and walked out into the cleansing mist.

<hr />

Hadrian shot upright in the bed, the echo of a scream dying on his lips, the shattering of glass ringing in his ears. Sweat slid down his chest, drenching the sheet he'd let drop to his waist. He wrapped shaking arms about himself, a solitary hug, torn between relief that he'd woken alone and a terrible fear that alone was what he always would be.

He raked a trembling hand through his damp hair. As always, his first thought upon waking from the nightmare was:

I have to have a woman. Sally kept a clean house and when she wasn't occupied with one of her regulars, she was always happy to oblige. When he had money he paid her and when he didn't, she did him for free. But going out in search of a quick coupling, soulless sex, struck him as entirely too great an effort to expend for such scant, temporary reward. He still wanted release, that hadn't changed, but he just possibly wanted something more, too. He wanted someone to hold, someone to hold him, to feel something, not just with his body but with his heart, too.

His thoughts turned to Callie, a condition that was becoming more and more common of late. By God she'd felt good in his arms, her generous figure fitting to him like a hand to a tailor-made glove. Though he'd yet to see her without her clothes, touching her through them had given him the feel of her. Imagination, his at least, was a potent force and his mind was more than capable of filling in the missing details.

Closing his eyes, he reached beneath the covers to take hold of himself, imagining the creamy whiteness of her thighs, the thick thatch of curls framed between them, the moist inner lips hidden inside. In his mind's eye, he saw himself burying his face in that musky heat, pleasing her with lips and tongue and teeth. The fantasy was becoming so real he could swear he tasted the brine of her on his tongue.

He squeezed his eyes tighter, letting his imagination carry him further along as he worked his turgid flesh. Eventually he would enter her. He would wait until he felt the first telltale tremors tickle his tongue and then he would take his mouth away and replace it with his cock. He was large, he knew, and very thick, not a conceit on his part but a simple acknowledgement of fact. One look at his open trouser front and the women he'd brought upstairs with him hadn't been able to get their clothes off fast enough.

Callie, however, would be a virgin. He'd never been with a virgin, but he imagined that she would be very tight at first, perhaps a bit dry. He would take care with her, be gentle but not overly so. At the core of all pleasure was some degree of pain and if she was anything like him, she would prefer to take hers sharp and fast. He would breach her with one clean thrust and then hold himself back until she got used to him. Once she did he would ride her, slowly at first and then faster until she was as wild for it as he was and then and only then would he let himself go.

Hadrian's eyes shot open as the first spasm overtook him. *Oh, God, Callie.* A few more rough strokes completed his release. He fell back against the pillow, wiping his hand on the empty sheet next to him.

Oh, Callie, do you sleep soundly, the slumber of perfect innocence, or lie awake in your lonely bed as I do?

Were he a normal man with an intact heart to offer, Callie Rivers would be very easy to love. As it was, how could he possibly work to destroy someone so pure of heart, so perfectly *good*?

Dinah jumped up on the counterpane, butting her head against his chest. He reached out and stroked her silky back until she arched, mimicking the silhouette of a perfect witch's cat. "What am I to do about her, Dinah? More to the point, what am I to do about me?"

One Week Later:

"Callie, my dear, what am I to do with you? These past days, you've not been yourself at all." Lottie looked up from the typed letter she'd just folded into precise thirds.

Callie hid a yawn behind her hand. She'd passed yet another restless night but then at this point she'd stopped counting. They were at the Langham Place office. She'd shooed Harriet and the volunteers off to lunch, not because she was being noble but because she wanted to be alone with her thoughts. Lottie, true to form, had refused to budge. By way of a compromise, they'd sent out to the sandwich shop across the street.

Seated across from her at the mahogany conference table cluttered with typewriter, stacked petitions, and the handbills advertising the upcoming march on Parliament freshly back from the printer, Callie quipped, "If not myself, then whom do I seem?" She knew she sounded snappish but lately she was too restless to care.

Lottie's knowing look cast that assurance into grave doubt. "If I didn't know better, I'd say you very much resemble a young woman in love."

"As I am neither young nor in love, I'd suggest you go back to reading your tea leaves." A pause and then, "Oh,

Auntie, I am sorry. I'm a beast to speak to you so and especially when you're sacrificing your day in this stuffy office to help with our mailing."

"Think nothing of it, pet. But you are in the doldrums, I can see it."

Callie made no move to deny it, though missing Hadrian wasn't entirely the cause. The day after the match-factory strike had descended into rioting, she'd gone to the magistrate's office and sworn her statement that Hardcastle had directed his henchmen to attack. After that, there'd been nothing left to do but pay the women's fines and pray the press didn't get a whiff of her involvement before month's end when the suffrage bill came back before Parliament. On a personal note, she'd penned Iris Brown a letter of introduction to a Manchester factory owner known for his fair practices toward workers. As Iris was the ringleader of the strike, Hardcastle would never take her back. It seemed little enough given the depth of trouble into which she'd led them all. But then again, as with most matters in life, only time would tell.

Lost amid her thoughts, she struggled to pick up the thread of what her aunt was saying, something to do with a ball and cheering her up. "Why not come with me to the benefit for the Tremayne Dairy Farm Academy? It's to be held at the Covent Garden Opera House the evening after next. There's to be an auction early in the evening followed by a ball and buffet supper."

Social gatherings such as this were apt to be famous bores no matter how worthy the cause and these days she couldn't seem to think much beyond her next "session" with Hadrian. At some point the sittings had become simply a vehicle, an excuse, for seeing each other. They'd make a show of posing her, only to end up talking for hours until at some point he'd glance toward the window and announce they were losing their light; it was winter, after all. "In that case, shall I come back tomorrow or the day after?" she'd ask, and they'd both smile and agree that yes, yes she should.

Never mind that by now he must have taken enough pictures to fill an entire album. It was a game, a lovely diversion from the stark reality of real life. Some days no matter how hard she worked at juggling, she couldn't manage to break away. Those were dark days indeed, although until now she'd fancied she'd made a rather good show of hiding her true feelings.

Of course they couldn't go on as they were forever. A man like Hadrian must have scores of women vying for his time and attention. She was a novelty at present but eventually he would tire of her, sooner rather than later—or so she suspected. A wise woman would wean herself from him before he cut her off, and yet she couldn't find the willpower to do so any more than a drunkard could dole out his stash of gin. Even though dwelling on the futile fantastical hope that their "relationship" such as it was might somehow blossom into something greater and grander than mere friendship wasn't remotely good for her, she wasn't prepared to stop. Not just yet. To no longer see him, hear his voice, or brush against his sleeve gave rise to a sense of sick emptiness she couldn't shake off. Even the low whistle he was wont to launch into when puttering with his camera equipment had grown familiar to her—and very dear.

Distracted as she was, it was a moment or two before the import of Lottie's words sank in. "Why, that is the vocational school Lady Stonevale founded, is it not? I must admit to being skeptical at first—but from what I've heard the school does quite good work training former prostitutes for gainful employment."

Lottie nodded. "That is so, and by all accounts her ladyship retains the closest of ties with the school. Her sister-in-law serves as its headmistress, in fact. To be seen to support it can only help advance your cause. It is common knowledge Stonevale dotes on his wife as though she was a new bride rather than a matron of a quarter century. Who knows but you might just have the occasion to bend his lordship's ear in your favor."

Lord Stonevale was Simon Belleville, former MP for Maidstone in Kent. Years before he'd distinguished himself among his fellows by pushing to extend the borough franchise to increase representation among the townships. Only when his grandfather, the old earl, died did he leave the Commons to take his rightful place in the Lords, and then with regret. His word held tremendous sway with his colleagues in both Houses. Though a highly respected leader among the Conservatives, he'd been known to cross the floor on more than one occasion to back the opposition's bill when he deemed the cause to be just. The welfare and protection of women and children were particular concerns of his, or so Callie recalled.

Reaching across the table for a fresh stack of letters, Lottie elaborated, "It promises to be the charity event of the year. Oftentimes a change of scene can work wonders to elevate one's mood. Besides Stonevale and his lady, there will be any number of influential persons in attendance, including several Members of Parliament who have not yet taken a public position on the suffrage bill. It might well be that this is your golden opportunity to bring them around."

"I'll go, of course. I can't very well let my dear auntie attend unchaperoned, now can I?"

"Actually, I rather suppose it is I who will be chaperoning you and your escort."

That woke her up. "My escort?"

Lottie clucked her tongue. "It's a formal function, Callie. For a woman of your youthful years and position, you cannot very well go alone."

"But I won't be alone. I'll be with you."

Lottie finished wetting the postage stamp before answering with a shake of her head. "It's just not done, my dear. You're not on the shelf yet no matter how high you button your shirtwaists."

Callie grimaced. It was far too early in the day to reprise this old argument most especially when the problem was so easily solved. "Oh very well, if I must go, I suppose I shall ask Teddy."

Callie had expected the discussion to end there, but instead Lottie looked at her for a long, thoughtful moment before saying, "Is there no one else you might ask? You seem to spend a great deal of time these days with that nice young photographer."

Callie felt herself bristling, for hadn't Teddy said as much just the other day, but with a sobriquet other than "nice young photographer"? "I told you, Mrs. Fawcett commissioned him to make a portrait series of me. I am in the way of being his client. I can hardly impose on him to squire me about town."

Lottie tilted her head to the side, gaze piercing. "Has it ever occurred to you that perhaps Mr. St. Claire might wish to be imposed upon, as you put it, or that he might not necessarily view a pleasant evening spent in the company of a lovely, intelligent young woman as an imposition at all?"

She was about to demur when a thought, too awful to bear contemplation, hit her. "Lottie, you wouldn't dare."

"On the contrary, I would dare a great deal to see you happy. If losing the person I loved best on Earth has taught me anything, it is that life is entirely too short and too precious to waste on foolish pride—or brooding on past ills, for that matter." Her sharp-eyed gaze honed in on Callie's face. "Take a chance, Callie. Be brave in this as you are in so many other ways. Ask Hadrian St. Claire to be your escort."

Callie smiled, she couldn't help it. "Auntie, you have the face of an angel and the cunning of a fox. You ought to run for office yourself."

Lottie grinned from ear to ear. "Why, that's just what my dear Edward used to say."

CHAPTER TEN

"I say, mister, here's me and my mate wants our
fotergruffs took; and mind, we wants 'em 'ansom,
cos they're to give to two ladies."
—*Punch*, "Photographic Beauties," 1858

Charlotte Rivers was not the sort of woman who
believed in leaving matters of the heart to chance.
She'd married Callie's uncle, Edward Rivers, after
contriving to get the poor, dear man drunk as David's sow and
into her bed. Though he'd been too muzzy-headed to make
so much as a move once he landed there, she'd been ruined all
the same. Even that starchy family of his finally came around
and agreed that a wedding was the only honorable recourse.
So had commenced forty-odd years of connubial bliss.

So despite her promise to Callie to leave off meddling,
the next afternoon she directed her carriage driver to let her

off at Great George Street. Big Ben tolling out the hour, she came upon the shingled sign announcing HADRIAN ST. CLAIRE, PRACTICAL PHOTOGRAPHIC ARTIST. Standing on the sidewalk, she peered through the plate-glass shop window, squinting to make out the small print of the framed advertisement.

A correct and lasting likeness!

Sitting generally occupies no more than one second.

Backgrounds representing a variety of landscapes, Grecian temple, the interior of a library, et cetera.

Price of a single portrait, usual size, one guinea. Portraits and groups taken on plates of an enlarged size. An immense stock of gold and bird's-eye maple frames to select from; also best silk velvet, fancy morocco cases, lockets, and brooches made expressly for portraits. Your absolute satisfaction guaranteed.

Displayed on the velvet-lined shelf were samples of the gentleman's work including pocket-sized photographs of the society models known as Professional Beauties. With the possible exception of Lady Katherine Lindsey, none of the young women depicted could hold a candle to her Callie. If only her niece would cease hiding her light under the proverbial bushel, or in Callie's case, those dreadful high-necked shirtwaists and monstrous hats. On the bright side, she had been leaving off the spectacles more often of late and wearing her pretty hair in a soft chignon rather than scraped back into that tight, unflattering bun. Might a certain photographer be the cause for these small transforming steps from caterpillar to butterfly? Lottie heartily hoped so but then there was only one way to find out for certain.

The shop bell gave off a soft tinkle as she stepped inside, the door falling closed behind her. She stood on the threshold a moment, surveying the scene from dusty glass counter to rustic worktable to bare floorboards. When no one approached, she cleared her throat.

The tall, broad-shouldered specimen of male stepping out from behind the curtained off area had her catching her breath. Now here was a man who knew his way around women, she could see that straightaway. Taking in his confident carriage, bedroom blue eyes, and sculpted features with a practiced eye, she only hoped for Callie's sake he wasn't a cad.

"Good afternoon, madam." Wiping his hands on his apron, he came toward her, rolled up shirtsleeves showing off strong forearms dusted with golden hair to match the thick mane curling about his collar.

Finding her voice, she said, "Mr. St. Claire, I presume?"

He hesitated as though not quite certain whether or not to own up to his name. "How may I be of service?"

"Actually I am here on behalf of my niece." She paused for effect before adding, "Caledonia Rivers."

Judging from the way his pupils widened, he was startled if only momentarily. "Callie's all right, isn't she?"

Lottie prided herself on her judgment of character and his concern certainly seemed genuine. And he'd said *Callie*, not Caledonia or Miss Rivers, another promising sign.

"Oh, she's well enough though she drives herself too hard by half, up until all hours of the night hammering out this article or that speech, then back at it early the next morning. And now, of course, there are her sessions with you." She recalled his advertisement's promise of a second's only sitting, and couldn't resist asking, "How is her portrait progressing? You two have been at it for some time now, nearly two weeks is it not?" Indeed, by now he should have taken enough photographs to fill several books if, indeed, photography was how they truly spent these so-called sessions of theirs. Lottie had her doubts.

His gaze shuttered. "It's to be a series of photographs, actually, and we are making headway, though she is still not altogether comfortable posing before the lens."

That she could well believe. "My niece has never had a proper appreciation for her looks. An unfortunate remark made long ago has put it into her head that she is plain when, I'm sure you will agree, nothing could be farther from the truth. Ah well, I am certain you do all that you can to put her at ease." Her gaze rested on his face, and though he didn't look away, she spotted a muscle jump in his jaw.

Recovering his smile, he invited her to sit. She started to refuse—really, Callie would have her head on a pike were she to catch her out—but before she could, he walked over to the pine table and drew out a chair for her. Resisting the urge to take out her hankie and dust off the rattan seat, she sat down.

He stripped off his apron and tossed it over his chair back. "May I get you some refreshment, tea or—"

She waved a hand in dismissal; she was on a mission,

after all. "Thank you but no, I'm afraid I haven't the time. I only dropped by to invite you to a function."

Seated opposite her, he looked across the table's scarred surface, his handsome face an open question. "A function?"

She nodded. "A benefit ball to raise funds for the Tremayne Dairy Farm Academy. I don't suppose you've heard of it, have you?" When he shook his head, she elaborated, "The school is located in the countryside, but most of its pupils are fallen women from the London streets. They are taught how to read, write, and cipher as well as a trade so that they may make a fresh start in life."

He swallowed hard, throat muscles working. "No, though I have some knowledge of a similar sounding establishment that operates as an orphanage," he finally said. "Those who engage in such noble work have my heartfelt respect, but I must be honest and say I haven't the funds at this time to make a proper donation." He looked down to his folded hands, and she gathered the admission pained him.

Following his gaze, she took note of the chemical stains on his right thumb and forefinger and the loss of pigment marring the broad back of the other hand; the latter looked to be scarring from a nasty burn. Although she knew little enough about photography, she suspected most professionals hired an assistant to take on the more mundane, menial tasks to do with the development process. Despite his fashionable address, it was evident Hadrian St. Claire was hurting for money, which explained his shop's spartan and somewhat shabby interior.

"On the contrary, Mr. St. Claire, I am not here to solicit a donation but to ask you to attend as my guest and," she paused, "my niece's escort."

He looked sharply up. "Perhaps it would be best if Callie asked me herself."

She looked at him. Really, men could be so terribly obtuse. "Of course, but she likely never will."

Settling back in his seat, he met her gaze, and she fancied a look of understanding passed between them. "Too proud?"

"On the contrary, too shy."

She was determined Callie should make a splash at the benefit ball to overcome the disaster of her come-out when countrified couture had caused her to be branded a wallflower. Callie's mother, no fashion plate, had dressed her tall, curvy daughter in watery pastels and fussy frills that made her look and, Lottie suspected, *feel* like an ungainly girl rather than a lovely young woman on the brink of a bright future.

She hesitated, wondering how much more, if anything, she dare say. "If she seems prickly at times, I only caution you not to be put off by it. It's her way of armoring herself against getting hurt again."

"Again?"

She slanted her gaze to the door. "I really should be on my way. I've taken up too much of your time as it is." She pushed back her chair to leave.

Hadrian St. Claire was on his feet in an instant. Holding her chair for her, he said, "On the contrary, I'm honored you called as I will be honored to accompany you both to the ball

. . . that is, if you're quite certain Callie will want me there."

Rather than give answer to the highly delicate question hidden in that statement, Lottie said, "Before I go, I'll risk speaking out of turn yet again and admit to your being a pleasant surprise from what I was expecting."

One dark blond brow edged upward. "And that was?"

She fixed him with an open, unwavering stare. "You are an exceedingly handsome young man, Mr. St. Claire, and charming as well, a combination I suspect serves you well with the women you encounter. Yet I also sense there's more to you than good looks and dash, that you are one of those rare men possessed of the gift, the *vision*, to spot a diamond and know its true worth even if it may not appear on first glance to be as smoothly polished as other stones aglitter with false luster."

"Why is it I don't think you're speaking of gemology?" he said, tone touched with irony.

Lottie did not deny it. Looking him in the eye, she answered, "My niece may think and speak and at times even dress in a mannish manner, but never doubt she has a woman's heart. And a woman's heart, Mr. St. Claire, can be a very fragile thing particularly once it's been broken." She snapped open her reticule and took out the gold-embossed invitation. Leaving it on the table, she started for the door. "I know it's customary for the gentleman to do the calling, but I've purchased a new carriage, very well-sprung, and I'm positively mad to show it off." A tactful way of settling the dodgy subject of transportation, for she knew full well the best he could have provided was a hired hansom. "May Callie and I call for you around seven o'clock tomorrow evening?"

Smiling, he accompanied her to the door. Opening it, he stood back, sketching a bow worthy of a Buckingham Palace courtier. "Seven o'clock shall suit me most admirably, Mrs. Rivers."

Callie looked over the stacks of papers topping her desk to see her aunt sailing into her office, turned out in a fur-trimmed carriage dress with leg-o'-mutton sleeves, their maid, Jenny, in tow. Smile bright, Lottie announced, "Callie, dear, I knew I would find you here. I've come to drag you away from duty for an hour's jaunt to the shops."

Callie fitted a hand over her brow where the beginnings of a headache had begun to pulse. "Auntie, I can't leave now. With the meeting with Lord Salisbury scheduled for this Friday, shopping is the very last thing I've time for." *Or mooning over a man I can't have*, she added to herself.

In truth, her feelings for Hadrian were growing every day. Worse still, she was beginning to suspect that those feelings went considerably deeper than mere animal lust, although there was certainly that in abundance. Though they'd left off touching since the week before when she'd come perilously close to letting him tumble her in a whore's bed, it was there all the same, hot enough to melt wax and thrumming between them like electrical current.

Lottie dismissed her protests with a wave as if meeting with the prime minister was of trifling consequence. "Fiddlesticks, you have a secretary, don't you, and a staff of able volunteers?" She glanced about the office to the half-dozen women, all brisk and busy. "Surely Harriet can mind the shop for the few hours we'll need to find you a proper ball gown, is that not so, Harriet?" When the secretary had only nodded and gone to fetch her coat, Callie had known her ship was as good as sunk.

Their carriage turned the corner of Bond and Oxford Streets, and Lottie directed her driver to let them out at Maison Valen, a fashion house in operation since Napoleon's time. Well-known as one of the few older ladies willing to spend the money required to dress à la mode, she had no difficulty in catching a shop clerk's eye the moment they crossed the threshold.

Beckoning a young girl with a mouthful of pins to her side, Lottie launched into an explanation of the problem at hand. "We need a ball gown for my niece and it is imperative it be ready in time for tomorrow evening."

Eyes widening, the girl gave an effusive shake of her head. Spitting pins, she said, "But *madame*, it is not possible."

From the vicinity of the marble-topped counter on the room's other side, an authoritative voice called out, "On the contrary, Genevieve, for my good friend, Madame Rivers, all is possible."

Lottie turned her approving gaze on the tall, slender woman crossing the Oriental carpet toward them. Dressed all in black and with silvered hair swept into a soft chignon, the modiste was the very embodiment of elegance.

"Hortense, you are kindness itself." She turned to Callie. "Allow me to introduce my niece, Caledonia Rivers." Lottie's smile was a rival for the electric lights shining forth from the crystal chandelier overhead.

If the modiste knew who Callie was, she gave no sign of it. She backed up several paces and ran her gaze over her from head to toe and back again, then motioned for her to remove her coat. Before Callie could comply, Lottie and Jenny were on either side of her, tugging the outerwear free.

"Ah," Madame Valen intoned. A finger to one side of her mouth, she slowly circled as though Callie had no more sentience than one of the dressmaker's forms anchored about the shop floor.

Callie gritted her teeth, perilously close to marching out the door. This was precisely what she'd dreaded: this bloodless, dispassionate appraisal that brought the bad memories flooding back, starting with her court presentation during which she'd tripped over her train and fallen, sending the feathers from her headdress flying and making the Queen sneeze. From that day on, she'd been a laughingstock, an oaf. The "season's leavings," Gerald's friend had called her, and he hadn't been far off the mark. It had been an extraordinarily painful time of her life, and in no mood to relive it scene by scene, she felt her upper lip stiffening.

"*Pas mauvaise.* Not bad, not so very bad."

The modiste's eyes were riveted on her breasts, and it took

every whit of her hard-won confidence not to cross her arms over her chest. Within the confines of the shop's silk-papered walls, she wasn't a suffragette, she wasn't even a leader. She was simply a plain woman bordering on middle age, with broad hips and a blousy bosom.

She turned to Lottie and whispered, "Truly, Aunt, that navy gown of mine will suffice."

If Lottie heard her, she chose not to let on. To the modiste, she said, "Hortense, you are the expert among us. What do you advise?"

Expression thoughtful, the dressmaker turned back to Lottie, her oval-shaped face weighted with the gravity of a magistrate about to pass sentence. "What we want is something with a minimum of stuff and nonsense, classically simple and timelessly elegant." She craned her neck to look at Callie's behind. "And we will be certain to leave off the bustle."

"A tactful way of saying I'm already so big there," Callie snapped, feeling utterly out of sorts.

Under cover of her coat, Lottie swatted her in the side. "Really, Caledonia, do try to be more positive."

Not Callie but Caledonia. She really must be wearing on Lottie's nerves, which was only fair, she supposed, since she was within an inch of taking her aunt's slender throat in her hands.

The dressmaker's thin lips lifted into a chilly smile. "Such a lovely bottom as *mademoiselle*'s requires no embellishment."

Mademoiselle. Callie hid a huff. Beyond flaring the nostrils of her Gallic nose and tossing out the occasional foreign phrase, Madame Valen didn't look or sound any more French than the rest of them.

Addressing Lottie, the dressmaker asked, "You are familiar with the gown worn by Madame X in the Sargent portrait?"

Lottie thought for a moment. "I believe so. All black with delicately jeweled shoulder straps, nipped-in waist, and narrow skirt?"

"Just so, and I believe I have the very gown. It will need a bit of alteration, of course, but my head seamstress can manage whatever we wish. Come, I will show you."

Arms linked, the two older women disappeared into the velvet-curtained dressing room. Jenny had likewise drifted away to finger the bolts of fabric stacked against the far wall. Accustomed as Callie was to being the one leading the charge, she felt as though she'd faded to invisibility.

Like an active beehive, the sights and sounds of activity buzzed all about her. Female shoppers draped themselves over divans and damask-covered chairs, sipping tea and offering advice to friends posing atop carpeted pedestals and frowning into pier glasses, snapping at harried seamstresses to put a move on. Callie sank down onto the cushion of a velvet-covered settee, an onlooker to the scene much as she'd been in her debutante days. She snatched up one of the several ladies' fashion magazines fanned across a nearby reading table and began furiously flipping through. What she found there was scarcely any comfort. The models depicted in the fashion plates all had heart-shaped faces, neat bosoms, and tiny, nipped-in waists. Closing the magazine, she told herself she never should have allowed Lottie to drag her here, particularly when there was the meeting with Lord Salisbury scheduled for the week's end. Her aunt had been angling to dress her for years and until today Callie had always held firm in her refusal. Why had she weakened?

As was the case with so many aspects of her life of late, the answer came back to one word, one person. Hadrian. The remarks he'd made on her clothing during their first photographic sitting had stayed with her. If she must go to this ball, and given the important guests in attendance it seemed she had little choice but to go, she didn't want to look "positively funerary" as he'd called it. Yet the last time she'd made any effort to transform herself, she'd ended up a laughingstock with poker straight hair curled into fussy ringlets and a frilly pink gown that had proven woefully out of step with London standards. Glancing about the well-appointed shop to the elegantly dressed women milling about, she tried telling herself that this time she was in far better hands, but the old shame was slow to die.

On the bright side, if she looked a fool, at least Hadrian wouldn't be there to witness it. She never had gotten up the nerve to ask him, and given how she was feeling, that was likely a blessing.

As if sensing the maudlin turn of her thoughts, Lottie poked her head outside the dressing-room curtain. "The gown is spectacular. You must come for a fitting." She beckoned Callie back.

Biting back a groan, Callie set aside the magazine and

rose. "Coming, Auntie."

Once she was on the other side of the curtained alcove, Lottie drew the curtain closed and asked, "By the by, dear, what did that nice young photographer say when you asked him to escort you?"

Turning away to unbutton her shirtwaist, Callie scarcely gave a glance to the sleek black gown with its straps of paste brilliants hanging on the back of the door. "I've been so busy, I haven't had the chance to speak with him, but I can hardly ask him at this late hour."

She tensed, anticipating a well-deserved scold, but instead Lottie only reached out to retrieve the discarded linens. Smile beatific, she said, "No worries on that score, pet. I already have."

Callie wasn't the only one in desperate need of eveningwear. Fortunately Hadrian and his barrister friend, Gavin were of a similar height and build. A gentleman born, Gavin's finely tailored suits might have come from Harrods and his hats from James Lock and Company, yet he wouldn't hesitate to strip the shirt from his back if he deemed a friend needed it more. As much as Hadrian hated to take further advantage of Gavin's generous nature, the prospect of taking the blood money he'd got from Dandridge to outfit himself held even less appeal.

More and more of late, he found himself scouring his

brain for ways he might find the funds to repay Dandridge and call the whole thing off. Barring that, with only one more week to go, he'd have to work bloody fast at fulfilling his end of their bargain. That he'd let any number of opportunities slip by set off a chorus of alarm bells inside his head, casting grave doubts on his ability to exact ruthless ruin on someone whom he'd come to own as one of the most goodhearted human beings he'd ever known.

A woman's heart, Mr. St. Claire, can be a very fragile thing particularly once it's been broken . . .

Meeting Callie's aunt had only deepened his dilemma. Now there was a woman whose respect, under other circumstances, he would very much have liked the chance to earn. What she would say of him once she learned that his true intent was to ruin her beloved niece, to pick up where apparently some brute had left off years before in breaking Callie's heart, was enough to send him searching out the gin.

But instead of drinking away his cares as he once might have done, he'd spent the past few hours since her leaving pacing his studio, too edgy to sit still let alone concentrate on his work. Finally, he gave up, stripped off his apron, and set out on foot for Gavin's. It was coming on dark by the time he reached his friend's rented rooms at the Inns of Court. With luck, he would find the barrister at home rather than working late in his office.

Only when Gavin's manservant showed him into the flat's small sitting room, he found that his friend wasn't alone. Their old Roxbury House mate, fellow orphan Patrick O'

Rourke lounged on the leather-covered couch, cigar in one hand and glass of whiskey in the other.

Sighting Hadrian on the threshold, he set down his drink and shot to his feet. "Harry, man, we were just talking about you." Broad-shouldered and barrel-chested with a shock of thick, ginger-colored hair, Rourke enfolded Hadrian in a bone-crushing hug.

Hadrian hid his awkwardness at hearing his true name yet again behind a smile. "No wonder my ears were burning. What has it been, an age and a day?"

Pulling back, he surveyed his old friend. Loosened neckwear, rolled-up shirtsleeves, and rumpled silk vest aside, the Scot had done well for himself, Hadrian could see that straightaway. The diamond stud winking from the lobe of one ear was the genuine article, not paste, as was the large emerald set in gold on the middle finger of his work-roughened right hand.

Impeccably dressed in a dark flannel suit and folded neck cloth, Gavin rose from the wing chair in front of the fire. "Our mate, Harry, styles himself Hadrian St. Claire these days." Hadrian shot his friend a grateful look. Trust Gavin to smooth over any awkwardness to do with his dual identities.

If Rourke wondered at the reason for him taking a new name, he kept it to himself. "Ah, Hadrian is it? Verra fancy. I'll be sure to mind that."

"What can I get you?" Gavin asked, already at the liquor cabinet.

Walking over to the fire, Hadrian answered, "I don't

suppose you've any gin lying about?"

It was a well-worn joke between them, a way of tweaking Gavin over his blue-blooded lineage, and yet as always it served to bring out Gavin's rare smile. "I'm afraid not. Will brandy do?"

Hadrian nodded and Gavin poured three fingers' worth into a crystal snifter. Handing it over, he waved Hadrian to an empty chair.

When they'd settled in with their drinks, Gavin said, "Rourke was just telling me how he's been keeping himself these past years. It seems our friend here has returned to us rich as Croesus."

Rich as Croesus! Blast, but if only Rourke has resurfaced a fortnight ago, how very different Hadrian's life might be now. Sipping his drink, he looked across the room at the Scot and mentally asked himself if he dared ask a friend he hadn't set eyes on for years to loan him what amounted to a minor fortune?

Over the next half hour, Hadrian listened with half an ear as Rourke brought them up to date on his life over the past seven years. After leaving Roxbury House, he'd headed north to Scotland to search for his mother's family. To keep himself, he'd signed on to one of the railway crews, working his way up from the blistering labor of laying tracks to foreman to principal shareholder and finally to full owner.

Finishing his story, Rourke shot Hadrian a wink. "Not bad for a braw Scottish lad who started out as a purse snitch, aye?"

Hadrian agreed it was so. Indeed, their common past

as petty thieves had been a big part of their early bonding as boys. When the leader of the flash house from which Rourke worked was picked up by the law, he'd saved himself by turning over Rourke instead. The plucky twelve-year-old had been on his way to Newgate when luck and a stranger's benevolence had landed him in Roxbury House instead.

Mind on his own troubles, Hadrian asked, "So, my friend, other than looking up your old mates, what brings you back to London?"

Gavin answered for him. "It seems our friend here is trolling for an heiress."

Wondering why a rich man need marry for money, Hadrian turned to Rourke and asked, "Have you anyone in particular in mind?"

Rourke answered with a slow nod. "I've my eye on Lady Katherine Lindsey."

"Kat Lindsey!" Startled, Hadrian almost choked on the swallow of spirit he'd just taken.

Rourke's gaze narrowed. "Aye, you know her, then?"

Hadrian nodded. "She's one of the reigning Professional Beauties. Society ladies who model for me," he clarified when Rourke's mouth flew open.

"You've no touched her, have you?"

Taken aback by the ferocity of the Scot's gaze, Hadrian hastened to reassure him. "Hardly. Lady Kat is about as warm as a cake of ice and has the temper of a wildcat when crossed. If it's a fortune you're after, you'd best look elsewhere. Rumor has it her father is a gamester who's landed the family deeply in debt."

A rumor he knew to be true given that unlike the other society beauties he'd photographed, Katherine Lindsey sat for him for money, not acclaim. Yet something inside him, what he might have termed honor were he a better sort of man, held him back from revealing the terms of the private arrangement between the two of them.

Seemingly satisfied, Rourke settled back into his seat. Stretching his muscular legs out to catch the fire's heat, he yawned and said, "Nay matter. It's the lady's blue blood I'm after, no her purse."

So Rourke wanted a highborn wife to serve as a breeder. Stubborn as the day was long, the Scot loved nothing more than a challenge and courting Lady Kat would certainly provide him that and more.

Then there was Gavin sipping his drink and quietly observing the byplay. Orphaned after his parents perished in a tenement-house fire, he'd come to Roxbury House only to be reunited with his maternal grandfather. Restored to his rightful place in society, Gavin would one day inherit a baronetcy. In the interim, he'd followed in the footsteps of his forbears in reading the law, a profession he professed to despise despite his fast-growing reputation as a crack barrister. Looking between his two old friends, at the solid successes they'd made of their lives, Hadrian felt ashamed at the depth of his envy.

Rising to refill their drinks, Gavin asked, "By the by, what brings you here in the middle of the week?"

Hadrian handed over his empty glass. "A visit from a lady actually."

"No surprise, that." Rourke grinned. "We always did call you Handsome Harry for good reason."

Considering he might have done better for himself had he been gifted with less looks and more brains, Hadrian shrugged. "A friend's widowed aunt, actually. She's invited me to a benefit ball tomorrow evening." He reached inside his coat pocket and pulled out the invitation, which he handed around.

Taking it, Gavin glanced down. "The Tremayne Dairy Farm Academy is an excellent cause, to be sure. I'm going myself, family duty and all that." He grimaced as though being the heir to title and fortune was a good deal less amusing than one might imagine. "Given the cachet of Lord and Lady Stonevale as sponsors, members from every top-drawer family in London are sure to attend."

"Every top-drawer family, you say?" Reaching for the embossed invitation, Rourke fingered it for a moment, before venturing, "How might a charitable fellow like myself go about wrangling one of these?"

Gavin's dark brows shot upward. "I've an extra invitation. You can go as my guest if you like, only since when do you fancy formal affairs? My God, you scarcely can bring yourself to tie on neckwear."

Rourke glanced to Hadrian and grinned. "But then it's not so much a ball as a hunt, only my quarry isn't deer or elk but a certain Wild Kat in want of taming."

CHAPTER ELEVEN

"Oh! Isn't it jolly
To cast away folly
And cut all one's clothes a peg shorter
(A good many pegs)
And rejoice in one's legs
Like a free-minded Albion's daughter."
—BARBARA BODICHON, circa 1850

Callie stood before the floor-length dressing glass in her bedroom stripped down to her dressing gown.

Jenny had just left from arranging her hair into a soft upsweep she had to admit became her. She turned her head from side to side, checking to make sure the paste diamond brilliants remained in place. The ornaments matched the stones in the thin straps of her gown almost exactly. At Lottie's urging, she'd even applied a light touch of cosmetics. Perhaps it was only the benefit of the encroaching evening shadows but her eyes looked a deeper green, her mouth moist and inviting, and her skin luminous rather than simply pale.

She glanced to the back of the door where her evening gown hung. At any moment, Jenny would be back to help her dress and then she would join Lottie downstairs. Together they would go in her aunt's carriage to Hadrian's shop and from there to the Covent Garden Opera House. Before the thought of walking into a formal function wearing something so very revealing would have been the stuff of nightmares, but she found she could scarcely wait to put it on.

Her aunt's words of a fortnight before rushed back to her. *Take a chance, Callie. Be brave in this as you are in so many other ways.*

Take a chance. Be brave. If not now, this night, then when?

<hr />

"Who's the goddess?" Gavin asked Hadrian, looking across the chandelier-lit ballroom to where Caledonia stood deep in conversation with a clutch of evening-clad gentleman.

"Caledonia Rivers," Hadrian supplied, sipping from his flute of champagne.

They were standing in the main opera room of the Covent Garden Opera House, the great crystal chandelier in the center of the dome and myriad incandescent burners ablaze with light, the tiered boxes festooned with flowers, the floor a veritable crush of London's well-heeled. Earlier that evening, the queue of carriages had extended down Wellington Street and far up the Strand. It had taken beyond a half hour for the Rivers' driver to wend their way to the entrance. He felt as though he'd been holding his breath ever since he'd entered.

As for Callie, since they'd made their way through the receiving line the hour before he hadn't been able to get close enough to her to say two words. The sight of her looking sleek and beautiful, laughing and relaxed, sipping champagne and seeming utterly at ease should have pleased him enormously. This was what he'd wanted for her, after all. Nonetheless, the fact that his caterpillar had blossomed into a splendid butterfly without so much as a glance his way bothered him more than he cared to admit.

Gavin's blue eyes widened. "*The* Caledonia Rivers? The suffragist?"

Against all reason, Hadrian found himself bristling "Yes, what of it?"

"Not a thing, my friend. I quite admire the lady protestors' dedication even if at times I question their methods."

"Meaning?" In an instant, protectiveness blossomed into full-blown alarm. If there was trouble brewing, Hadrian meant to find out from his friend all he could and warn Callie.

"There's a small but militant branch of the movement that espouses employing such tactics as hunger strikes and property destruction to advance their cause. There were several women from Manchester arrested last year and who, when taken, declared they would embark on a hunger strike until released."

"Were they released?"

Gavin hesitated, and then nodded. "Eventually but in the interim to prevent them from starving themselves, they were subjected to force feeding. As you can imagine, intubation is a ghastly experience and some of the women claim to have sustained lasting damage to their throats and digestive organs. I would hate to see your Miss Rivers become mixed up in any such unpleasantness."

Hadrian thought back to the episode at the match factory, to how selflessly Callie had set aside any consideration for her own wellbeing to pitch in and help the strikers, and a chill swept over him. That day he'd been there to hurry her away to safety, but what if the next time . . .

"Callie has too sound of a head on her shoulders for that," he said reflexively, hoping that were indeed the case.

"And a verra handsome set of . . . *shoulders*, they are, too." Grinning, Rourke sidled up to join them.

Against all reason, Hadrian felt jealousy rising. "She's off-limits, Rourke."

Pulling at his starched cravat as though it were a hangman's noose, the Scot gazed out onto the packed floor. "Dinna fash, man. Bonny as your Miss Rivers is, I've set my cap elsewhere."

Hadrian followed his friend's open stare to where Lady Katherine Lindsey held court amongst a circle of bedazzled admirers. Hadrian had photographed her any number of times, but this was the first he'd seen of her out of his studio. Though she stood a full head shorter than the men surrounding her, there could be no doubt that she was in complete possession of both herself and them. All in all, she was just the woman to give his friend, Rourke, a fair run for his money.

Turning his attention back to Rourke, Hadrian was taken aback by the look of raw longing on the Scotsman's rugged face. Wrenching his gaze away from Lady Katherine, he turned back to them and added, "If you'll excuse me, there's a lady who's promised me the next dance . . . only she doesn't know it yet."

Gavin's eyebrows rose. "Pardon me for asking but since when do you dance?"

Rourke grinned and backed away. "Since now."

Watching their friend push a path through the crowd as the orchestra struck up a waltz, Gavin and Hadrian exchanged amused glances. Hadrian had to admire the way Rourke inserted himself dead center into Lady Katherine's circle and then proceeded to steal her straightaway. It seemed that street cunning won out over blue blood at least on this occasion. Lady Katherine laid her slender gloved arm atop his and followed him out onto the dance floor without a backward glance to the men staring balefully after her. As for Rourke, Hadrian doubted he'd looked any more triumphant when he'd acquired controlling shares in his railway company, perhaps not even then.

Gavin turned to Hadrian. "It seems Cupid's arrow has found purchase in our friend's crusty heart."

Hadrian chuckled. "Patrick has a heart?"

"Apparently . . . as well as two left feet." Frowning out onto the dance floor, Gavin added, "I only hope he doesn't crush her toes, at least not before she's had the opportunity to discover his finer qualities."

"Call it artistic instinct if you will, but I have an inkling she has on some impressively high-heeled slippers this evening and isn't above using them to stomp on Rourke's foot, especially if he manages to put it in his mouth first."

"I rather see her as more the knee-to-the-groin type, but then I'm only a barrister, after all." Gavin's amused gaze left Hadrian to settle on a spot at the far end of the room. "The delectable Lady Katherine isn't the only one to draw an entourage of admirers this evening. Your Miss Rivers seems to be making quite a splash. I suspect that within twenty-four hours that rather striking gown of hers will be copied by every dressmaker in London."

Feeling inexplicably on edge, Hadrian shot back, "She's not my Miss Rivers and if you must know, the gown is a copy of the one worn by Madame X in the Sargent painting."

"I thought it looked familiar though I don't recall Madame X looking nearly as sumptuous."

"If you'll excuse me, I had better go and rescue her."

"Indeed." The mirth flickering in Gavin's gaze did little to lighten Hadrian's mood. Turning, he forded his way across the packed room.

He approached in time to hear Callie say, "Yes, of course, Mr. Winston, I agree with you but only to a point. Far too many husbands do exert undue influence over their wives, including squelching their right, even their ability, to form independent opinions. That said, the same holds true of many fathers and their adult sons and yet the British government does not deny impressionable young men the right to vote. I therefore cannot comprehend how your argument can be used, in good conscience, to deny the franchise to women, be they single or married."

"She has you there, Winston." The man with the boyish face and ginger-colored side whiskers chuckled.

The man, Winston, sketched a brief bow that not coincidentally placed him at eye-level with her bosom. "Touché, Miss Rivers. You have bested me, and now I have no choice but to cede defeat and humbly lay my sword at your feet."

Reaching out, Hadrian tapped his pudgy shoulder. "You'd do well to keep your sword in your pocket, Winston, and while you're at it keep it buttoned up as well."

"Hadrian!" Callie's face was suffused with pink.

Watching all that lovely heat travel down the long column of her throat to beyond where the gown touched the high slopes of her beautiful breasts, Hadrian felt his groin tighten and his mouth go dry. Judging by the bug-eyed looks and clearing throats firing off around him, he was far from alone in noticing.

He reached for her gloved hand, not waiting for her to offer it. "Gentlemen, if you'll be so good as to excuse us, I believe this dance is promised to me."

It was a lie. He hadn't bothered to reserve so much as one. He'd assumed all her dances, if indeed she ventured onto the floor at all, would be his for the taking.

Callie turned her face up to his. Her mouth, tinted with a touch of pale rose paint, looked moist and full and infinitely kissable. "As I was just telling these gentlemen, who were kind enough to ask me, I'd really rather watch the dancing than join it."

He stared at the half-full champagne flute in her hand and wondered how much it contributed to this new gay Callie he scarcely recognized but very much wanted to get to know. "A glass of punch, then?"

Not giving her a second opportunity to refuse, he took her elbow and steered her away to a relatively private spot on the other side of the room. Releasing her, he said, "You look perfectly lovely tonight."

She looked down at her bosom, restored once more to porcelain perfection. "What I feel is perfectly naked but thank you."

Not yet but soon, Callie. Soon, he thought but dare not say. "Glad you came?" he asked, his smile hinting he already knew what her answer would be.

Beaming, she answered, "Need you even ask? Tonight has exceeded any expectation I might have had. And . . . being here with you is the very best part."

He grinned, charmed by her shy-eyed admission. "In that case, dance with me."

She surrendered her champagne to a passing waiter and turned to him. "Very well, but if I lame you, mind you refused to heed my warning."

"Duly noted, but if you lame me, you'd best be prepared to nurse me back to health. I'll wager you'd look almost as fetching in a sister's bibbed apron as you do in that dress."

Laying her right hand in his, she followed him out onto the floor just as the orchestra struck up the strains of a waltz. She stepped into his arms and he settled his other hand on the small of her back.

She smiled up at him, the electric light from the chandelier overhead playing on the red hues in her glossy coil of dark hair. "I regret to inform you my schedule doesn't allow time for spooning up broth to self-indulgent libertines."

"Ouch." He made a show of mock hurt before turning serious once more. "Any chance of your stealing away tomorrow afternoon for an hour or so?"

The little telltale frown line appeared on her forehead, a sure sign that duty and pleasure were once again warring inside her. "I have a committee meeting in the afternoon and then I've to run through what I'll say to the prime minister with Harriet." He groaned when she shook her head. "I could break away around teatime."

He smiled, relieved. A quiet meal before the fire would be the perfect setting for a seduction but even better, it would be his best opportunity to discuss with her what Gavin had said. If Callie was being steered toward activities that might lead in her arrest—or worse—he meant to do all he could to keep her safe. Persuading her to see reason would be his first tactic, not that he held out much hope for its success. She was a stubborn woman and more passionately committed to her ideals than anyone, male or female, he'd ever encountered. For the second time in the last hour, a warning siren set off in his head. Just when had securing Callie's safety taken precedence over seducing her?

"In that case, I'll assemble a feast to tantalize your palate, delight your senses, arouse your—"

"Stop!" She brushed a gloved hand over the tightly cinched fabric at the waist of her gown. "Assuming I ever have the courage to wear this again, it *will* fit."

"In that case, what say you to toasted bread and cheese and a good bottle of wine?"

"I'd say that sounds heavenly." Something, or rather someone, beyond him caught her eye. Jealousy flared for a second time, doused by her exclamation, "Oh good heavens, there goes Lady Stonevale."

Whomever Lady Stonevale thought she was, or whatever she was trying to communicate, was irrelevant to Hadrian. He could have happily gone over, planted a smacking kiss on her cheek, and not given the matter a moment's thought.

Apparently oblivious to his idiocy, she supplied, "Her husband, Lord Stonevale, is a front bencher in the Lords. Before inheriting his title, he sat in the Commons, one of Disraeli's key protégés."

"And you're no doubt thinking that a word in the ear of his wife may be just the chance you've been waiting for?"

"Oh, but Hadrian, our dance—"

"Will be the first of many more," he said, not at all certain that was true. He steered them to the perimeter of the dance floor and released her. At her hesitant look, he gently nudged her away. "Callie, it's your chance. Who knows, but it may be the very thing that tips the scales to victory. You've worked too hard to let it go by without trying. Now off with you."

She took a few steps away and then turned back. "Hadrian, are you sure?"

"Go." He shot her a wink to cover the inexplicable emptiness that had overtaken him the moment he'd let her free from his arms. Unlike him, Callie belonged to the larger world. These sweet, stolen moments with her were just that—stolen. Once she found out who and what he was, she wouldn't care to set eyes on him ever again. "I'll be waiting when you come back."

Callie found her aunt sipping a glass of punch in the shadow of a potted palm and talking animatedly to a dashing older gentleman with white whiskers and a lance straight stance. Hating to interrupt, she turned back before Lottie caught her eye and beckoned her forward.

"Callie, dear, there you are." Turning to her companion, Lottie said, "Allow me to present my niece, Caledonia Rivers. Callie, this is a dear friend of mine, Maximilian St. John."

Callie fancied the older gentleman looked at her with something less than approval, but, no doubt for her aunt's sake, he managed a stiff smile and bow. "Miss Rivers, you must know your aunt is your most devoted admirer."

"That is so," Lottie said, looking between the two. "But then again there is much about Callie to admire."

"My aunt is, as usual, far too kind to me." Callie acknowledged the gentleman's courtly bow with a smile and a nod. Turning back to her aunt, who looked rather flushed she thought, she said, "Auntie, I hate to interrupt but might I beg a word with you alone?"

"Certainly, dear," Lottie replied. "Max, if you will excuse us?"

"But of course," he said though Callie didn't miss the reluctance with which he backed away. When he was out of earshot, Callie leaned in and whispered, "I was hoping you might introduce me to Lady Stonevale."

"Of course, where are my manners? I should have offered before now." Taking light hold of Callie's elbow, she ferried them across the ballroom.

Elegant in a gown of amber silk, Lady Stonevale held court amidst the milling crowd, a tall, dark-haired young man at her side. As they approached, Lottie explained that the gentleman was her eldest son, Simon, so-named after his father. Unfortunately Lord Stonevale had come down with the head cold and his eldest had stepped in to serve as host in his sire's stead.

Introductions made the rounds and then Lottie tactfully withdrew along with Lady Stonevale's son, who promised to return with glasses of punch. When they were alone, Lady Stonevale turned to Callie. "Miss Rivers, what an estimable young woman you are. I have been following your progress in the newspapers." Her ladyship's speech carried the hint of the West Country in her vowels.

"Your ladyship." Callie hesitated, wondering if a curtsy might appear a tad overdone.

She was saved from awkwardness by Lady Stonevale, who proffered a satin-gloved hand and a gracious smile. "Please, call me Christine."

Warmed by the unexpected familiarity, the complete lack of artifice, Callie shook hands. "I would be honored. And I am Caledonia, though my family and friends call me Callie."

"As I hope we shall be very great friends indeed, with your permission I shall call you Callie." Again that soft smile, the antidote to any awkwardness. "I'd like to hear more about this cause of yours."

"As I would like to hear more about your school."

Lady Stonevale inclined her head toward a velvet-covered cushion ledge. "In that case, let us sit, shall we?"

"It would be my honor . . . Christine."

<hr />

"The purpose of the school is the betterment of our fallen women through education, both academic and practical. But having spoken with you, it occurs to me that education may be only one piece of the puzzle."

Seated at Lady Stonevale's side, Callie nodded, feeling she'd met a kindred spirit. "Indeed, milady, among women disenfranchisement knows no class boundary. A woman is still largely under the control of her husband or father, be she bred to great wealth or the gutters, educated or unschooled." Callie stopped herself. "Oh dear, I've gone rambling again."

Lady Stonevale shook her head. Threads of silver shone in her simply dressed honey brown hair, but her smooth face was that of a much younger woman. "On the contrary, I find your candor refreshing. Tomorrow is my 'at-home' day, as these Londoners love to say. You must call on me if you are free. I will arrange for my husband to be there as well. The poor dear man is abed with the head cold, but hopefully by tomorrow he will be sufficiently recovered."

"I would be delighted." She stood as Lady Stonevale's son returned with a glass of punch in either hand.

Lady Stonevale rose as well. "In that case, two o'clock would be best. Accepting the punch glass from her son with a smile, she said, "In matters of politics, my husband and I do not always see eye to eye, but I can assure you he is the most reasonable and feeling of men. Make your argument to him as you have done to me, and I would be highly surprised if he didn't throw his support behind your bill."

Spirits high, Callie left Lady Stonevale and struck out in search of the ladies' retiring room. She needed a moment to gather herself before she returned to the ballroom—and Hadrian. Try as she might to minimize her feelings for him as base animal attraction, lust, whatever *it* was, it was on the verge of careening out of control and taking her with it. Indeed, she felt like she was living a fairytale—something as beautifully fragile as the bubbles rising from the bottom of her fluted champagne glass. Knowing that at any moment the bubble might burst, she vowed to enjoy every moment without reservation or regret.

A trio of women gathered about the gilded wall mirror, reticules lying open on the marble-topped dressing table. Instinctively Callie stepped back, but it was too late; they'd seen her.

"Ladies." She entered, stepping within striking distance of three sharp pairs of eyes.

"Why Miss Rivers, pray don't allow us to chase you away. We are only powdering our noses as an excuse to have a bit of a chat. Won't you join us?"

Callie recognized the speaker as Miss Isabel Duncan, eldest daughter of one of the Honorable Herbert Duncan III, a crony of Josiah Dandridge and one of the more vocal opponents of the suffrage bill.

Her sister, Miss Penelope Duncan, settled her unblinking gaze on Callie. "What a lovely gown, Miss Rivers. I meant to remark upon it earlier. I for one wouldn't have the courage to wear something quite so . . . revealing." Miss Penelope's gaze settled unmistakably on Callie's breasts and her rosebud mouth formed a smirk. "But then again I suppose daring not to care what others may think is the privilege of age."

The third woman, a gaunt blonde swathed in pale pink, chimed in with, "Indeed, given your choice of color, one might wonder if perhaps you'd suffered a recent loss."

The elder Miss Duncan let out a peel of laughter that cut Callie to the quick. "The only loss Miss Rivers suffered occurred a good ten years ago when her fiancé cried off, is that not so, Miss Rivers? But then given Miss Rivers's unfeminine *proclivities . . .*" She let the word hang in the air a full moment, before adding, "Who can fault him for it?" The kittenish pout she'd exhibited earlier in the ballroom when gentleman were about twisted into a sneer.

The Callie of ten years before would have fled the room in tears. Instead she pulled her shoulders back and lifted her chin. "I very much doubt that sacrificing independent thought for feigning so-called womanliness parades as any great virtue. As for age conveying certain privileges, you have the right of it. I call on it now in allowing myself the liberty, the *pleasure*, of telling you all to go to the devil."

"Well, I never," one of them sniffed although Callie neither saw nor cared whom. One by one, they turned and filed out of the room, noses pointed north.

From the door of the lavatory, a loo flushed. "Brava! What a pack of bitches. Were I you, I shouldn't mind a single word any of them said."

A petite and very familiar-looking brunette sidled up to the counter, dipped her hands into the bowl of rose water, and then accepted a linen hand towel from the attendant standing silent as a statue in the corner. Callie recalled seeing her briefly in the ballroom on the arm of one of Hadrian's friends, the Scottish chap with the charming brogue and the laughing eyes.

Turning to Callie, she smiled and said, "I'm Katherine Lindsey, only do call me Kat. That is how my family and friends address me, and I have a suspicion you and I will be great friends indeed."

Callie took a moment to study her latest acquaintance up close. A delicately molded but slightly longish nose added interest to otherwise symmetrical features. Honey-brown curls piled high and artfully arranged around a pearled tiara afforded the illusion of height.

Drained after taking her stand, Callie sank down onto the tufted pink velvet settee. "Why is that?"

Lady Katherine joined her. "We're both rebels in our way, you because of your politics and I because of my refusal to become leg-shackled to some man simply because every woman of a certain age and station is told she must."

Leg-shackled—now here was a kindred spirit. The warmth in Lady Katherine's intelligent brown eyes invited confidences. Shoulders drooping, Callie admitted, "I feel such a fool. I shouldn't have lost my temper as I did."

"Nonsense, you'd every right to give that lot the dressing down you did but then again I'm known to have a bit of temper myself. As to the rubbish about your gown and looks, pay it no heed. You've managed to draw the undivided attention of every male in the room—the breathing ones, at any rate."

Callie angled her companion a sideways gaze. "Not quite every male, I should think."

Lady Katherine's lovely face took on a pensive expression. "If you're speaking of Mr. O'Rourke, I assure you I've done nothing to encourage his suit."

"It would seem you need do nothing at all. He is quite clearly smitten."

"Hmm, I rather think the same could be said of Hadrian. Oh, Mr. St. Claire, I should say."

Suddenly Callie recalled why the piquant face should look so strikingly familiar. "You're one of his PBs, Professional Beauties, aren't you? His bestseller, in fact."

Lady Katherine shrugged her slender shoulders. "It's a great deal of stuff and nonsense; but, then again, it pays the accounts."

Wondering why someone such as Lady Katherine would need to work as a photographer's paid model, Callie was too tactful to ask.

Lady Katherine popped up from her seat. "Shall we go back in? I for one could do with a drink."

❦

When the call into the buffet supper came and Callie still hadn't returned, Hadrian grew restless. Though it was gauche and simply not done, he struck out in search of her. After going down more hallways and stairwells than he cared to count, he finally spotted her emerging from a side door with Lady Katherine. The two looked to be in deep conversation.

He walked toward them. Acknowledging Lady Katherine with a brief bow, he turned to Callie and said, "When the supper bell rang and you hadn't returned, I wondered if something might have happened."

Lady Katherine looked between them. "Supper, you say. Thank God, I'm famished." Turning to Callie, she smiled. "Miss Rivers, how glad I am we met at last. I do hope we shall see each other before long. Who knows, but one of these days I might even attend one of your rallies."

"I would like that very much."

Lady Katherine swept off in the direction of the supper room. Turning to Callie, Hadrian remarked, "You and Lady Kat look to be fast friends."

She nodded. "She's a bright, spirited woman with some refreshingly modern ideas. It's a bit premature to say, but I have a feeling we may become friends at some point. At least I hope so."

Gazing at her face, which had dimmed considerably from the short while ago when she'd left him on the dance floor, he said, "Something did happen, didn't it?"

When she didn't deny it, Hadrian lost no time in steering them inside a small sitting room adjoining the cloakroom. Closing the door behind them, he walked over to her and said, "Tell me. I want to know." If some man had dealt her an affront or worse yet, touched her, he wouldn't rest until he had the cad's name.

She shrugged those lovely shoulders of hers, bare save for the thin sequined straps. "It's nothing really. Some silliness I took too much to heart. There were some women who said some unkind things, deliberately so."

"What sorts of things?"

She waved a hand in the air as if it were all of no consequence though her eyes told him otherwise. "Oh you know, personal comments on my gown, my age and er . . . size." The latter admission had her hedging her gaze away.

"Callie, look at me." Propping her chin on the edge of his hand, he lifted her face up to the light.

Feeling foolish, she tried looking away, but with her heeled slippers they were of a height and when Hadrian moved closer still there was nowhere to look but in his eyes. Giving in, she quickly told him what had transpired with Isabel Duncan and company.

"So, you see, it actually turned out to be a good thing. It forced me to confront some old demons I've never really had the chance to release, and now that I have I'm all right, really."

"Isabel Duncan is a silly goose, a little idiot without a brain in her empty head," he said, the ferocity in his voice surprising him. "She only said those things because she was jealous." He paused, gaze sweeping over her face, throat, the satiny flesh of her shoulders and high-sloped breasts. "And I can't blame her. You're stunning. When I led you out onto the dance floor, I was the envy of every man in that room. I could feel their eyes stabbing into me like sabers."

"You're being very good to me, very kind."

He shook his head, looking sad suddenly. "Don't you know by now, Callie, that I am neither particularly good nor kind? But despite my more obvious defects, I am still a man with two working eyes, a photographer's eyes. When I look at you as I'm doing now and tell you how utterly beautiful you are, you ought to believe me."

"If anyone is the object of envy and admiration, it is you, sir. Black suits you. You . . . you look very fine in that tailcoat." She touched his lapel, an unaccustomed boldness.

He grinned. "I am glad you approve of something about me."

He didn't kiss her, not at first. He reached down and with one long finger traced the outline where the satin piping of her bodice met the heat of her skin. A single finger, just a whisper of a touch, but it was all it took to make her wet. Beneath the thin drape of her gown, the slit of her silk drawers felt warm and sticky as syrup.

Callie looked down at Hadrian's hand and this time she let her gaze linger, willing him to read her thoughts. She wanted that finger inside her, she wanted Hadrian inside her, and even as she tried to blame her wantonness on the champagne she'd drunk, she knew it would be a lie. It was him. All he need do was press her back against the wall and slide one of his clever hands beneath her skirt and she would let him. Let him take her; have her, in any way, in *every* way he would. She tilted her face up to his, an open invitation.

"Do you want me to kiss you?" His hair was a well of banked moonlight, his mouth a curved smile all but brushing hers.

"Yes." Oh yes, she wanted him to kiss her. But she wanted, needed, so very much more.

A moan, hers, cut through the muted sounds of the revelry taking place just a few feet away behind the closed doors to their back. She took hold of his hand, pressing it to the juncture of her thighs, pelvis jutted upward to meet his touch. "I want—"

"Hush, love, I know what you want, what you need. What we all need."

His other hand found her breast, thumb flicking over the satin-sheathed tip, the hardened nipple stabbing into the stays she wished desperately to be rid of. *So this is what it means to be vanquished*, she thought, and touched her mouth to his.

Against his lips, she said, "Take me home, Hadrian. Now. Please."

All his regret poured out in one rueful sigh. He drew back to look at her. "In that case, shall I find your aunt and call for her carriage?"

Callie hesitated. *Take a chance. Be brave.*

Moistening lips gone suddenly dry, she searched for the courage to say, "Not to my aunt's, not yet anyway. Take me back to your flat. Take me home with you."

CHAPTER TWELVE

"Now, the fact is that seduction is, and ought to be, mutual. No love is without seduction in its highest sense."

—VICTORIA WOODHULL AND TENNESSEE CLAFLIN, *Woodhull & Claflin's Weekly*

By unspoken accord, they didn't talk during the hansom ride from the opera house to Hadrian's. They sat facing each other on the cracked leather seats, the only physical contact the occasional brushing of knees when the coach hit a rough patch of road. But not speaking, not touching, only served to build the anticipation. By the time they halted at his flat, Callie felt as fragile as an egg left too long to boil and just as likely to crack.

The hansom halted, the driver calling out their fare. Reaching into his pocket, Hadrian looked across the darkened carriage to her. In the semidarkness, their eyes met.

"You're sure?"

She managed a steady if slightly breathless reply. "Yes, I'm sure."

They stepped down into the street swirling with clouds of yellowish gray vapor, a proper London fog. Crossing to Hadrian's shop, the mist weighing the folds of her caped cloak, Callie felt equal parts terrified and elated. She was about to enter a man's lodgings. Alone. Unchaperoned. After midnight. Although she'd been in his upstairs flat on several occasions now, this time it was with the full intention of going to bed with him. A man who was not her husband, not even her fiancé or steady beau. She was spending the night with Hadrian St. Claire of the sexy grin and laughing eyes and shadowed past. For one glorious night he would be all hers. The thought sent a thrill shooting through her.

But as they climbed the creaking stairs of his walk-up, flinty logic crept in. To spread your legs for a man and take him inside you was the ultimate submission, the ultimate gamble. And her intended lover wasn't any man but Hadrian. He was so attractive, so sophisticated, and so altogether comfortable with what men and women did together she couldn't help feeling gauche in comparison. The glimpses she'd had of his clothed erection suggested he was well endowed, possibly enormous. What if she was unable to take all of him? What if he hurt her? Worse yet, what if she disappointed him? That prospect terrified her most of all.

The door opened on a creak. "After you," he said, moving back for her to enter.

Callie stepped inside as she'd done on at least a half-dozen separate occasions, only this time was different. This time she was entering for the express purpose of lying with him. The act would be premeditated and preplanned, and no matter what happened afterward, she couldn't ever fall back on saying she'd been tricked or seduced.

She started on the hooks of her velvet evening cape, fingers clumsy with eagerness and nerves. Behind her Hadrian drew the door closed.

"Here, allow me." His hands, warm despite the chilly carriage ride they'd shared, found the tops of her shoulders.

"Thank you." She stood still and let him slip the cape off, his hands lingering for a whisper of a moment before he turned away to hang the garment on a peg.

"Make yourself comfortable." He draped his tailcoat over the back of a chair and then went to turn up the lamps.

A warm smoky glow suffused the room. Rubbing her bare arms, she drifted over to the table. Fitting one hand to the edge, she looked across to where Hadrian bent to the grate, busy rekindling the banked fire. She caught herself ogling his back, the way his buttocks and thighs molded to the soft wool of his tailored trousers. Despite the chill in the room, she felt a sliver of sweat slip down between her shoulder blades and silently prayed to whatever saint whose charge it was to watch over soon-to-be-fallen women that it wouldn't leave a telltale stain on her gown. For one night in her life she wanted to appear calm and collected, elegant and poised. She wanted to feel carefree and sexy and yes, just a little happy too.

Needing to breach the edgy silence, she called across the room, "You should know I've never propositioned a man before tonight."

"I didn't think you had but thank you for saying so," he answered over his shoulder, and she was warmed by the smile in his voice. "Not that you wouldn't have been met with a great number of acceptances." He straightened and turned to cross the room toward her, gaze holding hers. "You're so beautiful," he said and the warmth in his voice and in his eyes left no doubt he meant it. "Seeing you standing there in profile and dressed as you are, I can't help thinking Sargent's Madame X pales in comparison." He slid his gaze slid down the length of her, taking thorough measure of the heart-shaped bodice molding her breasts, the satin skirt cinched at her waist, the "V"-shaped fold of skirt draped snugly over her pubis.

Callie felt the brush of his eyes like a caress. She should have felt ashamed. She should have felt shy. But instead what she felt was a bold, pagan excitement coursing through her. "You make me feel beautiful."

Coming to stand before her, he slid one of the jeweled straps down off her shoulder, fingers trailing the edge of her forearm and sending fireworks shooting down her spine. "And you have the softest skin. Like rose petals," he added and then smiled at what an idiot he'd become.

Who would have thought that Harry Stone, whoreson and erstwhile thief, would be mooning over a woman's skin like some love smitten swain ramping up for his very first fuck? Incredible. Ludicrous.

Wonderful . . . wonderful beyond words.

Yet whatever shred of honor he still possessed prompted him to step back and say, "We don't have to do this, you know. There's still time to walk away. I'll never say a word to anyone, I promise."

Her eyes lifted to his. "I don't want to walk away. I want this. I want you."

He settled his gaze on her face. "You need to know I'm not a marrying man."

Callie's eyes flashed fire, a reminder of their first photography session when she'd sparred with him like a knight of yore. "What makes you think I'm a marrying woman? Men gratify their physical desires outside of marriage all the time and no one faults them for it or expects them to forfeit their independence. Why should it be different for a woman?"

A woman's heart can be a very fragile thing . . . Callie's aunt's words had haunted him ever since her visit to his shop. Hearing them now in the echo inside his head, he said, "Because it is. If we go to bed, it won't be long before you'll want more from me, the promise of something permanent. And I'm telling you now, Callie, I'm not capable of giving you or any other woman more than this."

She tilted her head and regarded him. "Have you ever tried?"

He lifted her hand and carried it to his mouth, pressing a kiss into her palm. "You've a whole wide world out there just waiting for you to save it. The salvation of one scapegrace would be a waste of your time and considerable talents."

"Shouldn't I be the one to decide that?"

He shook his head, a hank of hair falling over his one eye, making him look younger, boyish even. "You don't need me, Callie. I'm no good to you. If you're even half as intelligent as I know you to be, you'll go now and never come back."

Reaching up, she combed back the golden strands with her fingers. "I want to make love with you, Hadrian. I think I've wanted to almost from the moment I set eyes on you in Parliament Square. I'm not asking you to promise tomorrow, only give me tonight."

He kissed the curve of her neck. "In that case, no apologies, no regrets." His life's guiding mantra, only now he was giving it to her.

He'd tried to send her away, truly he had. He wanted her. He was shaking with the need to be inside her, to be one with her, to be a part of her life if only for this one night.

Stepping back from her, he held her gaze and said, "Your hair, take it down for me."

She reached up her arms—such lovely long limbs she had. Her hands went to her hair, fingers pulling at the pins, and he saw she was shaking. *Oh Callie* . . .

Hastening to reassure her—political pamphlets aside, how much did she really know about how it was between men and women—he hastened to set her at ease. "You don't have to worry about there being . . . consequences. I have a tin of French letters by my bed."

Tossing the pins on the table, she looked at him askance. "You've slept with a lot of women haven't you?"

Threading his fingers through the silk of her hair, he didn't deny it. "I can bring you to climax any number of ways. I don't have to breach you to make you come. You can have as much or as little as you want. It's your choice."

She took a deep breath and then released it very slowly, her magnificent breasts pulling at the short stays she undoubtedly wore beneath her gown's plunging neckline. "All of you. I want all of you."

His chest felt as though it were swelling, not with pride but with something else. Something deeper—finer—than anything he'd ever felt until now. "I've never been with a virgin before, but I won't hurt you, Callie. I'll go slowly with you, let you get used to me, and once you have, I'll give you as much or as little as you want."

He wasn't prepared for the raw vulnerability washing over her face. "Oh, Hadrian, I feel such a fraud."

He couldn't begin to guess at what she might mean, but he recognized the look of hurt, the bald self-hatred, at once for hadn't he confronted the same demons in his shaving mirror every day since he could remember?

She shook her head, the very picture of misery. "The press calls me the Maid of Mayfair because I'm so pure, but I'm not, I tell you, I'm not." The quaver in her pitched voice told him she was perilously close to crying.

"Callie, love, what are you saying?"

"That I'm no maid, not of Mayfair or anywhere else. I'm not a virgin and haven't been for ten years. Oh Hadrian, I've been pretending all along."

"I'm a hypocrite, Hadrian, the very worst sort."

In the ensuing minute or two since her confession, Hadrian had guided her over to his bed. Sitting side by side on the edge, he felt Callie's misery as a palpable thing, a dull throbbing that might as easily originated inside his own chest.

He stroked a hand down the curve of her bared back—she really did have the smoothest skin—and said as gently as he might, "I doubt that very much but go on."

Head in her hands, Callie began her story. "I was engaged a long time ago. I was young, just nineteen, and up from the country for my first season. My come-out had been nothing short of a disaster. The other girls that season all seemed to be blond and petite and the eligible men all my height or shorter. I think I came to dread being noticed and ignored in equal part. Every ball was a misery to me and even knowing that going home without an offer would brand me as a failure, I still didn't care. I just wanted to go home."

Gently, very gently, he pulled her hands away and turned her chin so that she was looking at him. "But you did receive an offer, I take it?"

She nodded. "I met Gerald at a *musicale* held at the home of a friend of my aunt's. He was pleasant, ingratiating even. When he confided to me that he too hated to dance, I felt at ease for the first time in months. The next day he called at the townhouse we'd let and asked Father's permission to court me. I have to admit it, I was flattered."

"Did you love him?" It was foolish, he knew, but for whatever reason he had to ask.

She hesitated. "Looking back, I think I was more infatuated than in love. He was young and good-looking and . . . virile in the way of country squires. My parents had started to despair of having a spinster on their hands, and Gerald seemed to satisfy all their requirements for a son-in-law. His family was solid, respectable, and well, it wasn't as though I was any great prize."

"I beg to differ but go on."

"The only person who didn't care for him was Lottie."

"Wise woman, your aunt."

She nodded. "Indeed. We'd courted for several months when he proposed."

"And you said you weren't a marrying woman." He stroked a hand down her cheek and shook his head if only because she looked so adorably earnest sitting there making her "confession."

"Oh, I'd read a few feminist tracts and attended the odd lecture, but I wasn't active in the movement. Gerald assured me that once we wed, I wouldn't have time for such silliness. His patronizing grated, but still I never thought of refusing him, that I might do something with my life other than be someone's wife." Her face darkened. "No sooner did I have his ring on my finger then he began pressing me."

"For sex." It wasn't a question and absurd as it was, he felt jealous.

She looked away. "I put him off for a while, not that I wasn't thinking about it as well. We'd kissed, that was all, but I'd liked it. I have to admit I was . . . curious."

He reached for her hand—touching any other part of her just now would have seemed wrong in some way he couldn't quite define. Lacing his fingers with hers, he said, "You're a passionate woman, Callie. There's no sin in admitting you wanted sex or that you enjoyed it."

That raised a thin laugh. She lifted her eyes to his, and he could imagine how she must have looked all those years before, untried and unsure and so vulnerable in her innocence that he felt his heart turning inward.

"Mostly I was nervous—and terribly shy. The embarrassment of being dragged out onto the dance floor was nothing to what I felt when Gerald unbuttoned my shirtwaist and exclaimed over how . . . how large I am."

The bastard! He gave her hand a reassuring squeeze. "He hurt you, didn't he?"

She bit her lip and looked away to the chipped globe of his bedside lamp. "He wasn't a monster if that's what you're asking, but he'd been drinking. I think it's fair to say he was . . . less than patient with me. When I asked him to please go more slowly, he laughed and said something about pain being the legacy of Eve, and if I liked I could close my eyes and think of something else until he'd finished."

"Good God." He wrapped an arm about her and pulled her to him as tightly as he could without hurting her—she'd been hurt so much already. "Please tell me you broke it off with him then."

Against his shoulder, she shook her head. "I should have, only I didn't. As I said, I was young and, despite my politics, still rather conventional. I'd as good as handed him my virginity on a silver platter. What choice had I but to see the thing through?"

"He broke it off, then?"

"Not exactly." She grimaced and he sensed then that the truly painful part was yet to come. "We were at our engagement ball. Now that he'd had me, I can only describe his attitude as coolly civil. We danced the obligatory opening dance and then went our separate ways. I imagined a lifetime of such nights with us together yet apart, and I knew I had to get out of that room if only to think. I'd only been in the garden a few minutes when Gerald and one of his cronies stepped out onto the balcony for a smoke. It was coming on dark, and I was about to make myself known and go back inside when I realized the girl they were talking about was me."

"I gather whatever they said wasn't particularly complimentary?"

"Hardly. Oh, I've blocked out a large portion of it but words like "milcher" and "beast" will always hold a place in my memory. Afterward there was nothing Gerald could do or say, nothing my parents could threaten, that could induce me to go through with marrying him. The only person who stood by me was Lottie. She let me come up to London and stay with her until things blew over. That was ten years ago. Rather a long visit, wouldn't you say?"

He raised their joined hands to his lips and brushed a kiss over the top of her knuckles. "Oh, Callie, my sweet, lovely girl, if can't you see how beautiful you are, then let me show you. Let me make you happy if only for tonight." He pinned her gaze with his. "Tell me what you want."

She smiled that small Mona Lisa smile of hers he'd grown to love and shook her head. "Beyond being with you I'm . . . I'm not certain."

He made a tsking sound and slid a hand beneath her fall of silky hair, cradling her nape. "Caledonia Rivers not certain of what it is she wants? I don't believe that for an instant."

She bit her lip. "Very well then, I want you . . . inside of me."

He broadened his smile. She really was adorable and, if not a virgin, certainly a lady to her very core. "Might you be more . . . specific?"

Jade green eyes glared up at him, a striking contrast to her very red face. Responding to his challenge, she lifted her chin and said, "Your . . . cock, I want it inside of me. There, satisfied?"

Hadrian angled his face to hers, their mouths but a hair's breadth apart, their shallow breaths joining. "Not yet but before long we both will be."

***

Finding the tapes of Callie's all-black gown in the semidarkness was no easy feat but eventually Hadrian got the thing off her. Stepping out of it, she turned away to shed her stays and corset and finally her short shift of soft handkerchief linen. That left only her black stockings and garters.

Hadrian came up behind her. Laying hands on her shoulders, he leaned close and whispered, "Turn around. I want to look at you. All of you."

Callie hesitated and then slowly pivoted to face him. There was something innately erotic, and more than a touch dark, about a lovely woman standing before him stripped down to her garters when he hadn't so much as loosened his neckwear. But in this case the beautiful woman was Callie, *his* Callie, and when he saw her hunch her shoulders and fumble to cover herself, he couldn't help but take her in his arms and hold her close against his chest.

Palm pressed to the curve of his shoulder as if to hold him at bay, she shook her head. "I'm nervous. I'm sorry. I didn't mean to be."

Her downcast gaze had him lifting her chin on the edge of his hand. "In that case, help me with my buttons," he said against the silk of her hair.

He'd only offered to distract her from her embarrassment, to return them once more to equal footing. Or, more properly, as equal as they could ever be, for Callie was entirely too fine for the likes of him. But now that he was holding her, he could no more ignore the sexual heat rolling off her than he could the rapid-fire pounding of his own heart.

She managed the three buttons of his waistcoat with

relative ease but when she got to the buttons fronting his pleated shirt, her fingers were cold and clumsy against his flushed flesh.

Sliding the shirt off his shoulders, she stepped back. "You're the one who is beautiful," she said, fingers skimming his chest, voice intoned with something akin to reverence.

"I've more buttons, Miss Rivers. You're not quite finished with me yet." Taking hold of her hand, he guided it down to the front of his trousers where the ridge of his erection strained to be free. "Do you feel how hard I am for you, how much I want you?"

Without waiting for her to answer, he bent his head to her beautiful breasts, blessing the high slopes with feather-light kisses, taking the tips in his mouth. He could have gone on suckling and tasting her there for some time but remembering what she'd told him about her fiancé, he moved on rather than risk resurrecting hurtful memories.

Shucking off the remainder of his clothes, he pushed her down on the edge of the bed and then knelt before her as he had so many times in his fantasies. Only this time she wasn't a figment of his fevered imagination but flesh-and-blood real, gloriously so. Spreading her thighs wide, he took her with his mouth, tongue flicking over her vulva, pink and glistening and fragrant with musk.

Moaning, she raised her hips to meet him, her hand settling at the back of his head, urging him closer. "Hadrian, I never knew. I never imagined."

"Lie back and let me make you happy. Let me show you

good it can be."

She obeyed, going back against the mattress. Dark hair splayed on the counterpane and creamy skin glowing, she arched to meet him. Still kissing her intimately, he lifted her stocking-clad legs until her feet were braced on his shoulders. He slipped both hands beneath her, cupping her buttocks and then pulling the firm lobes gently apart. Mouth hot on her sex, he found the ring of puckered flesh with his thumb and circled.

She moaned and bit down on her bottom lip. "Hadrian, what are you doing to me?"

"Pleasing you or at least I hope that's what I'm doing." He flicked his finger once more. "Do you like this? Does it feel good?"

"Yes, but—"

"No buts, only pleasure." He slid a finger inside her and pressed gently inward even as he circled her clitoris with the tip of his tongue.

"Oh God!"

She came then, little pulses that sent her woman's flesh fluttering against his mouth like the beating of butterfly wings. Staring down at the rosy pink of her throbbing sex, Hadrian knew he couldn't wait so much as another moment.

The tin of French letters was tucked away in his bedside table. Yanking open the drawer, he reached for them now, urgency warring with his heartfelt desire to make it good for her. Better than good. Magical. Knowing she wasn't a virgin somehow doubled his responsibility toward her. A bad

237

sexual experience was a good deal harder to overcome than no sexual experience at all, and that her former fiancé had used sex to degrade and humiliate her increased Hadrian's resolve to bring her as much pleasure as she would allow.

He lifted the lid and took one of the prophylactics out, unfurled the condom and rolled it over his turgid flesh as he had countless times before. Only this time was different, entirely so, than any other before it.

This time was with Callie.

When he turned back, she lay in the center of the bed watching him with large, luminous eyes. Eyes he knew would haunt his dreams for the rest of his days.

He climbed onto the mattress and straddled her, slipping hands down to knead her belly. "You have beautiful skin," he told her for the second time that night, both because it was true and something she desperately needed to hear.

Fitting himself to her, he glided inside, filling her in one sure stroke. She rose up to meet him, wrapping silk-sheathed legs tight about his waist. It had been a while since he'd been with a woman, and the sudden movement, coupled with the ghost tremors still firing off inside her, nearly pushed him over the edge.

When he could trust himself, he started to move back and forth very slowly, watching her face.

Callie eased back against the pillow, eyelids squeezed closed and body taut as a drawn bowstring. If they had time, another night at least, he would teach her to trust him enough to let him lash those lovely wrists of hers to his metal bedposts and show her just how sweet submission, total submission, could be. For now, he resolved not to waste so much as one second of their time together mourning what could never be.

He increased the pace, the pressure, slipping in and out of her slickness fast and hard as he touched her face, her throat, her breasts. "Open your eyes, Callie. I want to look into your eyes when you come." Reaching down between them, he found the rosy bud of her clitoris with his thumb, flicking over it once, twice . . .

Callie's eyes flew open. "H-a-d-r-i-a-n."

The spasms rocketing off inside her sent Hadrian over the edge. A final thrust was all it took to complete his climax. Coming hard and fast, he collapsed against her, head resting facedown on the pillow of one lovely flushed breast.

Callie was the first to recover. "Thank you." She ran a kneading hand down his sweat-sheathed back, fingers slipping in the slickness.

"My pleasure." He lifted his head and looked up into her sweet, sated face. "Has anyone ever told you before how delicious you are?"

He made a show of smacking his lips, which had her laughing and blushing in turns. She shifted her head from side to side on the pillow, a pantomimed "no."

"Pity, because you are. Absolutely succulent, in fact, speaking of which . . ."

He moved down the front of her, and found her with his mouth, again, spearing her with his tongue.

Her eyes shot open. She lifted up on her elbows to look down on him. "Hadrian, I'm spent, really, I don't think . . . I can't possibly. . ."

He raised his head from the tent of her splayed thighs and grinned up at her. "Is that a dare, Miss Rivers?"

⁂

Sometime later Hadrian lay propped on one elbow and turned on his side. Leaning over her, he circled the areola of one breast with a single finger. "Ashes of roses," he said so softly she couldn't be sure if she'd heard him properly.

"Sorry?" Callie cracked open an eye. She hadn't been asleep, not exactly, but rather catnapping, a delicious sort of slipping in and out of awareness.

"You are, just there. The same lovely dusky pink the London dressmakers call 'ashes of roses'." He lightly scratched the surface with his fingernail.

A delicious shiver shot from her breast to her toes. "Pinch me, will you?"

Looking up, he grinned. "With pleasure; but why?"

"Because that way I'll know I'm not dreaming, and that this is all real, that you're real."

"I'm real enough, make no mistake about that."

Before the situation went any further, she needed him to understand what he was coming to mean to her. Turning on her side to face him, she blurted out, "I think I've been waiting for you all my life."

His gaze shuttered. "You don't even know me, not really."

Rather than dispute that, she said, "Then tell me something about yourself, something personal."

His eyes met hers and despite being halfway to in love with him, the ice she saw there chilled her. "You should be careful, Callie. You might just get a taste of what you're asking for and find you don't like it overmuch."

"But I want to know everything or at least more than I do now which isn't all that much, not really."

He sighed. "You're like a dog with a bone, aren't you? You don't mean to give up 'til you've gnawed me down to the marrow." He rolled onto his back, stretched his arms and crossed them behind his head. "Very well, then, if you must know, Hadrian isn't my real name."

"Sorry?"

His mouth twisted, more grimace than smile, and for reasons unknown Callie felt a frisson of fear land in her belly and lower, those very areas that a moment before had been languid and pulsing. "Hadrian St. Claire, he's a persona, an invention 'if you will. For all intents and purposes, he doesn't exist."

She pushed up on one elbow. Gaze on his face, she pressed, "You're serious aren't you?"

"Yes."

She thought back to the day when he'd insisted on walking her about Bow. Both the street woman in the market and Sally Potts, the brothel madam, had called him Harry, at least at first. Was he some infamous criminal in hiding?

How bad could it be? He wasn't Jack the Ripper, surely. If so, she'd have been eviscerated long before now. As it was, the only organ she stood in peril of losing was her heart.

"Why change your name?"

"Because . . . well, why the devil not, there's no law against it. Theater people take stage names all the time. Why, look at that music-hall girl who's all the rage in Paris right now. Delilah du Lac she styles herself, but never think that's her real name. But it sounds all right, doesn't it?"

She'd set him on edge. She ought to leave off now but it was too late, she couldn't stop herself. "That woman in the marketplace and your friend, Mrs. Potts, they both called you Harry. That's you real name, isn't it?"

He nodded slowly. "Harry Stone."

"That's what they knew you as when you lived in Bow, before you went to the orphanage, the nice one in the country."

Looking almost relieved, he nodded again. "Roxbury House. It sounds odd, I know, but being sent there was the luckiest thing that ever happened to me. Until then I'd never seen a true patch of blue sky before or tasted fresh milk or picked wild strawberries from an open field or . . . well, you grew up in the country. You know what I mean."

She leaned over him and brushed blond hair back from his brow. "I rather fancy you as a Henry." She tried to sound light, teasing even, but the magic was lost to them now. Her fault, of course, for throwing open the lid on Pandora's Box.

A frown marred the brow she'd only just left off touching. "Pity then because the name's Harry. Just plain Harry"

"I like plain Harry well enough. It suits you. Shall I call you Harry, then?"

"Don't even think about it." He rolled over and then atop her, trapping her beneath him. "You asked me to tell you something personal, and I have. To my way of thinking, I must have some sort of reward coming my way for baring my blackguard's soul." His hands found her wrists, and he lifted her arms above her head. Her heartbeat quickened, and the heat between her thighs began to build.

She looked up into his eyes, intent on her face, and said, "But I've already bared my soul to you, haven't I?"

He glanced down to the sheet she'd pulled over herself. "Indeed, and a beautiful soul it is, I'm sure, but I'd much rather you bared those magnificent breasts instead."

Now it was his turn to spoil the moment. She turned her head, swallowing against the thickness in her throat.

He let her loose and then lifted her chin on the edge of his hand so that she was looking up at him. "I suppose you think that, like your oaf of a fiancé, your breasts are all any man sees when he looks at you?" When she let silence answer for her, he said, "Yes, your breasts are very beautiful, but then so is all the rest of you."

She gave a soft snort. "Really Hadrian, I do own a mirror."

"I can see you want for convincing. Very well, then, sometimes I lie abed at night and think of you lying in yours. What you might be wearing, what you really look like beneath all those layers of clothes. If the rest of you is as creamy and soft as your throat looks to be, how much the delectable fullness of your bottom owes to a bustle, and yes, how lovely your breasts must be—to touch, to kiss, to suckle."

"Hadrian, I—"

"Don't want to hear it, any of it, I know. You see, you've just asked me to tell you something personal, something intimate, and now you're doing your level best to shut those pretty ears of yours because you don't fancy what you hear. Well, too bloody bad, Callie, because if I have to pay with my honesty, then so do you."

She lifted her chin, trying to look braver than she felt. "Very well, what do you want me to say?"

"That you've thought of me in the same way. That you've lain in your chaste little spinster's bed and spread those lovely long legs of yours and fucked yourself with your fingers and pretended it's me you're feeling—my lips, my tongue, my cock."

"You're being deliberately vulgar." She tried to sound strident but there was no honesty in it, no point in pretending. What he's said was exactly what she had been thinking, *doing* all these past weeks.

"Undoubtedly, but what I'm also being is honest." He slid a hand between her thighs, slipped a finger deep inside her. "Confession time, Callie, can you give as good as you get?"

Without looking down, she could feel how wet she was, how hot, how ready for whatever it was he might be moved to give. His finger inside her started to slide in and out, back and forth. Her mouth opened on a moan. "W-what is it you want me to say?"

He stilled his hand, calculated torture. "I want you to tell me all the things you think of doing with me, of me doing to you, of our doing together. I want you to touch yourself as you do when you're alone; only this time you won't be alone, Callie. I'll be here, watching you pleasure yourself, watching your face when you cry out my name and come."

CHAPTER THIRTEEN

"Nothing is so burdensome as a secret."
                                        —French proverb

awn lights were streaking the winter sky when Callie crept into the house on Half Moon Street, draped her rumpled gown over the back of a chair, and slipped beneath the chilly sheets of her own empty bed. She felt tired as well as deliciously tender in spots she could scarcely name but what she mostly felt was wonderful, wonderful beyond words. For the first time in her life, she'd made love, truly made love, and the potency of that act was beyond her wildest imaginings.

She had to believe that Hadrian had felt it too, that force of nature connection that had run between them like electrical current, uniting not only their bodies but their minds and souls, too. How else could he have touched her with such tenderness, such *care*, as though she were made of Dresden china rather than flesh-and-bone? For her part, never before in her life had she felt such a compulsion, an absolute need, to touch another person. Afterward when he'd walked her out to the main street and flagged down the sleepy-eyed hansom driver, it had been very hard to leave him. With her face shielded by the hood of her evening cape, she hadn't been able to resist one last reckless kiss. Weary as she was, already her busy brain was engaged in plotting how soon she might break away and be with him again.

In the interim, there was the afternoon tea with the Stone-vales to be got through and then the long anticipated meeting with Lord Salisbury the following day. Even on an ordinary morning, her routine was to be washed and dressed and down-stairs by seven. She would help herself from the sideboard and then take her place at the table, forking up her buttered eggs and sipping her three cups of strong black coffee while skimming her stack of daily newspapers in quick succession.

But this morning she had the rare notion of being good to herself. So even though her thoughts were racing far too fast and furious for sleep, she stayed put in bed. Curled up like a cat beneath the patchwork quilt, she lay there reliving the past hours with Hadrian—his tongue teasing her breasts, the stroking fingers that had driven her wet and wild, the delicious pressure when he'd entered her, filling her completely. The knock outside her door startled her from her dreamy thoughts.

Thinking it must be her aunt—and certainly Lottie was far too canny to have believed her headache excuse for so much as a moment—she pulled herself up on her elbows and called out, "I'm awake. Come in."

The door opened and Jenny breezed inside carrying a breakfast tray and wearing her customary smile. "Good morning, miss. Your aunt thought you might fancy breakfast in bed. On account of your being out so late last night," she added with a wink.

"How lovely," Callie said. Fighting a blush, she waited while Jenny set the tray on her lap and then plumped the pillows.

Breakfast in bed was a delicious decadence usually reserved for special occasions like her birthday, but then knowing how thoroughly modern Lottie was when it came to matters of the heart, she'd likely reckoned that Callie's taking a lover after ten years of abstinence was as worthy of celebration as any holiday.

Jenny busied herself with tidying the room, including shaking out the crumpled evening gown with a giggle and murmured exclamation of "My, my," confirming Callie's suspicion that both the maid and her aunt knew full well what time she'd got in. Averting her eyes, Callie surveyed the contents of the tray where all of her very favorites were assembled: a basket of oven-warm muffins and scones, a succulent hot house peach and a pot of creamy chocolate in lieu of her customary coffee. When Jenny assured her she'd be back directly with her newspapers, Callie hesitated for a moment and then told her not to bother. There would be plenty of time later to hear all the spoiling news. For one morning out of her life she wanted to linger over her breakfast and let the world feel fresh and full of newfound possibilities.

The door clicked closed. Once more alone with her thoughts, Callie tucked into her breakfast. She hadn't realized how ravenous she was until she took her first bite. Then again she had missed supper the night before albeit for the very best of reasons.

Hadrian. Chewing, she asked herself what word he'd used to describe her figure. Oh yes, *generous*. At the time she'd rather thought he was the one who was generous but now curiosity compelled her to have a look for herself. Licking the butter from her thumb—and really, why not when there was no one about to see—she set the tray to the side, kicked back the covers, and got up. Barefoot, she padded across the floor to the mirror, reached up and pulled the flannel nightgown over her head. Tossing the garment over the chair, she took a deep breath and stared into the mirror.

The wide-eyed woman with the mussed hair trailing her back wasn't a sylph by any means but nor was she the hulking beast, the *milcher*, she'd imagined ever since the night of her engagement ball. Her breasts were full—all right, *large*—but not particularly bovine. They were, if anything, firm and rather nicely shaped. Moving on to examine her middle, she had to admit that though her waist wasn't exactly narrow, at least it cinched in where a woman's waist ought. Were she to bear children, it would likely thicken, but that would be years away, if indeed it ever happened at all. Her legs were long, her thighs and calves firmly muscled, not unlike the photographs she'd seen of the music-hall girls in their fishnet stockings and shortened skirts. An image of herself similarly clad for an audience of one, Hadrian, flashed through her mind, and she felt her face heat even as a giggle tickled the back of her throat. That left her posterior, the last but hardly the least of her. She took a bracing breath and turned sideways. Not small there either, not by any means, but also not nearly as hideous as she'd envisioned.

Yet for so many years she'd viewed her body as ugly, the enemy. Starting today, this very moment, she was calling a truce with her physical self. More than a truce, she meant to make her peace with the past, lay to rest her old insecurities and fears once and for all. Hers was a woman's body, neither grotesque nor goddess-like. It had its good points and its bad, but it was healthy and she could appreciate the inherent beauty in that, in herself. For the first time in more than ten years she saw what others saw, what Hadrian seemed to see: a healthy still-young woman with a healthy young woman's needs and desires.

Desires which last night he had fulfilled beyond her wildest imaginings, her most secret fantasies. Even so, she wanted more from him than the mechanics of mere physical release. She wanted him to be her lover in every sense of the word. She wanted not only his body, glorious gift that it was, but his mind and soul, too.

If we go to bed, it won't be long before you'll want something more from me, something permanent. And I'm telling you now, Callie, I'm not capable of giving you or any woman more than this.

For the first time since leaving his bed, she felt her euphoria dim. Rationally, she knew she ought to be content with whatever little of himself he was willing to give. Fair was fair, after all, and it wasn't as if he hadn't warned her. Yet now that she'd had this taste of bliss, how could she possibly go back to her old ways, her old life?

Always wanting more, hadn't that ever been her fatal failing?

Callie wasn't the only one to spend a sleepless night. Hadrian had spent the hours since depositing her in the hansom walking the London streets. Eventually his rambling footsteps led him to Gavin's door.

When Gavin's manservant showed him into the flat's small dining room, he wasn't surprised to find Rourke there. The two men looked up from plates heaped with deviled kidneys, buttered eggs, and toast when he entered.

"Harry, by God, you look bloody awful." Impeccably dressed though it was scarcely nine o'clock, Gavin rose from the head of the table. "Have a seat and some breakfast before you keel over."

Ignoring the sideboard of silver-covered rashers, Hadrian pulled out a chair and sat. "Got anything to drink?"

From across the table, Rourke shook his head. "I dinna think he means coffee. Here lad, this'll wake you up." Rumpled shirt rolled over muscular forearms, Rourke handed over his flask. "The finest Scotch whiskey. No true Scotsman would think of leaving home without it."

Hadrian accepted the flask and downed a fiery swallow. Replacing the stopper, he handed it back. "Better, thanks."

Gavin studied him, expression thoughtful. "For a man who disappeared before supper last night with the lovely Caledonia in arm, you look less than glowing."

"I took her home, end of story."

"Aye, but to who's home, hers or yours?" The Scot shot Hadrian a conspiratorial wink.

Mindful of his promise to Callie he'd not tell another living soul, he asked, "How went it with Lady Kat?" Anything to turn the subject from his own sorry self.

Gaze sobering, Rourke shrugged. "She'll come 'round. I'm growing on her, mind."

Hadrian winked. "Like a vine of poison ivy, no doubt."

Rourke reached across the table and dealt him a good-natured cuff upside the head that brought him back to when they were boys.

Pouring more coffee for them all, Gavin interjected, "In point, we were just discussing the nature of love when you walked in. Our flinty friend here"—he nodded toward Rourke—"maintains it either doesn't exist or exists only as a form of temporary lunacy. I, on the other hand, am a proponent that every soul has its one perfect life's mate." Ignoring Rourke's snort, he went on, "By way of a case in point, my parents were deeply, passionately in love. When my mother defied her family to marry my father, she walked away from absolutely everything—her family and friends, standing in society, and yes, money—and not once did I hear her utter so much as a word of regret. In retrospect the walk-up where we lived was a dreary place, but they made it more of a home than most grand mansions will ever be."

His voice dropped off and he made a show of stirring sugar into his coffee, no doubt carried back to the day when, as a boy of ten, he'd returned to his family's East End tenement to find the building ablaze. Both of his parents and baby sister had perished, leaving Gavin orphaned and with a lifelong need to save everyone and everything in trouble that crossed his path. Even as a boy, Gavin had exuded an ethereal quality that had set him apart from other children. "Saint Gavin," they'd jokingly called him, although as far as Hadrian knew there weren't any saints by that name. Though Hadrian loved him as a brother, he'd never really understood Gavin in the way he understood Rourke.

Unstoppering the flask, Rourke poured a generous measure of the spirit into his cup. "That's a verra touching story, and perhaps your parents were the rare exception to the rule, but I still say 'tis an addle-pated man indeed who'd let himself fall in love with the likes of Kat Lindsey, or any woman. All I want of Lady Kat or any wife is for her to warm my bed, birth my bairns, and grace my dinner table, and I'll consider the bargain well met. Right, Harry?"

Hadrian hesitated. A few weeks before, he would have found himself agreeing with his friend wholeheartedly. But since Callie had come into his life, things had changed. *He* had changed. For a man who'd grown up thinking of sex as a service, something done to earn one's keep, making love with all his mind and body and yes, heart engaged was a life-altering experience on par with Saul's journey on the road to Damascus or Daguerre's discovery of a method for fixing the images from a *camera obscura*. Miraculous. Wonderful. *Terrifying*.

But because he'd come too far to turn back now, because he'd sooner let Dandridge have him torn apart limb by limb than see so much as one hair on Callie's head harmed, he swallowed his pride and admitted, "I'm in trouble."

Gavin and Rourke looked at him and then exchanged worried glances. Never one to waste words, Rourke said, "Go on with you, then. Out with it, man."

Without sparing himself, he recapped the chance meeting with Callie in Parliament Square, the episode in the alleyway with the two gaming-hell henchmen, and finally Dandridge's visit to his shop and the terms of the bargain they struck.

He'd scarcely finished when Rourke slammed his beefy fist atop the table, sending plates and cutlery bouncing like rubber. "Jesus, Mary, and Joseph, what were you thinking, man? I would have loaned you the tin. To hell with loaned, I'd ha' given it to you outright. I *will* give it to you outright. Give Dandridge back his blunt and tell him to go to the bluidy devil."

Hadrian shook his head. "If only it were that simple. I know too much for him to allow me to live. He's as good as threatened to off me, not that my life at this point is worth terribly much. But if I don't come up with the photograph he's after, it'll only be a matter of time before he finds some other way to get at Callie, *vanquish* her as he cares to call it. If this suffrage bill of hers makes it to a third and final read, her life may be even more in danger than mine."

"Bastard!" Jaw blanketed with reddish-brown stubble and hair still bearing the imprint of last night's pillow, Rourke made a ferocious sight indeed. "We could go to the papers."

"Right now it's my word against that of a respected Member of Parliament. Given our respective backgrounds, whose story do you think would hold greater weight with the Fleet Street lot, his or mine?"

Gavin, quiet until now, spoke up, "He has a point. We have to find another way." Fixing Hadrian with solemn eyes, he added, "Of course you have to tell Caledonia the truth, the whole of it, if only to warn her."

Hadrian scraped the fingers of one hand through his mussed hair, thinking how good Callie's gentle fingers had felt on his scalp and indeed everywhere else. "I know I must. She'll hate me, of course, but then that's no more than I deserve."

Gavin shook his head. "I shouldn't be so certain of that were I you. At least give her the chance to forgive you. She just might surprise you."

Rourke grinned. "Aye, if she doesna cut off your bollocks first."

Feeling marginally better now that he'd unburdened himself, Hadrian rose and headed for the door.

Gavin looked back over his shoulder. "Where are you off to now?"

Lost soul though he might be, he'd be damned indeed before he'd drag Callie down to hell with him. "Back to my flat, to make myself presentable before I see Callie." He drew the door closed on their astonished faces.

Stepping out into the bracing air, it occurred to him that before Callie sex had been something that took place outside of him, a means to an end or an interlude into which he'd wandered without much or any conscious thought. His body had been engaged but his brain had been far, far removed. As for his heart, well, it had been a very long time since he'd given *that* particular organ any consideration.

But loving Callie had changed all that. Even if he never set eyes on her again after this day, these past weeks together had altered him. Irrevocably. Forever. He'd never be remotely the same and though his heart hurt like hell and he was scared shitless, he also felt . . . relieved. Keeping up with Hadrian St. Claire now struck him as a hell of a lot of work, more trouble than it was worth, and in general a royal pain in the ass. Whoever Harry Stone was, he was finally ready to welcome him back to life.

❦

Lord and Lady Stonevale kept a modest Georgian-style townhouse on Arlington Street. Walking up the marble steps to the façade of mellow brick, Callie felt her first pang of nerves. Contemplating the brass doorknocker shaped in the head of a dog, she mentally reviewed what she knew of Stonevale's political career. Before inheriting his earldom, his lordship, then plain Simon Belleville, had been a protégée of the late Conservative prime minister, Benjamin Disraeli. During his fifteen years in the Commons, he'd earned a reputation as being both shrewd and fair-minded. On more than one occasion, he'd crossed the House floor to back a Liberal bill concerned with the welfare of women and children.

Keeping that latter thought foremost in her mind, she felt her confidence rise sufficiently to let the knocker drop. The butler who answered was a pleasant-faced chap with a wide smile and a broad girth, scarcely the starchy, svelte sort she would have expected to find in the employ of a Parliamentary front bencher. Instead of having her wait in the hallway while he ferried her calling card forth, he simply bowed and beckoned her to follow him with a, "This way, if you please, miss."

He led her through the tiled foyer to the back of the house, bypassing the front parlor in favor of the oak-paneled library. The door stood open. Looking over the butler's shoulder, Callie saw Lord and Lady Stonovale holding hands before the library fire, a tabby cat curled upon her ladyship's lap and a black-and-white-and-tan mongrel dog with floppy ears lounging at his lordship's feet. Chockfull of bric-a-brac, framed photographs, and the miscellaneous clutter of family life, the library apparently functioned as the heart of the house. Indeed, peace and contentment seemed to float in the very air.

Laid out before her like the backdrop to a diorama, the

homey scene helped set Callie at ease, but it also caught at her heart. Before her was the very reason that centuries of poets and philosophers had expended so much paper and ink extolling the virtues of hearth and home. In the past, she'd viewed such writings as sentimentalized rubbish to rationalize female subjugation, but now she considered that perhaps she'd missed the point. As busy as the Stonevales were with their respective careers and causes, they had this oasis to come home to. They had each other.

She was almost sorry when the butler's light rap brought the homey tableau to a close as lord and lady turned to the doorway.

"Callie . . . Miss Rivers, I am so very pleased you were able to call." Smile radiant, Lady Stonevale set the cat on the empty seat cushion beside her and rose.

Lord Stonevale stood as well, and seeing them side by side, Callie was struck by what an exceedingly handsome couple they made. Tall, broad-shouldered, and athletically built, Stonevale could easily have passed for a man in his forties rather than one coming on sixty. As for her ladyship, dressed in a simple tea gown that complimented her sylph's figure, she glided across the floor to shake hands with the natural grace of a born dancer.

Lady Stonevale ordered tea to be sent in, and then gestured Callie to one of the pair of overstuffed wing chairs set on either side of the mantel. Seated once more, his lordship honed his keen-eyed gaze on Callie's face. *He's taking my measure*, she thought, and made certain to hold her shoulders back and her spine straight.

They chatted about desultory topics, including the weather, until at length he said, "I have been following your efforts and the progress of your proposed bill with great interest, and since meeting you last night, my wife has talked of little else. I assure she is not easily impressed, which is why I agreed to meet with you."

"I am honored, your lordship, and I appreciate both you and Lady Stonevale taking the time to see me."

"My wife speaks highly of you, Miss Rivers, and I assure you she does not give her endorsement lightly."

The arrival of the tea tray stalled further conversation. While Lady Stonevale poured and passed around cups and plates, Callie contemplated what she knew of Stonevale's private life gratis of Lottie. He had met and married his wife under unconventional if not precisely scandalous circumstances. After twenty-five years, five children, and several grandchildren, the couple was said to still be famously in love. Catching the warm looks that passed between them, Callie could well believe it.

Once they'd settled in with tea and finger sandwiches, Stonevale picked up the thread of conversation. "As I was saying, Miss Rivers, while I can appreciate the merits of your argument, I do hold some reservations."

Looking up from her steaming teacup, Callie met his flinty gaze. "And they are, milord?"

"There is a certain contingent of your group who seem to think smashing shop windows and other destruction of property is a fine means of getting their point across. I can assure you that such methods find you few friends in Parliament or elsewhere."

He was testing her. She sensed it in the intensity of those dark eyes trained on her face. Determined to hold her own, Callie replied, "I assure you, Lord Stonevale, that such militancy is not countenanced by either the London Women's Suffrage Society or the national confederation with which we are aligned. That said, the ladies' frustration is not without basis. It has been more than twenty years since John Stuart Mill first put forth a Parliamentary bill for women's suffrage and still we continue without representation, without voice. Plainly put, it is a case of taxation without representation, a circumstance on par with what prompted the American colonies to revolt more than a hundred years ago. It is quite simply *wrong*, milord, and with all due respect, the time for change is now."

He shook his head, toying with the untasted tea biscuit on his plate. "Female suffrage on the national level is a radical concept to many. Like all young people, Miss Rivers, you have yet to learn the art of patience. If there is anything my time abroad in the Orient has taught me, it is that the British are glad enough to impose change on others but painfully slow to accept it on their home shores."

Callie took a sip of her tea before answering, "And yet, milord, our countrywomen have held voting privileges in most localities for two years now, and British society is none the worse for it."

Balancing his cup and saucer on his knees, Stonevale answered, "You put forth a compelling case, Miss Rivers, and yet I must admit that in my bachelor days I likely would have opposed such a measure. Nevertheless, a quarter of a century of marriage to an intelligent, brave, and wonderful wife has opened my eyes to many things, not the least of which is the amazing strength and compassion of women." Casting a fond look at Lady Stonevale, he reached for her hand on the cushion between them. "Christine is my most loyal supporter as well as my most honest critic. She is more to me than wife, helpmate, and mother of my children though she is all of those things in abundance. Above all, she is my conscience, my heart. There are precious few issues on which I do not seek her wise counsel."

Callie glimpsed the sparkle of tears in her ladyship's amber-brown eyes and felt her own eyes moistening as well. To be wanted like that, respected like that, *loved* like that, must be a wondrous thing indeed. As grand as it had been to spend the night before in Hadrian's arms, she knew she wanted more from him than a single night or even a succession of nights. She wanted him by her side through thick and thin, good times and bad, year after year.

Tearing her gaze away from her husband, Lady Stonevale looked to Callie and said, "What Simon is a long time in saying is that he has decided to throw his backing behind your suffrage bill, is that not so, darling?"

"As always, my dear, you are the very soul of brevity." Smiling, Stonevale raised their joined hands to his lips.

Brushing a kiss over the tops of his wife's slender fingers, he looked across to Callie. "Indeed, I've a meeting with my old friend, Lord Salisbury, at our club later this evening. Before supper is through, the prime minister will know that I support your female suffrage bill unequivocally."

The most Callie had hoped for was that Stonevale would not dismiss her arguments outright, that after careful consideration he might quietly cast his vote in their favor. Never had she thought he would go so far to agree to stand as their champion before the prime minister.

Overwhelmed, she very nearly let her plate slip from her lap. Gathering herself, she said, "Lord Stonevale, you cannot imagine what your support means to me personally but more importantly to the thousands of British women who have fought for decades to secure the parliamentary vote for, if not themselves, their daughters and granddaughters. I assure you, sir, time will show that your confidence in me, in us, was not misplaced."

Stonevale nodded. "In that case, Miss Rivers, you have my word that I will do everything in my power to see that your suffrage bill carries through to a third and final read, including being among the very first to rise from my bench and proclaim 'Votes for women now'."

CHAPTER FOURTEEN

"You may fool all the people for some time, and some of the people for all time, but you will never fool all the people for all the time."

—ABRAHAM LINCOLN

When Hadrian left Gavin's, he headed for Callie's office at Langham Place only to learn from the hawk-eyed secretary guarding the front desk that she'd not been in all that day, an oddity or so everyone within earshot agreed. Knowing how late or rather how very early she'd left his flat, Hadrian wasn't nearly as surprised. If she'd decided to treat herself to a day in bed at home, she more than deserved it. Weary as he was, the mere thought of Callie in bed was all it took to make him hard. Only too glad to exit the office and escape the scrutiny of all those pairs of sharp female eyes, he walked out onto Regent Street and flagged down a hansom.

Directing the driver to the Rivers' house on Half Moon Street, he leaned back against the leather seat and mentally rehearsed what he would say once he got there. Several scenarios played out in his head, but the truth was the truth regardless and, in his case, none of it was remotely complimentary. Callie was going to hate him, that was a given, but at least putting her on to Dandridge would make her safe or at least as safe as any controversial public figure might hope to be. If so, the sacrifice would be well worth it.

Nerves drawn tight as piano wire, when the driver pulled up in front of the Rivers' gated front yard, Hadrian felt poised to spring jack-in-the-box style out of his seat. The bright-eyed young maid who answered his knock shook her capped head when he handed her his calling card, explaining that "Miss Callie" was not at home. Hearing that, he wasn't certain whether or not to be grateful for his reprieve or fearful for what that so-called reprieve might signify. Could it be Callie who had entertained second thoughts about their night together—and was even now hiding out in the house to keep from seeing him? Worse yet, had Dandridge grown tired of waiting for him to produce the damning photograph and moved forward with other, more expedient means to vanquish her?

Callie, he had to warn her but before he could he had to find her. Backing away, he had one foot off the stoop when Lottie Rivers appeared in the doorway, calling him back. "Mr. St. Claire, do come in. Callie isn't here at present, but we two can have a nice cozy chat while we wait."

Myriad excuses came to mind but when she assured him that his showing up on her doorstep had saved her from calling on him there was nothing to do but accept as graciously as possible. Besides, if anyone knew where Callie was, it would be her aunt.

He'd no sooner crossed the entrance threshold than the little maid was stepping behind him, pulling the coat from his shoulders and whisking away his hat. Feeling very much like the lone fly caught in a spider's web, he relinquished his outerwear and followed Lottie Rivers into her snug little parlor.

"I am so very glad you called, Mr. Rivers," she said once they were alone. "I was just about to have a spot of sherry and I abhor drinking by myself. You will join me, won't you?"

He nodded. "Yes, thank you." The dram of scotch he'd knocked back at Gavin's had worn off long ago, leaving him solidly sober and taut as a bowstring on the brink of snapping.

She moved to the marble-topped wine table where a crystal decanter and glasses set out on a silver tray. Over her shoulder, she said, "I'm afraid I can't say when Callie will be back. She's a private meeting with Lord Stonevale, and Heaven only knows how long that will last."

The meeting with Stonevale, of course! Mired as he was in his problems, he'd as good as forgotten Callie's triumph of the night before, the invitation to tea at the Stonevales. Were he alone, he would have smacked his hand against his forehead, not once but several times.

Lottie's voice called him back to the present. Back to him as she poured out the wine, she said, "I do so appreciate your bringing her home last night. These sudden headaches can be trying, and I know she was loath to ask me to end the evening early as well."

Rather than be put in the position of having to lie, he crossed over to the fireplace under pretense of warming his hands. A pair of silver-framed tintypes flanked either side of the cream-colored mantel shelf, sundry bric-a-brac sandwiched between. With nothing else to occupy himself, professional curiosity had him picking up the nearest one. A younger Charlotte Rivers smiled back at him, her arm linked with that of a tall, gaunt-looking gentleman of late middle years. Behind them, a gondola glided along crystalline water, the arrested motion causing the background to blur.

Coming up beside him, she said, "My late husband Edward, God rest his soul. That photograph was taken in Venice along the canal the year before he passed. His physician thought the dry Italian air might benefit his lungs. Knowing it was likely the last trip abroad we would ever undertake together made it a bittersweet moment for us both."

He turned to accept the glass of sherry she held out. "Ill though he was, I'm sure he counted himself the most fortunate of men to spend his final days with you."

She took a sip from her glass, her profiled face wistful if not exactly sad. "I count myself the fortunate one, Mr. Rivers. To love and be loved in return is a wondrous state of being. Whether that love lasts for decades or but a single day, it is a precious gift all the same." She turned to face him, knowing gaze meeting his full-on. "It saddens me to think that there are those who let life slip by without ever reaching out for that sort of happiness."

Uncomfortable under her scrutiny—if she had a clue as to whom or rather what he was, surely she'd send him bouncing out her door—he picked up the remaining photograph, this one of a very young couple. The woman, scarcely more than a girl, sat stiffly in a high-backed chair, her flounced skirt's festooned with lace and a great many bows. The man, bull-necked and bandy-legged, stood beside her, one hand resting on the back of her chair, the other concealed inside his coat pocket. Hadrian glanced back to the girl's face, thinking she looked familiar indeed when it struck him. Callie! Her chin in the portrait was more rounded than squared, the lovely high cheekbones present but less pronounced, the full mouth pulled into a tight, almost pained smile, and yet still it was her. He could only imagine the torture she'd endured to transform her thick, straight locks into that silly confection of corkscrew curls and yet somehow he very much doubted that her coiffure accounted for the unmistakable sadness in her eyes.

Next to him, Lottie said, "That was taken a few weeks before her twentieth birthday."

"I take it the man was her fiancé?" Again, he felt that irrational surge of jealousy that had him all but slamming the photograph down on the mantel shelf.

Her eyes widened. "She told you she'd been engaged?" At his mute nod, she shook her head and sighed. "They never would have suited, a blind man could have seen that straightaway, but her parents pushed her into it, too afraid they'd have an old maid on their hands to give a fig for her happiness. I only set it out because it's the one photograph I have of her. Until Mrs. Fawcett commissioned you, she was adamant never to come near a camera lens again."

Poor Callie. No wonder she had such a poor opinion of men and marriage, as well as such a keen dislike for posing for photographs. The latter must have been nothing short of torture for her. Now that he understood all she'd been through, the humiliation she'd endured not only from her scapegrace fiancé but her family, he would be the last to blame her.

Lottie took the picture from him and gave it a long look. "Gerald Dandridge was only a younger son, but the family is considered if not exactly top-drawer then the nearest thing to it. Even so, she is well rid of him. Well rid."

Hadrian nearly choked on the swallow of sherry he'd just taken. "Did you say Gerald *Dandridge*?" At her nod, he pressed, "What relation, if any, is he to Josiah Dandridge?"

Gaze trained on his face, she replied, "Why, they are father and son. By all accounts, Gerald will stand for his father's seat in the next election."

He'd always thought the MP's hatred for Callie went beyond the political and now he understood why. To Dandridge's way of thinking, Callie had jilted his son, an affront that an overly proud man such as he would take very personally indeed.

Not yet sure how he might use this latest information to

his advantage, or more properly to Callie's, he knew he had to get away if only to think. He set his glass down atop the mantel and turned to go. "I'm afraid I must be on my way, Mrs. Rivers. You'll tell Callie I called?"

"Of course, but Mr. St. Claire wherever are you dashing off to now?" She glanced down to his glass, still more than half full. "Why, you've hardly touched your drink."

"The three of us will have a toast in celebration shortly, I dare say. For now, though, I have to see a man about crying off a business deal."

He shot out into the hallway, nearly barreling into the maid who'd been standing outside the door, ear cocked. Heading out into the main hallway, he snatched up his things. He was hurrying down the steps and buttoning his coat when the screech of the front gate had him looking up.

The slender dandy in a bottle green coat and handlebar mustache entering the yard looked vaguely familiar though where Hadrian had seen him before he couldn't immediately say. He didn't think he'd ever photographed him. Even so, he never forgot a face.

He was about to continue on his way with a nod when the man stepped in front of him. "I say, you're that photographer chap, aren't you? The one Callie's been sitting for."

His narrowing gaze had Hadrian hesitating before answering, "Yes, I'm St. Claire, what of it?"

"I'm Theodore Cavendish though my friends all call me Teddy."

Looking the man up and down, Hadrian heartily

doubted he would find himself among their number. Temper short, he almost said as much but bit back the caustic reply in time. Whoever this man was, he was obviously a friend or acquaintance of Callie or her aunt, perhaps both. Despite his haste, there was nothing to be gained by being rude.

Beneath the waxed mustache, a pink tongue darted out to moisten cracked lips. "If you'll pardon my asking, what is your given name?"

Wondering if this was some sort of trick question—if this was Dandridge's snitch, his loud clothing hardly had him blending into the backdrop—he answered, "Hadrian, though I don't know what the devil my name should mean to you."

"Hadrian St. Claire." The man's too friendly smile dimmed and his narrow shoulders drooped. "That would make your initials H.S. H.S.," he mumbled under his breath, his watery eyes making him appear close to tears.

Placing him finally, Hadrian recalled seeing him once or twice before at suffrage functions. Being one of the few other men present as well as having a proclivity toward brightly colored jackets and bold prints had made him stand out from the crowd.

"Oh, right. You're Callie's friend from the rally in Parliament Square."

"Quite." The two men eyed one another and then Teddy stepped closer to confide, "Actually Callie and I are a great deal more than friends if you take my meaning." He punctuated the statement with a wink.

"I'm afraid I don't. Perhaps you'd care to explain."

A sly smile, a glance from side to side to see if anyone was about to overhear, and then, "We're to be married shortly."

Hadrian suddenly felt as if the paving stones beneath his feet had caved in, sending him hurtling toward oblivion. Callie to be married! Keeping his tone even, he said, "But I've just come from visiting her aunt, who said nothing of a wedding."

Theodore—Teddy—dismissed that statement with a shrug of his narrow shoulders. "We've had an understanding for months now but what with the press dogging her every movement, Callie understandably wanted to hold off on making any announcement. As soon as this whole bloody business with the bill is resolved, though, we'll be proclaiming our happy news to all and sundry. Until then, though mum's the word."

Hadrian felt numb in a way that had nothing to do with the chill seeping through his clothing. Standing there with hands stuffed into his coat pockets if only to keep from wrapping them about Callie's "fiancé's" scrawny neck, he struggled to instead wrap his mind about this latest news. Callie to wed this popinjay of all persons! Then again, perhaps after her past experience with Dandridge's brutish whelp, the effete Theodore held some bizarre appeal.

"In that case, allow me to be the first to wish you happy." Manners dictated that he offer his hand, but as he still didn't entirely trust himself, he held back.

Leaning forward, Theodore slapped Hadrian on the

shoulder as though they were old friends. "Thanks, old man. I do appreciate it. If those pictures you've taken of Callie turn out to be any good, I may just commission you to make our wedding portrait. There'll be a nice tip in it for you, too, no worries there."

"I'm afraid I can't take on any more commission work at this time." Indeed, were he down to his last crust of bread, photographing Callie in bridal white, her arm intertwined with that of her "Teddy" would be beyond him.

Feeling ill, he turned to go. If Callie's fiancé had a mind to stop him a second time, he wouldn't hesitate to knock the stripling to the ground. He must have looked ferocious indeed because this time the other man stepped quickly out of his way. Too bloody bad. Stalking toward the street, it occurred to him that stepping over a prostrate "Teddy" would have been a short-lived satisfaction but satisfaction all the same.

Leaving the Stonevales' residence, Callie was hard-pressed not to skip down the street. The interview had gone even better than she'd dared to hope, setting her up for success on the morrow when she met with Lord Salisbury. Millicent would be ecstatic. Eager to share the good news with her mentor, she almost stopped off at a telegraph office but superstition held her back. Counting her goslings before they were hatched, what better way to tempt Fate than that? Superstition aside, if there was one thing political life had taught her was that there were any number of hidden variables that could surface to alter an outcome in your opponent's favor—or yours. Far more prudent to keep her good news to herself, or at least not transmit it across the Atlantic, until victory was reasonably assured.

Lottie, of course, could be trusted implicitly, although the person with whom she most wanted to share her day was Hadrian. After just one night in his arms, already she was weaving schoolgirl fantasies that had them strolling hand in hand through the years, finally holed up in a cozy library not unlike the one from which she'd just come, pets and knitting and children and grandchildren's photographs ranged about.

But of course, such a lovely fantasy was just that, a flight of fancy, a dream not ever meant to be. Hadrian's coming into her life was a gift, to be sure, but he wasn't nor would he ever be hers to keep. The best she could do was savor whatever time he chose to give her and then when the time came let him go with as much grace as she could muster. Even so, God willing, that time was yet to come. In the interim, she meant to embrace life, and Hadrian, with all the joy she might.

In high spirits, she stepped inside the entrance to her aunt's house to find Teddy waiting in the parlor. Tamping down a disloyal pang of disappointment, she said, "Teddy, what a lovely surprise."

Lottie, smile wooden, rose from her chair by the fire. "I'll leave you two young people alone." On her way out the door, she whispered to Callie, "I'll be in the kitchen with Jenny if you need me."

As soon as they were alone, Teddy turned on her and said, "That attaché case you purchased earlier this month, it was for him, wasn't it?"

Had Hadrian confronted her with such blatant jealousy, she would have been tickled down to her toes. But this was Teddy, a dear friend but only that. Reminding herself she owed him no explanations, she said, "That rather depends on precisely what *him* you've in mind."

"You know well enough. Hadrian St. Claire, you're in love with him, aren't you?"

"What rubbish."

Squaring his narrow shoulders, he took another slug from his sherry glass. Glancing to the near-empty decanter, she wondered just how many he'd had. "That's not an answer."

"No, it isn't, is it?" Chin raised, she held her ground. "I wasn't aware I owed you one."

They stared each other down for a long moment and then all at once he folded like a balloon on the receiving prick of a pin. "Even if he disappeared, you still wouldn't marry me, would you?"

Seeing him so sad-eyed and dejected, she felt her annoyance ebb. "No Teddy, I'm afraid not. Whatever I may have said or done to give you false hope, I am sorry, so very sorry."

And she was sorry, truly she was. Whatever his name, she loved Hadrian with all her being—body, mind, and heart. That he didn't return that love, and likely never would, made her feel for Teddy all the more.

He sank down onto the chair seat. "Not as sorry as I

am, old girl."

She hesitated, wondering if she should lay a hand on his slouched shoulder or if touching him under the circumstances wouldn't just make everything that much worse. Deciding it was likely to be the latter, she held back, waiting. When he still didn't speak, only buried his head in his hands, Callie could bear it no longer.

"Oh, Teddy, we've been friends for years now. Can't we just forget all this nonsense about you wanting to marry me and go back to the way things were?"

Uncovering his face, he looked up at her, eyes streaming. "No, I'm afraid we can't."

This time she did reach for him, she couldn't help it. "Oh, Teddy, why ever not?"

"Because once I tell you what I've just done, you're going to despise me."

"I could never despise you. Whatever you've done, it can't be that bad." Even as she said so, she felt a pang of anxiety.

He looked up at her, eyes bleak. "I shouldn't be so sure of that, old girl, I shouldn't be so sure."

***

Back at his studio, Hadrian could do little more than pace the shop floor. Callie to marry that fop! Try as he might, he couldn't credit it. Yet what right had he to approve or disapprove? None, he knew which only made him feel that bloody much worse. He was the one who'd made a point of saying he wasn't a marrying man, that they had no future together. Certainly she was under no obligation to make an accounting of her personal life to him.

While he hadn't made any promises to her, she hadn't made any to him either. Small wonder the night before she'd accepted his terms so readily. She'd already promised to marry "Teddy" of the limpid eyes and waxed mustache. In that case, she'd like as not considered one night of passion before tying the knot as no more than her due. Or perhaps she was like the other society matrons he'd known over the years who fancied they could have their cake and eat it too — appearing in public with their staid, conventional husbands while keeping a lover on the side. Likely he was the worst of hypocrites, but the thought that Callie might view him as little more than a whore to service her made him sick inside. Rationally he knew he hadn't the right to jealousy, and yet he felt it burning a hole through him all the same.

Would they end up as a cliché, the proverbial two ships passing in the night, their contact limited to him reading newspaper accounts of her or the occasional posted letter? Or perhaps she'd had a change of heart and meant to retire from public life altogether and set up her nursery while there was still time. She'd certainly seemed taken with those rugby-playing lads in the park. Perhaps she would stay in occasional touch, even bring her growing brood into his shop from time to time to have their portraits made. The latter image sufficed to send him searching out the gin, and yet hadn't he been the one to tell her what a wonderful mother she would make?

So why then did he feel so patently empty, so abundantly ill?

The clanging of the shop bell roused him from his moribund musings. He looked up to find Josiah Dandridge hobbling through his front door.

"Where the devil have you been? When I came by earlier, your sign was turned over to CLOSED."

"Your snitch must be falling down on the job, Dandridge, otherwise you'd know, wouldn't you? It's just as well you're here—you've saved me a trip."

"You've the photograph, then?"

During the long walk back from Gavin's to clear his head, he'd decided to swallow his pride and accept the money from Rourke as a loan. No doubt it would take him years, perhaps the better part of his lifetime, to repay his friend, but at least he would be off the hook with Dandridge so far as money went.

"There won't be any photograph, not now and not ever. I'm calling off our arrangement. I'll need a few more days, but I mean to repay you the money in full. Consider us finished."

He'd expected Dandridge to be furious but instead the older man tossed back his head and laughed. "Oh, I don't think so, Mr. St. Claire . . . or should I say, 'Mr. Stone'?"

Hadrian froze. Like the photographs drawing in his darkroom, he felt raw, naked, *exposed*. He raked a hand through his hair, the fingers cold as snow against his scalp.

Dandridge's bloodless thin lips twisted into a farce of a

smile. "Does it surprise you that I know your true name? Do not, young man, imagine for a moment that there is so much as a single day of your history I do not know in full. I know not only who you are but what you are. Fail me and I will make certain all of London knows it, too. I very much doubt the son of an East End whore, a former pickpocket, would find many well-heeled patrons willing to let him photograph their wives and daughters."

Exposure, ever the worst of his adult fears, and yet now that he found himself facing it, Hadrian felt strangely . . . calm. Shrugging, he said, "I'll take my chances."

Dandridge scowled. "Don't be a fool. Play the game out and you can still have a bright future ahead of you. If you don't fancy staying on in London, there's no reason not to go to Paris, set up there. Now be a good lad and get me that photograph."

Be a good lad, a good lad, a good lad . . .

Without warning, the voices from the past came back to Hadrian with crystalline clarity.

"Keep away from me mum, you bastard."

"Sir, J.D., please, I'm begging you. He's only a boy."

Only a boy, a boy, a boy . . .

Like the slides projected from a Magic Lantern, the bits of fragmented memory rushed back—Mum cowering in the corner, the dark bruise blighting the smooth skin of her cheek; his beloved box camera, the one he'd built from scratch from the scraps he'd scrounged along the river bank, reduced to bits of broken wood and shattered glass; the soul-sinking feeling of being pushed down onto that rocking mattress, finger tracing the rose and ivy counterpane pattern while he searched for places to hide out in his mind.

Josiah Dandridge. The bad man he'd grown up knowing only as 'J.D.,' the well-heeled regular at Madame Dottie's who'd taken a fancy to his mum. The same man who'd beaten her and then smashed his camera when he'd tried to use it to give evidence against him. The pederast who'd raped him of his innocence, showing him just how very bad a bad man might be.

He swung around to the MP, now shrunken with age, and said, "My God, it's you. It's been you all along. You're J.D. No wonder you know my name, you bastard!"

He vaulted across the room, grabbed Dandridge by the collar and, plowed his fist into that patrician nose, more than a decade of fury fueling the blow. Blood spurted, a near perfect arc. Hadrian let go. Dandridge folded to the floor, no longer the villain of his youth but an arthritic old man near to helpless without his cane.

Cupping his bleeding nose, Dandridge looked up to where Hadrian towered over him, arms folded and legs spread. "You've no proof, Stone. It's my word against yours, the word of a whore's by-blow against the distinguished record of a respected Member of Parliament, a pillar of society. No one will ever believe you."

For the span of several heartbeats, Hadrian gave serious thought to killing the cock-sucking bastard. Were it not for Callie, he well might have. But as much as he'd enjoyed making the MP bleed, finishing him off wouldn't help Callie or him, either. He'd be hauled off to jail, maybe worse. How then could he hope to protect her?

Reining in his temper, he cracked his knuckles for effect and said, "I wouldn't be so certain of that, Dandridge. I may just have more proof than you credit. And know this, if you ever try to harm Caledonia Rivers in any way ever again, I will expend my last breath on Earth ensuring that you live to regret it as will your dear son, Gerald." The MP blanched and pressing his advantage, Hadrian continued, "Ah yes, I know all about the broken off engagement. It would seem that brutishness runs in your bloodline."

Taking advantage of Dandridge's stunned state, he reached down, hooked a hand about the old man's thin arm, and hauled him to his feet. Dragging him across the shop floor much as he'd been dragged all those years before, he opened the door and shoved him out onto the sidewalk, tossing his cane after him.

"Stay away from Caledonia Rivers, Dandridge. Stay far, far away."

He slammed the shop door amidst the clanging of the bell. Bolting it behind him, he felt as if he were shutting the door on the past with all its pain. Though the future might be far from secure, he no longer need be haunted by his history. After fifteen years of hiding, Harry Stone was finally free to live his life. Smiling to himself, he allowed that no matter what else befell him, that was a very good feeling indeed.

CHAPTER FIFTEEN

> "I speak only for myself individually who are of
> the opinion that women have not the voice they ought
> to have in the selection of the representatives of the
> kingdom; but I warn you that there is no question at
> present which divides parties more completely, and
> I am not certain even whether I express the opinion
> of the majority of my own party . . ."
> —ROBERT GASCOYNE-CECIL, Marquis of
> Salisbury, Address to the Primrose League, 1896

For Callie, the meeting with Lord Salisbury had been the cause of a great many sleepless nights. Now that the day was upon her, she found herself quite simply glad to get the thing behind her. As she followed Salisbury's personal secretary up the grand double staircase of the Foreign Office and then leftward down the first-floor corridor with its barrel-vaulted ceiling and stenciled walls, her thoughts drifted back to Teddy's revelation of the night before. At first she'd been furious with him for so egregiously misrepresenting their relationship, but anger had been quick to ebb, particularly when he'd tearfully confessed that like his idol, Oscar Wilde, he was guilty of "the love that dare not speak its name." He'd fought against his true nature all his life and in desperation thought that marriage to a woman who was also a dear friend might serve as the cure. Looking back, she suspected she'd always known his devotion didn't go deeper than friendship, and yet he'd been a good friend to her in so many ways. As eager as she'd been to seek out Hadrian and set the misunderstanding to rights, she couldn't very well toss Teddy out the door in such a state. They'd sat up talking late into the evening, and for the second day in a row, she'd missed supper. At this rate, she'd be winnowed down to a sylph in no time at all.

Yet despite precious little food or sleep, barring the errant abdominal butterfly, she felt calm as she walked down the drafty hallway leading to the PM's cabinet room. Footfalls ringing off the marble floor, she considered the reason for her newfound sense of peace. The answer came down to one word, or rather one person—Hadrian. Before him, the suffragette cause had served as her *raison d'être*; she had quite literally eaten, drunk, and slept solely in its service.

In the short span of three weeks, all that had changed. Having something, or rather someone, in her life not involved in politics had afforded her a perspective, a *balance*, that only in retrospect did she own had been sorely lacking for the past decade, perhaps the whole of her duty-driven adult years. Because of Hadrian, she'd come to see there was a great deal more to the art of living than the tangible measures she'd used to gauge success. While she still remained wholly committed to doing her utmost to sway Salisbury to their side, if today's meeting failed to yield that sought-after outcome, at least she and the other delegates had put forth their very best effort. That would be some satisfaction at least.

His secretary's knock yielded the anticipated call to enter and Callie caught herself holding her breath. No doubt in deference to his overriding interest in foreign affairs, notably British possessions in Africa, Salisbury had broken with tradition by opting to run his government from the Foreign Office, not 10 Downing Street. That being the case, certain of his remarks in the recent past could be construed as support, albeit tepid, for female suffrage. But then again, he was a politician, after all.

The door opened on a large, high-ceilinged room stenciled in olive and gold, with red and gold borders.

Lord Salisbury rose from behind the polished mahogany desk. Of late middle years, he had a heavy face framed by a fringe of white hair that put Callie in mind of a monk's tonsure and a closely clipped salt-and-pepper beard. The deep-set eyes studying her looked not so much unfriendly as fatigued but then he had combined his role of PM with that of Foreign Secretary, a demanding double job. Slope-shouldered and stout, he nonetheless cut an imposing figure as he crossed to the front of the desk and came toward her, gesturing her to one of the leather-upholstered chairs.

"Pray be seated, Miss Rivers. My esteemed colleague, Lord Stonevale speaks highly of you. Given all I have heard to recommend you, I am please to be able to meet with you at last."

Taking her seat, Callie inclined her head in acknowledgement of the compliment. "You are most gracious, milord, to consent to meet with me."

He raised a dismissive hand to indicate that his presumed graciousness was yet a subject of some debate. "Yet you must appreciate the difficulty of my position, Miss Rivers. As prime minister, I cannot risk my Party's majority for the sake of a cause that, by your own account, some British women themselves do not embrace."

The past decade on the periphery of the political arena had taught Callie that there was a time to smile and nod and a time to take bold if calculated action. Judging this to be one of the latter occasions, she drew a deep breath and said, "With all due respect, my lord, I rather think your government's primary directive is to safeguard and uphold the rights of all British subjects, regardless of party affiliation, gender . . . or circumstance," she added, thinking of women such as Iris Brown for whom gender was but one obstacle to be surmounted in the struggle for a better life for themselves and their children.

Salisbury shook his grizzled head. "Yet I hear reports of women embarking on hunger strikes, smashing shop windows, in some cases going so far as to chain themselves to fence posts so that police with hacksaws must be called in to remove them bodily. This government cannot endorse violence, Miss Rivers. We cannot and will not no matter how worthy the cause."

In addition to foreign-policy matters, Salisbury had made his mark by bringing unity to the various fractious Conservative party factions. Regardless of any personal sympathy he felt toward female suffrage, he was not likely to champion a cause that might threaten that hard-won unity.

He was alluding to Emmeline Pankhurst, who along with her husband, Richard, had formed the militant Women's Franchise League the year before. Based out of Manchester, the League regularly made headlines in the scandal sheets.

Knowing her response could well determine the outcome of the interview, Callie took care in framing her reply. "Extremes are to be found among the ranks of any movement as well you know, my lord, and sadly female suffrage is no exception. That said, please allow me to assure you that violence in any form has never and will never be countenanced by the leadership of our organization." It was fair near the same promise she'd made to Stonevale the day before, and one she meant to do everything in her power to keep.

Bracing stubby fingers on the desk's highly polished surface, he said, "As I'm sure you are aware, there is considerable concern among my colleagues, Liberal as well as Conservative, that enfranchising females on a universal basis could result in women voters outnumbering men. I will tell you plainly that amending the language of your current bill to limit female suffrage to older adult women who own property in their own right or through their husbands would greatly increase its chances of passage." He raised one bushy eyebrow and regarded her, waiting.

Callie hesitated. Tying suffrage to property ownership had always been a dodgy business, an issue on which the NUWSS member organizations continued to be split. Although she had always believed wholeheartedly in universal suffrage for both sexes, a few weeks before she might have been willing to settle on the basis that the proverbial half-loaf was better than none.

But thinking again of Iris Brown and her fellow match-factory workers gave her pause. Did Iris really have any less of a right to express herself politically than Callie did simply because she owned only the clothes on her back? And what of Iris's daughter, June? What chance would that little girl and the many others like her have for a better future if deprived of their voter's voice? Could Callie work to procure the vote for privileged women while consigning poor women to continued enslavement?

After a moment's pause, she said, "I cannot in good conscience attach such caveats myself. Until female suffrage is placed on the same basis as that afforded to men, there can be no true justice, only varying degrees of tyranny."

"You are frank, Miss Rivers, an estimable quality that precious few leaders of our modern age exhibit. If you can muster sufficient support to see your suffrage bill through to a vote, I will promise you this much, I will do nothing to oppose it."

That evening, Hadrian closed the door on his darkroom where he'd left the last of the photographs of Callie drying on the line. Once she'd let down her guard, Callie had made a lovely and arresting subject. Callie, eyes flashing fire and chin held aloft, giving him his comeuppance that first day in his studio when he'd deliberately baited her. Callie standing alone in the park, face wistful in profile as she looked out onto the boys playing ball. He had to marvel that what had started out as a ruse had resulted in a first-rate photographic portrait study, worthy of any exhibition-hall showing. Most savory were the myriad more-personal images he held onto if only in his mind's eye—Callie, bold and beautiful, standing on her soapbox outside the match-factory gates, Callie running hell for leather alongside him as they raced through the warren of East End streets, and last but hardly least, Callie looking up at him from his pillow, eyes wide and face stark with wonder, just after she'd come.

Stripping off his apron, he looked toward the stairs leading up to his flat. He would wash up and then set out for her aunt's house. By the time he got there, she should be home or at least on her way. No point in putting off the inevitable confession any longer. Despite his bluff, he really had no proof of Dandridge's past misdeeds. And after last night, satisfying though it had been, the MP wouldn't rest until he saw Hadrian ruined. Soon Callie, along with everyone else in London, would know the sordid truth of just who and what he really was. The very least he could do to atone for his sins, past and present, was to tell her himself before she found out elsewhere.

He would have sought her out earlier only he remembered that today was the much anticipated meeting with the prime minister, the culmination to all her sacrifice and hard work. He hadn't wanted to upset her beforehand and telling her just how he'd colluded with Dandridge to dupe and destroy her would most certainly do that. His confession made, he would say goodbye and walk out of her life for good. Surely by then she would be only too glad to see the back of him, especially as she was on the brink of starting a new life with another man.

Yet those soulful eyes of hers would haunt his dreams for a long time, quite possibly forever, because . . . well, because he was in love with her.

Ironically it was his encounter with the fiancé that finally had freed him to own the truth of his feelings. Ordinarily he didn't deal in absolutes, moral or otherwise. To say "I love you" was lunacy pure and simple; add "forever" to the mix and you bloody well deserved whatever slice of hell fate served up. Or so he'd thought before . . . Callie. Lost to him though she was, he couldn't help his feelings any more than he could help the color of his eyes or the breadth of his shoulders.

A tail swishing his legs had him looking down to where his cat followed him across the room. Dinah's green-eyed gaze met his and she opened her mouth on a loud meow, reminding him that though his life might be falling to bits, there was still dinner to be dished up. Reaching down to scratch beneath her chin, he said, "Well, Dinah, what say you to Paris next? Or maybe it's Venice you fancy, eh?"

From the top of the stairs, a female voice called down, "I'm rather fond of London myself."

Callie? Heart pounding, he bounded up the stairs two at a time to the half-cocked flat door. He entered, the room bathed in the soft glow of candlelight.

Wearing his silk dressing gown, dark hair flowing about her shoulders, Callie stepped out from the shadows. "Not planning on going on holiday anytime soon, are you, Mr. St. Claire?"

His heart stopped for what felt like a full moment, but her teasing smile had it resuming beating. She hadn't found him out, not yet at any rate; otherwise she'd never have come, certainly not like this.

Closing the distance between them, she wrapped urgent arms about his neck and pulled him down for a passionate kiss that sent the room about them spinning. Against his lips she said, "Can I possibly tempt you to join me in an indoor picnic, Mr. St. Claire?" He looked over her shoulder to where a bucket of iced champagne and a wicker hamper set out on the table along with the bank of candles, all the accoutrements of seduction.

Oh, she could tempt him, all right, in more ways than he cared to admit. He was already hard, a condition that couldn't possibly be lost on her given how she pressed against him. Yet remembering "Teddy's" self-satisfied smirk, he held back at the door and said, "That rather depends on what your fiancé would say if he knew you were here?"

He'd expected to startle her but instead she only sent him a soft smile and shook her head. "As I don't have a fiancé, only a dear but rather desperate friend, I'm much more concerned with what you've to say on the subject." She slid warm hands up his arms, palms coming to rest on his biceps.

She quickly explained the circumstances surrounding her friend's ruse. Embarrassed to have been so easily duped, so quick to think the worst of her when it was he who was the liar among them, Hadrian could only shake his head. "I'm a rum fool. I should have known."

"Were you terribly jealous?" She tilted her face up to his. Eyes dark with mischief and mouth moist, she looked every bit the part of the tantalizing seductress.

"Terribly." Though he'd told himself upon entering he'd stay stoic and strong, weak man that he was, he reached for her. Laying hands on the slippery silk at her waist, he pulled her flush against him, his erection pressing into the soft flesh of her belly.

"If I were a better person, I shouldn't be glad of that, but I am glad. So very glad."

Reaching between them, her hands found his trouser waist. Any trace of the previous night's reticence was gone as she slipped eager fingers inside and tugged his shirttail free.

"Callie, wait." He took hold of her wrists, bringing her hands down to her sides. Letting her go, he looked into her eyes and asked, "Do you remember the other night when I told you I'd changed my name once I got back to London?"

"Uh-huh." She nodded, but her nimble fingers were already working on undoing the buttons fronting his shirt, her attention riveted on the chest she was rapidly laying bare.

"Callie, hold. I never got 'round to telling you why."

"It doesn't matter. It's in the past. You don't have to explain yourself to me." She punctuated each sentence with a shake of her head, making him wonder which of them she was working hardest to convince.

"But it does matter, Callie. I thought a new name would mean a fresh start, a new life with a clean slate." Clean. God, he'd wanted so much to be that.

He started to say more when she opened his shirt and found his nipples with her mouth. "Hmm," she murmured against his sensitized flesh and try as he might to do the right and noble thing, thinking past the pull of those lips, that laving tongue, was quite simply beyond him.

She took her mouth away to smile up at him, her chin resting on the broad plain of his breastbone. "We've plenty of time later for talking. For now, take me to bed or better yet . . ."

Raining kisses over his mouth, his jaw, his neck, she backed them across the room until he bumped against the wall. She reached down between them to the buttons fronting his trousers. Without looking down, he knew that the telltale ridge of his erection would be straining those buttons to the point of popping. Before they might, she had them undone and open. Her hand closed about his cock. "You're so beautiful here and everywhere else," she whispered, lifting her face to kiss him even as she stroked the moistened tip with her thumb. "Does this feel all right?"

Biting back a groan, he managed, "It feels better than all right."

"Am I doing it properly, then?" Again, that devilish smile that told him she knew exactly what she was doing to him.

In the throes of his need, he almost laughed. "Yes, though the word 'proper' doesn't exactly come to mind. Exquisite, more like, though if you keep stimulating me as you're doing, I'm going to lose control. I'm going to climax."

"That's the point, isn't it?"

"Not yet. Not if I'm to please you, too."

"But you are pleasing me. It pleases me just to look at you, to touch you like this. I've thought of little else since leaving you the day before. I could scarcely attend to what Salisbury was saying, all I could think was that after our session, I could come back here and be with you."

She released him but only for the handful of seconds it took for her to slide down to the floor to her knees. Hadrian held in his breath as she guided him inside the warm, wet cavern of her mouth.

Looking down onto the crown of her dark head, her hair sweeping over one shoulder to expose the creamy arc of jaw and throat, he thought he might come then and there. "Callie, you don't have to do this."

She paused to look up at him with lazy-lidded eyes. "I

know I don't *have* to, but I want to. Is that so very difficult for you to believe?"

He started to answer, but her lips slipped over him again and he couldn't recall whether his reply was no—or yes.

"Hmm, you taste nice, delicious even." Her eyes drifted closed again, long lashes brushing the tops of her cheekbones.

She was awkward at first, finding her bearings, finding her way. Aside from offering an encouragement or two, Hadrian declined to direct. Instead he braced his back against the wall and gathered a handful of her hair to keep it from falling in her eyes. In the throes of his torture, it occurred to him that though he'd performed sexual acts with long Latin names, done things that in retrospect shocked even him, never before had he taken the care to hold a woman's hair back from her face. But then the lovely woman kneeling at his feet wasn't just anyone. She was Callie, his heart's desire. The woman he loved.

On the brink of climax, he knew he couldn't bear it any longer. Callie must have read his mind. She stood and reached into his robe pocket for one of the prophylactics he kept at his bedside. Watching her roll it over him, her beautiful mouth pursed in concentration, the peaks of her perfect breasts standing out against the silk of his robe, he couldn't wait to much as a moment more.

He bent down and reached for her. "Wrap your legs about my waist and hold on."

She obeyed, robe falling open to reveal all that lovely opalescent flesh, full breasts and full thighs crowned with the triangle of dark curls damp with dew. "So beautiful," he moaned, lifting her high against him so that they were on eye-level, the points of her nipples chafing his chest, his penis pulsing against her dewy pink woman's flesh.

Reaching down between them, he tested her with his fingers. She was ready for him, more than ready, as he'd known she would be. Back braced against the wall, and hands cradling the lush swell of her bottom, he entered her in one smooth, clean thrust.

Hands atop his shoulders, she tossed her head back, all that lovely long hair trailing down her back and teasing the top of his arm. "Hadrian, Harry, I don't care what your name is, I love you. *I love you!*" Squeezing her thighs tighter still, she rocked forward, any trace of shyness washed away in the lava-like heat sweeping over them both.

It was too perfect, *she* was too perfect. She met him thrust for thrust, and though Hadrian had been with more women than he cared to count, never before had he moved with anyone with such perfect unspoken understanding, such peerless rhythm. Lost in a sea of sensation, he could scarcely credit the murmured endearments slipping forth from his mouth—"so beautiful," and "God, you feel so good around me," and "Callie, I never knew—" Suddenly he did something he'd never done before; something he'd thought himself incapable of doing. He stared into her eyes and concentrated not on him or on her but on *them*, how good they were together.

"*Oh, God, Callie!*" He came so fast and so hard it took

several minutes for him to realize that the metal coating the inside his mouth was blood.

They lay spoon-style in Hadrian's bed, the wrinkled sheet loosely tossed over them. Reaching over to Hadrian's side of the bed, Callie used the edge of her thumb to blot the blood from his lip. "Better?"

"Much." He lifted her hand to his mouth and pressed a kiss into the palm before returning it to rest on his chest, the left side just over his heart. Her other hand was occupied with tracing invisible patterns on the curve of his bicep. Even after they'd collapsed together into an exhausted heap, she couldn't seem to get enough of him.

She lifted her head off the pillow; she had to be sure. "Do you get tired of me touching you?"

His face half-hidden by the pillow, she caught the curve of his sleepy smile. "I could never tire of your touch, not in a million years."

Not exactly *I love you*, but a million years seemed a promising place from which to start building the foundation for it. "Good, I'm glad because I'll never tire of touching you."

Smiling, she pressed a kiss to the back of his neck and snuggled closer, satisfied for the moment at least. There'd been no more talk of love, a sentiment he'd yet to return in words at least, and yet wishful thinking though it might be, she fancied she'd felt it pouring forth from him in abundance—

the melting gazes he'd sent her way ever since she'd met him at the door, the tenderness of his touch when he'd parted her thighs and slid a testing finger inside, the way he'd called out the shortened version of her name, Callie, again and again just before he came.

In the light of the guttering candles his skin glowed like polished marble, his bones closer to the surface than hers were, his body pared down to its core essence. With no will or need to resist, she ran her hand over the smooth plane of his back, tracing the "V" his shoulders joined to make, reveling in the ripple of warm, taut flesh beneath her fingertips, the dance of light and shadow on the sculpted planes. Brushing a kiss over his shoulder, she followed the downward line of his spine to the sheet riding his waist. Beneath it were, she knew, firm buttocks and thighs and calves muscled as those of any athlete. There wasn't so much as a pound of extra flesh on him, at least not anywhere she could see, and yet she couldn't say he was skinny. Just right or rather better than all right. Perfect in the way that Michael Angelo's David could be said to be perfect.

Thinking her thoughts aloud, she said, "You're so beautiful. I could look at you all day."

Glancing back at her over the landscape of one broad shoulder, he smiled his lazy smile, the one that had used to irritate her—only now it didn't anymore. "Only look?"

That smile, and the reflection of it in his eyes, had her slipping a hand around the front of him and beneath the sheet. As she'd suspected, he was rock hard and velvet smooth and more than ready for her.

Feeling herself growing wet in response, she ventured, "I've heard that a woman can take a man inside her in any of three places. It occurs to me we've tried all but one."

Holding her hand in place, he turned on his side to face her. "Callie, what are you saying?"

Fighting back the old shyness, she forced her gaze to his. "The other night when you entered me back there with . . . with your finger, I liked it. I don't know why only that I did."

He glanced downward to where, beneath the covers, she'd curved her fingers about the pulse point of his erection. "My penis is a great deal thicker than a finger, Callie. Even with cream to ease you, I won't be able to keep from hurting you, not entirely."

He looked so serious, so altogether concerned that she reached up and smoothed the frown line between his eyes with the pad of her thumb. "I don't care. I want to be with you, Hadrian, in every way I can."

The drawer that housed the tin of French letters was also home to a jar of lubricating cream. Reaching across her, Hadrian produced the vessel of cobalt-colored glass and unscrewed the lid.

Sinking two fingers into the cream, he rolled her onto her side. "Let's begin with a massage, shall we?" Settling his hands on her shoulders, he started working the juncture of her neck. "Do you know I love everything about your body, from your glorious breasts to your tight little tail?" His stroking hands slid down the curve of her spine to her buttocks, which he began to knead. Callie tensed. As if reading her thoughts, he said, "You have a beautiful ass, Callie, voluptuous and full. I'm very much looking forward to fucking you there. Do you know why?"

Turning her head to look back at him, she said, "Because you fancy women with big bottoms?"

"You're only partly correct—I do fancy you. As for your ass, there's this delightful little indentation just here"—he traced the curve where her left buttock met her upper thigh—"that I'm particularly enamored of." He ran his finger down the jointure between her buttocks, using the tip of his finger to gently scratch against the puckered flesh.

Callie shivered.

He touched her again. "Do you know that when I touch you there, just there, the little curve trembles?"

No surprise that as her entire body trembled when he touched her anywhere but especially here.

"So beautiful." He pulled her buttocks apart. Cool air kissed her backside, sensitized from the cream. Then, dear God, he was blowing his breath on her. She shivered, whole body on tenterhooks, poised for the moment when he would enter her, desire pounding through her, making her forget about being sore or even recently sated.

She was so relaxed she barely felt his finger slip inside her. Instinctively, she crawled onto her knees, pushing against the invading digit, wishing that they might be longer still, thicker still, wanting to take them all the way inside her if only she might.

Hadrian's breath was hot on her back. "More?" He'd curved his arm about her middle and pulled her against him so that she could feel the heat and strength of his erection pulsing against her.

"More," she breathed and lest he doubt her, she rolled her hips backward, driving his finger as deep as it would go.

"Two fingers it is?"

A slight blunt pain that wasn't quite pain and then oh, lovely, he had a second finger inside her and along with the other was moving it scissor fashion. There was a moment's pause, during which he drew his arm away from her waist and she wriggled in helplessness, a fish caught on a snare— and yet her only thought was how to get closer rather than escape. Then cool prickly heat, more this time. He must have used his free hand to reach for the jar because there was more of that lovely cream now, and he was using his free hand to slather it between her damp buttocks.

He bit down on the edge of her ear, not hard enough to hurt, but it got her attention. "Shall I stop now?"

To have her prize snatched away after she'd come this far didn't bear consideration. A bead of perspiration struck the side of her neck, and she arched back, grabbing firmer hold of the metal bedposts. "No . . . oh, no, please."

He took hold of her hips and entered her, not in one clean thrust as he had before but slowly, carefully, inch by gloriously inch. He'd been right in cautioning it would hurt but somehow the blunt pain brought other senses to life as well: the smell of their commingled sweat; the bleached bed linens pleasantly stiff beneath her knees; the slapping of flesh striking flesh. And beyond everything was the incredible first time feeling that she was beautiful, every part of her.

"God, you're lovely," he breathed into the shell of her ear. He reached a hand around to the front of her and fondled her breasts, milking their fullness, pulling on her aching nipples, and then rolling them between his thumb and forefinger until she thought she would scream from the pleasure of it.

"Oh, Hadrian, I—"

His hand left her breasts and slid down the front of her. Fingers, again, two of them, found their way inside her there too, sliding inside the rawness, at once easing her and bringing her to life.

Doubly impaled, joined to him at front and back, her senses screamed for release and yet she could do little more than moan little snatches of phrases—"please" and "dear Lord"—but mostly his name, or at least the one she knew him by, "Hadrian," again and again, her pleasure, her want building with each breathless utterance.

He bent his head and gently bit the back of her neck. "Scream if you like. There's no one to hear you but me."

CHAPTER SIXTEEN

"The wounds I might have healed, the human sorrow and smart,
    And yet it was never in my soul to play so ill a part,
    But evil is wrought by want of thought, as well as by want of heart."
                    —MARY LEE, *South Australia Register*,
                                April 2, 1890

Eventually hunger drove them to rummage the contents of the food hamper. Downstairs the blinds were drawn, the shop's sign turned over to CLOSED. Confident in their concealment from the outside world, Callie roamed the studio in lace-edged camisole and knee-length drawers, sipping champagne from a jelly jar while perusing works she must have seen any number of times only now viewed with fresh eyes. Eyes wide open to the possibility of passion.

"Miss Rivers has anyone told you of late you look a picture."

She turned away from the platinum print she'd been admiring, the one of the nude, to see a warm-eyed and smiling Hadrian coming down the stairs with a plate of bread, fruit, and cheese. Her mouth watered but not due to the food. Hair mussed and wearing only the braces and wool trousers he'd hastily pulled on, he was a glorious six feet, four inches of near-naked male; and, for the time being, he was entirely hers.

Emboldened, she stepped forward. "In that case, take my picture."

"I've done little else but take pictures of you these past weeks."

Holding her glass up to his lips, she said, "Not that sort of picture but the other kind, like this one, the reclining nude."

He choked on the sip of champagne he'd just taken. Swiping a hand across his chin, he said, "You want me to photograph you in the nude?"

Oh God, just when she thought she was immune to humiliation, this sort at least, the old shame rose up, keener now than ever before because this time it wasn't only pride at stake, but the whole of her heart. For the first time in her life she was well and truly in love, in love with Hadrian. Though he might not love her back, not yet at any rate, the thought that she wasn't beautiful to him, that he'd made love to her out of boredom—or worse yet, charity—was altogether too bitter to bear.

Crossing her arms over the bosom she'd forgotten to

hide, she backed away, searching for a graceful means of retreat. "Never mind, it was a foolish fancy I had that's passed. Please, forget I mentioned it."

He set the plate down on the table and crossed the room toward her. Laying warm hands atop her shoulders, he looked into her eyes and said, "I'm not about to forget and it wasn't foolish. I only want to know why the change of heart when until now I've counted myself fortunate to coax you into posing without your glasses."

"Because . . ." She shot a furtive glance to the photograph. All that perfection—how had she hoped to possibly compete? Yet it wasn't meant to be so much a competition as a validation that she was all right as she was; desirable, yes, but beyond that, worthy of being loved. "I know I'm not as young as she is nor nearly so lean and lovely but being with you tonight and the time before, you've made me feel . . ." The rest of her hastily assembled speech died in her throat, and she would have given the world to turn away only Hadrian wouldn't let her.

He caught her face between his hands, turned it up until there was nowhere for her to look but at him. "Oh, Callie, my sweet foolish girl, surely you must know you're myriad times more beautiful to me than that slip of a girl could ever be? You have a bosom most courtesans would envy as well as legs worthy of a music-hall dancer. Only, Callie . . . why now?"

"I suppose I'd like something by which to remember us. A memento I can take out of the bottom of my drawer years from now when I'm old and gray and truly on the shelf."

When you've moved on, long gone from my life.

"Even gray-headed, you'll always be beautiful."

"You don't have to say such things to spare my feelings."

He answered with a fierce shake of his head. "Not to spare your feelings, but because it's the truth, every bloody word." He drew her to him, shaping her body with his big, sensitive hands. "God, Callie, if only you knew how true."

She reached up and stroked a hand down the side of his face, a measure of the new confidence returning. "In that case, take my picture, Hadrian. Make it as a remembrance of our beautiful night together, of how it was between us before the world and all its folly had the chance to intrude."

"You're sure?"

She didn't hesitate. "I trust you, Hadrian."

He swallowed hard, a long ripple traveling the length of his corded throat. "In that case, I would be honored to photograph you."

<hr />

I trust you, Hadrian. The blind faith shining forth from Callie's eyes had been like a razor slashing at his heart, for wasn't it only the day before that he'd finally broken it off with Dandridge? Knowing this would be his parting gift to her, Hadrian was determined that everything should be perfect, down to the very last detail. He carried his best camera and tripod upstairs to the divan, and then spent some time arranging the scene, positioning pillows and draping fringed silk scarves, until it finally struck him that a simple backdrop would be best. One of the cardinal rules of photographic portraiture was that any props and scenery should enhance the subject, not distract from it. Looking as she did now, so lovely and so free made his heart both ache with longing for what could never be and swell with pride at how very far she'd come in just these few short weeks.

Even so, he would keep the lighting subtle, soft, both to set her at ease and to show off to best advantage her lush curves and satiny skin. Accordingly, he went about the room turning up some lamps and turning down others, suffusing the chamber in a warm, smoky glow, then dragged over a pier glass and positioned it to the side to maximize the reflected light, all the while aware of Callie looking on.

Once he was satisfied, he gestured for her to take her place on the divan. "Position yourself as feels natural to you."

She came forward and sat, lifting her long legs onto the seat. Stretching out on her side, she paused and then draped one elegant arm over the furniture's serpentine back. Once she'd settled in, he made a few minor adjustments— smoothing back a stray strand of hair, draping a colored scarf on the furniture back to achieve greater subject contrast, slipping one silky camisole strap down off her shoulder to expose that perfect curve of shoulder and high-sloped breast. Hating to leave her, he backed up to where the camera set on the stand, framing the shot in his mind's eye as well as between his open hands.

She turned luminous eyes on to his face. "Is it all right?"

He smiled at that. "I'd say it's a good deal better than all right. I wish you might see yourself now as I see you. You are beyond beautiful."

Rather than argue as she would have done just a day or so ago, she smiled at him, a smile of such unadulterated brilliance that he felt warmed by it, not only his heart but the whole of him. Eyes alight and skin aglow, she met his gaze, the camera lens, without a hint of anxiety or hesitation. And then she did what he wouldn't have expected her to do and would never have dared request. She tented her left leg out from her body ever so slightly and slid a finger inside the open slit of her drawers.

Slipping beneath the camera cloth, Hadrian felt as if the heat in the room had spiked several notches. Mouth dry and brow damp, he called out, "Are you sure?"

Rather than answer, she began moving that finger slowly in and out, back and forth. Even peering through the camera's viewing screen and positioned several paces away, he couldn't possibly miss how slick she was, how ready, and how utterly sure of exactly what she was doing.

Feeling the ache of desire weighing between his thighs, Hadrian cried out, "Hold," and yanked the striking cord down.

Their idyll, no matter how sweet, couldn't go on indefinitely. When upon waking late the next morning Callie regretfully told him she had to get back—the march on Parliament overlapping with the suffrage bill's final reading the day after—Hadrian knew he couldn't put off telling her any longer. Coward though he was, he waited until they were in the hansom headed for Half Moon Street before breaking the news.

For the sake of discretion, they sat in opposing seats though the urge to touch was strong enough to have them reaching across. Callie, gaze soft, gave his gloved hand a squeeze. "It was a good of you to see me home, but you needn't have, you know."

Swallowing against the tightness at the back of his throat, he said, "Callie, I've something to tell you, something I should have told you days ago, weeks actually, only I couldn't find the proper time or the words."

His serious tone had her sobering. Looking up from their joined hands, she said, "Very well, then. I'm listening."

He hesitated. Just how to tell the woman you loved that you'd accepted money to destroy her? "Why didn't you ever tell me the man you were engaged to marry was Gerald Dandridge?" It was an inelegant beginning but a beginning all the same.

She hesitated. Taking back her hand, she reached down to pull up the carriage blanket slipping off her knees. "No particular reason. I suppose I never gave his family all that much thought."

"Unfortunately they have given you considerable thought, or at least his father, Josiah has."

Frowning, she waved a dismissive hand in the air. "Josiah

Dandridge is nothing but an old starched shirt, a Conservative from the old school who thinks women, like children, ought to be seen and not heard. The word is that his health is poor, that he means to retire before much longer and cede his seat to Gerald not that the latter will necessarily be any great improvement. At any rate, he has been one of the more vocal of our opponents, but I doubt there's anything personal behind it."

"On the contrary, it is personal, Callie, personal indeed. You might even say it's a vendetta."

That got her attention. "Hadrian, what are you saying?"

Knowing the moment of truth was upon him, he steeled himself to say, "Josiah Dandridge paid a call to my shop three weeks ago just a few hours after you and I met by chance in Parliament Square." He reached across the seat, took both her hands in his. "Callie, you have to understand I was desperate, beyond desperate really. I'd got myself into a rare scrape, ran up a large debt at a gaming hell in Bow. The proprietor sent on two of his thugs to collect, but I hadn't anywhere close to the tin to repay him. I managed to wrangle another week's grace period but after that they'd be coming for me and when they did, they'd collect their debt in blood. I was at my wit's end as to what to do when Dandridge presented himself."

She pulled her hands free of his and sat back against the seat. "What's any of this to do with me?"

"Dandridge hates you Callie, personally because you cried off the engagement to his son and politically because of the power you wield in bringing the suffrage issue to the forefront of the public's conscience. He means to see you ruined, shamed to the point that you'd have no choice but to retire from public life entirely. But to create scandal on that par, he needs evidence, tangible evidence he can take to the Fleet Street press."

"Such as a photograph, you mean?" She stared at him, expression not so much horrified as frozen . . . blank.

He nodded. "He offered me five thousand pounds, a small fortune. To earn it, all I need do was deliver a compromising photograph of you into his hands before your bill came before Parliament a final time. He paid me money to ruin you, vanquish you as he likes to call it, and until a few days ago I'd agreed to go along with his scheme."

Turning away from him, she flung open the carriage window. Icy air rushed the interior. She stuck her head out the opening and rapped sharp knuckles against the coach's lacquered side. "Driver, pull over just there. Stop, I say. Stop!"

"But I can't just yet, miss," he called down from the box. "We're in terrible traffic, mind you."

"Just do as I say." She pulled back inside and, a hand braced to the leather-covered wall, started to rise.

Alarmed that she meant to leap out while they were moving, Hadrian reached and grabbed hold of her wrist. Pulling her back down into her seat, he said, "Callie, what the devil do you think you're about?"

She jerked free as though his touch had scorched her. "Don't you dare lay a hand on me. Not now and not ever again."

The coach lurched to a halt on the side of the road. Casting a quick look out the window, Hadrian saw they had just turned the corner onto Regent Street, still a fair distance from their destination.

Seeing her eyeing the door handle, he moved to block her. "You never let me finish. I saw Dandridge the day before last and told him our deal was off."

"Really, how noble of you. Was that before or after you fucked me, Mr. Stone?" He thought he'd prepared himself for her inevitable anger, but the venom in her voice stung more than he might have imagined.

Hands shaking she opened her reticule and fumbled inside. Above them, the driver barked, "In or out, what's it to be?"

"In," Hadrian shouted. To Callie, he said in a high whisper, "There's nothing to be gained by catching your death walking home in the cold. Calm yourself and let me see you home at least."

Ignoring him, she called, "Out."

She had the purse open now, a fistful of paper notes in hand. Without counting it out, she threw the money at Hadrian.

He scarcely glanced at the bills scattered across his lap, the leather seat, and the dirty floor. "Callie, what the devil? I'll pay the fare, for God's sake." He tried to hand it back, but she only shook her head.

"The money's not for the driver, it's for you, payment for your services of last night and the time before. If it's not enough, you've only to send your bill 'round with that of the other tradesmen."

Stunned as much by her hard-eyed stare as her words, this time when she reached for the door handle, Hadrian didn't make a move to stop her.

After Callie stalked off, Hadrian couldn't bear facing his empty flat, where the intimate signs and scents of her recent presence would be certain to haunt him. Instead he directed the disgruntled driver to one of his old haunts, a tavern at Mile End. Only there didn't seem to be enough gin in the world to make him drunk, let alone to cut the pain knifing through him. Callie as he'd last seen her, eyes bright with held-back tears and mouth trembling, haunted him no matter how many drinks he downed.

Eventually he left and just started walking. With no particular destination in mind, he somehow found himself standing outside the entrance to the former Madame Dottle's, the brothel he'd once called home. Now that Sally ran the place, it had a far friendlier feel. Oh, the infamous two-way mirrors were still there for those who fancied that sort of thing . . . but Sally saw to it her girls were well fed, decently clothed, and received the regular care of a physician. Anyone who wished to leave knew she might do so freely and without fear.

He knocked on the door. Three sharp raps, the old signal. Wearing a peach-colored peignoir and with her hair still in curling papers, Sally answered it. "Why Harry, this is a surprise."

He saw at once by her painted and powdered countenance that this was a working night and stepped back to go. "I shouldn't have come."

She looked him up and down. "Whatever's the matter, love? You look like death warmed over and stink like a gin palace."

Meeting that keen-eyed gaze, he knew there was no point in dissembling. "Oh hell, Sal, you might better ask me what could possibly be right."

***

They bypassed the parlor with its plush velvet settee and satin-covered wing chairs, heading through the mirror-lined hallway to the kitchen, their respite when they were children.

Sally poured two mugs of freshly brewed coffee, stirred in liberal quantities of sugar and cream, and handed one over to Hadrian. Taking her seat across the planked table from him, she said, "Out with it. I want to hear it all."

Hadrian stared into the well of his mug and admitted, "I don't know where to begin."

"At the beginning, of course, and then straight on through to what brings you here. It's Callie, isn't it?"

He shook his head, not in denial but in defeat. "Oh Christ, Sally, I've ruined everything, any chance of making things right between us."

"Why not let me be the judge of that? We women are a forgiving lot, you know."

"Not this time. Were I in her shoes, I don't think I could ever forgive me for what I've done."

"That bad is it? Best take a deep breath and let it out."

Hadrian took a bracing swallow of scalding coffee and then set it aside. These past weeks he'd been navigating such a web of lies, he scarcely knew where to begin.

Gathering his thoughts, he recounted his and Callie's unplanned and as-then entirely innocent meeting in the park, the encounter shortly thereafter with Boyle's henchmen, and finally his desperate acceptance of Dandridge's devil's bargain.

Heedless of the curling papers, Sally dragged a long-nailed hand through her hair. "Oh, Harry, why didn't you come to me? I've a bit set aside, not four hundred pounds surely, but enough to have gotten you out of London for a time until things blew over."

"My mate, Rourke said nearly the same thing only he's been out of the country, and I didn't know how to contact him. As for Gavin, I've already taken so much from him; I didn't know how I could possibly ask for more, especially when I'd brought the whole bloody mess on myself."

"So you agreed to ruin Caledonia instead. Oh, Harry."

He hung his head. "I know, I know. When I first agreed to Dandridge's terms I meant to see the thing through only . . ."

"You've gone and fallen in love with her, haven't you?"

No point in denying it. He scraped a hand through his hair. "Christ, Sally, I'd gladly trade my life for the chance to make things right for her, keep her safe only it's too late. I confessed everything to her, and she never wants to see me again, not that I blame her."

"Like as not that's the shock talking. Give her time. She'll come 'round."

"Time is the very thing I don't have. Now that Dandridge knows I won't be providing any photographs, it's only a matter of time before he sends one of his henchmen after me." He looked up from tracing the mug's rim to regard her. "So you see, I may just have to take you up on that offer of going into hiding, for the near future at least."

Expression thoughtful, she leaned in and dropping her voice said, "I've something for you. Something I meant to give you a long time ago but never got around to it."

"What is it?"

Rather than answer, she said, "Wait here. It's upstairs in my room. I'll just be a minute."

No longer able to sit still, Hadrian got up to pace the slate floor, the scene in the hansom playing back in his head. He was no stranger to insults or pain, either for that matter. He'd been born in a brothel, a whore's son, and then spent his early years as a beggar and a thief. Yet never had he felt so low in all his life as when Callie threw her money at him and as good as called him a Judas, a betrayer, a whore. Not that he blamed her. Likely letting her go on hating him was the kindest thing he could do, and still there was a part of him that wasn't prepared to entirely give up hope, not yet. She had said she loved him after all, and though that frantic utterance had come in the heat of passion, he couldn't think Callie would say such a thing lightly. God alone knew how he'd longed to clasp her to him and say those magical and oh-so-true words straight back. *I love you.* Yet knowing that he wasn't free, that he hadn't the right, he'd held back even as he'd given her everything his body could give.

Mired in his musings, he didn't hear Sally return until she cleared her throat. "Mind you don't wear out my floor."

Standing in the doorway, she handed him a small square swathed in cotton wool and smelling of cedar. "This is my gift to you and Callie." He started to unwrap it, but her hand on his arm stayed him. "No, not now." She darted a worried look to the open doorway. "Wait until you're alone. Better yet, open it with Callie. You'll know what to do then."

"Sally, is everything all right with you?"

"Right as rain, now go on with you." A hand on his shoulder, she steered him out the door.

Callie, he had to get to her, though what the devil he would say to her once—*if*—he got the chance was a mystery still. "But Sally, how can I begin to hope she'll forgive me, let alone take me back?"

Sally leveled him one of her good, long looks. "So long as a body's still breathing, there's always hope. If you're lucky she'll take you back today; and if not today, tomorrow; and if not tomorrow, maybe the day after." A single tear tracked through the cake of rouge and powder. "Just love her, Harry. The rest will follow."

CHAPTER SEVENTEEN

"Seldom, very seldom, does complete truth belong to any human disclosure; seldom can it happen that something is not a little disguised, or a little mistaken."

—JANE AUSTEN, *Emma*, 1815

Since leaving Hadrian in the hansom and going it alone on foot, Callie had spent the better part of the afternoon crying in her room. Eventually the wellspring of tears had run dry, temporarily at least. She'd risen from her sopping pillow, wrapped her still thawing body in an old quilt, and migrated to the parlor where the recently replenished sherry decanter called to her like a siren to a sailor lost at sea. That had been three glasses ago . . . or was it four?

It was in that fragile state between acute misery and semi-intoxication that Lottie found her later that day. Smartly turned out in a princess-cut visiting suit of rose-colored wool, she breezed in. "Why darling, there you are. When you didn't come home for tea last night, I was a whit worried, I must confess, but then again I suspect I knew where you'd gone."

The reference to confessions sent fresh tears welling. Looking away, Callie counted herself fortunate to manage a mute nod.

Drawing closer, Lottie ventured, "How went the meeting with the PM?"

Staring ahead into the fire lest her aunt see her puffy eyes and tear-streaked face, Callie tried for a normal tone and answered, "Better than I'd expected. Lord Stonevale has been most vocal in his endorsement, and his good opinion seems to hold considerable sway with the PM." She cleared her throat though she was so hoarse from sobbing she scarcely recognized her own voice. "I believe we may have a supporter in Salisbury though he will hold back to see which way the wind blows before casting his lot publicly."

Lottie rounded the settee on which Callie sat. Slipping slender hands out of her muff, she set the bit of fur and lace aside and said, "Why darling, this is wonderful news. But why the long face?"

Knowing that any further pretense was useless, Callie set her glass down on the gate-leg table and turned to meet her aunt's concerned gaze. "Oh Auntie, I've been such a bloody fool. I actually had myself believing he cared something for me, that perhaps he might even be on his way to loving me if only just a little."

"Lord Salisbury?"

"No aunt, Hadrian, or rather Harry Stone, if you must know."

Eyebrows lifting to her hairline, Lottie asked, "Who is Harry Stone?"

Callie shook her head, which was throbbing like a toothache. "He is Hadrian St. Claire, or rather, Hadrian St. Claire is he. Oh, Lottie, either way, it's the most dreadful mess."

Slipping onto the cushion next to her, Lottie wrapped a comforting arm about her shoulders. "If we're to sort it all out, I think you'd best begin at the beginning."

The compassion in her aunt's face was all it took to start fresh tears flowing. Hiding her face in her hands, she said, "In all honesty, I'm still struggling to sort it out myself."

Pulling her closer, Lottie patted her back. "There, there, pet. If I've anything to give you, it's time."

Sensing that time was of the essence, Hadrian left Sally's and took a hansom cab back to Westminster where his intention was to quickly shave and change before presenting himself at the Rivers' residence and begging both women's forgiveness. Although his hope that Callie might take him back was slim if not next to nil, as Sally had pointed out, it was hope all the same. But when he fit his key to the lock of his shop's entrance, the door swung ominously open.

Icicles freezing his blood, he stepped inside, every fiber

of his being on full alert. In one sweeping glance, he took in the smashed glass countertop, the overturned worktable and chairs, and the framed photographs wrenched from their wall hooks and heaped in the center of the room. Bloody hell!

Feet crunching on glass, he bounded up the stairs. Like his studio, the flat door stood ajar, the room inside in utter disarray. His heart dipped when Dinah didn't materialize to meet him. Whatever his just deserts might be, the thought that yet another innocent might be made a victim in his stead was almost more than even he could bear. Sick with anticipation over what he might find, he went about calling for her. After several heartrending minutes, an answering meow emerged from the vicinity of the pantry. Weak with relief, he went down on his hands and knees and crawled over to where she crouched behind the meat safe, terrified but apparently unharmed. Lifting her into his arms, he stroked her small, trembling body, cooing soft words of comfort before continuing his inventory of the destruction. The door to his darkroom closet stood open as well. Ordinarily that would guarantee the ruin of any recent work, but the only photograph he'd made in the past twenty-four hours was the nude he'd shot of Callie. Eager to see the finished piece, he'd developed it before they'd gone back to bed.

Callie! Heart in his throat, he set Dinah down and dashed into the darkroom. A cursory search confirmed the room had been picked bare. Unwilling to face what that must mean, he searched every nook and cranny, not once but several times, until there could be no doubt as to what had happened. The intruder had made off with the boudoir photograph of Callie.

Dandridge! For the span of moments he stood in the center of the closet of a room and ran a shaking hand through his sweat-dampened hair. The MP must have hired someone to turn over his apartment. Whether that person had found the intimate photograph by accident or design scarcely mattered at this stage. Hadrian had carried out his Judas mission after all, delivering Callie to Dandridge on the proverbial platter.

Shaky, he made his way back into the main room. Someone had slit the upholstering of his divan and hacked away. Sitting down amidst the stuffing, he considered what his next move might be. Call in the police? But no, if they wouldn't have believed him before, what chance had he now when admittedly he'd been a party to Dandridge's plan? Even if by some miracle they did credit his story, he would have to admit that such a photograph of Callie existed and that would never do.

No, there was only one course of action that made any sense to him, and carrying it out called on the talents of Harry Stone, not Hadrian St. Claire. If Dandridge had ordered the photograph stolen, he would simply have to steal it back. He'd been a crack thief in his day and though snitching purses wasn't quite house-breaking, the same core skills applied. And if he were caught, and there was a good chance he would be, what of it? At this point, he really had nothing to lose. Dandridge had seen to that, stripping his fledgling life as bare as any wintertime tree. Whether he called himself Hadrian St. Claire or Harry Stone no longer mattered in the least. Either way, he was a man with no prospects and no future—and that made him a very dangerous man indeed.

"For Chrissake, man, make your move, why don't you, and put us both out of our misery? I've taken your queen a'ready and your king is but one move away from being in my pocket. You've naught to lose at this point."

Pointer finger hovering above the onyx chess piece, Gavin looked up from the board into Rourke's frowning face and admitted, "I'm distracted with thinking about Harry. I didn't care for the look of him when he left the other day. I think he may have gotten in over his head this time."

They were at the Garrick, Gavin's club, sipping glasses of Madeira in the card room, its plasterwork walls flanked with portraits of playwrights and other past and present luminaries of the stage. A few other gentlemen had wandered in to play cards or talk quietly; otherwise the club had mostly cleared after the supper hour.

An eye cocked on Gavin's finger, which for the past ten minutes and counting had yet to commit to any move, Rourke said, "Och, Harry's like a cat with nine lives. He's got through other scrapes before. He'll get through this one. Betimes, I've my man-of-affairs working on having that bank draft ready by noon tomorrow. As soon as he pays Dandridge back in full, he should be in the clear." He looked about, and dropping his voice, added, "Despite the blackguard's threats, I canna ken he'd go so far as commit murder over a vote on a wee bill."

Gavin shook his head. During his short time as a barrister, he'd witnessed cases where murder had been done over as little as a coveted hat or a pie left to cool in a window well. When it came to mankind's capacity for committing acts of folly and senseless destruction, next to nothing surprised him. In this case, the "wee bill" to which Rourke referred had the capacity to significantly altar the landscape of the British electorate for centuries to come. It was no trifling matter.

"I wouldn't be so sure of that, my friend. Even if Dandridge is bluffing, a great deal of mischief can be made in twenty-four hours time."

"Are you suggesting we pay a call to Harry's shop and make sure he's tucked in safe and sound?"

Finger still circling the piece, Gavin said, "I wasn't suggesting any such thing, but I must admit that sounds a capital plan."

Rourke shifted in his chair, a straight-backed affair upholstered in hard leather that, Gavin privately admitted, felt easily as uncomfortable as his barrister's bench. "In that case, you maun as well make your move or forfeit; either way, your goose is cooked."

Gavin felt a smile tugging at the corners of his mouth as all at once the sought-after pattern emerged with crystalline clarity. "I wouldn't be so certain of that were I you. The old adage about patience being a virtue isn't without merit, after all." His hand settled on the piece, which he slid into place without hesitation. Looking up from the board to his friend's stupefied face, he said, "Checkmate."

By the time Callie finished her story, her aunt had joined her in hitting the sherry. Seated side by side, glasses in hand and the near-empty decanter on the table between them, Lottie said, "I can't help but think there's more to all this than meets the eye."

Setting her empty glass aside, Callie said, "Meaning?"

"If Hadrian is truly the bounder we make him out to be, then why would he cry off with Dandridge and confess all to you knowing you might never speak to him again?"

Callie shook her head. Despite the quantity of spirit she'd imbibed, she felt depressingly sober. The only tangible result of all that drinking was an aching head to match her aching heart. "Perhaps he's come down with a case of cold feet and was afraid he'd get caught or . . ." All at once, Hadrian's remark from the previous day came rushing back to her.

"Well, Dinah, what say you to Paris next? Or maybe it's Venice you fancy, eh?"

He'd been speaking aloud to his cat, as yet unaware of her presence upstairs. At the time she'd been too much passion's prisoner to give the statement a second thought, or even a first, but in the context of all she'd since learned, it stood out as an important clue indeed.

"Or what, Callie? Pray don't leave me on tenterhooks." Sitting on the edge of the seat cushion, Lottie moved to top off both their glasses.

Callie could no longer contain her misery. "I think Hadrian may mean to leave the country."

Replacing the decanter's crystal stopper, Lottie said, "But dearest, if he cried off with Dandridge, surely that means he has to give back the money. If it was a dire want of funds that drove him to accept the villain's proposal in the first place, how could he possibly finance a trip abroad now?"

"Take my picture, Hadrian. Make it as a remembrance of our beautiful night together, of how it was between us before the world and all its folly had the chance to intrude."

Had Callie been standing rather than seated, the fist-grip on her heart would have sufficed to drop her to her knees. Sinking hard fingers into the sofa arm, she managed to choke out, "I'm not entirely certain he did cry off."

Turning to her, Lottie's face formed a question mark. "What do you mean, Callie? I thought you said—"

Dropping her head into her hands, Callie felt the sobs she'd struggled so hard to keep down pushing up the back of her throat. "Oh, Auntie, when I'd said I'd been a bloody fool before, I didn't know how true a statement that was."

It was coming on dark when Hadrian made his way to Dandridge's house in Hanover Square. The brass front doorknocker, aptly cast in the form of a serpent, was turned up, indicating that the MP was within and "at home" to callers. Dressed in all black, with boot blacking on his face, Hadrian slipped around to the back alley. Crouching behind the low stone wall, as yet unlit lantern in hand, he bided the time for full darkness to descend.

While he waited out in the cold, recollections of Callie invaded his thoughts. That soft smile, those gentle hands, the habit she had of lifting her chin just so, the way her eyes lit up when she laughed. Odd how he hadn't fully realized just how much she'd come to mean to him, just how much he loved her, until now when she was as good as lost to him. Even so, the time they'd had together would always be a sweet gift to be treasured throughout the long barren years ahead.

In the interim there was one last gift he could give her and that was the retrieval of the photograph. Stamping frozen feet, he waited for the last upstairs light to dim before heading for the tradesmen's entrance. The lock pick he pulled from his pocket was a rudimentary tool but one that had served him well in the past when, driven by hunger, he'd broken into a grocer's shop and gorged himself on raw vegetables and uncooked meats. That had been more than fifteen years before, and yet he trusted the touch hadn't left him entirely. A few tweaks had the door giving weigh, gaining him admittance to the slate-floored kitchen.

Loud snores greeted him when he stepped inside, paralyzing him in place. He fell back into the shadowed corner, narrowly missing banging up against a peg from which a great many copper cook pots hung. Holding his breath, he craned his neck to see the source of the din, a fat woman in a stained apron slouched over the table, an overturned cup set by her dimpled elbow. The cook, he surmised, and relaxing fractionally, stepped softly past.

Dandridge's study would be the most reasonable hiding place for a photograph or indeed anything else. Coming out into the front hall, he turned right, guessing that the MP's sanctum would be on the main floor.

His hunch proved to be on the mark. He found the wood paneled room without incident, the door standing wide open. Darting a quick glance behind him, he slipped inside and pulled the door quietly closed.

Lifting the lantern aloft, he glimpsed the outline of twin built-in bookcases flanking a wide desk. The bookshelves alone presented innumerable hiding places though he rather suspected Dandridge would have the photograph sequestered in some sort of safe. If so, his lock pick would be put to true test.

"Looking for something, Mr. Stone?"

The now familiar voice had him halting in his tracks. Garbed in a dressing gown Dandridge rose from behind the desk, his rail thin figure casting ghoulish silhouette on the paneled wall behind. In the dim light, Hadrian took note of the bandage dressing the MP's swollen nose and wondered if that meant it was broken.

Heartily hoping that were the case, he lifted the lantern so that the cone of light hit the MP square on the face. "You tell me."

The MP only laughed. "You've got balls, I'll grant you that. A pity you lack the brains to go with them."

"You had my flat turned over."

Dandridge did not deny it. "For that, you've only yourself to thank. Were it not for your ill-conceived allusion to having proof of my past, I would never have thought to do so. Instead, we stumbled upon that deliciously damning photograph of the Rivers whore hanging out to dry in your studio's darkroom. Very fortuitous, don't you think?"

"I want it back, Dandridge."

"Even if you had anything to barter with, which you don't, it is too late, my friend."

Staring into Dandridge's reptilian eyes, Hadrian felt a sick foreboding sinking his stomach. "What do you mean?"

The MP shrugged his narrow shoulders. "The delightful image of Miss Rivers toying with her cunt is even now in the hands of the Fleet Street press. If all goes well, it should make the front page of every London daily newspaper by tomorrow morning, suitably censored, of course. Public morality is no trifling matter, after all."

Hadrian felt as if the room were spinning like a top. *Callie, what have I done to you?* To Dandridge, he said, "You bastard." With nothing more to lose, he launched himself across the study floor. Grabbing Dandridge by his lapels, he slammed his right fist into the old man's face, catching him in the jaw and sending saliva spurting.

He hauled back to hit him again, landing a second blow in the solar plexus that had Dandridge doubled over the desk, flailing hands clawing for the bell rope. Between wracking coughs, he said, "You'll pay for that, Stone."

"I've been paying all my life, Dandridge. It's high time you and your lot anted up."

Hadrian started to go for him again when hard hands grabbed him from behind. Fists raised, he spun about, the lantern crashing to the floor amidst three pairs of booted male feet. Ratcheting his gaze upward, he stared into the grotesquely smiling faces of Sam Sykes and Jimmie Deans.

Looking like a guard dog salivating in anticipation of the kill, Sykes said, "Good eve, St. Claire. Fancy meeting you 'ere."

Dividing his gaze between the two henchmen, Hadrian asked himself if Boyle and his lackeys hadn't been part of the plot to entrap him all along. He had only a handful of seconds to contemplate that likelihood when a ham-sized fist planted itself in his midriff. A second set of hands jerked his arms behind his back, an unbreakable human shackle. More blows caught him in the face, eyes, and gut until he doubled over, head hanging and eyes squeezed shut against a waterfall of snot and blood. Apparently not done with torturing him, someone drove a knee into his crotch. A lightening streak of pain, stark as a camera's flare, had his legs folding beneath him. He heard a heavy groan, a sound of unadulterated agony, and belatedly realized it had come from him.

"That's enough; cease." Dandridge's muffled shout rose about the eddying pool of dizziness and pain. "He's bleeding all over my Aubusson carpet. Get him out of here—now!"

The hands holding him up relaxed their grip. Hadrian dropped to the floor, a knee-bruising thud.

"Where . . . where d'ye want us to take him?" Even with eyes closed, Hadrian could tell it was Deans, as slow-witted as ever.

"That's what I pay you to figure out. Only see that you take him out the back through the kitchen."

Hard hands grabbed him under the armpits, drawing him back onto his feet. "Come on with you, you filthy bugger, we 'aven't got all night."

Between them, they dragged him as Dandridge had hauled him across the brothel bedroom all those years before. The next few minutes flickered in and out, snatches of consciousness punctuated by spells of blissful blackness. The screech of a door opening on rusted hinges; a rush of icy air hitting him in the face like a fist; the tang of sweat pouring down his face, stinging his swollen eyes and salting his wounds. Coming to, he wondered where the devil they were taking him. The weight of his head felt enormous, the effort to hold it upright nothing short of Herculean. Cracking open an eye, he saw they were crossing the cobblestone alley to the mews. A black-lacquered carriage stood at the ready, team in harness and driver seated atop the box. One of the henchmen, Deans, released him and went behind the conveyance to lift the boot. The next thing Hadrian knew, he was being pulled along to follow like a balloon on a string. It was then that he understood they meant to fit him inside like a corpse in a coffin. Panic flared, granting him the strength to struggle. He kicked out, his foot connecting with what felt like a shinbone.

A kidney punch had him doubling over again, lungs choking on frigid air. "Get inside, you bloody fucker, or else." The speaker was Sykes, not that it mattered.

A blow struck him from behind at the base of his skull. Stunned, he felt himself falling forward into the dark well, his captured arms powerless to break his fall. He landed and scrabbled to climb out but several well-placed punches stole the last of his will. They were going to kill him, he was going to die, and his only real regret was that he wouldn't have the chance to see Callie once more. He would simply disappear and she would live out her days hating him as her betrayer.

"Ye're a stubborn fucker, St. Claire, I'll grant 'ee that."

The boot slammed closed, leaving him entombed in musty darkness, elbows and knees pinned to his chest. For a handful of seconds, he teetered on the edge of madness, the closeness stealing what little breath he might draw. Then a strange peace descended. His life, or the little that was left of it, was about to come full circle. Hadrian St. Claire had been born on a similar winter eve fifteen years before when climbing inside a prime minister's carriage had seemed the start of a bright new future. Yet all his grand plans, fine airs, and fancy clothes had come to naught.

Hadrian closed his eyes, giving himself up to the darkness. Not so bright now.

CHAPTER EIGHTEEN

"It is never too late to be what you might have
been."

—GEORGE ELIOT

id you see that?" Rourke lifted his head from where
he and Gavin hid behind the hedge bordering the
mews behind Dandridge's townhouse. Their horses,
let from the lending stable, were tethered nearby but out of
sight. Turning back to Gavin, his breath came out in a puff
of steam. "Come on with you, man, 'tis two against two, an
even match. We can take 'em. Hell, I'm so bluidy mad, I can
take 'em both myself if need be."

He would have launched himself forward, but Gavin
grabbed his shoulder, forcing him back down. "Hold, for God's
sake. Unless you want to see Harry dead, you'll curb that Scot's
temper of yours and stay hidden for now. And *quiet*."

"But you saw what they've done to him as well as I did.

Christ, I've seen haggis in better form than he is. Now they've packed him into the boot like so much baggage."

Peering between the branches of hedge, Gavin watched as the bald henchman climbed onto the driver's box. The other, the bulkier of the two, stood outside the carriage, applying some substance, boot blacking he suspected, to cover Dandridge's crest.

Turning back to his impatient friend, he whispered, "For the present, he's alive and he'll stay that way until they get him to wherever it is they mean to finish him. If we make our move now, who knows how many more of Dandridge's bullies may pour out of that house to aid them. No, far better to follow and see where they take him, and then attack while the element of surprise is ours."

"Why, ladies, this is a lovely surprise, though it is rather late for a social call, do you not think?" Dropping the cloth-wrapped ice he'd been holding to his swollen face back in the champagne bucket, Dandridge rose to greet the two women his butler had just shown into his study. Thinking he'd got St. Claire cleared out and the blood cleaned up just in time, he gestured them toward chairs.

Staring him down from the other side of his desk, Caledonia lifted her chin. "This is no social visit, sir, as well you know. I believe you have something that belongs to me, and I want it back."

Beneath the blur of her hat veil, he glimpsed her puffy eyes and pale face, the irrefutable signs of female suffering, and hid a smile. It seemed that St. Claire had done his work even better than he'd credited. Not only would the chit be ruined politically and socially after tomorrow, but it appeared she already suffered the ill-effects of a broken heart—vanquished beyond even his fondest dreams. Despite his throbbing face, he could barely contain his glee.

"Really?" He tapped a finger against his lower lip, one of the few spots that didn't hurt, and pretended to consider. "I do not believe so," he said at length. "Might you be more specific?"

Charlotte Rivers, silent since entering, marched up to her niece's side like a mother lion prepared to defend her cub to the death. "Josiah, you know full well what we came for. Now where is it?"

Born Charlotte Smythe, Caledonia's aunt by marriage was still a very attractive woman though she must be his age or near to it. Dubbed "Lovely Lottie" at her come-out ball, she'd been the reigning queen of her season, a diamond of the first water who'd had even the most devoted bachelors contemplating a trip to the altar. He'd been set to offer for her himself when Edward Rivers had stolen her out from under his very nose. Not that he'd loved her, love for women wasn't in his nature, but he did have an appreciation for rare, beautiful things, and she was certainly that. Charming, lovely, and accomplished she would have made a far more adept political wife than that brainless country mouse he'd finally settled on marrying—yet another reason to despise the Rivers family.

He held his arms out at his sides as though inviting them to search his very person. "I'm afraid I am at a loss, although if you could only describe in some detail what of yours you think I have, perhaps I could be of more help." The latter was said by way of a dare. Casting his gaze on Caledonia Rivers, her photographed image flashed into his mind, and he barely bothered to contain his smirk.

Even fuming, Charlotte was a lady to her very core. "This isn't over yet, Josiah," she said, words dripping ice water. Turning back to her niece, standing frozen as a statue, she said, "Come along, Callie, we are obviously wasting our time. We cannot appeal to the honor of a man who has none." Hooking her arm through that of the younger woman, she steered them toward the study door. On the threshold, she paused to look back at him. "Josiah, whatever has befallen your face?"

For the first time since they'd entered, he felt his smile slip along with his mood. The bandage on his nose was bad enough but now there was his jaw, too, painfully swollen and likely still bearing the imprint of St. Claire's knuckles. "An unfortunate accident. I took a fall from my horse."

In truth, he'd had to give up riding years ago along with a great many other corporal pleasures, and the penetrating look she sent him told him she knew that and more, putting him in mind of just how shrunken and gouty and old he'd become, a veritable shadow of the man he once was. The latter though had him reaching down to cinch his dressing gown's velvet tie.

"That is most unfortunate indeed, Josiah. Why if I didn't know better, I could almost think you'd run afoul of someone's fist."

The snow pelting the back of his neck and the mewling of gulls overhead pulled Hadrian out of the blackness. He came to, not so much in pain as numb. Sykes and Deans had him between them, pulling him along the pier. Resisting the temptation to open his eyes, he kept them closed and let himself be carried along. Judging by the stench of fetid water and decaying fish, there were in the East End somewhere near the docks.

"Put a move on, why don't you? At the pace you're going, it'll be light before we get him to the water." The voice belonged to Sykes.

"I'm doing my level best," Deans complained, giving off a pungent whiff of leeks. "But he's heavier than he looks."

"He's dead weight is all or at least he will be soon enough." Sykes's barking laugh punctuated that pronouncement. Bracing him between them, they paused to catch their breaths. "Did you bring the rope?"

"What for?"

"For tying his hands and feet, idiot."

"Why bother? He's out like a light."

"He may not be once he hits the water, and Dandridge won't want us taking any chances. Betimes, St. Claire's like a cat. You never know what sewer hole he's liable to crawl back out of."

"All right, all right, rope's in the boot. I'll fetch it."

Eyes still closed, Hadrian let himself sag against the bully's bulk, keeping his ears trained to monitor Deans's retreating footfalls. It was his chance and though beaten as he was it would hardly be an even fight, he knew he'd never get a better one.

Silently he counted to ten and then opened his eyes. Next to him, Sykes was an ungainly silhouette backlit by the beach, moonbeam striking atop his billiard ball head. "So it's rise and shine time, is it St. Claire?"

"Rise . . . and *shine*." Whirling on him, he smashed his fist dead center of Sykes's fleshy throat.

The bully fell back with a groan, crashing into a stack of empty shipping crates propped against the side of a transit shed. Staggering like a drunk, Hadrian limped away, a thousand invisible pins needling away at his feet and legs. Willing himself to ignore the agony, he kept the brick warehouse ahead in his sights. He couldn't possibly outrun them in the open, but if he were lucky he might be able to lose himself in the maze of shipyard clutter until dawn when the stevedores and watermen showed up to work.

"Hold you, where do you think you're off to?"

Hadrian darted a look back to where Deans had rounded the coach, shouldering a coil of sailor's rope.

A voice, Sykes's, rasped, "Don't just stand there. After him!"

Deans hesitated, then dropped the rope and gave chase.

Heavy footfalls lumbered behind Hadrian, closing the distance on his narrow lead. Ordinarily he would have had no difficulty in outpacing the heavier man, but already his left leg was cramping badly, the muscles in both legs afire from his time folded into the carriage boot.

Still he kept on, one thought, one hope, one woman fueling his fight for survival. Callie. If he could only manage to escape, to find his way back to her, he would throw whatever was left of him at her feet and beg for her forgiveness.

Deans was at his back now, no more than an arm's length away, the warmth of his breath all but beating down on the back of Hadrian's neck. Heavy weight like a sandbag crashed into him, knocking him to the ground. Sprawled atop him, the henchman pinned him to the path, oyster shells cutting into his palms as the shattered camera glass had all those years before.

The memory roused whatever fight Hadrian had left in him. He knew he'd never escape now, but he resolved he wouldn't go down easy. No, he'd give them a fight they'd remember for some time to come; the rest of their miserable, misspent lives. He reared up, knocking Deans off balance. He was upon his knees when beefy hands took hold of his collar, pulling him back down. This time, though, he managed to wrangle his way on top. Several well-placed downward jabs had Deans's face looking little better than his own must have appeared. Knowing it was either kill or be killed, he wrapped his hands about the thick throat and found the fragile larynx with his thumbs.

The sharp poke of a blade in his back had him stilling his hold. "Leave off, St. Claire, or I'll run you through here and now." Sykes, voice husky, pressed the knife deeper between his shoulder blades, leaving him no choice but to pull back. "That's better." To Deans, busy dusting himself off, he barked, "Fetch that rope and bind him. We'll sit him down on that crate over there. No reason not to have a bit of fun before we feed him to the fishes."

Not content with drowning him, they meant to torture him first. Limp, Hadrian let them shove him back over to the crates. Whatever hope he'd harbored of escape was lost now. Setting one of the boxes upside down, they shoved him down onto the makeshift seat, then pulled his hands behind his back and wound the rope with punishing tightness about his joined wrists.

Deans, face bloody, grabbed a fistful of his hair and yanked his lolling head upright. "Shall I start by lopping off your ears or maybe that cock of yours would make a better trophy for the pickle jar, eh?"

Hadrian offered up a silent prayer to whatever God there was that he'd either pass out or bleed to death before they did their worst. Looking up into the two bullish faces looming over him, he said, "If you lads take my cock, at least you'll have the one between you."

"You were always too clever for your own good, St. Claire," Sykes said, shaking his head. "I wonder if you'll sound half as clever as a soprano." Face stretched into a hideous leer, he nodded to Deans, who dragged the point of his knife from

Hadrian's Adam's apple downward to rest between his legs. "It's moment of reckoning, fancy man."

Not caring to witness his own gelding, Hadrian squeezed his eyes shut. A pistol's booming report had him opening them in time to see the two henchmen drop to the ground. He looked across the beach to see the silhouette of two men striding forward, weapons drawn.

"I wouldn't count my trophies just yet were I you." A tall, dark-haired man elegantly turned out in a riding coat and breeches stopped a few paces away, smoking pistol in hand. His slightly shorter, brawnier companion stepped up beside him, his weapon cocked and a lantern in his other hand.

Looking up through a haze of blood and pain, Hadrian could scarcely credit the proof of his eyes. Gavin and Rourke? "What took you so long?" Dividing his gaze between his two friends, he cracked a smile, which set his swollen lips to bleeding.

The bullies were on their knees with their hands up. Sykes turned to Deans, and said, "It's only a single barrel he's carrying. He can't hit us both." Eying Rourke, he slowly got to his feet, Deans following suit.

The Scot broke into a toothsome grin. "Aye, 'tis true enough, but then at this close range, I canna be counted on to miss, either." Waving the weapon between them, he said, "Which one of you brave lads will it be, eh?

Exchanging looks, the pair wavered, all the time needed for Gavin to reload. "As they say, 'no honor among thieves,' and apparently not a great deal in the way of bravery either." A siren's blare had the two henchmen turning their heads sharply to the road above. In answer to their unspoken question, Gavin supplied, "That would be the police. The magistrate is an old friend of the family. I would have got here sooner, but I stopped to send a message 'round to his house. If you two lads don't mind holding tight a moment or two more, we'll have you safely tucked into the police wagon and slapped in irons in no time at all."

The visit to Dandridge had been a waste of time and breath as Callie had known it would be, but when her aunt had insisted they couldn't very well sit about quaffing sherry all night, she'd reluctantly agreed to go. Likewise, she'd put up only a fledgling fight when afterward Lottie had wanted to drive by Hadrian's shop on their way home. The shop windows were dark when their carriage pulled up to the curb.

It wasn't until Lottie pressed for them to disembark and knock on the very door that Callie had put her foot down. "Really, Aunt, I've subjected myself to sufficient humiliation to last another ten years, don't you think?"

Sitting on the carriage seat next to her niece, Lottie said, "We don't know for certain he's even turned over that picture. It might be in his possession even now."

Callie shook her head, which ached from grief and fatigue as well as a surfeit of sherry. "You saw Dandridge's face as well as I when we confronted him. The way he stared at me, one would think I hadn't on a stitch. Oh, he has the photograph, all right, and only because Hadrian gave it to him. By his own admission, he took money from Dandridge to ruin me. Really, Aunt, what more in the way of proof do you require?"

"I am only saying you owe it to yourself to confront him, hear what Hadrian has to say in his defense."

"I'm not terribly interested in anything he has to say in his defense or otherwise. Why, how could I possibly credit a single word he says? Hadrian St. Claire isn't even his true name. He took it so as not to be traced back to his . . . past." She stopped herself from saying more. Even now that she knew Hadrian to be the agent of her ruin, telling the secret of his past, even to her aunt, still struck her as terribly wrong.

In the shadows cast by the carriage lamp, Lottie regarded her, expression thoughtful. "Just as times change, people can change, too—if they want to badly enough."

Callie had the discomfiting feeling that the remark was meant for her. "Very well, Auntie, you win again. If Hadrian wishes to speak with me, I'll hear him out. Only this time, Lottie, it is he who must come to me."

The early morning streets were just beginning to come to humming life when Hadrian, Gavin, and Rourke stepped out of the magistrate's office, having just finished swearing out their statements. Connecting Dandridge to the night's deeds might take some doing, but knowing Sykes and Deans, Hadrian felt certain one or both criminals would soon confess rather than swing from the gallows rope.

Looking down at the Manton dueling pistol tucked into his pocket, Rourke chuckled, "Och, but that was quite an adventure."

"An adventure I can well do without repeating," Gavin added, "particularly as before last night Grandfather's dueling pistols likely haven't been fired since Napoleon's day."

Dividing his gaze between his two childhood friends, Hadrian said, "In case I neglected to say so earlier, my thanks to both of you for saving my unworthy hide, or rather what's left of it."

A cursory glance in the cracked mirror of the police loo had shown his face to be a mask of cuts and bruises that would render shaving pointless for the next week if not longer. A knot the size of a robin's egg was fast rising on his crown, and though he was no doctor, he was quite certain his nose was broken. Even so, he would gladly live with this battered face for the rest of his days if it meant Callie might take pity on him, and yes, take him back.

"Think nothing of it, Only Harry."—Gavin paused to scour his face with sober eyes—"the next time you take it into your head to go haring off like some knight errant, tell us in advance, will you? Just what did possess you to stake out Dandridge's townhouse?"

From the street corner, a newsboy's shouts of "Extra! Extra! Read all about it. Maid of Mayfair bares all" saved him from answering.

"What the devil." Wheeling about, he rushed forward

and grabbed the newspaper out of the startled boy's hands.

"Now see 'ere, guv . . ."

Hadrian scarcely registered the protest, his gaze, indeed his entire focus, riveted on the paper's front page. Splayed across it was the photograph of Callie, *his* photograph, the high slopes of her breasts and bare white thighs visible beyond the edges of the "censored" banner printed to cover them. Dandridge had made good on his threat after all. Ruined though the MP would shortly be, he hadn't gone down without first dragging Callie with him.

Reeling, he reached into his pocket for his money clip. "How much for the lot?"

The boy looked up at him. From the shadow of his wool cap, his mouth formed a shocked circle. "You want to buy 'em all?"

"Never mind, here, just take it all." Pressing the wad of notes in the boy's grubby palm, he swooped down and swept up the full stack of newspapers.

Coming up beside him, Rourke looked over to Gavin and shook his head. "That wee lump atop his head must be addling his wits."

Gavin came up on his other side. Reaching for his arm, he said, "Seriously Harry, let us get you to a doctor. You don't look at all well."

Hadrian answered with a fierce shake of his head that set the knot atop to fresh pounding. "That will have to wait. I've to pay a call on a lady first. Now help me flag down a hansom and pour myself into it because there's no time to lose."

The knowledge that it was only a matter of time, hours perhaps, before the proverbial axe fell had Callie lying awake to see dawn lighting the sky. When she heard the stirrings of life downstairs, she knew she couldn't put off rising any longer. Determined to face the day and whatever it had in store for her with as much dignity as she might, she washed her face, pinned up her hair, and dressed to come downstairs. The bill to extend the vote to women was slated to be read when Parliament convened for its evening sitting and the rally with the petition of more than three thousand signatures from women throughout the country would commence shortly after noontime. She could only suppose that Dandridge would see to it that the photograph of her surfaced sometime between now and the bill's introduction on the House floor. In the interim, she meant to carry on with her usual commitments as though this was any ordinary day, which of course it wasn't. Afterward she would step down from her leadership role in the Movement, quite possibly for good. What she needed now was time alone to take stock of her priorities, her goals, and most importantly her life.

On her way downstairs, she considered the part Hadrian had played in her imminent ruin. All these weeks he'd been tempting her, daring her to cast off her reserve, her ironclad self-control, and the starch-faced mask she'd taken refuge behind for the past decade much as she'd hidden behind her uncle's old spectacles. Now that she had left safety behind and stepped out into the open, albeit with disastrous consequences, she found she wasn't entirely sorry for having made the shift.

Her thoughts went out to Hadrian; she couldn't help that any more than she could help loving him, or at least the man she'd believed him to be. Soft feelings aside, certain of his actions were like missing puzzle pieces that simply didn't fit with the whole. That photograph, why then had he so resisted taking it, or had he been playing her even then? Under either circumstance, why bother confessing his unsavory association with Dandridge? She supposed she would never know the answers, and she supposed it didn't greatly matter. Either way, she was ruined.

Entering the breakfast room on that sobering thought, she saw that her place at the table looked oddly bare. Usually a stack of newspapers, ironed and folded, lay by her plate. Lottie, hair in curling papers and petite form swathed in her dressing gown, stood staring out the window to the street.

Drawing the drapes closed though it looked to be a fine, sunny day, she turned about. "Callie, dear, I thought I heard you up and about." Her grim face belied the sunny greeting. She crossed the room toward her, a newspaper fisted in one reed thin hand.

Callie looked down to the newspaper clutched in her aunt's hand and felt her heart beating like an executioner's drum. "How bad is it? I want to know."

"You might want to sit first. It's . . . bad, Callie." She

handed Callie the newspaper, a folded copy of the *London Times*.

Taking it from her, Callie sank into her seat lest her suddenly weak legs give way. She thought she'd prepared herself for the worst, but when she unfolded the paper and looked down, what she saw there sent her thundering heart falling through to the floorboards. The photographed face peering back at her in shades of halftone gray was her image and yet it wasn't. Languid gaze, swollen lips, and mussed hair all bore witness to a woman who had recently known carnal pleasure and been thoroughly sated. As for the body, all that pale skin and generous curves struck her as so very bare. The sole salvation was that the censored banner covered her wantonly straying hand.

How long she sat there staring in stunned silence she couldn't say but at some point Jenny entered with the morning post, her usual chipper good morning greeting silent on her lips. She glanced down at the mail tray in her hands. "I'll just set this down by you, Miss Callie."

Lottie answered for her, "Thank you, Jenny. That will be all."

"But what should I tell them reporter fellers who keep knocking on the door?"

"I said that will be all for now." Lottie's tone, uncharacteristically sharp, sent the maid scurrying out the door.

Callie waited until they were alone before asking, "What reporter fellows?"

Heaving a heavy sigh, Lottie nodded toward the window

she'd just left. "You may as well know that the press has been camped out on our sidewalk and front lawn since dawn."

"I see." Setting the newspaper aside, Callie glanced at the tray piled high with correspondence.

Cresting the heap was a note from Mrs. Fawcett due back from the States just the day before. Familiar with Millicent's usually precise signature, she could tell the letter had been penned in haste. Feeling numb, she broke the seal and perused the few short lines.

Standing over her shoulder, Lottie squinted to see. "What does she say?"

Callie cleared her throat, thick with emotions she'd yet to own. "Apparently I have become through my own 'wanton conduct and ill-advised actions' a detriment to the Cause. She goes on to say she has no choice but to make a public statement decrying my immoral behavior and disavowing any further association with me. Moreover, she has called an emergency meeting of the board of the NUWSS to propose that the London Society for Women's Suffrage be expelled from the coalition unless I step down as president, effective immediately. In the interim, she advises me against showing my face—or any part of my anatomy—at today's march."

"Callie, what will you do?"

Callie set the letter aside without bothering to refold it. "Step down, of course. Millicent's measure will most certainly carry, and even were that not the case, showing up at this point would only divide the membership."

"I meant afterward."

Callie rose to pace the room, her steps no match for the racing of her thoughts. "Oh, I don't know. Perhaps I'll take some time and travel abroad. I've a fancy to see France again. Isn't that what disgraced women do nowadays, decamp to Monte Carlo and divide their days between playing baccarat and staring at framed photographs of themselves in their glory days? On second thought, I believe I'll skip the photographs." She ended that thought with a ragged laugh.

Lottie regarded her. "My niece running away, I never would have thought it. Why, you could knock me over with a feather."

Callie whirled on her. "I am not running away, I'm . . . I'm retiring."

Arms folded in front of her, Lottie said, "Is that what you call tucking your tail between your legs?"

"If you'll recall my tail, along with the rest of me, is headlining the *Times* as well as God only knows how many other newspapers and scandal sheets. What would you have me do?"

"Stand tall and fight."

Callie shook her head, feeling at once terribly tired, terribly defeated, and more than a trifle old. "I've nothing to fight with and no future to fight for."

Lottie reached up and planted a palm on either of Callie's shoulders, stalling her sally about the room. Looking purposefully into her niece's eyes, she said, "Oh Callie, dearest girl, can't you see? No one can take away your honor unless you let them."

CHAPTER NINETEEN

"We have already women enough sacrificed to this sentimental, hypocritical prating about purity, without going out of our way to increase the number. Women have crucified the Mary Wollstonecrafts, the Fanny Wrights, and the George Sands of all ages . . . let us end this ignoble record and henceforth stand by womanhood. If this present woman must be crucified, let men drive the spikes."

—ELIZABETH CADY STANTON in response to criticisms of Victoria Woodhull, 1871

Extra! Extra! Read all about it. Maid of Mayfair bares all."

Standing at the breakfast room window overlooking the street thronged with reporters and photographers and sundry scandal mongers, Callie had to admit that the future, hers, looked decidedly bleak. Even so, now that the initial shock was wearing off, she felt an eerie calm descending. Knowing Hadrian had caused her to take a long, hard look at her life, and though their relationship had brought her harm as well as good, she couldn't help preferring the woman she was now to the walled-off person she'd been but a few weeks before. Just what could one say about a woman who'd been utterly at home lecturing to hundreds, and yet at a perfect loss when it came to carrying out a simple, honest conversation with a friend? A woman who'd known how to give orders but hadn't the faintest idea how to smile, who craved physical satisfaction with all her being and yet until a few days before hadn't the courage to let a man close enough to touch her in ten years. So even though she found herself ostracized by her suffragist sisters and polite society alike, she somehow fell short of feeling completely crushed. But before she stepped down, she meant to make a public statement the likes of which would not be heard again for some time.

The sound of a throat being delicately cleared had her turning her head to the breakfast room doorway. Lottie, restored to her customary elegance, stepped forward. "I delivered your message as you asked. Are you quite certain you want to do this?"

With a sigh, Callie let the fold of brocade drapery drop and moved away from the window. "Yes, quite, and the sooner better." She started toward the front hallway.

Lottie's voice stalled her in her tracks. "Will you want these?"

She glanced down to where the older woman held out

her late husband's spectacles.

Callie bent and pressed a kiss onto her aunt's smooth cheek. "Thank you, Auntie, but no. I don't think I'll have need of hiding behind Uncle Edward's eyewear ever again."

Fueled by the promise of a hefty tip, the hansom driver made it to Hadrian's shop in record time. As eager as Hadrian was to go to Callie and throw himself on her tender mercies, he didn't care to plead his case stinking like a dead fish and bleeding like a stuck pig. In the process of shucking off his putrid clothing, he heard a soft thud. Looking down, he saw that something had fallen from his inside coat pocket to the floor. Impatient to change and be on his way, he thought about leaving it lie until Dinah bounded up and started batting it about.

Cursing beneath his breath, he stiffly bent to retrieve the fallen object. Scarcely larger than a postage stamp, it was swathed in so much cotton wool as to make its shape indecipherable. Sally's gift, he'd all but forgotten. Remembering her admonition that he wait until he was with Callie to open it, he trusted that under the circumstances she would forgive him a small preview peak.

Swollen fingers clumsy, he unwound the wrapping and pulled out the thin square of pressed metal. Turning it over to view the imprinted image, a smile stole over his mouth, setting his scabbed lip to bleeding.

Oh Sally, were you here, I'd plant a big, smacking kiss on your cheek.

His old friend hadn't given him just any gift, but the key to his future, and quite possibly, Callie's, too.

Out in the front hallway, Callie draped a light shawl about her shoulders. Looking from her aunt to Jenny, she drew a deep breath and then nodded for Jenny to open the door. Tears in her eyes, the maid complied and then moved out of the way as a cacophony of voices poured inside the room on a draft of icy air. Cold wind rushing her face, Callie stepped out onto the stoop. Even though she'd been observing from the window, the scene stretched out before her momentarily stole her breath. The normally quiet street resembled nothing so much as a marketplace on fair day. In addition to members of the press and newspaper boys, a good many vendors had set up shop outside the wrought iron gate, hawking their wares of roasted chestnuts, hot cross buns, and gingerbread from three-legged barrows. And everywhere, absolutely everywhere, was the black-and-white image of her nearly naked self.

In the midst of the melee, a high-pitched voice piped up, "It's 'er, the randy Maid o' Mayfair."

Laughter greeted that remark. "Use your peepers, Jack. She's no maid as that *photogruff* shows."

Holding her head high and her shoulders back, Callie

motioned for silence. Clearing her throat, she began . . .

Coming to Half Moon Street, Hadrian all but jumped off the carriage step while the hansom was still moving. Calling down from the box, the driver said, "I'm that sorry, sir, but this is as near as I can take you. There looks to be some goings-on up ahead."

Heart in his throat, Hadrian paid the fare and jumped down to the street blocked by pedestrian traffic. Judging from the dull roar, it seemed that half of London congregated outside of Callie's front gate.

Determined, Hadrian elbowed his way through the crowd. It took considerable doing, but eventually he pushed his way toward the wrought-iron gate. Being tall afforded him the advantage of seeing over most of the crowd to the house's Palladian façade. A thick-waisted woman selling fresh-cut flowers blocked the gated entrance. When she wouldn't budge in response to his request, he pushed a five-pound note in her meaty fist and all but moved her aside bodily.

Circumventing her cart, he squeezed inside the gate door to join the dozen odd persons parading about the patch of frosted lawn. The gate had just fallen closed behind him when a hush fell and heads turned. He turned, too, in time to see the front door open and a tall woman with dark hair and large eyes step out onto the front steps. Callie!

Hadrian froze in mid-step. The crescents carved beneath

her swollen eyes spoke to her suffering, yet the dignity and self-possession that struck him the first time he set eyes on her was still there in abundance. But there was something different about her, too, something more than there used to be, a new ease that he noticed at once though she'd yet to speak so much as a single word.

"Dear friends," she began as though the reporters and the newsboys and even the hawkers selling newspapers and sundry savories at her expense were all friends and neighbors she'd invited over for a chat. "Before we begin, I would like to thank you in advance for this opportunity to be heard in my own way and my own voice. I know the day is cold and the morning hour grows late, so I promise you I will be brief."

From outside the gate, a cheeky male voice cried out, "Let's have a look at those lovely titties, love. We'll stand out 'ere all day for that."

Other than a slight flushing of her face, she ignored the heckler and continued, "I would like to say I deeply regret any embarrassment my recent behavior has brought upon the supporters of women's suffrage throughout the country, the London Society for Women's Suffrage specifically, and my most esteemed colleague and mentor, Mrs. Fawcett. I trust that our distinguished representatives in Parliament will continue to weigh the suffrage bill on its own merits and give it all due and fair consideration when it is brought before them later this day."

Inside his bruised chest, Hadrian's heart was swelling to bursting with pride and love. No, he would never be halfway to good enough for Callie nor could he expect her to forgive him let alone to take him back, but neither circumstance would stop him from loving her for the rest of his life.

"On the personal front, however, I can admit to having few—if any—regrets. I may not have loved wisely, but I have loved well. Yes, I have bestowed my body outside of marriage, but not without first having given the whole of my heart. And while I hold to my conviction that every British subject should be born with the right to vote regardless of sex, I have learned that the most precious things in life aren't the rights wrested from governments or granted by princes, but the inalienable gifts bestowed by the Creator. The free will to love where and whom our hearts direct us is the greatest gift, the greatest freedom, that any man or woman might wish for."

Callie, my splendid, brave girl, I love you. I've loved you all along.

And because he loved her, with all his body, mind, and heart, he couldn't let her stand up there alone for so much as a moment more. He had to get to her. Amidst the pop and flash of cameras and the scraping of pencil stubs across notepads, he pushed a path through the dispersing crowd, stiff leg dragging.

From the entrance, Callie's half-moon brows shot upward and her beautiful eyes widened. "Hadrian, dear Lord, what happened to you?"

Taking hold of the rail, he climbed up to join her. "I'll explain later but first things first." He reached the top and turned to face out onto the yard, shouting to be heard above the hubbub. "Hold, hold, I say. I am the photographer who took this picture. If you want the full story, you'll stay and hear me out."

From the crowd, someone demanded, "Who the devil is that?"

Turning back en masse, the spectators reassembled. Keenly aware of Callie's gaze on his face, he announced, "Foremost, you need to know that it was Mr. Josiah Dandridge, MP for Horsham, who caused that photograph to be commissioned—yes, commissioned. In fact, Dandridge blackmailed me into discrediting Miss Rivers whom, you also should know, is the most moral woman I've ever had the honor of knowing—or loving."

He slanted a gaze at Callie but her expression, riveted on his face, was unreadable.

That admission won the crowd's attention as well as hers. The raised voices dimmed to a collective whisper. Satisfied his voice would carry, he continued, "When I declined to carry out Dandridge's scheme by turning over the photograph, he had my studio ransacked and Miss Rivers's photograph stolen. I confronted Dandridge last night and demanded he return the photograph. The coward informed me he'd already turned it over to the press, and then called in his henchman to beat and then drown me."

Beside him, Callie's gasp found its way to his ear. He thought she said his name but couldn't be sure if it wasn't his own wishful thinking.

"If the battered face you see before you won't stand as

evidence enough of Dandridge's duplicity, I have proof—indisputable proof—that Dandridge is the very last person to be passing judgment on another's morality."

He reached into his breast pocket and pulled out the gift from Sally, the one photograph for which that Dandridge's lackeys hadn't thought to look. The faded but still discernible tintype was of a much younger Dandridge, his raised fist a blur of motion as it connected with the face of the cowering prostitute, Hadrian's mother.

Holding it up to catch the eye of the crowd, he said, "This tintype photograph was taken more than fifteen years ago by me and salvaged from my very own smashed camera by one Sally Potts, proprietress of a pleasure emporium in Bow." He paused to pat his chest where an inner coat pocket contained Sally's brief note. "Moreover, I have Mrs. Potts's admission, penned in her hand, that she has been fronting for Dandridge for years."

A collective gasp greeted that announcement. It was common knowledge that it was illegal in England for a man to own a brothel. Dandridge could very well face a prison term for pandering if he wasn't convicted already for commissioning murder. Regardless, his political career was finished. In seeking to ruin Callie, to vanquish her, he had seen that fate visited upon himself.

Slanting a gaze at Callie's pale profile, he resolved that brave though she was, she would not have to stand alone, not ever again. "Finally, I come before you not to pass judgment but to own the whole truth, to put the lies to rest once and for all, including my own. Dandridge, despicable though he is, is not the only person here guilty of deception. Though those of you who know me do so by the name of Hadrian St. Claire, my true name is Harry Stone, and that prostitute in the photograph is Annie Stone, my mother."

There, it was done and ruined though he was, what a relief it was to own his true self, to let go of the last of the lies. He'd scarcely caught his breath when a deluge of reporters and curiosity seekers pressed in on him. Next to him, Callie slipped her hand into his.

Angling her face to his ear, she whispered, "I think we've both stood out in the cold long enough, don't you?" Before he could answer, she turned away and opened the front door, pulling him in after her.

Once inside, they broke hands. The maid moved to bolt the door, and then turned about. Standing by the stairs, Callie's aunt regarded him, face fatigued but otherwise unreadable. Pinned by three airs of female eyes, Hadrian felt perspiration prick his palms. He turned to Callie, almost afraid to hope. Back braced against the door, she stared at him, tears tracking her cheeks.

He took a halting step toward her. "God, Callie, 'sorry' isn't much of an apology under the circumstances, but I am that and more. Sorrier than I've ever been in all my life."

She released the door handle and pushed away from the door. "Is that all you've to say to me? That you're sorry?"

He hesitated, and then shook his head. Recalling Sally's advice, he found the courage to forge ahead. "No, no it isn't.

You're within your rights to turn me out here and now. God knows, I wouldn't blame you if you did only you need to know . . . Callie, I love you."

"You love me?"

"With all my heart." He would have said more but before he could, she closed the short distance between them and launched herself into his arms.

"I love you, too, Hadrian," she whispered, brushing her mouth over his bruised lips, the sweetest of silencers. Pulling back, she sent him a watery smile. "I think I've loved you from that very first day when you barreled into me in the park."

Almost afraid to believe, he said, "But can you ever forgive me, sweetheart? Even though Dandridge stole that photograph from my studio, had I never put myself in the position of working against you, he would not have . . ."

She framed his face between her hands, her cool palms and gentle fingers balm to the bruises. "Oh Hadrian, don't you see? In facing down the press and revealing your connection to Dandridge, in owning up to your true self, you've done for me what no other man ever has. You've sacrificed your wellbeing, your happiness for mine, and if that isn't a measure of true love, I can't imagine what is."

Whether he called himself Hadrian St. Claire or Harry Stone, either way he was the most fortunate man in the world. In spite of the myriad mistakes he'd made, this amazing woman loved him. Cupping her cheek in his cut palm, he could only look at her in wonder. "Oh, Callie, I can't come close to ever deserving you but if you think you can truly forgive me, truly trust me again, I'll gladly spend the rest of my life finding ways to make you happy."

"You've already made me happy, happier than I ever thought I could be." Her arms slipped to his neck. "And Hadrian, you've taught me so very much."

Seeing she was serious, he shook his head.

"No really. Before I met you, I couldn't see beyond winning the vote for women. While universal suffrage will always be near and dear to my heart, I see now that the problems we face as a society, as a country, are so much broader than female emancipation. The issue, the cause if you will, isn't just a matter of women's rights but human rights, the dignity of all British subjects whether they be rich or poor, child or adult. Man—or woman."

"Oh, Callie."

"And I'd very much like to do something to advance that, only I can't do it alone. I'll need a partner for my new pursuit."

"A partner?"

Smile wobbly, she nodded. "An able photographer to help me publish a volume of photographic portraits of the East Enders as they really are—not just their poverty, but also their joys and aspirations, their wonderfully brave spirit in the face of adversity."

From across the years, Gladstone's gravelly voice came back to him, as clear as it had been on that snowy night fifteen years before. *Might you be that able young man?*

Face beaming, Callie said, "Oh Hadrian, I want so much

to show it all, but I'll need a partner, a helpmate to bring it about. I need you."

Heedless of his injuries, he swept her up into his arms and pressed fervent kisses over her dear, tear-streaked face. "Oh, Callie, my brave, beautiful, Callie, not nearly as much as I need you but for whatever it's worth, whatever *I'm* worth, you have me body and mind and soul."

Smiling through her tears, Callie cautioned, "In that case, there is one small condition of employment you must first agree to satisfy."

"Anything, my darling, you've only to name it."

For the first time since he'd seen her on the front steps, her confidence seemed to fold. Gaze searching his face, she hesitated, biting at her bottom lip. "You must let me make an honest man of you."

For a handful of seconds, Hadrian could only stare, heart so full that speech seemed not only impossible but needless. The most he'd hoped for was to someday earn Callie's forgiveness. Never had he expected to win the treasure of her trust, the bounty of her heart. The woman he'd set out to vanquish had turned the tables and vanquished him—with her honesty and integrity, her understanding and forgiveness, and most of all, her boundless, unconditional love.

Drawing her against him, he bent his face to hers and brushed his swollen mouth over her soft lips. Forehead resting against her brow, he said, "My darling, dearest Callie, are you proposing marriage to me?"

She answered with a slow nod. "Why yes, Hadrian, I do

believe I am."

From the vicinity of the stairs, Lottie and the maid exchanged smiling glances. One of them whispered "shackles of matrimony" and chuckled, but Hadrian couldn't have said who it was, for his ears, like his eyes, were all for the lovely woman wrapped up in his arms.

Smiling at her through his bruises, he said, "In that case, my love, I'll gladly promise you that and more—a passionate partnership wherein we shall be lovers, best friends, and soul mates every day for the rest of our lives."

EPILOGUE

"I love you not only for what you are, but for what I am when I am with you. I love you not only for what you have made of yourself, but for what you are making of me."

—ELIZABETH BARRETT BROWNING

Parliament Square, London
January 1918

The victory was decades overdue and tempered by political compromise and yet it was a victory all the same. After nearly thirty more years of hunger strikes, property destruction, and staged protests on the part of suffragists around the country (including the now-infamous Black Friday riot in Parliament Square), the government had finally granted the vote to women, rate-holders aged thirty years and older. Turning her face up to catch the rare warmth of winter sunshine, Callie couldn't help but smile. Lobbying to place women's voting rights on the same universal basis as men's would be the future frontier to be forged, but with the so-called Great War still raging, even the most militant feminists agreed the fight would have to be postponed. Now that the United States had cast its lot with Britain and the Allies in declaring war on Germany the previous April, hopes were high that the war soon come to a victorious close. With two sons fighting in the trenches to hold the boundary line known as the Western Front, Callie heartily prayed it would prove so.

Ironically, it was women's wartime service on the home front more so than the sensational tactics employed by militants like the Pankhursts that had overwhelmingly turned the tide of public opinion in favor of female enfranchisement. The example of British women of all ages and stations pitching in to undertake jobs in munitions factories, hospitals, and municipal offices had proven far more effective in marshaling support than had seventy years of protests and petitions.

From across the square, the sound of a beloved male voice brought her back to the present. "Callie, love, do *smile*."

She looked over to find Hadrian shaking his head at her, the very latest in roll-film cameras, which he'd ordered from the Eastman Kodak Company in New York, aimed in her direction. Given her husband's proclivity for taking pictures of her and their family whenever and wherever he would, thank goodness there were no longer any striking cords, chemical kits, or glass plates to haul about. And the new technology made photographic books such as Hadrian's and her expose of the poverty endemic to London's East End far more economical to produce than in the old days, when photographs had needed to be tipped in. A famous success, the book had just gone into its third printing, one of several such projects they'd undertaken together over the years.

Even after all this time, however, the sight of Hadrian cutting across the frost-parched grass at a brisk clip to reach her still had the power to set her heart aflutter. Coming to stand beside her, he said, "Has anyone told you lately you make a dreadfully uncooperative subject?" Before she could answer, he bent and brushed his mouth over hers. Grinning from ear to ear, he stepped back. "Now give us a smile, love. It's your day, after all."

Laying a gloved hand alongside the lean face that time's chisel had rendered only more handsome and dear, Callie had no difficulty in finding her smile. "I was smiling. I *am* smiling, but then I have so very much to smile about. Only it's *our* day, darling. This day, and every one hereafter."

HISTORICAL
NOTES

A degree of artistic license is part and parcel of most commercial historical fiction and *Vanquished* is no exception. The Bryant and May Strike took place in 1888, two years prior to *Vanquished*, and involved some 672 women and girls rather than the ragtag group of strikers I depict in these pages. Departing from the somewhat ambiguous scenario set forth in *Vanquished*, the actual strike had a quasi-happy ending. As is so often the case, the pen proved mightier than the sword—or even the striker's placard. An editorial entitled "White Slavery in London" by reformer Annie Besant in the weekly *The Link* detailed the B&M Factory's abysmal working conditions: the long hours, poor wages, system of fines, abuse by foremen, and generally boring, tedious, and dangerous nature of the work. The company threatened to sue the paper for libel and attempted to strong-arm the strikers into signing a statement denying the claims, but the women held firm. As a result, their leader received the sack. Public support, that most fickle of political gambits, came down squarely on the side of the workers. Within two weeks, the employers were forced to grant some concessions. The women (and ultimately the whole factory) walked out, supported this time by the trade-union movement. On July 18, the company conceded to all the women's demands, and on July 27 the women established the Union of Women Matchmakers. It was, if imperfect, the dawn of a new day.

The "happily ever after" for British women's suffrage was considerably longer in coming, but come it did. In 1918, catalyzed by the proactive role women had taken in filling the workforce gap left by men during the First World War, Parliament granted the vote to women over age thirty on the condition they were householders or married to householders. But it was not until 1928 that Parliament granted adult women (aged twenty-one and older) the right to vote, putting their franchise on the same basis as that of men's.

Sometimes progress takes time. Until next time . . .
Wishing you fairytale dreams-come-true,
Hope Tarr

Spring 2006,
www.hopetarr.com

If you enjoyed reading Vanquished,
you may also enjoy this special presentation of
By Honor Bound *available from Medallion Press:*

By Honor Bound

Helen A. Rosburg

A PERFECT TEN!

"In my opinion, BY HONOR BOUND is a must-read for any romance fiction fan, and assuredly deserves the distinction of a Perfect 10. It's just that good!" —*Romance Reviews Today*

Prologue

October 16, 1793

The final few steps were difficult. Though the injury to her leg had been a long time healing, and the pain had lessened greatly, it was still not gone completely. The last stairs to the ground floor had to be taken carefully, and Honneure leaned heavily on her cane. Finally at the bottom, she rested against the wall for a moment to catch her breath and wipe the moisture from her brow. As she did so, the hood of her cape fell back and she immediately stiffened with fear.

A quick glance up and down the narrow street assured Honneure that no one had noticed her. She pulled her hood back up, tucking in stray wisps of pale, wavy hair. The sidewalks usually teemed this time of day. No doubt the crowds had all gone to the square to witness the execution.

A wave of nausea coursed through Honneure's frail form, so strongly it rocked her. She fought to keep down the meager breakfast of bread and tea Dr. Droulet had pressed upon her.

She could not be sick now. She could not. She had to be at the square also. She had to be there, at the end. She could not allow her friend to die alone. No matter how great her own personal danger, the bonds of love could not, would not, be denied.

Honneure squeezed her eyes tightly shut. It was ironic, she thought. So ironic. All of her adult life she had lived for and served her queen. Again and again she had sacrificed her own wants and needs for her sovereign's. She had believed it to be her duty and had been bound by honor to fulfill it. Honor bound. All her life, honor bound. And now?

Honneure shook her head, a humorless smile on the curve of her mouth.

Once again she risked all for her queen. Once again she was about to take the chance that she would never again see her beloved Philippe. This time, however, it was not from a sense of duty, but out of love. It was a lesson she should have learned long ago. If she had she might, even now, be in the arms of . . .

No. She mustn't think that way. There was no going back, only forward. The choices she had made in the past had led her to this moment in the present. She had to take what she had learned and keep moving. For as long, at least, as she was able.

Another swift glance up the street assured Honneure she was virtually alone. Leaning on her cane, she started on her journey. She only prayed she would arrive in time.

The closer she came to the square, the more crowded the streets became. A few people glanced at her curiously. But perhaps it was only because of her limp. Or, because of the dark cloak and hood she held close at her throat on such a warm, fall day. She recognized no one, and no one recognized her. No one had the slightest clue that she was a fugitive from the revolution. No one could possibly guess that she, too, had been slated to be fodder for the hungry blade of the guillotine.

Nausea churned again in Honneure's stomach. She could almost feel the blood drain from her face. But she did not hesitate. With one leg in rhythm with her sturdy cane, she hobbled onward.

Urgency quickened her lopsided gait, however, when she heard a cry from just ahead.

"She comes! The Widow Capet comes!"

"The Austrian whore!" came another shout. "The whore meets Lady Guillotine!"

Urgency turned to rising panic. Honneure stumbled as someone jostled her shoulder. "Sorry," she mumbled under her breath, although it was not her fault. "Sorry."

An overweight man with grizzled hair scowled at her. "Watch where yer goin'," he growled. Several others around him turned in her direction, all with thunderous frowns riding their brows.

Honneure lowered her gaze and tried to push her way through the mob in the opposite direction. She was going to have to be very, very careful. The mood of the crowd was murderous, indeed.

"There!" a woman's voice screamed. "There she is!"

Honneure felt her bladder weaken. But the woman was not talking about her. Taking a deep breath, she dared to glance up from the littered ground.

All heads were turned to the left. Fathers hoisted little children up on their shoulders so they could see better. Women stood on tiptoes.

Honneure could see nothing. She was only able to hear the creak and groan of the tumbril's wooden wheels as it rolled through the crowded, cobbled square. Emboldened by her growing horror, Honneure elbowed her way through the massed and stinking bodies.

Irritated grunts and rude curses filled her ears. She ignored them. She had but one thought, one purpose. She had to get there in time. Her friend must know she did not die alone.

There was so much pushing and shoving by all that hardly anyone paid any attention to Honneure. Ducking, squeezing sideways, and pushing by turn, she managed to make her way to the front of the crowd. Only a few heads bobbed in front of her. She was able, at last, to see her Queen. Tears immediately rushed to Honneure's eyes.

She sat facing backwards, hands tied behind her back. Her posture was rigid, chin held high. The cart rumbled to a halt.

The former Queen had to be helped from the tumbrel. Honneure noticed her pretty plum shoes as she slowly climbed the ladder to the scaffold. Her white pique dress and bonnet were immaculate.

How like her. How very like her. A sob caught in Honneure's throat.

Though she remained erect, Antoinette began to tremble at last. The executioner seized her roughly and forced her to her knees. He tied her to the plank. The guillotine towered above her, blade glimmering in the sun.

"You're not alone," Honneure whispered. "Antoinette, dearest friend, you're not alone," she said a little louder. Heads turned in her direction, but she paid them no heed. Pressing closer still to the scaffold, she slipped the hood from her head.

For one brief moment, Antoinette raised her eyes.

"My Queen!" The tortured cry rasped from Honneure's throat. She stretched out her hand, cane clattering to the ground.

The blade fell.

Pandemonium erupted. A thunderous roar, as if from a single, giant throat, burst from the crowd. General cheering followed. A few screams punctuated the tumult as the mob surged forward, crushing a few of its own under its terrible weight. Honneure feared she would be carried along with them, but the few who surrounded her were not moving. They had noticed her when she cried out. Now they stared at her.

Though choking on her tears, Honneure quickly pulled her hood up. It was too late.

"It's the woman, from Tuileries!" a pock-marked crone cried out. "It's her, the one who escaped!"

"Who? Who is it? Someone asked. A small crowd within the crowd had formed.

Honneure tried to back away, but a hand grasped her skirt. "The bastard whore!" the scarred woman exclaimed. Honneure screamed as another pair of hands tore at her, ripping her bodice.

"No!"

"Get her! Don't let her get away!"

Searing pain shot through Honneure's head as someone pulled her hair. She saw a great handful of it come away.

"Leave me alone!"

Hands dragged at her, pulling her down. She was losing footing. A fist connected with her nose and blood splashed.

"No!"

Honneure screamed in denial.

But she could not save herself.

She was going to die . . .

By Honor Bound

Helen A. Rosburg

ISBN# 097436391X

Gold Imprint

US $6.99 / CDN $9.99

Historical Fiction

Available Now

www.helenrosburg.com

CATHERINE KEAN

DANCE of DESIRE

Desperate to save her brother Rudd from being condemned as a traitor, Lady Rexana Villeaux must dance in disguise at a feast for the High Sheriff of Warringham. Her goal is to distract him so her servant can steal a damning missive from the sheriff's solar. Dressed in the gauzy costume of a desert courtesan, dancing with all the passion and sensuality in her soul, she succeeds in her mission. And, at the same time, condemns herself.

Fane Linford, the banished son of an English earl, joined Richard's crusade only to find himself a captive in a hellish eastern prison. He survived the years of torment, it's rumored, because of the love of a Saracen courtesan. The rumors are true. And when he sees Rexana dance . . .

Richard has promised Fane an English bride, yet he desires only one woman – the exotic dancer who tempted him. Then he discovers the dancer's identity. And learns her brother is in his dungeon, accused of plotting against the throne. It is more temptation than Fane can resist.

The last thing Rexana wants is marriage to the dark and brooding Sheriff of Warringham. But her brother is his prisoner, and there may be only one way to save him. Taking the greatest chance of her life, Rexana becomes the sheriff's bride. And learns that the Dance of Desire was only a beginning . . .

ISBN#193281535X
Jewel Imprint: Sapphire
US $6.99 / CDN $9.99
Available Now
www.catherinekean.com

THE
SECOND
SEDUCTION

SHELLEY MUNRO

Though the gifts of second sight and a loving heart have made her an extraordinary healer, Rosalind finds her talent has also branded her a misfit and an outcast. When a marriage is arranged for her with the mysterious Viscount Hastings, heir to Castle St. Clare, she embraces what she sees as the last chance for a normal and secure future.

Lucien, Viscount Hastings, back from the dead and safe in the bosom of his family, has no time for the chit his family has arranged for him to marry. There is no room in his life, or his heart, for anything but vengeance for the death of his beloved first wife, Francesca.

Threats echo in every crash of the waves beating upon the cliffs on which Castle St. Clare stands. Whispers linger in the corridors during the still of the night. Malicious eyes track every move made by the spurned bride and her scarred, but handsome would-be husband.Is there a chance for two lonely hearts? A dark past collides with the present, bringing together family, truth and . . .

The Second Seduction . . .

ISBN#1932815198
Jewel Imprint: Sapphire
US $6.99 / CDN $9.99
Available Now
www.shelleymunro.com

For more information

about other great titles from

Medallion Press, visit

www.medallionpress.com